Beasts Beyond
the Fire

Beasts Beyond the Fire

Michael Jenkinson

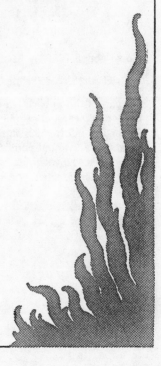

E. P. DUTTON • NEW YORK

For Hal Fore, Ned Judge, Karl Kernberger, Jack Loeffler, John Loehr, Sam Scott, and numerous other friends with whom I have swapped stories around a lifetime of campfires.

For Barrett Price and David Barnett, who have taught me that good stories should be shared.

Contents

Preface   ix
Acknowledgments   xi

1   The Sharks   1

2   Beasts of the Water   31

3   Some African Beasts   66

4   Man-Killing Cats   83

5   Scaly Things that Shuffle and Lurk   108

6   Killer Bees   130

7   Behold the Serpent   143

8   The Belled Vipers   171

9   Wolves   191

10 A Solitary Beast   213

    Selected Bibliography   243

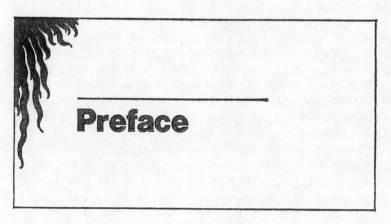

Preface

One of the most arresting news articles I have ever read concerned an Australian who was stalked by a six-foot-long tailless crocodile. The item, like so many of the more interesting newspaper stories, was haunting in its brevity. One learned that the victim worked in the outback of northern Australia and had been terrified of crocodiles all of his life. Because of his phobia he never ventured into backcountry waters more than ankle deep, and was obsessively vigilant. Despite his caution and fear, or perhaps because of it, a crocodile grabbed him as he bathed in ankle-deep water late one afternoon, and devoured him. His companions, backtracking the crocodile's tracks, determined that the beast had been following the victim for days, waiting for the opportunity to make his particular nightmare come true. The article, disappointingly, did not describe or speculate on how the animal had lost its tail.

Despite mankind's ability to create concertos and computers, not to speak of bottling Coca-Cola, anthropologists assert that our essential emotions are still little removed from those of our club-carrying forefathers who cowered in fear at the sound of a stick breaking under the foot of some prowling predator, out there just beyond the flicker of a campfire.

I have never experienced more genuine fear than when a grizzly lumbered back and forth in the dimness at the periphery of a camp in the Yukon Territory, apparently debating whether or not to charge. Although I know that I have been in much more danger, statistically, every time I had stepped into an automobile, there has been nothing remotely frightening about it on a gut level. The real possibility of a head-on collision is distant, impersonal—a matter of luck or lack of it. But the attack of a grizzly is somehow very personal. We know, perhaps without consciously remembering, that an ancient dreaded spirit has come to claim us.

We can read of hundreds of people being massacred in some political upheaval with a curious detachment; it is, after all, simply people killing other people within the framework of some struggle which makes sense at least to some of the participants. Yet when we read of a shark biting some hapless swimmer in two, we are fascinated, horrified, and in an odd way, outraged. It strikes at our sense of the natural order of things, our assumed place at the pinnacle of evolution. It taunts our notions of afterlife. To be buried in unhallowed ground is bad enough, not to be buried at all is worse, and to be eaten by a lion or crocodile is unspeakable.

The focus of this book is on the creatures we most fear, and an exploration of why we fear them. Why do snakes have such a powerful hold upon our imagination? What almost invisible creature is almost always fatal within minutes? Do wolves attack people? Why will certain African elephants attack a man on sight while most of these elephants are peaceable unless molested?

All of the events described in this book have been carefully checked for veracity, except those indicated as mythology or tall tales. It is my hope that this book not only addresses some of our deepest fears, but celebrates the animals who have created them.

M. J.

Santa Fe, N.M.
July 1979

Acknowledgments

I am grateful to several people who assisted in the research and preparation of this manuscript, especially my wife Constance, Gary Rosenberg, Polly Rose, and Dr. George Miller of the University of New Mexico Library, as well as personnel of the Santa Fe Public Library and the New Mexico State Library. I am indebted to my daughter, Jennifer, who sacrificed a lot of record-listening and television-watching time so that I would have silence while writing.

While much of the material in this book is drawn from old sources, I wish to thank the following individuals and publishers for their permission to reprint sections of more modern text: Peter Schub and the New York Graphic Society for material from *Eyelids of Morning,* by Alistair Graham and Peter Beard; University of Minnesota Press for excerpt from *They Shall Take Up Serpents,* by Weston La Barre; Harper & Row for material from *The Living Sea,* by Jacques-Yves Cousteau; Doubleday & Co. for a passage from *Octopus and Squid,* by Jacques-Yves Cousteau; Charles Scribner's Sons for material from *Through the Brazilian Wilderness,* by Theodore Roosevelt; and The Macmillan Company for excerpts from *The Man-Eaters of Tsavo,* by Colonel J. H. Patterson.

Beasts Beyond the Fire

1

The Sharks

On August 26, 1913, a shark was caught off Spring Lake, New Jersey. Sharks, as the fisherman knew, were prone to swallow all kinds of odd junk, in reality consuming the absurd objects mythically attributed to the diet of the terrestrial goat. So it was with something akin to a sense of whimsy that once the creature had stopped twitching, the angler opened its belly. He found a woman's foot wearing a knitted stocking and a tan shoe.

To be sure, when recounted ashore, the story of the foot in the tan shoe was a chiller; details of the catching of the shark and the gruesome discovery could hold habitués of a waterfront bar spellbound. But for the press the story had little interest. People drowned. Sharks were scavengers. Now if the foot could have been identified—say as belonging to a society woman who had been shoved off a yacht by a cuckolded husband—*that* would have been a story.

Almost three years later, on July 1, 1916, Charles Van Sant, a young Philadelphian, was swimming off Beach Haven, forty-five miles south of Spring Lake. He and his family had just arrived by train for a holiday. He had pivoted perhaps a hundred yards from shore, perhaps thinking this was about the right distance for the first swim of the season, and was leisurely stroking back when people on the beach noticed a triangular fin gliding behind and toward him. They yelled and gestured, but Van Sant apparently did not hear them, or took their antics as some game or prank. From the beach, people watched as the fin steadily closed the distance to the young man. Close to shore it reached the swimmer and there was a sudden blossom of red in the water around them. Van Sant was pulled to shore by a former Olympic swimmer. His legs were horribly mutilated and he died that evening.

The incident provoked no sensational press coverage, nor panic along the New Jersey beaches. A shark attacking a human being? Local experts scoffed. Possibly such a thing could happen in the tropics, but certainly not in northern waters. Thirty years before, a New York banker had offered a $500 reward for proof of a shark attack anywhere north of Cape Hatteras. Although $500 went a long way in those days, it was still unclaimed.

Spring Lake, close to where the shark had been caught with the woman's foot in its stomach, was a posh resort. Elegant hotels there catered to the sort of people who often flipped to the society page of a newspaper before perusing the front page, on the reasonably good assumption that they might be mentioned in it. Charles Bruder, a bellboy, had worked at various Spring Lake hotels for some twenty of his twenty-eight years. Wealthy patrons usually tipped him well, for he personified the attributes they admired in a person unfortunate enough to have been born without means. Personable and good natured, he was never heard to complain and supported both himself and his elderly mother in Switzerland by the fruits of his labor. On July 6, 1916, Bruder had an afternoon off and decided to take a dip in the ocean. He was a strong swimmer and lifeguards made no effort to summon him back when he passed the lines beyond which hotel guests were not permitted to swim.

A woman suddenly screamed. "He has upset! The man in the red canoe is upset!" The lifeguards, rushing their boat into the water and rowing quickly toward Bruder, glimpsed Bruder's agonized face as he reached an arm toward them. What the woman had taken for the reflection of a canoe was in actuality a spreading stain of blood.

"Shark. Shark got me. Bit my legs off!" he cried out, and fainted as they pulled him into the boat.

Mrs. George Childs, a pillar of Philadelphia society, saw a commotion on the beach below the private balcony of her suite at the Essex and Sussex Hotel. She asked her maid for a spyglass. Peering through it, she saw Bruder being gently laid out upon a coat. Mrs. Childs, although seventy-four years of age, did not faint as did several women on the beach. She promptly called the manager of the Essex and Sussex, calmly related what she had witnessed, and requested that her car be brought around. While Mrs. Childs sped north toward nearby Deal Beach to warn her daughter, who usually bathed at that time of day, the hotel telephone operator was calling central switchboards all along a twenty-mile stretch of the Jersey coast, warning of a prowling man-eater. This time the alarm was taken seriously. Hundreds of bathers began thrashing toward shore.

The personable young bellboy was dead. Within fifteen minutes after he had been carried off the boat, Colonel W. G. Schaffler, Surgeon General of the New Jersey National Guard, examined the body and stated, "There is not the slightest doubt that a man-eating shark inflicted the injuries."

There was panic along the beaches of New Jersey, not the least of which was shared by the resort owners, who saw sharks devouring the rest of their profits for the season. The evening after Bruder's death, motorboats probed the sea near Spring Lake with powerful searchlight beams. In the days to come, a flotilla of shark fishermen tried to lure the beast to hooks baited with fresh mutton donated by a Spring Lake meat market. Volunteer riflemen strode up and down the strand. Not a single shark was spotted. Elsewhere, however, a number of people claimed to have encountered sharks: a Bayonne policeman who emptied his revolver at a fin that seemed to be stalking some swimming boys; some Brooklyn men who claimed to have killed a shark in shallow water with oars, eel-tongs, spears, and spades. Resorts hurriedly began to erect protective steel nets. While members of the scientific community insisted that a shark's jaws were not strong enough to snap off a man's legs, as indicated in the medical report on Charles Bruder, others questioned whether sharks would attack at all.

Another, rather chilling, theory was that the attack on Van Sant was occasioned by a scarcity of fish off the shoreline. The killer was crazed by hunger. Having thus acquired an abnormal taste for human flesh, it had attacked Bruder. This was reassuring in terms of sharks in general—but what about that single shark, that even now might be gliding toward shore in search of another exotic meal?

Sharks were now prime newspaper copy. Like most people in the upper Atlantic states, the citizens of Matawan, New Jersey, read the accounts avidly, but with some detachment. Although only twenty-five miles from Spring Lake as a fish would swim, the town is eleven miles from the Atlantic Ocean proper. The only direct tie to the sea is a shallow, meandering tidal creek which empties into Raritan Bay. Six days after Bruder's death, a retired seaman, Captain Thomas Cottrell, was standing on a bridge which spanned Matawan Creek when he observed a large dark shape swimming up the creek with the incoming tide. Captain Cottrell, who figured he knew a shark when he saw one, rushed back into the town to sound a warning, especially anxious to stop groups of boys who were heading for the creek for a swim. It was a muggy, drowsy day, and the seaman's urgent warnings were largely regarded with amusement by the townspeople. A shark in Matawan Creek, which was shallow and only thirty-five feet across at its widest place? Folks decided he was a bit addled from the heat and continued about their business.

In front of some old pilings known as Wyckoff Dock, several youths were already enjoying the coolness of the water. One of the boys was about to climb out of the water when something bumped against his leg, almost causing him to lose his balance. In astonishment, he saw it was a huge dark fish, which was now gliding toward a companion, Lester Stilwell. As the fish struck Lester and dragged him under, it twisted over to reveal a white belly. Shark! The other boys thrashed out of the water and ran screaming into town. People, who a short time before had only smiled indulgently at Captain Cottrell's shark nonsense, now dashed toward the creek. Stanley Fisher, a husky young man who owned a dry-cleaning establishment, quickly took charge. He instructed some men to push off in boats to pole for the body, others to string a roll of chicken wire, weighted with stones, across the creek downstream from the dock. Fisher had a hunch that the shark, with Stilwell's body, was probably lurking in a deep hole on the opposite bank. He planned to dive into the hole and startle the shark into fleeing into shallow water and the chicken wire barricade. The people crowding the bank grew hushed as Fisher swam across the creek and then plunged under. After what seemed an agonized suspension of time, there was a sudden violent churning of the water where Fisher had dived. Men holding the chicken-wire barricade tensed, anticipating the rush of the shark. Instead, it was

Fisher who floated to the surface, flesh stripped off his right leg from groin to kneecap.

The injured man was taken from the water and carried by litter to a baggage car beside the Matawan Railroad, a quarter of a mile away. A doctor was found who did about all that could be done—preventing additional loss of blood until a train was flagged down. Throughout the wait in the baggage car and on the train, Fisher stubbornly clung to consciousness, trying to form faint words. Before he died, while being wheeled into the operating room, he managed to whisper his message. In the murk at the bottom of the creek he had wrestled the body of Lester Stilwell from the shark's jaws.

The chicken-wire fence, it was soon discovered, had only partially blocked the creek. Joseph Dunn, aged fourteen, and several friends were swimming in Matawan Creek off the dock of a brickyard, blissfully unaware of the horrors that were occurring a half mile up the creek. They were all in the water when someone dashed down the bank, warning them about the shark. Joseph, the last one out of the water, was just starting up the ladder when something he described as feeling like a pair of big scissors seized his right leg. He screamed. The other boys rushed to the ladder, grabbed him, and pulled upward in a desperate tug-of-war with the shark. "I felt my leg going down the shark's throat," Joseph would later recall. "I believe it would have swallowed me." Abruptly the shark let go. Only quick transport to a hospital and the efforts of a skilled surgeon saved both the boy's life and then his badly torn leg.

Two days after the three attacks, an 8½-foot shark was caught after a savage battle, in a drift net. In its stomach were fifteen pounds of flesh and bones, including a shinbone which was positively identified as belonging to a young human being. The shark was examined by ichthyologists. It was a great white, considered the most dangerous of all sharks.

Did one shark attack all five victims? Although it seems likely, no one will ever know. In retrospect, perhaps the most curious aspect of the 1916 New Jersey attacks was the initial disinclination of so many people, including erudite scientists, to believe that a shark could or would fatally maul human beings. The attacks in Matawan Creek silenced the last armchair skeptics even as locals were dynamiting the tidal flow from end to end, shooting pistols and rifles at shadows and hurling pitchforks toward anything that moved in the water.

Mariners have known of the shark as a creature to be feared for a long, long time. Fragments of a vase unearthed at Lacco Ameno, Ischia, believed to have been created about 725 B.C., depict a sailor being devoured by a huge fish. Vasco da Gama, the first European to voyage around the Cape of Good Hope to India, saw sharks off Sierra Leone in 1497. A companion, Antonio Pigafetta, wrote that they "have teeth of a terrible kind and eat people when they find them in the sea either dead or alive." Another adventurer, writing of his experiences on the long sea route from Portugal to India three years later, gives us a more detailed account:

> When a man fell from our ship into the sea during a strong wind, so that we could not wait for him or come to his rescue in any other fashion, we threw out to him on a rope a wooden block, especially designed for that purpose, and this he finally managed to grasp and thought he could save himself thereby. But when our crew drew this block with the man toward the ship and had him within half the carrying distance of a musket shot, there appeared from below the surface of the sea a large monster called Tiburón; it rushed on the man and tore him to pieces before our very eyes.

Up to this point most European references to a man-eating fish spoke of the tiburón (still the Spanish word for shark). In 1569, however, the swashbuckling, freebooting fleet of Sir John Hopkins triumphantly sailed back to England with the swag plundered from Spanish vessels. They also brought back a preserved shark which was placed upon exhibition. It would appear that it was about this time that the word shark became part of the English lexicon, and an educated guess is that it was initially slang borrowed from the German word *Schurke,* which means villain.

A report of the villain was logged by a seaman in 1595:

> This fish doth great mischiefe and devoureth many men that fish for pearls. . . . As our ship lay in the River of Cochin [India] . . . it happened that as we were to hang on our rutter . . . a Sayler beeing made fast with a corde to the ship, hung downe with halfe his body into the water to place the same [rudder] upon the hookes, and there came one of those Hayens [sharks] and bit one of his legs, to the middle of his thigh, cleane off at a bit, notwithstanding that the Master [ship's captain] stroke at him with an oare, and as the poor

man was putting down his arms to feel his wound, the same Fish at the second time for another bit did bite off his hand and arme above the elbow, and also a peece of his buttocke.

Yet not all early encounters with the villain were to end in numbing catastrophe. About the middle of the last century, the captain of the ship *Ayrshire* pitched overboard. His situation was classic penny-dreadful, silent-movie suspense. As his trusty Newfoundland threw himself into a furry arc of rescue, a shark glided sinisterly toward the floundering hero. In a harrowing rescue, both master and dog were finally hauled aboard, but not before the brave Newfoundland had lost his tail to the thwarted shark.

One of the finest eighteenth-century American paintings, *Brook Watson and the Shark,* by John Singleton Copley, was not a vision: it was commissioned by the victim himself, after he recovered from a shark attack in Havana harbor. Watson was so pleased with his narrow escape that he redesigned his family crest to symbolize a shark being fended away as it is about to devour its prey. Watson lost a leg in the encounter, and later, when he had become Lord Mayor of London, someone would occasionally inquire, with delicacy, as to what happened to his leg. The Lord Mayor would generally roar with laughter and exclaim, "It was bit off!"—to the total disbelief of any strangers within earshot.

The scientists who, at the time of Charles Bruder's death, doubted that a shark would attack man probably had not read the April 1, 1881, edition of the *Indian Medical Gazette,* in which a doctor reported that "more than 20 persons have been severely bitten by sharks this year. Almost all were fatal." In 1899 the medical officer of Port Said treated three youths for serious shark wounds within a three-hour period on the same morning. As with the New Jersey attacks, the notion that a single shark was responsible is more than possible.

Peter Gimbel, who filmed *Blue Water, White Death,* once wrote that sharks are "as well armed as anything alive, and they have a quality that's particularly dreadful that I always think of as the quality of an insane, passionless killer. You have no possibility of really anticipating what a shark will do. It's not a mammal and it's a form of life far removed from any mammal; it's an eating machine."

The anatomy of the shark is beautifully adapted to its calling. Nerve endings in the "lateral lines" which run the length of the shark can pick up erratic vibrations in the water from as much as 600 feet away. Thus alerted to the possibility of a meal, the predator may then precisely locate the object of its interest through a keen sense of smell which can track minute amounts of fish blood in the water. Streamlined and swift, the shark propels itself through the water with sweeps of its crescent-shaped tail fin.

The shark may well have been the first animal to develop teeth; it has obviously put them to good use ever since. There are virtually as many varieties of shark teeth as there are varieties of sharks, ranging from the serrated triangles of the great white, the stilettos of the sand shark, to the flat grinders of the gaudy wobbegong. Depending upon the species, there may be four to twenty rows of teeth embedded in the gums. When a tooth becomes broken or worn, the tooth behind it moves up as a replacement. A tiger shark may shed as many as 24,000 teeth in a ten-year period.

To accommodate their often large and bizarre meals, sharks possess distensible stomachs which can stretch to several times their normal sizes. Even more remarkably, they are capable of storing consumed objects for long periods of time without digesting them. Some scholars have suggested that Jonah was swallowed and later regurgitated by a huge shark rather than a whale.

Shark skeletons are formed of cartilage rather than bone, and unlike other fish, sharks do not have an air bladder to keep them afloat. Most sharks must swim constantly, never sleeping as we know it, or they would sink into the depths of the sea. They usually swim with mouth slightly open, so that water can wash through their gills and replenish oxygen. The reproductive system of the shark is not primitive. Unlike most fish, which discharge sperm and eggs into the water, the male shark ejects seminal fluid into the female by means of a pair of organs called claspers. The genital openings of maiden sharks actually have a sort of hymen. Ichthyologists are discovering that sharks have their own, fascinating Kama Sutra; the male cat shark, for example, coils around its partner during mating.

In most species, the newborn shark emerges as a fully developed miniature of its parents; it is ready to defend itself and begin a lifelong quest for food.

There are over 250 known species of sharks, which are members of a larger family which includes rays, skates, guitarfish and sawfish. Although encounters between sharks and men have most frequently occurred in tropical or mid-latitude waters, sharks apparently prowl most, if not all, of the seas upon Earth. The lethargic Greenland shark is caught by Eskimos using handlines dropped to great depths through holes chopped in the ice. Eskimo families who follow tradition cut their children's hair with sharktooth knives, as the use of iron scissors or knives is taboo. Sharks range in size from the three-inch length of a full-grown *Squaliolus laticaudus,* a denizen of the deep Pacific, to the gigantic bulk of the gentle whale shark. The whale shark, a sluggish monster which feeds upon plankton, grows to more than forty-five feet in length and may weigh in excess of thirteen tons. The basking shark, the other giant of the shark clan, also nourishes itself with plankton and other small marine organisms. It too is generally placid, although one of these behemoths once took umbrage at the presence of a 664-ton steamer and deliberately rammed it. As a 1937 issue of *The New York Times* was to relate: "The Clyde pleasure steamer *Glen Sannox,* thus raided, put into Glasgow from Arran the other day with two five-foot observation windows shattered, with glass and splinters cluttering her main-deck, and with her two hundred passengers in various stages of hysteria and emotion."

The shark's adaptability to different environments is a major factor in its passage through the ages with little evolutionary change. The freshwater Lake Nicaragua shark is a striking example. Geologists have postulated that the 100-mile-long lake was once an arm of the Pacific Ocean. Ancient volcanic activity sealed it off from the ocean, trapping sharks and other marine life in what is now an inland body of water. Over countless centuries, as fresh water flushed out the salt, sharks, as well as remoras, sawfish, and tarpons adapted to a fresh-water existence. Lake Nicaragua sharks grow to more than eight feet long. They are man-killers. Native fishermen claim at least one person a year is lost to sharks. Tradition has it that a good many years ago a Dutchman used to fish diligently for sharks after important native funerals. The bodies, bedecked with all the jewelry and gold the person had possessed in life, would be placed in the water as an offering to the shark spirit. The Dutchman, whose only reverence for spirits was for those of the potable variety, would extract jewelry from the sharks' stomachs and sell it. When they caught him, outraged Indians slit his throat; they did not dignify his body by giving it to the sharks.

Sharks have attacked people or been caught tens or even hundreds of miles up various rivers. They have been caught deep in the Amazon jungle, observed 200 miles up the Perak River of Malaya, and a 700-pound shark washed ashore at Marlboro on the Hudson River, fifty miles from New York Harbor. It had apparently been rammed by a steamboat. The Ganges River sharks are justifiably greatly feared. They feed upon the numerous corpses which Hindus place into the river, believing that the sacred waters will carry them to paradise. The sharks also frequently maul live worshippers as they stand in the river performing devotions.

Although virtually any species of shark, if provoked, can be dangerous to man, the species most frequently identified in attacks include the blue pointer, whaler, bull, mako, blue, hammerhead, and Australian gray nurse. About an equal number of severe injuries and deaths have been attributed to the tiger shark and the great white shark. Yet it is the great white, with its vast bulk, huge jaws, and round expressionless eyes (which make it seem as if it were looking out of a hood) that inspires our greatest horror.

A booklet published by the California Bureau of Marine Fisheries in 1950 commented that the great white shark was "uncommon at best in our waters, and, since it rarely comes inshore, it is a negligible hazard to California swimmers." At that time virtually no reliable sightings of great white sharks had been reported in California waters.

In October, 1955, a shark startled two skin divers when it appeared close to them off the pier of Scripps Institution of Oceanography at La Jolla, California. The shark soon swam off without molesting the divers. An ichthyology student witnessed the incident from the pier. He was convinced that he had seen a *Carcharodon caracharias,* commonly known as the great white shark. The next day, Arthur Flechsig, a Scripps specialist in sharks, managed to hook one close to the pier. The shark put on an awesome display of strength and frenzy, even gouging and biting at the skiff the men were in. The shark got away, but left the large telltale triangular teeth of the great white shark embedded in the wood of the boat.

The sudden appearance of the great white in California waters was as unexpected and inexplicable as had been its arrival along the coast of New Jersey in 1916. A number of shark encounters were now being reported, although the victims were generally unsure as to the species. Two men suffered minor injuries off Venice Beach, a scuba diver beat back the violent attack of a small, three-foot shark, and a surfer kicked free of a shark off Santa Monica. Peter Savino was swimming in Morro Bay when he was brushed by a shark whose rough skin drew blood on his arm. Thoroughly frightened, he and his companion, Daniel Hogan, began swimming steadily for shore. Hogan, who had stroked ahead, looked back to see how Savino was doing. There was no sign of him. No remains were ever found.

A spear fisherman in Monterey Bay was seized by a shark which stripped off the ankles of his wet suit, bit through his left swim fin and tore the right one entirely off. Miraculously, the diver escaped without injury. He was sure that the shark that had gobbled at his ankles had been a great white.

As the spring of 1959 slipped into summer, highways leading to California's beaches were choked with weekend traffic. Most residents of the state are no more than two hours' drive from the ocean, mountains, or both, and they frolic at these natural playgrounds with zeal. The afternoon of May 7 was a warm dazzle of sun upon water and sand at Baker's Beach on San Francisco Bay. Even at five in the afternoon the sand radiated heat, although the water, true to form at this time of year, was decidedly chilly. Eighteen-year-old Albert Kogler basked in the sun for a bit with a friend, Shirley O'Neill, and when the heat had seemed to press right through their flesh until it tickled their very bones, they ran to the water, splashing gaily and awkwardly until it was deep enough to lunge forward and swim. They swam out about fifty yards, paused to tread water, and had started back when O'Neill heard Kogler scream.

She was later to recall that "I turned around and saw this big thing flap up into the air. I didn't know whether it was a fin or a tail. I knew it was some kind of fish.

"There was a thrashing in the water and I knew he was struggling with it. It must have been pretty big. He shouted, 'It's a shark . . . get out of here!'

"I started swimming back. I swam a few strokes, but I thought to myself, 'I just can't leave him here.' I was scared and I didn't know what to do, but I knew I couldn't leave him.

"I turned around and took a couple of strokes back. He kept screaming. I could tell the fish was chewing him up. It was a horrible scream. All I could see was blood all over the water. He was shouting, 'Help me! Help me!' "

With a great effort of courage which so often characterizes the actions of people in the immediate vicinity of a shark attack, the girl swam back to her friend's side. His left arm was useless, almost bitten through at the shoulder. Placing an arm around him, she began to struggle toward shore. It would take her a nightmarish twenty minutes, during which time no one on the beach moved to help her until she was almost ashore. Fortunately, the shark had abruptly broken off its assault. Kogler died of his injuries three hours later. The wounds had unmistakably been made by the teeth of a great white shark.

On June 14 of that same summer, Robert Pamperin, an aircraft engineer, went diving for abalone off a rocky point near La Jolla. His companion, Gerald Lehrer, was a less experienced diver, and he glided above rocks closer in to shore as he searched for the prized shellfish. Over his head, where sunlight diffused in the clear water, was an inner tube with a rope and net to hold whatever abalone they might pry loose until ready to head back to shore. After a brief, exploratory dive, he surfaced to see a large dorsal fin cutting toward Pamperin. Even as he shouted a warning, Pamperin rose almost completely out of the water, his face mask gone, arms thrashing. He was then suddenly jerked underwater.

Lehrer swam to the spot, ducked under the surface, and stared in horror through his mask. A few feet below, Pamperin was gaping upward, the lower half of his body in the jaws of a twenty-foot-long shark. "It had a white belly and I could see its jaws and jagged teeth," Lehrer said. "I wasn't able to do anything more. So I swam to shore to warn the other swimmers."

From Lehrer's description authorities concluded Pamperin had been the victim of either a great white shark or a tiger shark. Although a search involving boats and a Coast Guard helicopter began immediately, all that was ever found was one of Pamperin's blue swim fins. Eight days later, a 12½-foot shark was caught in the vicinity of Santa Catalina Island, sixty miles north of La Jolla, in whose stomach there was a badly deteriorated man's watch. It served only to evoke mystery—Pamperin had not been wearing a watch.

More than a month after the Pamperin tragedy, a diver named Verne Fleet had his leg badly slashed by a shark some 300 yards from where Pamperin had been attacked. Yet Fleet insisted his assailant was a hammerhead, a shark whose eyes are at the ends of protruding head lobes, an unmistakable creature whose bizarre head might be a mask fashioned for some carnival of the deep sea. The proximity of the two attacks by obviously different sharks was disturbing; it made no sense. Nor did the two encounters which took place in the waters off Panama City, Florida, that same year.

In early summer a diver was pulled underwater by a shark. The victim jabbed at it ineffectually with his spear until finally, in desperation, he plunged his hands into the shark's jaws and attempted to pry them apart. The shark, which could have snapped the youth's arms like carrot stems, obligingly opened its jaws and allowed his victim to swim to safety, although it took seventy stitches to close all his wounds. Later in the summer, some scuba divers were spearfishing over the coral reefs of a seventy- to eighty-foot-deep sink known as the Warsaw Hole. Later, when they regrouped at the boat to compare catches, which were good, it was noted that one member of the party, Army Lieutenant James Neal, had not yet returned. Gary Seymour and other divers headed back down their shot line to the coral.

"I went on down the reef," Seymour later recalled, "killing several snappers and groupers. Then I met Jeff Sherman, who wrote 'SHARK' on the bottom and described it as a ten-footer." The divers carried their fish up to the boat. Neal had still not shown up. They returned to the reef. There was no sign of the missing serviceman. Seymour soon had other things to think about. "I was going along the reef with a string of fish tied to my belt. A big shark passed by about three feet away, and I made a fuss in the water to scare him away. Then another shark came from behind and missed me by about six inches. I'm sure it was a mako. The other could have been a blue or a gray shark. Both sharks made passes at me, and I backed against the rocks so I had only to watch in front of me." The diver cautiously made his way back to the shot line and surfaced.

Eventually, scattered over a 300-square-yard area of ocean, searchers found Neal's ripped swim fins, face mask, other pieces of diving gear, and shredded trunks and undershirt. There was no trace of Neal himself. In Panama City, as elsewhere, people pondered how one man might open a shark's mouth and struggle away unmolested even though bleeding from a number of deep gashes, while later, in the same vicinity, a man was apparently attacked with such ferocity that rescuers could find only some floating bits of rubber and rags. Once again, it made no sense. There was no pattern, no predictability.

It is this lack of predictability which gives rise to much of our horror concerning sharks, adding to our ancestral dread of being consumed by an animal, as well as the fact that we face it helplessly in its own environment. Actually, one of the curious things about shark behavior is that they attack men so rarely, given the frequency with which they inhabit the same stretches of water.

After two people were injured by sharks off Florida beaches in 1975, John Montazzoli, a television program supervisor, hired a plane to skim low over the shoreline, hoping to get some shark footage. Montazzoli later startled viewers with his report. "I frankly wasn't prepared for what I saw. During the flight we observed an even two dozen sharks just along a few miles of beach. Some of them were right in among the swimmers. One was so close to shore that there were people wading in the water further out. . . ."

When a shark estimated to be nearly twenty feet long dragged a fifteen-year-old boy from his air mattress off Lanikai Beach near Honolulu, killing him, concerned citizens raised money to outfit the *Holokahana,* a boat which would be used for catching, killing, and examining sharks in the vicinity of Oahu. On its shakedown cruise, sixty-three sharks were taken in forty-eight hours.

Although the phrase "man-eater" has a wonderfully dramatic ring to it, scientists are beginning to wonder if provocations other than hunger are responsible for many, if not most, shark attacks. There are, of course, well-documented and chilling instances of sharks devouring victims or repeatedly striking at them until the remains can be dragged ashore or aboard a boat. Yet in the majority of authenticated shark encounters, the victim is only hit one or two times; only slightly more than a third of them die. Given the size and strength of most sharks that attack man, and the lethal potential of their jaws, one wonders that more victims are not torn apart and eaten.

None of this, of course, makes the slightest difference to the victim who loses an arm or leg in a single, perhaps casual, snap of a shark and bleeds to death in the water or on the beach.

Sharks, as might be expected, feed mostly upon fish, seals, and other marine life, including smaller sharks. Great white sharks consume sea lions and even sea turtles, crunching through their thick, tough shells. From time to time, we hear of sharks attacking land animals which venture into their domain. Dogs have been devoured by sharks. Australian racehorses, which are customarily exercised in the surf, have been attacked. In the Kiah River of New South Wales, a shark lunged at a horse crossing the shallow waterway. The horse reared and bucked in terror, breaking its saddle girth and pitching its rider into the water. The man swam a nightmarish one hundred yards to shore, but the shark did not pursue the matter. During a 1959 drought in Kenya, a thirst-maddened elephant charged into the sea, apparently headed for a nearby island where perhaps it sensed there might be water. Cruising sharks tore it to bits.

The most astonishing things have been found in sharks' stomachs. In Australia, the stomach of a great white shark was opened to reveal the carcass of an entire horse, apparently scavenged after being dumped from a garbage scow. The stomach of a tiger shark contained, among other odd items, a raincoat, a pair of pants, a pair of shoes, the horns of a deer, twelve lobsters, the wire of a chicken coop in which there were still some feathers and bones, and a driver's license. Another tiger was found to harbor a keg of nails, a roll of tar paper, and a carpenter's square. No sign of the carpenter. Shark researcher David Baldridge discovered that a 1,015 pound tiger shark weighed no more than seven pounds in the water, due to the incredible buoyancy of the oil in its huge liver. Possibly the tiger shark, and other sharks, ingest undigestible objects for ballast, simply to give them more maneuverability.

In 1952 some Italian fishermen reported catching a shark in whose stomach was a bottle containing a wad of paper. It was a Frenchman's farewell note to his wife and children, tossed from the life raft upon which he was drifting and dying.

When Arthur Hobson, an Australian fisherman, checked a line he had set off Coogee Beach near Sydney in the summer of 1935, he pulled in a curious catch. A small shark had taken his baited hook, and a fourteen-foot tiger shark was in the process of devouring it. Hobson and his brother managed to get the large shark ashore, where excited spectators helped them drag it across the sand to an aquarium. For twenty-four hours the shark moved listlessly, but then, after oxygen had been pumped into the tank, it seemed to regain its vigor and began to eat the fish thrown into the pool. Five days later it stopped feeding and once again seemed to sink into a stupor. Suddenly, as fourteen railhangers watched, it lashed about the pool and then regurgitated the remains of a rat, an entire ghostly seabird, and a tattooed human arm with a severed rope clove hitched around the wrist. The tattoo on the muscular, well-preserved arm portrayed a boxer in red trunks confronting another in blue trunks.

The shark was killed, cut open, and was found to contain only fish bones and bits of the smaller shark. Dr. V. M. Copperson, who was not only a skilled surgeon but also an expert on sharks, examined the arm and concluded it had been severed from the body by a sharp knife. Police theorized murder, speculating that perhaps the arm had not fit into a trunk or other receptacle with the rest of the body, and had therefore been cut off by the killer and thrown into the sea lashed to a weight. The small shark had snapped it up before being gobbled by the tiger shark.

The fingertips were too shriveled from immersion to yield easy prints. Yet by peeling the skin, inverting it, and chemically treating it to remove the wrinkles, the victim was identified. The mysterious arm had once belonged to James Smith, a onetime amateur boxer who had been operating a billiard parlor at the time of his disappearance. Police began the traditional drudgery of an investigation, questioning dozens of people associated with the victim. They discovered that Smith, whose prints identified him only because he had once been arrested for illegal betting—a minor offense—had apparently been dabbling in some shady business ventures with Reginald Holmes, an affluent boat builder. They also ascertained that Smith was last seen while sharing a cottage in the fishing town of Cronulla with a man named Patrick Brady. When contacted, the landlord stated that his temporary tenants had left in a hurry, and that a trunk, a mattress, some rope, and sashcords were missing. Left behind was a can full of a foul-smelling liquid he thought might have been blood.

Brady was arrested and charged with murder. He was as talkative as a lump of lead.

Police investigated a speedboat which seemed to be powering out of control around Sydney Harbor. They managed to cut it off, and take its occupant to a hospital as he mumbled: "Jimmy Smith is dead. I'm nearly dead, and there is only one other left." It turned out to be Reginald Holmes, with a .32 caliber bullet flattened against the freakishly thick frontal curve of his skull. After a few days, doctors released him from the hospital, marveling at the capacity of the human animal to survive. *A .32 slug flattened against the cranium. Indeed!*

The same evening Holmes was found murdered in his car.

Patrick Brady was duly tried for the murder of James Smith and was acquitted. Legally, an identifiable arm does not make a body, even when delivered from the deep by a pair of reluctant sharks.

Large sharks are prey only for still larger sharks. A number of fishermen have battled sharks for hours, finally reeling them up to the sides of their boats where other sharks tear off great chunks before they can be hauled aboard. Great white sharks regularly devour other sharks as large as half their own size. A great white caught off Florida had ingested two entire sandbar sharks. And also two pumpkins, a wicker-covered scent bottle, and the foot of a man. The offspring of the sand tiger shark, which are hatched in the mother's uterus, are cannibals even before they are born. The first unborn shark to emerge from its egg devours its siblings as they break free of their shells. Since the sand shark has two separate uteruses, two sharks survive to be born.

Aside from man and his own kind, the only adversary of the shark is the porpoise. Maritime lore has it that the two creatures—one a fierce loner, the other sportive and gregarious—invariably battle whenever they encounter each other. This is not true, although porpoises will defend themselves against sharks and have been observed to drive them from feeding grounds. The porpoise uses its hard snout to ram the shark in its one soft spot, the gills. On the other hand, sharks and porpoises sometimes share the same section of sea without any apparent antagonism.

Scientists at the Lerner Marine Laboratory in Bimini conducted an experiment in which they placed sharks and porpoises in the same pen. Upon first observing a shark placed in the pen, the porpoises would emit a sort of chirping sound, and then would herd the sharks against the outside of the pen by swimming toward them while making clicking noises.

Shark frenzy! What sounds like the title of a low-budget adventure film is in actuality one of the most violent dramas of the animal kingdom. Divers from Jacques-Yves Cousteau's research vessel *Calypso* observed it in the Red Sea, where they were using fish as bait to lure sharks into a cage for observation. As Philippe Cousteau was to write later:

> . . . Things became confused very quickly, and the rhythm of events accelerated. Canoe and Jose succeeded in getting two sharks into the squaloscope at once, but by that time the scent of fish was acting on all the others like smoke on a bee hive. While Jose was putting the bait back in place I saw two fairly small sharks crash against the framework of the cage and rebound like ricocheting bul-

lets. The water around us was streaked with grey silhouettes flashing by in every direction. . . . I think it is the irrationality in this frenzy of sharks that strikes me most. It gives me a feeling of complete impotence, such as I never experience in any other circumstances. The shark is the most mechanical animal I know, and his attacks are totally senseless. Sometimes he will flee from a naked and unarmed diver, and at other times he will hurl himself against a steel cage and bite furiously at the bars.

Australian Theo Brown, who spent years attempting to develop an efficient shark repellent after witnessing a fatal shark attack, also reported on the fury of a feeding frenzy. To test the effectiveness of a chemical repellent known as the "Shark Chaser," he dumped forty-four gallon drums of blood and offal into clear waters off the Great Barrier Reef. For his experiment, he chose a place where the shallow reef sheered off into a cliff which dropped away into the black depths of an ocean trench; here great sharks would rise from twilight waters to feed upon schools of fish that wandered out of the sunny shallows. Bait, including an entire side of beef, hung from Brown's vessel. Numerous sharks soon began to circle the boat, and then rushed in to snap at the baits. Brown and his crew began to empty bags of "Shark Chaser" into the water. The repellent had apparently kept sharks at bay in a previous test, but here, where dozens of sharks were lashing the water in a quickening frenzy, the "Shark Chaser" had absolutely no effect. The sharks were devouring the bait, ramming the boat, slashing at each other, and greedily snapping up objects thrown into the water by the crew—bits of timber, empty cans, four-gallon metal drums, as well as bags of "Shark Chaser."

When there was nothing left in the water but uninjured sharks, the frenzy ceased, and the sharks left as quickly as they had gathered.

In *Blue Meridian*, Peter Matthiessen's excellent account of the expedition which filmed the documentary, *Blue Water, White Death*, the author describes a frenzy of a different sort. Hundreds of sharks had congregated to feed upon a dead sperm whale. The sharks, in great excitement, would rush to the underside of the whale, bite off several pounds of blubber or flesh, wheel off while gulping it down, and then return for more. The sharks, although feeding ferociously upon the whale, did not molest each other nor bother the filmmakers. Peter Gimbel even swam into the gaping wound of the whale where he was surrounded by gore, blood, and wildly feasting sharks.

Reflecting upon the sharks' astounding lack of interest in them, one of the filmmakers speculated that the sharks regarded them as companions in their predation. The sharks frequently bumped the divers, apparently to ascertain if they were alive. Finding the strange, black-suited creatures to be very much so, they were content to gorge themselves upon the obviously dead, and hence not dangerous, whale.

A number of tragic feeding frenzies have occurred in association with wartime disasters at sea. The *Cape San Juan,* a World War II troop carrier, was torpedoed by a Japanese submarine in the South Pacific. The *Edwin T. Meredith,* a merchant ship, managed to save 448 of the 1,429 men who had been aboard the stricken vessel, but not before numerous men in the water and on life rafts had been taken by the hordes of sharks which rushed to the blood- and oil-stained waters. One of the survivors had a harrowing recollection:

> I was sitting on the edge of a raft talking to my buddy in the darkness. I looked away for a moment, and when I turned back, he wasn't there any more. A shark got him.

Even as rescuers dragged men from the sea the horror continued unabated. As one rescuer stated:

> Time after time, I heard soldiers scream as the sharks swept them off the rafts. Sometimes the sharks attacked survivors who were being hauled to the *Meredith* with life ropes.

When a German U-boat torpedoed the *Nova Scotia* off the coast of South Africa in 1944, over 700 men were lost, most of them Italian prisoners of war en route to a penal camp. Although it is impossible to say how many men were killed by the explosion or drowned, eyewitness accounts indicate a great many victims of the disaster, perhaps the majority of them, were torn to bits by frenzied sharks.

> "It was sickening by day," a Scottish seaman told the *London Daily Sketch* in June of 1944, "but the worst of it came at night. At least you stood a chance in the sunlight, especially if it was your turn on the boat. But during the night every second in the water seemed to last an eternity. Just the sound of the waves slapping against the boat, the groaning of my mates and the stink of salt and open wounds. Then there'd be a scream a little way off, the water would

boil up and the screaming would go on and on and on. I would pray for them to die quickly . . . pray for them to drown . . . pray that I wouldn't be next."

Yet even in the nightmare of maritime disaster, there is no consistency in shark behavior. A pilot who was downed in the Pacific simply ignored four sharks that glided within twenty-five yards of him, and swam steadily, calmly, to the safety of an island, shadowed most of the way by his potentially deadly escorts. Another pilot who parachuted into the Pacific kicked at sharks which made repeated passes at him. At one point the sandpaper skin of a shark scraped past his legs. Even though he bled from the abrasions, he remained in the water for eight hours without being attacked.

Dr. George Llano, a shark researcher, found that only thirty-eight out of some twenty-five hundred survivors of wartime sea disasters mentioned contact with sharks. He could not, of course, interview or read reports of the vast numbers of men who were listed as being simply "lost at sea."

In efforts to dispel shark fears among American troops, survival manuals were issued at the beginning of World War II in the Pacific. Among other absurdities they noted that sharks were "slow-moving, cowardly, and easily frightened by splashing," and advised that after knifing the shark's vital parts one should "swim out of the line of his charge, grab a pectoral fin as he goes by, and ride with him as long as you can hold your breath."

It is doubtful if many troops confronted with sharks took advantage of this tome of wisdom, but in at least two instances downed airmen threw the worthless manuals at circling sharks, which promptly devoured the treatises. The information, or at least its format, apparently satisfied the sharks, as they made no effort to molest the men.

In 1958 a group of thirty-four scientists from four continents met in New Orleans to consider approaches for developing an effective shark repellent. The conference resulted in the formation of the Shark Research Panel, a consortium of scientists dedicated to researching shark behavior. One of the first major activities of the panel was to set up a process by which detailed data on authenticated shark attacks could be gathered. Over a period of nine years, the U.S. Navy, working in cooperation with the Smithsonian Institute, logged and analyzed some sixteen-hundred attacks, the earliest being the gory death of a seaman who fell overboard somewhere between Portugal and India in 1580.

The study dissolved several long-held myths. The presence of porpoises in the water does not necessarily mean there are no sharks about, and the notion that a porpoise will defend a human from an aggravated shark is pure pipe dream. Illustrators and writers have long titillated book and magazine readers with images of triangular fins circling a hapless swimmer as the sharks prepare to charge and mutilate en masse. In actuality, aside from the feeding frenzies which have accompanied a few maritime disasters, most attacks are made by a single shark which the victim did not even glimpse before being struck. Although the victims may be bleeding heavily, they are rarely struck by other sharks, even if they are in the vicinity. Some investigators are beginning to feel the stimulation of human blood upon sharks has been highly exaggerated; this is not to say that the shark's legendary sensory abilities have been overestimated, but is merely a conjecture that a skin diver towing a string of fish leaking blood and body juices may be in a lot more danger than a chap bleeding from a coral scrape, or a menstruating woman. Most people, in thinking of fatal or maiming shark attacks, tend to assume deep water and a huge shark, the classic horror of absolute helplessness. Yet two thirds of shoreline shark attacks take place in water no more than waist deep, and it would appear that in about half of the incidents the shark is less than six feet long.

The study carefully considered numerous factors surrounding attacks such as location, activities of victims, time of day, color of bathing attire, clarity and temperature of water, the species of shark when positive identification has been made. Conclusions were elusive: very few clear patterns emerged other than that attacks occurred in a rather direct proportion to the incidence of sharks and humans sharing the same waters. The great white and tiger sharks were identified as the most frequent villains. Yet both species frequent the shoreline, while the white-tipped shark, suspected of being the principal predator of men forced into the open ocean by maritime accidents or the deliberate destructions of war, may be far more dangerous. The abrupt and unpredicated great white shark attacks upon scuba divers in the chill, murky waters off northern California in the 1950s probably has much more to do with a change in man's pattern than in that of the shark. Great white sharks have probably been feeding on seals there for thousands, perhaps millions, of years.

Men in black wet suits, who might well from time to time be mistaken for a sort of malformed seal in dim cloudy water, have only entered that domain in numbers during the last three decades.

Some of the most extraordinary tales of the sea concern men who have been in the jaws of sharks and lived to tell of it.

Rodney Fox had no thought of sharks as he glided over a reef near Aldinga Beach, Australia, in an early December afternoon in 1963. The young, accomplished spear fisherman cautiously approached a twenty-pound fish, intent upon his prey. Fox, a contestant in the South Australian Skindiving and Spearfishing Championship, had brought sixty pounds of fish ashore during the morning—a successful kill on this fish might well give him the championship. Just as Fox was about to release his deadly missile at the fish, something smashed into his left side, gripping his upper body in a vise of pressure. It was a shark.

"I couldn't see the creature, but it had to be a huge one," Fox later recalled. "Its teeth had closed around my chest and back, with my left shoulder forced into its throat. I was being thrust face down ahead of it as we raced through the water." The blow had jarred his spear gun away; in desperation he poked at the shark's head with the fingers of his free hand, hoping to gouge an eye. "There was no pain, although I felt quite weak. My mind was very clear, and all I could think of was—you'd better get out of here."

Possibly one of his fingers did find an eye, for the shark released him. "Instinctively, I pushed at the shark and I felt my hand gash on its teeth . . . both my knees were against the shark's side, so I put both my arms and legs around it, thinking it couldn't bite me in this position. . . ."

This bizarre and terrifying underwater rodeo lasted for only seconds—Fox thrashed frantically toward the surface and air. The water was red with his blood. Moments later the huge rust-colored shark, which Fox could now identify as a great white, broke surface next to him and rolled lazily on its side. "If he has another go at me I'm finished," Fox thought. "I pushed at him with my foot, and I felt my flipper touch him."

The shark moved off as Fox helplessly awaited its next rush. A thirty-foot cord ran from his belt to a hollow fish float used by all contestants to minimize spreading of fish blood which might attract sharks. The cord suddenly tightened as the shark gobbled the float and the diver was once again being towed rapidly underwater. Lungs bursting, he thought, "Surely I'm not going to drown now." The line snapped. Fox, with a final reserve of energy, kicked to the surface where a patrol boat picked him up.

Transferred from boat to car to ambulance, Fox's ordeal was not over. ". . . They could see into a large gash in my side, which, every time I breathed, sucked in air. . . . My biggest problem was breathing. I remember that it was perhaps the hardest thing I have ever done in my life. I could have given up many times, but two friends of mine who were with me all the way to the hospital kept talking to me, and telling me to keep fighting and that I was going to be all right." Fox, through a combination of luck, willpower, and prompt medical attention, survived.

Other divers, seized suddenly and without warning like Fox, have at first been unsure of their assailant. In 1959 James Hay was diving for abalone off Bodega Head in northern California when he "felt a tremendous shake, and then a wiggling motion. I assumed that it was a sea lion. It dragged me down under the water and shook me . . . I was within an inch of its side, but could see no head or tail. All I could see was a white wall and what looked like black lines (possibly gill slits) down the side." The creature wagged the diver as a dog will a sock for about five seconds and then released him, swimming away. Hay's partner glimpsed a dorsal fin which he estimated to be two feet long. One of Hay's swimfins was gashed by teeth, identified as those of a great white shark. All Hay suffered was a twisted ankle.

Nine years later, Frank Logan was seeking abalone near Bird Rock at the southern end of Bodega Bay when he "felt this pressure on my left side . . . I thought it might be a giant clam—I glanced to my left—it was a shark . . . its body went clear out of sight in the murky water." Reminiscent of Fox's adventure, Logan's side and shoulder were in the shark's jaws and it swam fifteen or twenty feet with him in the water. Logan went limp, played dead, and prayed his assailant would not begin to shake him, sawing its razor-sharp teeth through his body. The shark did sever the diver's weight belt and it was later speculated that it might have fallen into the shark's maw. In spitting out the weight belt, the shark, so a theory went, released Logan and then decided not to continue the attack. Logan felt himself a lucky man, even though surgeons did have to take over two hundred stitches to close his wounds.

Logan and Hay were wearing black wet suits and operating in an area where great white sharks and other sharks were known to feed upon seal. The water was murky, visibility poor. It is not at all unreasonable to wonder if the divers might have been mistaken for seals, attacked, and then released when the sharks realized their mouthfuls were not the desired delicacy after all. The same may be true for a number of other California shark assaults.

Most people attacked by sharks suffer injuries to the legs or arms. Yet two men were almost decapitated by tiger sharks and lived to tell of it. Curiously, both were pearl divers working in the Torres Strait between New Guinea and Australia, even though the incidents took place twenty-four years apart. Around 1913 a native of Thursday Island nicknamed Treacle was diving toward a promising shell when he literally swam into the mouth of a shark which seemed to appear out of nowhere, jaws swung wide. Instinctively, his hands went for the shark's eyes. Badly gouged, the large tiger released him, and Treacle floated up to the surface with his head almost ripped from his body. Although the slashing teeth had deeply gouged his head and shoulders, as well as shredding the flesh of his neck so that his jugular vein lay completely exposed in places, the vein itself was not severed. The pearl diver somehow recovered and thereafter supported himself in a certain amount of style and ease by exhibiting his impressive scars to tourists, and recounting the events of that dive so often that they became a sort of ritual chant for him.

Iona Asai was also seeking pearls when a large tiger shark charged him over a rim of rock. He, too, miraculously lived to describe his plight.

> When I turned I saw the shark six feet away from me. He opened his mouth. Already I have no chance of escape from him. Then he came and bit me on the head. He felt it was too strong so he swallow my head and put his teeth around my neck.

> Then he bite me. When I felt his teeth go into my flesh, I put my hands around his head and squeeze his eyes until he let go me and I make for the boat. The captain pulled me into the boat and I fainted. They get some medicine from Jervis Island school-teacher.

An extremely tenacious shark bit thirteen-year-old Raymond Short at an Australian beach. Like many shark victims, the boy felt no pain at first. "I remember treading water when I felt something nudge my right leg," he recounted. "I kicked my leg, but it felt like it had something heavy attached to it." The attachment was an eight-foot three-inch great white shark. Short kicked at it, punched it, and finally, in desperation, doubled over and bit it hard upon the nose. No effect. A lifeguard arrived and clubbed at the shark with a surf-board—yet it doggedly continued to grip Short's calf. Only after life-guards had carried both boy and shark to the beach could the shark's jaws be pried open. Fortunately, there was a hospital only three hundred yards away, and Short survived his ordeal even though the flesh of his leg was badly torn and toothmarks pocked his shinbone.

Another zealous shark chased an Australian woman through shallow water. She made the beach safely and continued running, while the shark, either excited by its prospective prey or unable to check its momentum, heaved itself up onto the sand. A lifeguard killed it with a hammer.

The lady, at least, had some running room, unlike Captain Manuel Chalor of New Jersey when a large shark erupted out of the water to crash into the bottom of the dory from which he was fishing. "I didn't know what to do," the captain recalls. "There was a fifteen-foot man-eater right in the boat with me, thrashing about. I tried to keep out of his way, but the fish was too big and the boat was too small. His jaws kept snapping, and I tried to keep clear, but in doing so I slipped. He got one of my arms in his mouth, and I felt my skin rip." The fishing vessel was close by, and crew members began pelting the shark with loose timber and metal objects. The shark released Chalor's arm. "I was about to jump into the water to get away from him, but I finally decided I'd rather be in the boat with a shark than in the water with him. I'm not such a bad swimmer, but I'm not that good." For some ten minutes the beleaguered seaman dodged both the snapping jaws of the shark and the missiles hurled at it. Finally, after being struck upon the head with an old harpoon, the shark heaved itself back into the water, almost capsizing the dory as it did so. The captain's arm wounds were treated ashore and healed without complications.

In 1949, bathers at Miramar Beach at Tampico, Mexico, watched as the guns and depth charges of a U.S. Navy destroyer were demonstrated to Mexican officials. A shark, perhaps crazed by the commotion, leaped out of the water and bit a sunbather before companions could club it to death.

A number of documented shark attacks, especially among species which are usually docile around man, are the result of some provocation by the victim. Sharks, like all creatures, do not take well to being speared, poked at, or otherwise manhandled. A skin diver grabbed the tail of a five-foot nurse shark off Miami Beach in 1958, thinking to obtain an exhilarating ride. Instead, the shark clamped onto his thigh with an iron lock. Back in his boat, it took the thrill-seeker's companions ten minutes to force the shark to let go.

Several Australian spear fishermen have discovered to their extreme discomfort that the wobbegong, a lethargic bottom-dwelling shark with blunt teeth, will clamp onto the nearest limb of a tormentor with a grip as tenacious as that of the proverbial Gila monster. Diver Gary Greaves discovered the potential dangers of spearing a wobbegong the hard way: the shark refused to release his arm, holding him underwater, although he stabbed at it with his knife. A companion finally managed to pry the wobbegong's jaws open in the nick of time. As Greaves was later to comment, "Air never tasted so sweet as when I broke the surface."

So great is man's fear and hatred of sharks that occasionally a fisherman will take morbid pleasure in eviscerating or otherwise mutilating a shark and watching it die slowly. Such unfortunate beasts, when believed dead, have occasionally obtained revenge by taking off a hand or foot of the tormentor. An almost metaphysical form of retribution visited the sport who stuffed a large cherry bomb into the gullet of a small shark and threw it overboard off Quinby, Virginia, in 1970. As he was eagerly watching over the rails for the anticipated explosion, the shark swam under the boat and blew up with such force that a hole was punched in the planking. The forty-three-foot power launch promptly sank.

Sharks are an ancient species. As Captain Jacques-Yves Cousteau once commented, "Across the gulf of ages . . . the relentless, indestructible shark has come without need of evolution, the oldest killer, armed for the fray of existence in the beginning." Sharks similar to those which prowl the seas today existed more than one hundred million years ago. The great mountain ranges of our time—the Himalayas, Rockies, Alps, and Andes—had not yet started to rise, while brontosaurus and other gigantic dinosaurs made the earth tremble as they plodded across swamps. Some twenty million years ago a monstrous shark, *Carcharodon,* an ancestor of the present day great white, lived in a shallow sea which covered parts of what is now the San Joaquin Valley of California. In 1853 a geologist for the Pacific Railroad Survey discovered some *Carcharodon* teeth in a hillside near Bakersfield. Since then thousands of teeth have been recovered from the hill, as well as the remains of whales, dolphins, sea lions, porpoises, sea birds, and other marine life. Some of the teeth were six inches long, indicating to paleontologists that the sharks themselves were up to 120 feet long. Six standing men were easily accommodated in a set of *Carcharodon* jaws reconstructed by the American Museum of Natural History.

The movie *Jaws* stimulated a lot of speculation as to just how large great white sharks can grow. A 2,664-pound great white was caught off Australia by rod and reel in 1959 while a 4,500-pound great white has been harpooned off Montauk, Long Island. Bigger ones, naturally, have gotten away. A few years after the turn of the century some four-inch *Carcharodon* teeth were dredged up from the bed of the Pacific Ocean. The fact that they were covered by only a thin film of silt seemed to indicate they had been recently deposited. Yet *Carcharodon,* it was assumed, became extinct millions of years ago. Most scientists tended to dismiss the apparent freshness of the *Carcharodon* teeth as being impossible, yet a few of them reflected upon a strange little knife-jawed shark caught off the coast of Japan a few years previously. The goblin shark, as it was dubbed, seemed an unknown and mysterious species until its teeth were found to be identical to those borne by a shark thought to be extinct for over one hundred million years.

If the *Carcharodon* teeth dredged up from the Pacific are recent, gigantic sharks that would dwarf the mechanical villain of *Jaws* may still glide through the vast, mysterious depths of the Pacific.

Throughout the Pacific region, sharks have made a profound impression upon man. Shark images have appeared in Australian aboriginal rock art, and on South and Central American pottery. The Tlingit Indians of the northwest coast of North America build ceremonial shark lodges. Solomon Islanders once made human sacrifices and placed the bodies in the water to appease the wrath of a shark deity. Missionary William Ellis described shark worship in the Society Islands during the early part of the nineteenth century. Temples were built to honor the great blue shark. Offerings were made to insure protection for fishermen and other ocean travelers. Some tribes of New Hebrides live in a world of ghosts and spend much of their time in rich, complex ritual. In one ceremony a shark is buried, and then a mound in the shape of the shark is molded over it. The mound is decorated with white pigment and shark's teeth are placed in the mouth. In Samoa, the great white shark was considered an emissary of Moso, god of the land. Coconut shark figures were hung in bread-fruit and coconut trees as insurance against thieves. A person stealing from a tree thus charmed, it was believed, would eventually be eaten by a great white shark.

During the construction of a drydock at Pearl Harbor, the U.S. Navy dredged up lava blocks which had once been parts of a wall which surrounded a four-acre shark pen. Hawaiian legend has it that the enclosure was once the site of gladiatorial contests staged for the entertainment of the Shark Queen, who ruled the harbor as well as human royalty. A shark would be lured into the pen with fish or other bait, the exit blocked, and the designated warrior would then attempt to kill it by slicing open its stomach with a sharktooth dagger. It would appear that the Roman gladiators had considerably better odds.

Virtually every culture in the world has legends of men turning into animals and animals into men. There are many shark–man stories recounted on the islands of the Pacific. In Hawaii they speak of Kamo-hoa-lii, the shark god who fell in love with a beautiful girl, Kalei, as he watched her gathering shellfish in a secluded bay. Kamo-hoa-lii changed himself into a handsome young man, swam ashore, and struck up a conversation with Kalei. She was as taken with him as he was with her, and after an appropriate period of time had passed they married. Kalei became heavy with his child. Shortly before its birth, the shark god revealed who he was, and told his heart-broken wife that he must return to the sea. He assured her that their forthcoming son would be strong and healthy, but that under no circumstances should he ever be allowed to eat meat.

When the infant was born, Kalei's family drew back in terror at the shark's mouth which lay between his shoulder blades. But as time passed and he grew normally in every other way, their doubts subsided. Kalei made sure that his shoulders were always covered with a handsome cape, and that there was no meat in his food. But when Nanaue, as he had been named, grew old enough so that custom decreed he must eat alone with the men, his grandfather, forgetting that it was forbidden, gave him some pork.

As Nanaue grew older, he craved meat to the point of obsession; he could think of little else. One afternoon, fascinated by the brightly colored fish swimming in the cove where his parents had met, he flung himself into the water and was transformed into a shark. He chased and gorged himself upon fish before returning to shore where he became a man once again.

Time passed, and occasionally villagers would wonder about the handsome, reclusive young man who always wore a cape. But such thoughts were usually fleeting, for there were more serious things to be considered. Several villagers who had gone to bathe in the cove disappeared without a trace. Strangers were regarded with suspicion. It was thought that sharks might have attacked and eaten the missing villagers; yet no sharks had been seen in the area for some time.

Several months after the first puzzling disappearance, all the able-bodied men on the island were ordered to join work gangs which were farming the royal plantations. One afternoon, some of Nanaue's companions began to tease him about his cape, and during the horse-play, one of them snatched it off. When they saw the snapping jaws they realized that Nanaue, as a shark, had killed and eaten the missing villagers. They attempted to capture him, but he was strong and his shark jaws slashed several of them savagely before he broke away, ran to the ocean, plunged in, and was instantly transformed into a huge shark.

In this form Nanaue swam to the island of Maui. There he changed back into a young man and married the chief's daughter. They were happy for a time, until, as on Hawaii, he developed an insatiable yearning for meat. People began to vanish. Two fishermen finally surprised him in the act of pushing a young girl into the ocean, then leaping in behind her where he became a shark. From Maui he fled to Molokai, where he was able, for a time, to continue his gruesome shark–man habits of feeding on unwary, isolated bathers.

Frightened residents of the island eventually consulted a shark priest, who told them the answer to the mystery of their missing people lay beneath Nanaue's cape. They captured him on the beach, tore off his cape, and bound him securely. They sent word that a huge fire should be built in the hills to destroy him. Hearing this, Nanaue struggled desperately to thrash his way to the edge of the water. When he reached the rim of the beach, waves lapped over him, and he instantly became the monstrous, snapping shark of his other being. The islanders, however, bound him with ropes and nets, pulling him from the water and the chance of another escape. The monster was dragged to a fire made of bamboo from a sacred grove, and there he perished.

In the preface to his book *Shark Attack,* H. David Baldridge remarks that "shark attack is unique among human experiences. What could possibly equal being eaten alive by a monster fish?" As he and other researchers have observed, however, in the majority of well-documented shoreline attacks the shark only strikes the victim once or twice. Given their size and formidable apparatus for cutting, this is often enough to cause a fatality, especially if prompt medical attention is not available. Yet if the primary object of shark attacks upon people is food, one wonders at the number of victims a shark does not finish off after leaving them bleeding and splashing helplessly in the water and the rarity of attack upon their rescuers. It has been suggested, with good reason, that much shark aggression has to do with factors other than hunger, such as shifts in water temperature, the way man moves in the water, or even forms of territoriality which are greatly different from those practiced by land animals.

One notes the number of researchers who, in the course of their work, has swum among sharks without being molested, not to speak of the thousands of recreationists who frequently, if inadvertently, share water with sharks. It is estimated that annually more people die of bee stings in the United States than are killed by sharks in the entire world.

Yet our fear of sharks, if disproportionate, is very real. Encounters occur in their element, and in most cases the victim is as helpless as a shark flopping upon the sand would be in ours. Unlike most dangerous animals, there is little predictability as to whom a shark will attack, and why, where, and when. More precisely, we simply know very little about shark behavior.

Taken on its own, broader terms, the shark is a magnificent beast, a predator possessing such a superb functional design that it has survived with little evolutionary change for tens of thousands of years. It is one of the most graceful swimmers in the sea. In fierceness, it is one of the most awesome creatures ever to exist upon the planet; a constant reminder that some beasts, thankfully, will never be domesticated or cajoled into being our dependent pets.

2

Beasts of the Water

In August, 1817, a number of fishermen as well as two women on shore were astounded to see a huge, serpentine creature undulating its way into Cape Ann Harbor, just north of the seafaring town of Gloucester, Massachusetts. Not long after, the same odd beast was observed close to the entrance of Gloucester Harbor by a sailor named Amos Story. Story would later testify to an investigative committee that:

I, Amos Story of Gloucester, in the County of Essex, mariner, depose and say, that on the tenth day of August A.D. 1817 I saw a strange marine animal, that I believe to be a serpent, at the southward and eastward of Ten Pound Island, in the harbor of said Gloucester. It was between the hours of ten and one o'clock when I first saw him, and he continued in sight for an hour and a half. I was sitting on the shore, and was about 20 rods (330 feet) from him when he was the nearest to me.

His head appeared shaped much like the head of the sea-turtle, and he carried his head from ten to twelve inches above the surface of the water. His head at that distance appeared larger than the head of any dog that I ever saw. From the back part of his head to the next part of him that was visible, I should judge to be three or four feet. He moved very rapidly through the water, I should say a mile in two, or at most, three minutes. I saw no bunches on his back. On this day I did not see more than ten or twelve feet of his body.

Over the last five hundred years there have been numerous reported sightings of sea monsters, especially those which resemble snakes. Story's tale is notable in that several hundred people apparently saw the same creature. It was seen by bleary wharf rats, as well as respected sea captains, children and elderly people, a Justice of the Peace, and the entire crew of a ship. Although descriptions of the sea serpent varied from individual to individual, a consensus indicated it was about sixty-five feet long, with smooth dark brown to black skin. It carried its head a few inches to a foot above the water, and in most reports other parts of its snakelike body humped out of the water. The Gloucester monster was able to change its direction abruptly as well as sink quickly under the water.

The sea monsters of ancient mythology were often depicted as half human and half fish. Glaucus, the Greek god of the sea, was portrayed as possessing a long, fishlike tail, as was Dagon, the fish–god of the Phoenicians. Mermaids have long been a popular concept. In the sixteenth century, clever con men fashioned "Jennie Hanivers" or "Gullian Pokes" out of the underside of skates and rays. When dried, they were peddled to the gullible as the dead offspring of mermaids, objects of great magic. Sea monsters spouting twin jets of water, probably inspired by stories of whales, began to appear on nautical charts in the sixteenth century, a practice which some mapmakers continued until the advent of the twentieth century. Spanish illustrations sometimes showed a ship at rest upon the back of such a beast, while a priest celebrated mass for the crew. Other graphics depicted boats being swamped by the jets of water, after which the monster would rush forward to devour the boat and its unfortunate passengers.

Sea monsters appear in ancient tales of many different cultures. Rabbi bar Hannah described a curious encounter:

> At one time while aboard a ship at sea, we came to a gigantic fish at rest on the waters, which we mistook to be an island. We made a fire and cooked our meat. But the fish, on feeling the heat, rolled over,

and had the vessel not been nearby, we undoubtedly would have drowned.

Japanese fishermen once spoke in awe of Baku, a great sea dragon which would gradually swallow parts of each new moon as it nightly rose over the water, thereby saving the world from some vague but cataclysmic disaster. The Baku could also eat nightmares. A fisherman suffering from bad dreams would pay an artist to draw a Baku upon a piece of paper. When placed under a man's pillow, the image would feed upon unpleasant dreams, allowing the sleeper to concentrate upon soothing images or to sink into the emptiness of deep, dreamless sleep.

Although a wonderful array of such phantasmagorical beasts were still reportedly being sighted until well into modern times, by the eighteenth century, some highly respected mariners, backed by witnesses, were swearing under oath to having seen some strange creatures in the water.

Lorenz von Ferry, royal commander and pilot-general of Bergen, Norway, was being rowed to shore from his yacht on a calm summer day in 1746 when a "sea snake" appeared in the water in front of the boat. Von Ferry later described the animal:

> The head of this sea serpent, which it held more than two feet above the surface of the water, resembled that of a horse. It was of grayish colour, had black eyes, and a long white mane, which hung down from the neck to the surface of the water. Besides the head and neck, we saw seven or eight folds, or coils, of this snake, which were very thick, and as far as we could guess there was a fathom's distance [about six feet] between each fold.

Von Ferry fired a rifle at the beast, which immediately dove beneath the water, which reddened, indicating he had wounded it. Von Ferry not only wrote a lengthy description of the incident to the procurator of the court of Bergen, but two seamen who had been with him in the boat affirmed its truth by placing a hand upon a Bible and pointing heavenward with the other, a gesture not known to be associated with pranks in eighteenth-century Christendom.

During the nineteenth century, seafarers saw, or thought they saw, sea serpents in a wide variety of settings. Scientists were reluctant to become involved with, let alone defend, the reports of untutored seamen, who could not be expected to recognize the subtle anatomical differences between known sea creatures. Sailors, like gold prospectors and professed womanizers, were known to be masters of exaggeration. Most scientists of the century had a tendency to regard the sea as a space to be crossed en route to distant shores where there were exotic birds and plants to be discovered and classified, primitive people whose mores were more than quaint, as well as pyramids that cleverly, tantalizingly, were found to conceal mummified royalty and their riches.

In 1905, however, two eminent British naturalists, Fellows of the Zoological Society, saw a strange sea creature off the mouth of the Paraíba River in Brazil from Lord Crawford's research yacht, the *Valhalla*. E. G. B. Meade-Waldo's comments upon the incident are so methodical and restrained as to be a good deal more sensational, in the net result, than the vivid prose of feature writers covering sea serpent stories over the previous century.

He stated that:

On December 7, 1905, at 10:15 A.M., I was on the poop of the *Valhalla* with Mr. Nicoll, when he drew my attention to an object in the sea about 100 yards from the yacht; he said: "Is that the fin of a great fish?"

I looked and immediately saw a large fin or frill sticking out of the water, dark seaweed-brown in color, somewhat crinkled at the edge. It was apparently about 6 feet in length, and projected from 18 inches to 2 feet from the water.

I got my field glasses on to it (a powerful pair of Goerz Trieder), and almost as soon as I had them on the frill, a great head and neck rose out of the water in front of the frill; the neck did not touch the frill in the water, but came out of the water in *front* of it, at a distance of certainly not less than 18 inches, probably more. The neck appeared about the thickness of a slight man's body, and from 7 to 8 feet was out of the water; head and neck were all about the same thickness.

The head had a very turtle-like appearance, as had also the eye. I could see the line of the mouth, but we were sailing pretty fast, and quickly drew away from the object, which was going very slowly. It moved its head and neck from side to side in a peculiar manner: the color of the head and neck was dark brown above, and whitish below—almost white, I think.

"Shark Fishing" (From Louis Figuier, The Ocean World; *London, n.d.)*
*Mankind's fear of sharks is such that the capture of a large specimen often
elicits in the fisherman a sense of righteous warriorhood.*

"Watson and the Shark" by John Singleton Copzey. The painting was commissioned by the victim himself after he was attacked by a shark in Havana Harbor. Watson lost a leg in the encounter but recovered and later became Lord Mayor of London. (Gift of Mrs. George Von Lengerke Meyer. Courtesy, Museum of Fine Arts, Boston)

This old French print depicts a sea monster on the rampage. In 1817, several hundred people in the vicinity of Gloucester, Massachusetts, reported seeing a similar beast in the water. Unlike the sea monster portrayed above, the Gloucester monster was apparently more curious than aggressive.

Sea serpent, from the marine chart of Bishop Olaus Magnus, 1539. Magnus describes this creature in his History of the Northern People as an individual monster two hundred feet long and twenty feet through the body, which allegedly plagued the coast of Norway with its habit of attacking ships and devouring sailors.

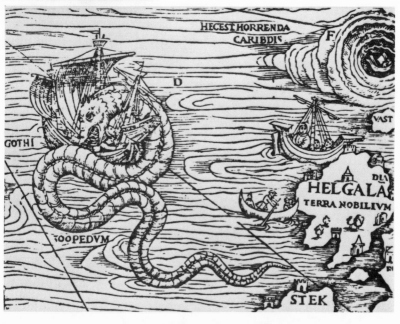

Harpooning a manta ray. From an old print. "A giant manta ray is one of the most graceful entities in the sea. . . . It may weigh more than 3,500 pounds."

A fighting sperm whale turns on his tormentors and crashes their whaleboat in his jaws. The whaleship is seen at left. From a painting done in 1879 by Charles S. Raleigh of New Bedford, Massachusetts, who knew whaling from firsthand experience. (Courtesy of Old Dartmouth Historical Society Whaling Museum)

It would have taken several men to provide a mouthful for Carcharodon, *a prehistoric shark. This set of jaws was reconstructed by paleontologists at the American Museum of Natural History in New York, using fossil teeth for scale. Such a beast would have been some eighty feet long.* (Courtesy of American Museum of Natural History)

For almost a thousand years, since the voyages of the Vikings, seamen have swapped stories of gigantic squid given to capsizing vessels by reaching into the rigging with their flexible arms. Although the peril to ships appears to be pure myth, some immense squid have been reliably reported. In 1878 a fifty-five-foot long squid with arms as thick as a man's body washed ashore at Newfoundland.

Although Meade-Waldo's reportage was tidy, it led to no neat zoological conclusions. Was the creature a reptile, sea mammal, or an odd sort of fish? It had certain characteristics of all three—yet taken in totality could be none of them.

A century after a goodly proportion of the citizenry in and around Gloucester, Massachusetts, were startled by the appearance of a sea serpent, the officer of the watch on the British troopship *Hilary* spotted a similar creature lolling on the surface of the mid-Atlantic. The ship's commander, who later commented that "We never missed a chance in those days to do a bit of anti-submarine practice . . . ," instructed his gunners to blast away at the beast with their six-pounders. They were not on target, and as the *Hilary* drew closer to it, the animal was observed to be serpentine, possess a dorsal fin, and to be about sixty feet long. The creature paid little attention to the shells which were plowing into the water around it until, finally, a direct hit was scored. The commander likened its response to ". . . a bather lying on his back in smooth water and kicking out with all his force to splash the water, only of course, the commotion on this occasion was on a vastly greater scale." The sea monster plunged back into the depths.

In retrospect, one cannot help but wish that the commander had been more interested in sighting in his binoculars than his guns, so that more might have been observed of the odd creature.

Over the years, military men have used some curious things for target practice, including the Great Sphinx of Giza, whose monumental nose has all but been destroyed by gunners of the Egyptian army.

In some maritime circles, the killing of a sea monster is considered flirtation with the worst kind of luck. Two days after shooting at the sea serpent, the *Hilary* itself was demolished by another kind of sea monster—a German submarine.

On July 30, 1915, another German U-boat torpedoed the *Iberian,* a British ship. George von Forstner logged the following account of the event:

> The ship, which was about 180 meters long, sank rapidly, stern first, the depth at this point being a few thousands of meters. When the steamer had disappeared for about 25 seconds it exploded at a depth which we could not know, but 1,000 meters would be a good safe guess. Shortly thereafter pieces of wreckage, among them a huge marine animal which made violent movements, were ejected out of the water, flying approximately 20 or 30 meters high.

At this moment there were six of us men on the bridge, myself, the two officers of the watch, the chief engineer, the navigator and the helmsman. We at once centered our attention upon this marvel of the sea. Unfortunately we did not have the time to take a photograph because the animal disappeared in the water after 10 or 15 seconds. It was about 60 feet long, looked like a crocodile, and had four powerful paddle-like limbs and a long, pointed head.

In the period between World War I and the present time, accounts of sea monsters continued to accumulate. Many were obviously hoaxes. Others were provided by individuals who might well have mistaken a line of leaping porpoises or the fronds of giant kelp as sea monsters. A number of weird creatures washed up upon lonely beaches proved, upon scientific examination, to be the decomposed remains of basking sharks.

Yet some reports, substantiated by several witnesses, left little doubt that there are mysterious creatures out beyond the harbor lights. In 1947 the Grace passenger liner *Santa Clara,* en route from New York to Cartagena, Colombia, cabled that they had struck and either wounded or killed a huge marine animal. Captain John Fordan, at the completion of the voyage, issued a detailed description of what his chief mate, navigation officer, and third officer, John Axelson, had observed:

Suddenly John Axelson saw a snakelike head rear out of the sea about 30 feet off the starboard bow of the vessel. His exclamation of amazement directed the attention of the other mates to the Sea Monster, and the three watched it unbelievingly as in a moment's time it came abeam of the bridge where they stood, and was then left astern. The creature's head appeared to be about 2½ feet across, 2 feet thick and 5 feet long. The cylindrically shaped body was about 3 feet thick, and the neck about 1½ feet in diameter. As the monster came abeam of the bridge it was observed that the water around it, over an area of 30 or 40 feet square, was stained red. The visible part of the body was about 35 feet long. It was assumed that the color of the water was due to the creature's blood and that the stem of the ship had cut the monster in two, but as there was no observer on the other side of the vessel there was no way of estimating what length of body might have been left on that side.

From the time the monster was first sighted until it disappeared in the distance astern it was thrashing about as though in agony. The monster's skin was dark brown, slick and smooth. There were no fins, hair or protuberances on the head, neck, or visible parts of the body.

In 1977 the *Zuiyo Maru,* a Japanese trawler, hauled up nets which had been set a thousand feet beneath the surface of the sea off of Christchurch, New Zealand. The nets contained the decomposing body of a bizarre, thirty-foot long creature. It had a small head, a long neck, somewhat thicker body, and four flippers. Overall, it resembled a crepe paper animal mascot of some university whose parade float had passed through a thunderstorm. The captain, fearing contamination of his cargo of mackerel, had the bedraggled, rotting corpse dropped overboard, but not before Michihiko Yano, a minor executive with a seafood corporation, had sketched and photographed it.

Professor Ikuo Obata of Japan's National Science Museum examined the sketch and photographs. He observed that the creature looked like a plesiosaurus, a marine dinosaur which had been extinct for some sixty million years. Although a number of other scientists, lacking vertebrae in hand, as it were, were cautious as to the identification of the *Zuiyo Maru*'s unusual catch, the ship's captain was roundly criticized for discarding what might have been one of the greatest scientific discoveries of our time.

It would appear that the sea contains some creatures about which we know little or nothing. An odd fish caught in the Indian Ocean in 1938 turned out to be a coelacanth, which scientists had thought to have been extinct for fifty million years or more. In 1930 Dr. Anton Brunn dredged up six-foot eel larvae from a depth of one thousand feet. If the larvae and growth patterns correspond to what we know about eels in shallower water, then we must assume that there must be eels of up to one hundred feet in length in the deep sea. A great many water creatures, including oarfish, sea turtles, sharks, whales, and colonies of sea squirts—which resemble ghostly, gigantic white worms—have undoubtedly been the objects of some sea monster sightings. Yet when Dr. Bernard Heuvelmans made an objective and in-depth analysis of 459 sea monster reports, he concluded that while 49 were definite hoaxes and 52 probable mistakes, there were 358 which were inexplicable in terms of marine biology as we know it.

We are only beginning to probe the mysteries of the animal life which thrives beneath the waters. As well as creatures about which we know little or nothing, there is a treasure chest of curiosities concerning creatures with which we are scientifically familiar.

In the Bible we read that:

> The Lord prepared a great fish to swallow up Jonah. And Jonah was in the belly of the fish three days and three nights. Then Jonah prayed unto the Lord his God out of the fish's belly and said ". . . I am cast out of thy sight, yet I will look again towards thy holy temple. . . ."

> And the Lord spoke unto the fish and it vomited out Jonah upon dry land.

On August 25, 1891, the whaling vessel *Star of the East* was cutting through the mid-Atlantic when the lookout spotted several sperm whales. Boats were lowered and the chase began. One of the boats, commanded by helmsman James Bartley, closed upon one of the behemoths and a harpoon was hurled into it. The wounded whale rushed at the boat and crushed it with long, powerful jaws. All of the men except Bartley managed to leap into the water to safety, but the helmsman was swept into the whale's gaping maw. The whale sounded as Bartley's crewmates struggled toward the other boats. Obviously, there was nothing to be done about Bartley; it was one of the calculated risks of whaling.

Several harpoons had been driven home into some of the whales and the captain of the *Star of the East* cruised the area for several hours, hoping that at least one of the whales had been mortally wounded. Finally, a huge hulk floated up to the surface, dead, and the men lashed it to the side of the ship. For two days the crew cut away strips of the blubber with long flancing knives. One of the men speculated that this might be the whale which had swallowed Bartley, and proposed opening its stomach and intestines to see if there were any remains which might be buried at sea. Most of the crew were hesitant, figuring that even if this were the same whale, what would be left after the jaws and powerful digestive juices had done their work would not be retrievable. Nevertheless, they cut through to the stomach where, to their astonishment, the shape of a man could clearly be seen bulging against the stomach wall. Very carefully now, they cut open the final membranes, so as not to mutilate their companion's corpse.

The man was covered with whale blood, a ghastly purple hue—but was alive! Some of the crewmen started to administer artificial respiration to the unconscious man, while others forced his mouth open and splashed small amounts of brandy into it. Gradually, Bartley revived, although delirious for some time. He suffered from nightmares, but eventually recovered from his ordeal.

When the *Star of the East* returned to England, the story of Bartley's curious experience was understandably met with skepticism. Yet everyone associated with the incident, from captain to lowest cabin boy, testified under oath as to its veracity. The editor of the respected Paris periodical, *Journal des Débats,* spent five years reviewing the facts, interviewing the men who had been aboard the *Star of the East,* and obtaining medical opinions before publishing an account of the event. Bartley related that:

> The very moment I jumped from the boat I saw the whale turn right round so that its open mouth was right underneath me. Within seconds I felt my feet touch something soft and spongy. I knew I had entered its huge mouth and I remember going down into what seemed like a canvass covering of pinkish-white, feet first, and then I realized I was being swallowed by the whale.

> I went lower into its body and a wall of flesh surrounded me, but the pressure of this was not great and the flesh actually seemed to give way against my slightest movement or touch.

> Suddenly I found myself in what was like a tremendous sack, much larger than my body. All was totally dark. I felt about and my hand came into contact with several fishes, some of which seemed still to be alive, as they squirmed away at my touch . . . I felt a great pain in my head, and my breathing became difficult. At the same time I felt a dreadful heat . . . like being in an oven . . . I believed I was condemned to perish in the belly of the whale. I tried to rise, to move my arms and legs, to shout out . . . my brain was quite clear and then, with the realisation of my awful fate, I finally lost consciousness.

Thus, perhaps the greatest fish story of all concerns the man who got away, rather than the fish (or marine mammal, to be precise).

There is evidence that sharks have swallowed men whole, although, understandably, none have escaped to tell about it. The giant grouper, known too as the Australian black rockcod, jewfish, or sea bass, has also been suspected of making a single-bite meal of a man. The grouper, which resembles an overgrown version of the freshwater largemouth bass, seems an unlikely villain. Alhough capable of short bursts of speed, it is generally a languid creature which hovers about reefs, rock grottoes, and sunken ships in tropical waters. Its coloration tends to echo that of its environment—some wear the brilliant hues of the coral in which they live—and many varieties can change their colors as quickly as if they were objects in a conjuring trick.

Skin divers enjoy observing groupers. Each fish, at least the larger ones, seems to have a territory staked out, and if not molested by spear fishermen, they may be curious, even friendly, around divers. One researcher who fed them tidbits of fish reported that they would come up to him and poke into pockets of his diving gear as if they were household pets. Groupers can grow to gargantuan proportions; spear fishermen and anglers seek them not only as trophies but for the excellent flavor of their flesh. Specimens weighing between one hundred and four hundred pounds are not uncommonly reeled in by patient fishermen. Aficionados of sport fishing, one of whom once remarked that its fight was only slightly more vigorous than that of a snagged tree bole, do not celebrate the grouper.

What gives a sinister edge to the friendly grouper has to do with size. Truly immense groupers are never swept up in nets, as they lurk in natural or man-made crannies. They seem to like the iron legs of deep oil rigs. Suited, deep-sea divers report that the deeper their work takes them, the larger the groupers they encounter. Flancer Burton, a master diver who services oil rigs in the Gulf of Mexico, claims to have seen groupers which he estimates run around two thousand pounds. Such fish, he asserts, "could easily have swallowed a Volkswagen."

A giant grouper's mouth opens and closes in rhythm with its breathing. When prey—fish or shrimp—swim past it, the grouper sucks a surge of water into its gaping mouth, and the prey is helplessly drawn in with it. Philippe Cousteau reports seeing a twenty-pound barracuda thus vacuumed into the mouth of a relatively small grouper. Over the years, the *Sydney Herald* of Australia has reported incidents of deep-sea divers being attacked by immense groupers, and even being swallowed by them whole—helmet, weighted shoes, and all. Aside from this, a number of other divers have simply disappeared, the boat crews reeled up severed air hoses. Some were undoubtedly cut by sharp coral or jagged metal, yet were others chomped off by gigantic groupers? It is certainly possible.

None of which is to say that we should regard the giant grouper as anything more than it is, a huge, fascinating fish capable of chameleon color changes and a curiosity about human divers. If one of the gigantic specimens which apparently do exist occasionally has sucked up a human under the delusion it was just another fish, some prey, we can only assume the Lord neglected to tell the grouper about man's opposing thumb, history, philosophy, and place upon the pedestal of evolution, and excuse the mistake.

I am sure no malice has ever been involved. Only dinner.

The mola mola, or ocean sunfish, is one of the most curious and little-known inhabitants of the sea. They grow to immense size. A mola mola that became stranded on the sand at Comodoro Rivadavia, Argentina, weighed 2,640 pounds. Out of the water, this bizarre creature, sheathed with grisly, elastic flesh, resembles the decapitated head and front fins of an even larger fish. The mola mola's spinal cord never exceeds an inch in length; its great bulk, covered with barnacles and other crustacean parasites, is directed by one of the least intelligent minds of the fish world. Mola molas usually float languidly upon the surface of tropical waters, although when hungry they may dive to depths of a thousand feet in quest of shrimp and small fish. On the surface, the mola mola sometimes aimlessly revolves around and around. They have large, gentle eyes, tiny mouths, and have been known to make a groaning sound when harpooned and drawn up to the side of a ship.

At night, the mola mola gleams with a ghostly phosphorescence, and might well be taken for a sea monster. Fortunately for the mola mola, and those who are fascinated by the diversity of animal life in the sea, this huge docile fish has little commercial value or interest to the sportsman.

The helmeted diver, who has outlasted a mutiny and a typhoon above the surface of the water, and vanquished a large shark beneath it, now leadfoots his way toward the bars of gold which can be seen through a rent in the sunken galleon's side. The reef is contorted, rocky, and one of our hero's legs slips into a crevasse, the scalloped edges of which suddenly clamp shut, trapping him. Giant Clam! On the surface, the hero's blonde and busty girl peers anxiously over the rails of the charter boat, and the mate with the scarred cheek, sensing disaster, is already leering at her.

The perilous potentials of the giant clam have long been appreciated by the creators of low budget adventure films and comic books. A good many years ago, an East Indian story goes, a pearl diver had his hand snapped off by a giant clam. Much later, the clam was pried up and hauled to the surface, cut open, and found to contain the hand, now coated with mother-of-pearl. The hand was owned by several wealthy people over the years, each of whom, as they found the hand enabled them to commit evil deeds, became progressively more vile themselves. The mother-of-pearl hand now resides in the National Library in Bombay. It is not known if the regulars of the reading room have been infected with dark passions and greeds.

An ancient Indian scroll describes the plight of another pearl diver who had an unpleasant encounter with a giant clam. "Whereof he knew not whence the danger cometh, a limb was crushed within the vise of a shelled mischief-maker and thereupon he suffocated with surrounding waters."

Although such tales abound, there is not a single documented case of a person dying in the clasp of a giant clam. Giant clams live in Australian waters as well as parts of the Indian Ocean. These giant mollusks grow to over four feet long and weigh in excess of five hundred pounds. Once shut, the only way a giant clam can be forced to relax its grip is by sticking a knife through the valves and severing the powerful muscles which hold the two halves together. Formidable as all this may sound, in order to close itself, the clam must first expel the water from between its lips. Although this takes only a matter of seconds, there is plenty of time for an alert diver to remove his hand or foot from danger.

One of the most fascinating things about giant clams, aside from their size, is the fact that a plant lives within the host's skin, utilizing carbon dioxide given off by the mollusk. In return, the plant increases the amount of oxygen available to its host. The giant clam has lenses in its skin which intensify sunlight, speeding up the process and thus benefiting both plant and animal. Some giant clams have colorful mantles which completely hide the shells.

Several tropical, maritime peoples have legends about giant clams. In Fiji, they tell of the time when a boy stepped into one of the mollusks at low tide. The boy, who was in charge of all the chickens of his island, had brought his large flock to feed upon the snails, worms, and other tidbits of the reef. The clam was a dignified old cuss, and resented the squawk and flutter of the chickens in his orderly domain. He determined to hold the boy until the tide should rise and drown him. After instructing his chickens to fly back to land, the boy tried to flatter the clam, and thanked him for teaching him a lesson about other creatures' sensitivities. The clam was not appeased. The water rose higher on the boy as the tide returned. Nimble of mind as well as desperate, the boy apologized to his captor for mistaking him for a clam when its was obvious he was an oyster. The clam, astonished, asked the boy why he thought so.

"Because of the pearl inside of you," the boy responded. "Only oysters have pearls." When the clam opened his shells to look for his pearl, the boy swam free. Meanwhile the chickens had been calling frantically, urging their guardian to hurry ashore before high tide should cover him. And to this day the advent of high tide in Fiji is signalled by the crowing of roosters.

As with the giant clam, filmmakers and authors of watery adventure tales have often pictured the moray eel as one of the most vicious denizens of the deep. Indeed, the sight of a moray, or a brace of them, swaying sinuously out of a rock cranny like macabre puppets of doom, is unsettling to a diver. History has not helped their image. In ancient times it was believed horsehairs which had fallen into salt water would later become eels; around the turn of the last century a researcher concluded that eels lay their eggs in the depths of the Sargasso, that legendary eye of becalmed mid-Atlantic waters where rotting ships were once thought to drift with skeleton crews, hopelessly entangled in kelp. Horace, the Roman poet, tells us that morays were kept in special reservoirs and fattened upon the bodies of dead slaves. A large moray eel—which may grow to more than eight feet long—will very likely lash out if molested. They have sharp teeth, strong jaws, and the myth that the only way to induce one of them to release its bulldog grip is to cut off the head perhaps has more than a grain of truth to it.

Although the moray is capable of a nasty bite if startled or otherwise provoked, it is generally shy and unaggressive around man if he keeps a tolerable distance. Some divers report them to be friendly creatures if convinced of the visitor's good intentions. Like the giant clam, the moray eel suffers from its myth, as well as the kind of face we have come to associate with evil incarnate.

Mythology, both classical and tribal, embraces the notion of opposites among siblings—the kind and beautiful woman whose sister is ugly and evil, as well as the lovely, sinister woman whose sister is loving and drab (at least until discovered by a prince, whose touch transforms her into a traffic stopper). The family *Scorpaenidae* includes the stonefish, perhaps the most grotesque creature in the sea, and the zebra fish, quite possibly the most gorgeous. But both siblings of *Scorpaenidae,* better known as scorpion fish, are the de' Medicis of the sea; they are poisoners without peer. The stonefish and the zebra fish inhabit the shallow waters surrounding the rim of Australia, that botanical paradox where the quantity and diversity of shoreline marine life seems almost a compensation for the scorched and largely barren interior of the continent.

The blunt-nosed, warty stonefish with its cockscomb of highly venomous spines, camouflages itself with the dull colors of the mud, sand, or rock in which it lives. The zebra fish, gently propelling themselves through the bright horns and slabs of coral reefs, have long delicate fins which are so featherlike that they might be taken for brilliantly hued tropical birds which have plunged into the water after fish. They, too, have lethal spines. Neither fish is a menace to man unless molested. Yet, if a spear fisherman unwarily brushes close to a zebra fish, or if a wader accidentally steps upon a stonefish, poison from the spines can cause convulsions, delirium, gangrene, and even death within hours.

Stepping upon a stingray, which like the stonefish is a master of concealment in sandy shallows, is rarely fatal, but can be excruciatingly painful.

While a high school student in southern California, I was once playing touch football in the shallows of Newport Bay when I slipped down and my hand came in contact with a stingray on the murky bottom. The flat, rounded stingray was no larger than a good-sized frying pan, although its whiplike tail, containing a poisonous spine, more than doubled its length. The spine itself only grazed my hand, but a small barb broke off under the skin. Within half an hour my hand became a pulsing core of agony. Although I have broken several bones in my life, none of them resulted in this sort of breathtaking pain. I was delirious by the time friends could get me to a doctor.

The French naturalist Pierre de Latil described a similar case in which the victim had only been scratched on the thumb. He suffered immediate, intense pain, high fever, and his arm was moderately numb for three months. It has been estimated that some fifteen hundred people are treated for stingray wounds each year in the United States.

Greek lore has it that Ulysses was killed by a spear tipped with a stingray barb. Pliny, in his *Historia Naturalis,* commented that: ". . . There is nothing that is more to be dreaded than the sting which protrudes from the tail of the Trygon (stingray) . . . a weapon five inches in length. Fixing this in the root of a tree, the fish is able to kill it; it can pierce armor, too, like an arrow, and to the strength of iron it adds the venom of poison."

Modern researchers have yet to see such a ray, or observe a tree toppling after being stung. Pliny also asserted that the stingray "lies lurking in ambush and pierces the fish as they pass." We now know that stingrays feed mostly upon worms and crustaceans. They use their barbs strictly for defense. When wading in water where the presence of stingrays is suspected, it is a good idea to shuffle your feet, which will usually cause the unaggressive rays to flee.

The giant manta ray, or devilfish, is one of the most graceful entities in the sea, in spite of its great size. A manta may weigh more than thirty-five hundred pounds, and flaps through tropical waters on pectoral fins, resembling wings, which may be twenty feet wide. It is of no danger to man unless accidentally enmeshed in a net, in which case the sheer bulk of the animal could swamp a small boat. Mantas are known for their soaring leaps out of the water. A harpooned mother was once observed to eject an embryo while in flight. The newborn manta spread its pectoral fins and fluttered like a bird as it dropped back to the sea. Researchers are unsure if the manta's wild leaps are made out of sheer exuberance or to rid themselves of the small parasites which cling to their skin. Perhaps for both reasons. A German zoologist has observed that pilot fish clean out the parasites from inside the manta's mouth. The manta, grateful for the service, does not harm the pilot fish.

Marine researcher Russell Coles once observed a pair of lesser devil rays in the act of mating. "Copulation," he reported, "was not accomplished by a vertical motion, but by a graceful, serpentine lateral curvature of the spine, as the male alternately advanced one of his *mixopterygia* (claspers) as he withdrew the other." During the leisurely mating, the couple would sometimes disengage, swim about and jump out of the water before returning to each other.

In small Mexican villages on the Gulf of California, small mantas are sometimes speared for food. Steaks cut from the wings taste to me rather like mildly fishy pork chops—quite tasty when served up with a stack of hot tortillas and washed down with a *Pacifico* or *Tecate* beer.

The sawfish, a relative of both the shark and the ray, is another curious creature of the sea, as well as a number of large rivers such as the Amazon. Its flattened snout is edged with sharp teeth, giving it the appearance of a double-edged ripsaw. A twenty-foot specimen may have a saw which is six feet long. Sawfish will slash at a school of fish with their formidable weapons and then feed upon those it has killed or wounded. Predictably, the sawfish has a fearsome niche in the lore of the sea. Archbishop Claus Magnus of Sweden asserted that sawfish "will swim under the ships, and cut them, that the water may come in, and he may feed upon the men when the ship is drowned." Assuming that all hands would perish of such a doleful experience, one wonders where the good Archbishop obtained his information. Be that as it may, contemporary accounts of sawfish aggression towards man are almost nonexistent. We do have a reliable account of a three-foot sawfish which made an "unprovoked" attack upon a diver in the Yucatan. Since the teeth of the saw "were scarcely larger than the blade of a small scalpel," the diver suffered but minor lacerations, and, as he was in the process of spearing fish, the "unprovoked" nature of the assault might be questioned.

The barracuda, with its needle-sharp teeth, underslung jaw, and glaring eyes like those of a disturbed man in a bar about to break a chair over someone's head, appears to be a dangerous customer—and is. Although documented attacks on man are rare, most divers are cautious around a giant barracuda, which may be eight feet long, or a school of smaller specimens. Jacques-Yves Cousteau has described being surrounded by a "bulkhead of barracudas [which] extended from the ocean's floor to the surface. Alone and bare-handed, I could not suppress a tremor of panic. We had never paid attention to barracudas, and I had dismissed them in print as being of no danger to divers. Now, in this confrontation, I was not sure. They might have a mob psychology that would produce a sudden, irreparable act at any moment." Cousteau forced himself to be calm and the mass of barracudas eventually swam away.

Barracudas can strike with the speed of a torpedo. In 1953 a wader at Juno Beach, Florida, was savagely bitten on the leg by a barracuda. Nine years later, in water less than a foot deep off the coast of Mexico, a barracuda all but took off a man's foot. In his *Natural History of the Antilles,* Lord de Rochefort wrote in 1665 that: "Among the monsters greedy and desirous of human flesh, the Becune (local name for barracuda) is one of the most formidable." Sailors sometimes catch barracuda by trailing a strip of white cloth behind their ship. In the Windward Islands, a seaman was rowing toward the victory line in a dinghy race when something underwater slammed into one of his freshly painted white oars with such force as to knock it out of his hand. Retrieving the oar, he discovered a four-foot-long barracuda clamped to the end of it. He was compensated for the loss of the race by his unusual catch, which he ate.

The transparent or translucent bells of jellyfish are one of the most beautiful sights in the sea—unless you happen to be swimming in a mass of them. Their trailing tentacles are lined with stinging cells with which they paralyze small fish and other prey. Depending upon the species, swimmers brushing against jellyfish tentacles may suffer anything from a mild stinging sensation or a skin rash to severe shock with paralysis and convulsions. The tentacles of many jellyfish dangle or trail more than fifty feet through the water. Indians warned early American settlers to be wary of jellyfish; a bather was killed by them in Virginia's Rappahannock River in 1750.

The largest jellyfish live in the polar regions. Eskimos have reported seeing jellyfish some ten feet across with ten- to fifteen-pound fish immobilized in their tentacles. Yet ounce for ounce many authorities consider the sea wasp, a small, almost transparent creature which lives in Australian waters, to be the most deadly creature in the world. Its venom, far more deadly than that of a cobra, can cause death in three to ten minutes, often before the victim has a chance to struggle back to the shore. In recent years, scientists have attributed a number of deaths to the terrible touch of the sea wasp.

Professor E. Ford, director of the School of Public Health and Tropical Medicine, Sydney, Australia, made the following report in 1938:

> . . . A half-caste boy aged 12 years, was bathing in the local swimming baths [Darwin, Australia]. He dived into the water and when he came to the surface he was distressed and just able to reach the beach. He said that he had been stung by a jellyfish. He died shortly afterwards . . . witnesses stated that the jellyfish was still sticking to

the boy when he staggered to the beach. This specimen was submitted to the Australian Museum and identified as *Chiropsalmus quadrigatus* Haeckel, commonly known as the "Sea Wasp."

Like jellyfish, Portuguese man-of-war catch their prey with stinging tentacles which cause painful welts on any humans who brush against their potent, trailing ribbons. They may also be fatal. The *Cairns Post,* an Australian newspaper, carried a story of a jellyfish attack in its issue of January 21, 1937:

> Within eight minutes of being stung by the deadly Portuguese man-o'-war while bathing at Bramston Beach (40 miles south of Cairns), 12 miles from Mirriwinni, this morning, D. W. T. (19) collapsed and died. Young T., who had been holidaying with his aunt at Mirriwinni, was in the water with a friend. They waded out waist deep and almost instantly the man-o'-war tentacles became wrapped around the victim's abdomen. His companion helped to free him and assisted him to the shore. T. staggered about 50 yards and collapsed. He was dead within eight minutes. . . .

The Portuguese man-of-war is actually a merged, closely functioning colony of animals rather than a true jellyfish. Some of the animals which make up a man-of-war are responsible for stinging, others for digestion, and yet others for reproduction. Each of the separate entities of this remarkable creature smoothly cooperates as if they were one animal. The nomeus is a small fish which spends its life darting through the tentacles of the man-of-war without being stung. Scientists are still unsure if this is at the pleasure of the man-of-war, or if the nomeus has acquired immunity by nibbling at the tentacles. While true jellyfish pulsate their umbrellas for locomotion, the man-of-war sails before the winds with its crested, air-filled bag.

A few years back, my wife, two of our three children, and I visited the Mexican port of Topolobampo. We had neither the time nor the money to go out on a proper fishing vessel, but spontaneously decided to pay a genial young Mexican to carry us across the bay to a small beach in his skiff. My son, prepared for any eventuality, brought along some line and hooks. Close to some rocks, we fished briefly with droplines and landed some good-sized triggerfish. Back at Topolobampo we offered our catch to our friend with the boat, as we had no way of conveniently carrying them back to our hotel in

Los Mochis. Our man politely declined with a shrug, telling us in Spanish that they were not very tasty. Disinclined to waste food of any kind, we tried to give them away to people hanging out around the dock. Their response, like that of our boatman, was merely that they were not the best of fish for eating.

Later we read that triggerfish can be highly poisonous.

Throughout the world there are numerous fish which are toxic to man, especially in tropical waters. The situation is confused by the fact that some species which are not only safe but delectable in one region or season may be poisonous in another. Many varieties of pufferfish, which can inflate itself to three times its normal size when alarmed or irritated, are deadly.

For more than a century and a half, the Japanese have been flirting with fatal indigestion every time they raise their chopsticks over a dish of fugu, a local variety of pufferfish. They not only consider the fugu a delicacy—they are willing to risk death for it. The secret of surviving a fugu feast is in its preparation. The back of the fish is not poisonous, but it must be carefully separated from the rest of the fish, which is. Although the cooks who work in restaurants which serve fugu not only go through rigorous training and must pass examinations and be licensed, an estimated two hundred Japanese gourmets die from eating fugu every year. The ultimate disgrace for a fugu cook is not to have the dish returned to the kitchen but to have the customer carried out of the restaurant.

In spite of the danger, or perhaps because of it, fugu connoisseurs continue to flock into restaurants which specialize in the exotic dish. It is not only dangerous, but frightfully expensive, thought to possess certain aphrodisiac qualities, and even tastes good. As if all this were not enough, fugu chefs artistically serve the flesh of the fugu in shapes of beautiful birds and flowers.

In a world where puffers and other questionable fish are simply tossed back into the sea, it is refreshing to know that some people still know how to make a silk purse out of a sow's ear.

The most renowned sea monster has been cut off from its ocean homeland since the end of the last ice age and a date some five thousand years ago. At least, this is the theory of a great many men and women who believe that a gigantic creature with a long neck lives in the depths of Loch Ness when rising land changed that body of water from a saline fiord to a freshwater lake. Numerous people of respectability, including clergymen, have reported sighting the beast. There have been hazy photographs of it. The tools of twentieth-century technology, including sonar, telescopic camera lenses, and even a small yellow submarine, have been pitted against the elusive monster with inconclusive results which have only served to further tantalize the believers and harden the cynicism of nonbelievers. In this, the believers share the frustrations of flying-saucer buffs; the nonbelievers refuse to take any of it with proper seriousness unless the Loch Ness monster is captured and transported to Marineland, a UFO pilot appears upon a television talk show, or an intact flying saucer has been trundled into the Smithsonian for exhibit.

Although "Nessie," the Loch Ness shy violet, is the most publicized lake monster, there are others. *The Dublin Irish Evening Herald* once interviewed a sixteen-year-old student, Gay Denver, who witnessed a beast coming ashore from the depths of Glendarry Lake in the wilds of County Mayo.

"It was moving in a sort of jumpy way like a kangaroo," stated the lad. "It had a long head like a sheep and a long neck and tail. The hind legs were bigger than the front ones." He elaborated that it was "much bigger than a horse. I got a terrible fright, jumped on my bike and rode away as fast as I could."

There is a Loch Morer monster, who is said to reside in his own deep lake in Scotland, only twenty miles away from Loch Ness; there are monsters apparently gliding through the depths of lakes in New Brunswick, British Columbia, and Alaska. It would seem that most lake monsters prefer waters which are too cold to attract bathers, unless lake resort owners in warmer climates have managed to suppress stories of their own monsters, as unfavorable word might spread among water skiers.

People in the vicinity of Lake Utopia, New Brunswick, first became aware of their monster over a hundred years ago. Since then there have been a number of sightings of a huge, long-tailed beast with a peculiarly full-beaked head, rather like that of a parrot. The *Illustrated News of Canada* reported that it "was sending up logs, spruce edgings and other material and causing the water to boil and foam as if a geyser had suddenly broken loose."

Years after the *Illustrated News* story appeared, Mrs. Fred McKillop was to recall an incident for the press: "It was a clear, beautiful day. The men had all gone fishing and had left me to sit with two of my grandchildren. We were all watching the lake and it was beautiful. It was so clear it resembled glass and there wasn't a ripple showing.

"Suddenly, as I watched, the water commenced to boil and churn, and make waves which came in and broke on the shore. Then a huge creature of some sort emerged from the water, at least it showed part of its head and part of its body. It resembled a huge black rock, but it moved and churned all the time."

Pending further evidence, I suspect the jury will remain hung upon the existence of lake monsters. There is, however, another freshwater monster whose reality cannot be doubted. It has not only been caught, but cooked, eaten, and declared tasty (a test to date which no mythological beast has passed). I refer to a fish as small as its legend of diabolical viciousness is great—the piranha.

The piranha thrives in a four-million-square-mile South American domain which includes most of the Atlantic watershed between Caracas and Buenos Aires, the tropical rain forest and savannah which takes up the better part of the continent. Throughout much of this region the piranha is called the *caribe,* which alludes to the tribe of Indians who once lived along the rim of the Caribbean Sea. They were cannibals. *Capaburro* is another common name for the piranha. It means "donkey castrater." The some twelve species of piranha rarely get larger than a man's hand and are often striking in coloration—silver lamé and a vivid red which covers the throat from the lower jaw to the belly. It looks like blood and this distinctive marking is sometimes covered with blood when the scalpel-sharp tricuspids of the fish are biting into some animal which has wandered into the water. A larger, darker piranha may grow to eighteen inches long and weigh five pounds.

It is quite true that a school of frenzied piranhas can and occasionally do reduce a cow to a skeleton within minutes, although the tradition that vaqueros will usually drive an old or sick animal into the water downriver from a ford so that the rest of the herd can cross in safety while piranhas are distracted by the sacrifice, is a myth. The lethal potentials of the piranha came to the attention of the general public in the United States and Europe largely through Theodore Roosevelt's account of his epic trek through the outback of Brazil in 1913. At one village, he was told of a twelve-year-old boy who had recently been "literally devoured by them." His guide, noted explorer Colonel Candido Rondon, had lost one of his toes to a piranha. When one of Rondon's men on a previous expedition failed to return to camp, a search party found his remains in a nearby stream, the gentle current eerily ballooning the untorn clothing around the missing man's stripped bones. On a tributary of the Paraguay River, some of Roosevelt's companions

> . . . found a deepish pond a hundred yards or so long and thirty or forty across. It was tenanted by the small caymans and by capybaras —the largest known rodent, a huge aquatic guinea pig, the size of a small sheep. It also swarmed with piranhas, the ravenous fish of which I have so often spoken. Undoubtedly the caymans were subsisting largely on these piranha. But the tables were turned if any caymans were injured. When a capybara was shot and sank in the water, the piranhas at once attacked it, and had eaten half the carcass ten minutes later. But much more extraordinary was the fact that when a cayman about five feet long was wounded the piranhas attacked and tore it, and actually drove it out on the bank to face its human foes. The fish first attacked the wound; then, as the blood maddened them, they attacked all the soft parts, their terrible teeth cutting out chunks of tough hide and flesh. Evidently they did not molest either cayman or capybara while it was unwounded; but blood excited them to frenzy. (From Theodore Roosevelt, *Through the Brazilian Wilderness* [New York: Charles Scribner's Sons, 1914].)

Piranhas eat piranhas as well as other species of fish. Many an angler in South America, hooking a fish, has ended up reeling in a catch which has already been half devoured. Indians net piranhas, prizing them as food. They usually handle them with care. Other people have not been cautious. Henry Wickham, whose export of Brazilian rubber seeds in 1876 began the rubber industry of the Far East, was splitting a piranha down its back when it sheered off one of his fingers. A lieutenant on one of Colonel Rondon's expeditions dynamited a pool to obtain fish, a common backcountry practice to this day in Latin America. He and his companions hurriedly waded in to gather the dead and stunned fish which had floated to the surface of the water. His hands full, the lieutenant placed one of the fish in his teeth, much as a man might hold a nail to free his hands. The fish was a piranha. It revived and took off a chunk of the lieutenant's tongue. He almost bled to death.

There was the gandy dancer who, taking a noon break from laying track beside the Amazon, plunged into the water for a cooling dip.

His enthusiastic splashing was cut short as he screamed. He was dead before he could be dragged ashore. Numerous natives of the Amazon basin wear scars the size of silver dollars, legacies of piranha attack.

As with all beasts which inspire terror, however, there is another side to the story. Anthropologist Harald Schultz spent some twenty years in piranha country, yet wrote, "In all these years I have never had a harmful experience with these greatly feared piranhas." Adventure classics to the contrary, attacks by single piranhas are apparently far more common than those of a blood-crazed school. Only four species of the fish are known to attack man, and even their inclinations to voraciousness seem to vary from stream to stream, and to be affected by swiftness of current, the piranha breeding season, and even the tides in coastal areas (they are deemed to be dangerous only after the ebb tide). A naturalist recently observed an Indian, bitten by a piranha while netting fish, merely bind the wound with a chewing tobacco poultice, and then wade back into the water to resume fishing.

The paradox of the piranha is perhaps best summed up in the frustrations of a French film crew who placed a cow carcass in a pool where they expected it to be skeletonized by piranha. Nothing happened. The filmmakers bloodied the water. Still nothing happened. Finally, giving up after two hours, they had started to pack their gear when the water exploded in a frenzy of feeding fish. The cow was consumed so fast the film crew barely had time to reset their cameras.

An American who has waded and swum in innumerable streams of the Amazon basin without so much as ever receiving a nip from a piranha once wryly commented that he never entered the water unless preceded by a local Indian who had all of his fingers and toes intact.

In certain marshy lakes and sluggish streams which meander through the jungles of South America there are blind, ten-foot-long creatures with strangely crude and unformed features as if they were objects which children had started to mold out of clay before abruptly abandoning their projects. They move about after nightfall, and can discharge enough electric shock into the water to knock a man or a cow unconscious, causing them to drown. Traditionally, they have been called electric eels, although scientists now place them in a family all their own. Much of their long tubular bodies are packed with the electric cells by which they guide and defend themselves, sense the presence of prey, and then stun it. Electric eels are born with sight, which they lose as they mature. Lacking well developed gills, they must surface for air, the soft splash of which must be an ominous sound to a man wading a darkened jungle slough.

Curiously enough, this odd creature of nocturnal waters is a distant relative of the goldfish which circles pet store bowls.

The Vikings were bold seafarers, venturing across the Atlantic in small wooden boats almost a thousand years ago. When they returned from their explorations and conquests, there would be feasting and strange tales to be shared, none of which were more spellbinding than those concerning the *kraken*. The *kraken* was a monstrous sea creature whose numerous flexible arms were known to reach up into the rigging of a ship and pull it over, causing it to sink. Most of the curious beasts of mythology were combinations of known animals or humans as well as fanciful interpretations of creatures sighted which were unknown at the time. Yet the *kraken* of legend was actually a gigantic version of the squid, an elongated invertebrate with eight arms and two longer tentacles which they shoot out to grasp prey and bring it in to their powerful beaks. Small squid had been caught for food and bait for centuries, and most scientists of the seventeenth and eighteenth centuries brushed off reports of *krakens* as myth. Still, for a myth, it was persistent.

An Icelandic journal described a sea monster that washed up on a beach in 1639 as having a boneless body as large and thick as a man's and seven tails with "buttons like eyeballs" (a picturesque allusion to suckers). The monster had yet another arm which was sixteen to eighteen feet long. In 1673 an Irish showman exhibited two suckered eight-foot arms which he had taken from a stranded sea monster. Toward the end of the eighteenth century New England whaling captains were telling of recovering severed arms from the mouths of sperm whales, some of which had suckers the size of dinner plates. Sailors reported seeing giant squid in a number of parts of the world, but by the middle of the nineteenth century most of the scientific community remained highly skeptical.

In the winter of 1861 a French gunboat, the *Alecton,* was cruising off the Canary Islands when its crew noticed a large floating mass in the water. When the commander edged his ship in closer for a better look, the object was seen to be a brick-red squid. The *Alecton* gave chase and finally managed to sink a harpoon into the viscous body. It appeared to have been previously wounded, was probably dying, and smelled strongly of musk. As a noose was secured around it, its length from tail to beak was estimated at fifteen to eighteen feet, its arms reaching out for an additional five or six feet.

As it was being hauled aboard the body broke off from the tail and sank. No matter. When the report of the *Alecton* was filed ashore, the *kraken* had passed from myth into reality; the existence of giant squid became widely accepted. As if to punctuate this acceptance, a number of giant squids began to wash onto the shores of Newfoundland, New Zealand, and Ireland. Most of these creatures were already beached, dead or dying, when discovered. The *Canadian Illustrated News* of October 27, 1877, however, described a specimen which was very much alive when it became beached on the shore of Trinity Bay.

> In its desperate efforts to escape, the ten arms darted about in all directions, lashing the water into foam, the thirty-foot tentacles in particular making lively play as it shot them out and endeavored to get a purchase with their powerful suckers, so as to drag itself into deep water. It was only when it became exhausted and the tide receded that the fishermen ventured to approach it. It died soon after the ebb of the tide, which left it high and dry on the beach.

Another large squid was spotted by fisherman Theophile Piccot in October, 1873, off Portugal Cove, Newfoundland. He indiscreetly jabbed it with a boat hook, whereupon the beast curled a tentacle over the edge of the small dory and began to pull it over. Piccot's twelve-year-old son snatched up an axe and flailed away at the rubbery appendage, severing it some ten feet away from the body of the advancing squid. The fishermen hastily rowed back to shore, with twenty-five feet of writhing, suckered tentacle in the bottom of the boat.

At least fourteen huge squid came into the shallows of Newfoundland to die during the decade between 1870 and 1880. No one is quite sure what brought them up from the deeps, although an abrupt change in water temperature is a possible explanation. The most immense squid of the lot made a dramatic appearance in the winter of 1878. Reverend Moses Harvey, considered by scientists of the day to be a reliable man, described its capture for the *Boston Traveller:*

On the 2nd day of November last, Stephen Sperring, a fisherman residing in Thimble Tickle . . . was out in a boat with two other men; not far from the shore they observed some bulky object, and, supposing it might be part of a wreck, they rowed toward it, and, to their horror, found themselves close to a huge fish, having large glassy eyes, which was making desperate efforts to escape, and churning the water into foam by the motion of its immense arms and tail. It was aground and the tide was ebbing. From the funnel at the back of its head it was ejecting large volumes of water, this being its method of moving backwards. . . .

Finding the monster partially disabled, the fishermen plucked up courage and ventured near enough to throw the grapnel of their boat, the sharp flukes of which, having barbed points, sunk into the soft body. To the grapnel they had attached a stout rope which they had carried ashore and tied to a tree, so as to prevent the fish from going out with the tide. . . . At length it became exhausted and as the water receded it expired.

The fishermen, alas! knowing no better, proceeded to convert it into dog's meat. It was a splendid specimen—the largest yet taken—the body measuring 20 feet from the beak to the extremity of the tail. . . . The circumference of the body is not stated, but one of the arms measured 35 feet. This must have been a tentacle.

From what we know of squid proportions, an animal the length of that hacked into dog meat at Thimble Tickle would have had arms thick as a man's body, suckers four inches wide, and a beak nine inches in diameter. One can imagine a diver confronting a creature fifty-five feet long, with glaring eyes which were roughly the size of a man's head. The *Guiness Book of World Records* echoes most oceanographers in regarding the Thimble Tickle squid as the largest of its kind as yet reliably reported.

With squid of this size prowling about, people remembered old tales of them rising out of the sea to entwine the masts of sailing ships. In 1874 *The Times* of London reported that a 150-ton schooner, the *Pearl,* had been attacked in the Bay of Bengal by a squid which "squeezed on board between the fore and mainmast, pulling the vessel over and sinking it." According to the article, the event was witnessed by crew and passengers of the *Strathowen,* a steamer bound from Columbo to Madras. The squid's body was estimated to be as large as that of the schooner. Since the *Strathowen* was not even listed in *Lloyd's Register* for that year, the entire business sounds rather like a hoax. In fact, with the single exception of a sailor said to have been dragged away from a life raft following the sinking of the troopship *Britannia* during World War II, believable accounts of men being killed by squid are almost nonexistent.

Aggression toward man aside, might there, in the perpetual darkness of the deep sea, be squids even larger than that seen at Thimble Tickle? Prince Albert I of Monaco, a dedicated marine biologist, used the royal yacht as a research vessel. On a cruise to the Azores in 1895 as he observed whalers killing a sperm whale, he was startled to see the victim "vomit several octopi or squid of a colossal size. Evidently these had been gathered during the whale's last excursion into the abyss . . . a mouthful that had hardly time to be swallowed."

Although no doubt thinking the Prince a bit daft from too much royal inbreeding, the whalers allowed Albert's assistants to dissect the odoriferous innards of the catch after they had stripped away the commercially valuable blubber and flesh. They found large squid, some of them unknown to science at the time, as well as observing curious round scars upon the skin of the whales. Albert, quite reasonably, assumed they had been inflicted by the squid during the course of titanic battles which must have taken place in the depths of the ocean.

Seaman Frank Bullen, while standing a late watch on a whaler cruising the Indian Ocean in the 1870s, claims to have witnessed such a struggle. In his *Cruise of the Cachalot,* he states that upon hearing a great commotion off upon the moonlit surface of the sea, he focused night glasses upon:

a very large sperm whale . . . locked in deadly conflict with a cuttlefish, or squid, almost as large as himself, whose interminable tentacles seemed to enlace the whole of his great body. The head of the whale especially seemed a perfect net-work of writhing arms—naturally, I suppose, for it appeared as if the whale had the tail part of the mollusc in his jaws, and, in a business-like, methodical way, was sawing through it.

By the side of the black columnar head of the whale appeared the head of a great squid, as awful an object as one could well imagine even in a fevered dream. Judging as carefully as possible, I estimated it to be at least as large as one of our pipes, which contained three hundred and fifty gallons; but it may have been, and probably was, a good deal larger. The eyes were very remarkable from the size and blackness, which, contrasted with the vivid whiteness of the head, made their appearance all the more striking. They were, at least, a foot in diameter, and, seen under such conditions, looked decidedly eery and hobgoblin-like.

All around the combatants were numerous sharks, like jackals round a lion, ready to share the feast, and apparently assisting in the destruction of the huge cephalopod. So the titanic struggle went on, in perfect silence as far as we were concerned, because, even had there been any noise, our distance from the scene of conflict would not have permitted us to hear it.

Thinking that such a sight ought not to be missed by the captain, I overcame my dread of him sufficiently to call him, and tell him of what was taking place. He met my remarks with such a furious burst of anger at my daring to disturb him for such a cause that I fled precipitately on deck again, having the remainder of the vision to myself. . . . The conflict ceased, the sea resumed its placid calm, and nothing remained to tell of the fight but a strong odor of fish, as of a bank of seaweed left by the tide in the blazing sun.

In his *Follow the Whale,* zoologist Ivan Sanderson points out that while the suckers of the largest known squid, such as the giant of Thimble Tickle, were no more than four inches in diameter, circular scars of eighteen inches in diameter have been found upon captured sperm whales. If these were, as we have every reason to believe, made by deep sea squid which are anatomically similar to those which washed into the shallows of Newfoundland a century ago, then we cannot ignore the possibility that in the deep rifts of the sunless sea there may be pale, tentacled creatures as large as any of those described in *kraken* myths of the Vikings.

Victor Hugo and other novelists have depicted life-or-death struggles between men and giant octopi. In actuality, although some octopi do grow large enough to threaten a diver if so inclined, they are shy, reclusive creatures. Researchers have found them to be the most intelligent of the invertebrates, learning things readily, and retaining what they have been taught. They are also curious, as more than one diver has discovered to his discomfort. A salvage diver named Lee Jones once watched apprehensively as a large octopus slowly made its way down his air hose, pausing every so often to nip at the rubber hose with its parrotlike beak. Apparently finding the knit cotton layers which sheathed the hose unappetizing, it continued to haul itself downward, gripping the hose with the suction cups of its arms. Jones had backed into a corner of the shipwreck in which he was working when one of the octopus's arms crawled across his shoulders and another tugged at his leaded boots. In lieu of a scream, Jones touched his chin to an emergency button which abruptly released a mass of air bubbles. Startled, the octopus propelled itself off into the dim water. The diver lost no time in signaling to be brought to the surface.

Although an octopus resembles nothing as much as an octopus, perhaps the next closest thing would be an inflated bagpipe with the expressive eyes of an aged and somewhat bored Shakespearean actor. They are among the most abundant creatures of the sea, and are thought to date back some four hundred million years. They are essentially hermits who reside in rock caves which they often partially seal with barricades of stone. They propel themselves in short bursts by forcing water through a siphon. Crab, shrimp, and other shellfish make up their diet.

Rather than monsters, octopi might more properly be regarded as magicians. Alarmed, they can instantly change color or throw out a cloud of ink. They have an astonishing ability to squeeze through the most minute cracks, stretching and flattening like rubber; it is almost as though they are able to transform themselves into liquid. Although they usually move backwards, they can move in any direction and, on occasion, have been known to venture out onto land for brief periods of time.

There is only one species of octopus which presents any danger to man. Like its relatives, the blue-ringed octopus is a retiring rock dweller.

On an autumn day in 1954 an Australian skin diver named John Baylis spotted a six-inch octopus, playfully grabbed it and let it crawl around his body. Surfacing, he tossed the small octopus, its arms frantically waving, to his companion, Kirke Dyson-Holland. The octopus landed upon Dyson-Holland's shoulder, moved gently across his back, and plopped into the water. The two men swam back to the beach. Dyson-Holland complained of his mouth being dry, then, puzzled, said he was having difficulty swallowing. Baylis noticed a thread of blood upon his friend's back and a small puncture wound. Dyson-Holland became violently ill and lost coordination. As Baylis rushed him to a hospital, Dyson-Holland muttered, "It was the little octo-pus." He lost consciousness en route to the hospital, began to turn blue, and there, died fifteen minutes after being placed in a respira-tor. This could be shrugged off as a violent allergic reaction except that another diver, pierced by the tiny beak of the same variety of oc-topus in Australian waters, also exhibited identical symptoms before dying within the same time frame.

If such a tiny octopus is capable of dealing death to a man who handles it, what might a truly large one do? When Jacques-Yves Cousteau and his team of divers came to Washington's Puget Sound to investigate the largest known variety of octopus in the world, spe-cialists from the Seattle aquarium warned them that the bite of such a huge octopus might cause death. Possibly so. Yet Cousteau's divers found that these octopi—which can be thirty feet in diameter and weigh up to two hundred pounds—had no aggressiveness towards them. At first the divers from Cousteau's research vessel *Calypso* found that the octopi would not venture from their rocky caves, al-though watching the intruders curiously. Accompanied by a local diver, Joanne Duffy, they eventually persuaded some octopi to emerge from their lairs. Held gently by the young woman, a large oc-topus turned bright red, then calmed and became paler as she stroked it on the mantle and head before releasing it. Another diver was immediately encircled by the arms of an octopus which he led away from the rocks. Calmly, the diver carried it back to the rocks, to which the suckered arms transferred themselves as they gradually released the diver. The octopus had gripped the man for support rather than in violence. As Cousteau remarked:

Thus, the divers of *Calypso* had their first confrontation with those mythical beings who, for centuries, have been "monsters" to land creatures and have held an honored spot in the folklore and legends of the West.

Face to face with the largest octopuses in the world, our team was able to measure the strength and estimate the danger which they represented. And it has been demonstrated that, for an experienced diver, it is possible to handle a cephalopod weighing 125 pounds and measuring 20 feet in diameter. Once our prejudices have been de-molished, man and octopus will be able to live together in harmony in the same sea. (From Jacques-Yves Cousteau, *Octopus and Squid* [Garden City, N.Y.: Doubleday & Co., 1973].)

Are the octopi of Puget Sound really the largest of their kind? There are scattered reports and tales of much larger octopi living in the depths of the sea, below the range of conventional scientific collecting apparatus. In 1956 F. G. Wood, a marine researcher, hired a Bahaman fishing guide named Duke to assist him in gathering marine specimens. Wood was greatly impressed with the man's knowledge as to where fish and other sea creatures might be found at a given time, as well as with his sincerity. Recalling tales he had previously heard of giant deep-water octopus in the region of the Bahamas, he asked Duke what he knew of them. His guide matter-of-factly mentioned several sightings, giving the place and the person. When asked as to how large they were known to grow, Duke indicated a boat house some seventy-five feet away, and stated their arms would reach from the boat to that structure.

Tasmania, a mountainous island cut off from the mainland of southeastern Australia by the often turbulent waters of Bass Strait, harbors a number of unique and curious life forms. There is the Tasmanian Devil, a fierce marsupial which looks rather like a small bear and gives voice with an eerie screaming howl. The Tasmanian wolf, also a marsupial, looks like a lean, striped dog. The Tasmanian wolf hunts by night, chasing its prey until they collapse from exhaustion. In the summer of 1960, three cattlemen trailing across a lonely beach came upon a huge inert lump of what apparently had once been some sort of sea creature. They estimated it at twenty feet long and eighteen feet wide, and figured a weight of between five and ten tons. Although there seemed to be a mouth opening, eyes were nonexistent, and the entire ivory-colored mass was so tough and rubbery that a zoologist would later have to use an axe to cut away tissue samples, as he had difficulty penetrating it with a knife.

The remains of a similar creature had been found at Rottnest Island, off the coast of Western Australia, in 1934.

The Tasmanian ranchers' story was a good one, and no doubt earned them many a free beer at the local pubs, but the location was too remote for folks to go and look for themselves, and it was not until two years later that the Australian scientific community paid serious attention to it at all. Finally, zoologist Bruce Mollison trekked out to the beach, and cut samples from the disintegrating blob. At the time, he estimated its weight at a ton.

Samples of the flesh were sent to the marine biologists working for the Australian government's chief research agency. After testing it, they concluded that it ". . . consists throughout of tough, fibrous material, loaded with fatty or oily substance. The material did not contain any bones, spines or other hard structures. . . . In view of the fact that this material has been stranded for a long time and is much decomposed, it is not possible to specifically identify it from our investigations so far. But our investigations lead us to believe that the so-called monster is a decomposing portion of a large marine animal. It is not inconsistent with blubber. . . ."

In other words, although hedging their bets, scientists who had not seen the strange lump upon the beach, at least until it had greatly disintegrated, hesitantly put their money on it as being part of a whale. Mollison, the first proper scientist upon the spot, disagreed, confident from his observations that it could not have been a portion of a whale.

His notion is that it was the remains of a sea creature as yet not known to, or classified by, science.

In 1957 F. G. Wood, the marine researcher whose guide had told him about gigantic squid in deep channels around the Bahamas, happened upon an old newspaper clipping, an illustrated feature entitled "The Facts about Florida." The caption beneath a sketch of an octopus stated:

In 1897, portions of an octopus, said to have been more gigantic than any ever before seen, were washed up on the beach at St. Augustine. Professor Verrill, of Yale University, who examined the remains, which alone weighed over six tons, calculated that the living creature had a girth of 25 feet and tentacles 72 feet in length.

Wood was intrigued. Not only was St. Augustine Beach, where the monster's remains reportedly washed ashore, only sixteen miles away from the Marineland Research Laboratory where he worked, but Professor Verrill had been a leading authority on squid. Wood pursued his investigation with the patience of a detective. The clipping carried neither date nor newspaper, and none of his associates could recall reading or hearing of such a monster. The building in which the St. Augustine newspaper had been housed had burned many years before; the clipping morgue had gone up in flames. Eventually, Wood received a photocopy of a page from the *Florida Times Union* of December 1, 1896, which he had traced through the state librarian. It gave the dimensions of the creature and said it was "apparently a portion of a whale. . . ." A man named Webb, president of the local scientific society, disagreed, positive he had examined the remains of an octopus.

An inquiry to the local historical society identified Webb as Dr. DeWitt Webb, a knowledgeable physician with an interest in natural history. A story which appeared in the *New York Herald* on January 3, 1897, stated that the monster had been dead for some time and was considerably mutilated, presumably from scavengers and decomposition. It went on to say that:

> Its head was nearly destroyed, and only the stumps of two arms were visible . . . the body, as it lies somewhat embedded in the sand, is 18 feet long and about 7 feet wide, while it rises 3½ feet above the sand . . . the weight of the body and head would have been at least four or five tons. If the eight arms held the proportions usually seen in smaller species of the octopus, they would have been at least 75 to 100 feet in length and about 18 inches in diameter at the base.

Wood deduced that this had been written by Professor Verrill based upon information supplied by Dr. Webb, although there was no byline. In a letter which appeared in the March 14 edition of the *New York Herald,* Verrill repudiated an earlier story he had written on the St. Augustine monster, and stated that after analyzing tissue sent to him by Webb, he no longer felt it could be that of either a squid or an octopus. He stated, "We must conclude, therefore, that the creature was a vertebrate animal, probably related to the whales. But I am unable to refer this immense, closed pouch-like mass to any part of any known whale, or, in fact, to any other animal. . . ." Verrill made a similar about-face in scientific journals. In an issue of the *American Journal of Science* he ventured the opinion that the creature was a giant squid; in a later story he agrees with Webb that it is indeed a huge octopus and mentions Webb's excavation of "the stump of an arm . . . still attached, thirty-six feet long and ten inches in diameter where it was broken off distally." In a later issue of the same publication he reversed his position, giving the reasons cited in the *New York Herald* story, although defending his earlier view, noting that colleagues had agreed with it.

Webb remained convinced that the St. Augustine creature had

been an octopus. In letters to W. H. Dall, former curator of mollusks at the National Museum, he described his struggles to excavate and protect the creature's remains (entrepreneurs tried to cart it away piecemeal for exhibition). After Verrill's change of mind he states that the "animal is simply a great bag and I do not see how it could be any part of a whale." In another letter he says that ". . . the hood is so tough that when it is exposed to the air an axe makes very little impression on it. Judging from the difficulty of moving it, it must weigh six or seven tons for twelve men with a block and tackle ought to move anything else . . . there was no caudal fin or any appearance as if there had been any. There was no pen to be found nor evidence of any bony structure whatever." In closing, the physician with a love of natural history, who had invested a great deal of energy, time, and money out of his own pocket in trying to interest the scientific world in a mass of flesh on a Florida beach, requested that Dall and Verrill come to examine it in person. Dall politely declined, citing lack of museum budget, and Verrill's response, if any, is unknown.

The remains of the mysterious creature finally washed out to sea, and the story of it was all but forgotten. Aside from some magazine articles, newspaper stories, and letters, the only evidence that it ever existed was a photograph of it and some lumps of white flesh in a large bottle filled with a Formalin solution in the basement of the Smithsonian Institution—the samples Dr. Webb had sent to a skeptical scientific world.

As with all sciences, the study of marine biology has made quantum leaps between the end of the last century and the beginning of this decade. Tissue identification, for example, has become much more sophisticated. The final phase of an investigation which began when F. G. Wood read an undated, yellowed clipping from an unknown newspaper took place in 1971 when marine specialist Joseph Gennaro, Jr., placed some slides under his microscope. They contained tissue from the lumps of flesh which had been stored those many years. Comparing the structure of these minute scraps of former life with modern sections of whale, squid, and octopus, Gennaro came up with the answer to an old, almost forgotten riddle.

The remains which washed ashore at St. Augustine were unmistakably those of an octopus.

From the tip of one tentacle to the tip of the opposite tentacle it must have measured two hundred feet, which is—to say the least—something to contemplate.

The oceans are filled with a diversity of life. Much of it is known; some of it is not. As we probe deeper into its secret depths, we find gigantic versions of smaller creatures we know from the shallows, and we find forms more bizarre than those with which science fiction writers use to populate Mars. We know almost nothing about the behavior of some of these creatures, except that they can be lethally dangerous to man, and yet, oddly enough, rarely are.

In the perpetual night of the deep sea, creatures thought to have been extinct for millions of years may still savagely feed upon each other, and no man can say now how many creatures will pass from the domain of myth into scientific acknowledgment during our lifetimes.

Quite a few, I suspect.

3

Some African Beasts

Few things are more terrifying than the charge of an enraged African elephant. It may lurch forward with a shrill trumpeting. The great ears flare out. The trunk, dexterous enough to pick up a single peanut but strong enough to hurl a man into the air or dash him to death against a tree, usually curls tightly between the tusks. The tusks themselves can be used to impale a man or even neatly punch their way through the side of one of his vehicles. Likely as not, this concentration of fury will stand better than nine feet at the shoulder and weigh several tons.

Quite a number of people have been the object of such a charge and lived to tell of it; either they or their companions were able to kill the animal with well-directed, high-caliber rifle bullets or the elephant was bluffing. Threat charges are especially common with old cows protecting a herd of younger females and calves. Quite a number of people have not lived to tell of it. Johnny Uys was a man with a great deal of experience around wild African elephants, having been a professional hunter and game warden before becoming a guide for camera safaris. He felt, with some justification, that he could read an elephant's reactions well enough to guide clients close enough for good photographs while maintaining a margin of safety. And he did, except for his last safari when a cow's threat was not a bluff and he was driven into the earth and killed.

Billy Pickering was an affable poacher of steady nerves who had maintained his composure and aim in the face of several elephant charges. He once shot an elephant bearing tusks of ivory weighing 190 pounds each, among the heaviest on record. But the charge of an elephant is not something one can ever get used to. Soon after the hunter obtained the giant tusks, an elephant struck him with such fury as to decapitate him and trample his torso into the dust. It was discovered that Pickering, a superb shot, had frozen as the maddened creature bore down upon him, and had not even pulled the trigger.

As with all wild herbivores, the African elephant regards man only with curiosity unless he is perceived to be a threat. Man, seeking meat, has always been something of a threat, hunting elephants with poisoned spears or driving them over traps—skims of light vegetation through which they crashed to be impaled upon sharpened, poison-smeared stakes. Elephants began to be tracked and slaughtered in vast numbers during the last century, when the world beyond the African continent came to value ivory. By the turn of the century an estimated one hundred thousand elephants were killed every year. The largest land creatures on earth were being massacred for billiard balls and piano keys.

Like humans, elephants are relatively immature at birth and they learn much of what they will know about the world and how to deal with it from their mothers during the first ten years of their lives. There seems little doubt that fear and hatred of hunters can be passed on from generation to generation. One of the first European hunters to lay waste the fauna of South Africa, Roualeyn Gordon-Cumming, noted that: "The elephant entertains an extraordinary horror of man, and a child can put a hundred of them to flight by passing at a quarter of a mile to windward; and when thus disturbed, they go a long way before they halt. It is surprising how soon these sagacious animals are aware of the presence of a hunter in their domains. When one troop has been attacked, all the other elephants frequenting the district are aware of the fact within two or three days. . . ."

When there is nowhere to flee, elephants may react differently. The region which is now South Africa's Addo Elephant National Park contains a forest. The elephant herds which lived in the forest took to foraging in adjacent farms and orchards. In 1919, the farmers hired a professional hunter to eradicate the massive creatures. Over a period of months, the hunter picked off the elephants wherever and whenever he could get a shot at them. By the time the original population of some 140 animals had been reduced to two or three dozen, the survivors had become uncommonly wary and difficult to locate, only emerging from the deep recesses of the woods at night. When the hunter was able to get close to them, the elephants would charge at him from dense cover. After several narrow escapes, the hunter gave up. Today, more than half a century later, the descendants of these elephants are protected, but the herds have not forgotten. Unlike most African elephants, they still usually come out from cover to feed only after dark, and will charge a man on sight. They are considered to be the most dangerous group of animals in Africa.

Elephant herds are matriarchal family units, presided over and protected by the older cows. Bull elephants, once they come of age, are expelled from the herd, and wander about on their own or in loose association with other bulls. Even in the same region, there may be pronounced differences in how a family of elephants, or even individuals, will relate to people. In their remarkable study of wild elephants, Iain Douglas-Hamilton and his wife Oria found some animals to be inquisitive and friendly while others remained shy and aloof. Douglas-Hamilton had begun to feel relaxed and at home around the elephants of the Lake Manyara region of Tanganyika until he encountered a family led by cows who did not share the gentle persuasions of the elephants he had previously encountered.

The zoologist, two assistants, and a friend in the Peace Corps, Katie Newlin, were observing some familiar elephants from a Land-Rover, when they noticed some strange animals back in the foliage. They drove toward them. Abruptly, one of the unfamiliar cows charged the vehicle and drove her tusks to the hilts through the side of the vehicle. The two assistants, whom the tusks had narrowly missed, piled out of the Land-Rover and scurried off into the bush. The elephant withdrew her tusks and again thrust them through the side of the Land-Rover. Now other elephants, trumpeting wildly, rushed at the car, goring it with their tusks. Even a calf butted ineffectually. A gigantic newcomer drove the Land-Rover backwards for thirty-five yards before it crumpled against an ant hill. At last, concluding that the curious, metallic animal was dead, the elephants withdrew.

Douglas-Hamilton had dramatically met the belligerent family he would dub the Torone Sisters after the strident queen of Greek mythology. The Douglas-Hamiltons, who were threatened by none of the other Lake Manyara elephants, would have other terrifying encounters with the Torone Sisters, as would other visitors to the area. As Oria was to muse: "Any time, anywhere, one or more of the Torones might be out like a flash to get their hated enemy. They must have been shot at a great many times for the smell of a human being or the sound of the car to arouse their immediate hostility."

More than twenty years before the Douglas-Hamiltons came to know the elephants of Lake Manyara, bow-hunter and photographer Howard Hill almost became a victim of one of them. Hill and a companion were watching an elephant herd moving through some trees at the edge of a meadow. A huge cow was aware of the men in the idling jeep and, trumpeting furiously, tried to hustle the laggards along. The herd streamed over a knoll and were lost to sight. Hill knew that there was a wide gulch beyond the slope, and he waited for them to emerge back into sight on the other side of it. The trumpeting ceased. The herd, obviously bunched up behind the hill, did not emerge. The photographer suddenly realized that the great matriarch who had been prodding the herd had not followed them over the slope. In the rather ominous silence, Hill's companion suggested they move on.

Suddenly, Hill spotted the huge cow approaching them with remarkably quiet stealth through the dense acacia trees. Her trunk was raised and her ears stood straight out from her head as if hung from invisible wires. Even as the two men realized they had been stalked, the elephant charged, blaring her shrill anger. The pounding animal was only twenty yards away as the jeep lurched forward, tires spewing gravel and grass. The murderous tusks were less than ten yards from the rear of the jeep before it gained enough speed to pull away.

There is little doubt that Hill and his companion had met one of the Torone Sisters, very likely an aged herd protector who was already dead by the time the Douglas-Hamiltons encountered the clan.

Fictional man-killers of the Dark Continent are never portrayed as aggressive (or admirably defensive) family units, as with the Torones or the elephants of the Addo Forest; they are merciless old bulls, the classic rogue elephant. Perhaps this is because of our romantic notions; if a man kills a mother elephant, we feel that the orphaned baby must and will forgive us and then the story will come out right. This is not to say that there are not rogue elephants. One of them killed twelve people in Zulu territory during recent years. It would appear that some rogues, after the fashion of mankind and certain other intelligent creatures, simply go insane, deviating from the predictable patterns of their fellows. Others, also sharing a prerogative of the higher orders, occasionally become raging and dangerous drunks. The fermenting fruit of the plumlike *marula* tree most frequently does the damage.

Still and all, most rogue elephants are animals that have been painfully injured by inept outside hunters or expert native poachers whose weaponry may be little more than chopped, rusty nails and melted-down bottle caps spewed out from an ancient muzzle-loader which is as much a threat to the triggerman as it is to the target. The worst wounds are those to the long roots of an elephant's tusk; the abscess from a piece of embedded metal can cause the animal to live a nightmare of unrelieved agony. A tiger suffering an old gunshot wound may turn man-eater simply because it can no longer catch swifter prey. A pain-wracked rogue elephant is still a herbivore. It will tense at the distant smell of a man and try to tramp him into jelly if he comes too close because it cannot forget or forgive the creature which inflicted the pain. The so-called Dabi killer, a rogue that once rampaged through settlements south of the Zambezi River, would ambush natives as they walked along paths, wrapping the screaming victims in its trunk and then dashing them against tree trunks.

The dangers of wounding an elephant, even one of an affable disposition, should be obvious. The results may be only mildly discomforting to the animal and a terrifying inconvenience to the person. A case in point involved a man who swung his vehicle around a curve of a rough dirt track after nightfall and inadvertently bumped the back legs of a departing elephant. The elephant ponderously, almost wearily, squatted on the hood of the car, crushing it, and blowing both front tires. Apparently none the worse for wear, she then lifted off and wandered back into the bush. The car required major assistance.

A seriously wounded animal is another matter. In the winter of 1790 and 1791, Jacob van Reenen, founder of the Cape Colony, trekked into the interior of South Africa in search of survivors from a wrecked vessel. His diary noted the following:

Wednesday, December 1, 1890 . . . a big bull elephant appeared at the wagons, which we at once began to hunt. After he had received several bullets and had already fallen to the ground twice, he crawled into a thorn bush thickly covered with undergrowth. Tjaart van der Walt, Lodewijk Prins and Ignatius Mulder rode up to the bush thinking that the elephant had been finished off, when the elephant charged furiously from the bush and caught Lodewijk Prins, struck him from his horse's back with his trunk, and trampled him to death, and pierced him, Lodewijk Prins, right through the body with one tusk, threw him fully thirty feet in the air and away from himself. Tjaart van der Walt and Mulder, seeing no way of escaping with their horses, leapt from them and hid in the undergrowth. The elephant, seeing only van der Walt's horse, pursued it (they were all within an ace of being crushed to death by him). After having pursued the horse for some distance he turned again to the spot near to where the dead body was, looking for it. Then we all began shooting at the elephant in order to drive him away from the place or to shoot him dead, whereupon he finally, after a great deal of shooting, hid in the thick thorns. When we thought he was far enough away, we began to dig in order to make a grave for the unfortunate man, and while we were busy with this the elephant charged us again and chased away all who were remaining by the grave in the open plain. Tjaart van der Walt, once again riding past him at a distance of 100 yards, shot at him again. The fury of the animal was indescribable. We shot at him again with our entire force until at last he left the spot, and then let him be followed by the Hottentots who shot him to the ground once more and he remained lying there.

Arthur Neumann, an English hunter, was once gored by a wounded bull elephant which left him for dead. One tusk had pierced his upper arm, passing between the biceps and bone. His other injuries were extensive. At the time, Neumann was several hundred miles from the nearest outpost of civilization in what was by and large unexplored territory. Yet somehow Neumann managed to survive, continued to hunt, and eventually to return to England to write his memoirs.

Other hunters have had close calls. Some of them have ripped off a jacket or other garment which the pursuing elephant has paused to tear and trample while its owner sprinted to safety. Hunter Murray

Smith was tossed by an enraged animal which then drove its tusks into the hard earth on either side of his prone body. The great bows of ivory prevented the elephant from mashing him with its forehead. After withdrawing them, the rogue sauntered back into the forest. Another hunter, Samaki Salmon, was hurled up into the trees. The branches broke his fall and by an extraordinary stroke of luck he landed next to his rifle. He picked it up and killed the elephant.

Occasionally an elephant will cover a victim, either dead or alive, with leaves or other debris. No one is quite sure why they do this. An African woman who was sleeping under a tree was buried in this fashion, although once the elephant which had so solicitously covered her had left, the frightened woman was able to dig herself out. Elephants display concern for their own dead and may nudge them with their trunks, as if to lift them back to life. Once the hyenas, jackals, marabou storks, vultures, ants, and other scavengers have reduced an elephant corpse to bones, its companions have been known to carry off a large bone or one of its tusks. Yet the fabled elephant graveyard is merely legend. Part of its origin may lie in the fact that many old or infirm animals become bogged in the mud of swamps or riverbanks, die, and the heavy bones and tusks sink quickly into the ooze.

The charge of a black rhinoceros, like that of an elephant, is a display of awesome power. Of the five species of rhinoceros, only the black rhinoceros has a reputation for ferocity, much of it undeserved. The slow-thinking animal, which in one form or another has been around for sixty million years, has excellent hearing and sense of smell, but is pathetically nearsighted. A disturbed black rhino will often fake a charge, pausing in the middle of it to ascertain if its adversary has taken flight. They usually do, as a two-ton, twelve-foot-long creature in full gallop has a remarkable potential for dramatic impact. The truly dangerous thing about black rhinos is that there is absolutely no way to judge whether any given charge will be aborted as a bluff or if the animal is deadly serious. Nor is there any way to tell if the beast will charge a second time.

A black rhino once charged the line of native porters of a large safari. They scattered, and it missed them in its headlong burst. Wheeling, the rhino stormed back toward the fleeing men and tossed an Austrian sportsman with its horn. The victim, badly wounded, lay motionless, while the rhino snorted and charged about, probably unable to make out the still, prone form with its weak eyesight. It finally trotted away, unable to relocate the objects of its wrath. The victim was lucky, he survived; many people are killed by rhinos each year.

In his book, *The Man-Eaters of Tsavo,* Colonel J. H. Patterson described an encounter with a black rhino. Having spied the animal, Patterson wriggled through the grass in an attempt to get close enough for a shot.

. . . at length I got within fifty yards of the spot where the huge beast was resting. Here I lay and watched him; but after some little time he evidently suspected my presence, for rising to his feet, he looked straight in my direction and then proceeded to walk round me in a half circle.

The moment he got wind of me he whipped around in his tracks like a cat and came for me in a bee-line. Hoping to turn him, I fired instantly; but unfortunately my soft-nose bullets merely annoyed him further, and had not the slightest effect on his thick hide. On seeing this I flung myself down quite flat on the grass and threw my helmet some ten feet away in the hope that he would perceive it and vent his rage on it instead of me. On he thundered, while I scarcely dared to breathe. I could hear him snorting and rooting up the grass quite close to me, but luckily for me he did not catch sight of me, and charged by a few yards to my left.

As soon as he had passed me, my courage began to revive again, and I could not resist the temptation of sending a couple of bullets after him. These, however, simply cracked against his hide and splintered to pieces on it, sending the dry mud off in little clouds of dust. Their only real effect, indeed, was to make him still more angry. He stood stock-still for a moment, and then gored the ground most viciously and started off once more on the semi-circle round me. This proceeding terrified me more than ever, as I felt sure that he would come up-wind at me again, and I could scarcely hope to escape a second time. Unfortunately, my surmise proved correct, for directly he scented me, up went his nose in the air and down he charged like a battering ram. I fairly pressed myself into the ground, as flat as ever I could, and luckily the grass was a few inches high. I felt the thud of his great feet pounding along, yet dared not move or look up lest he should see me. My heart was thumping like a steam hammer, and every moment I fully expected to find myself tossed into the air. Nearer and nearer came the heavy thudding, and I had quite given myself up for lost, when from my lying position I caught a sight, out of the corner of my eye, of the infuriated beast rushing by. He had missed me again!

A rhino, if agitated enough, will charge at anything. One of them once attempted to bowl over the engine of a train. Patterson related the story of a queue of twenty-one slaves who, attached by long neck chains, were being prodded by overseers on the long trek from the interior to the coast. A rhino charged the helpless men, impaling one of them on its horn. The necks of the other slaves were broken by the impact. It has been claimed that one can sidestep a charging rhino since once committed it will rush straight ahead blindly. There are people who have done this. There are also people who have discovered, to their ultimate discomfort, that a charging rhino can and sometimes will turn on a dime and hook to the right or left. Tree climbing, rather than a bullfight flourish, is advised for the traveler who finds that a rhino is paying inordinate attention to him.

Like all mammals, including man, the rhino can be testy if interrupted during amorous activity. During the mating season, most male mammals wage fierce battles for individual females or to obtain and defend harems. By and large, rhinoceroses take exception to this pattern in a forthright style which should delight those who champion women's rights. When in season, a black rhino cow makes a shrill whistling noise. If more than one male gallantly trots up, they may square off, but usually the female chooses one of them before they actually tangle with each other, and the rejected suitor wanders off in hopes that his charms will be more properly appreciated elsewhere. Although chosen, the bull is not immediately accepted. The cow often will deflect his amorous advances for hours with her horn. Sometimes, in surrender, the female will allow the bull to softly rub his horn against hers. Mating may last for up to an hour.

Most zoologists consider it a minor miracle that the rhinoceros has not already been annihilated, although some species are on the brink of it and all rhinos are threatened. During the Middle Ages the rhino was identified as the living embodiment of the mythical unicorn, and their horns were in great demand for supposed magical properties. Powdered rhinoceros horn was considered an essential ingredient of many plague cures and was hoarded by alchemists. Hollowed-out horns were used as goblets by nervous members of the aristocracy, in the belief that the horns would have an unmistakable effect upon liquids containing poison. Despite scientific evidence to the contrary, millions of Asiatics still believe that ground rhino horn has remarkable aphrodisiac qualities. A single horn will still fetch up to $2,000 on the black market.

As the elephant was slaughtered for its ivory, the crocodile for its hide, the horn of the rhino has all but precipitated its extinction. Unlike the more intelligent elephant, which soon learned to avoid man as much as possible, changing its habits and retreating into terrains least hospitable to man, the rhino was unable to adjust to its peril, although it still survives in protected game preserves.

Invariably, when conversation turns to the "most dangerous game," the Cape Buffalo is singled out as being at the top of, or close to the top of, everyone's list. For a fact, a wounded or startled buffalo can be as deadly as any creature on earth. Most perilous or fatal encounters with buffalo occur on its home turf—thick brush where a man may not even see the animal until it crashes upon him and has little chance of fast movement even if he does. A buffalo is a tough, durable animal, and during the pioneer era of South Africa, countless animals were wounded. These injured beasts would charge to kill, and there was a heavy toll among homesteaders attempting to clear brush for fields. In places they undoubtedly killed more people than the crocodiles did.

African white hunter John Hunter once hired a native tracker who had been severely gored by a buffalo. The man had been walking through high grass en route to a bee hive when he all but stumbled upon a reclining bull. The startled animal hooked the man in the groin, hurling him upward. In a bizarre sequence of events, the man landed upon the buffalo's back, grabbed an ear and a tuft of hide, and clung desperately as the beast galloped for some sixty yards. He was swept off of his unwilling mount by a branch of a thorn tree. The bull pivoted to gore him again, then left the unconscious man for dead.

The native came to. He was sprawled next to a stream, and managed to inch forward to it. One hand was broken, but with the other he could scoop water to drink and splash over his burning injuries. For two weeks, almost helpless, he lay by the stream, subsisting on what grass was within reach. He could hear elephants and rhinos when they came to the stream to drink. Hyenas laughed and wailed maniacally in the nearby brush and crocodiles glided up the stream to within a few feet of him. None of these wild creatures molested him. His wounds were healing well when other honey gatherers stumbled upon him. They brought him back to the village where he had long since been given up for dead.

Occasionally a man is murdered in the bush and the crime is concealed by making it appear that a wild animal was responsible. In the past, such killings were sometimes ceremonial, associated with a leopard society or other secret cabal. Far more often, the murder would have more universal motives such as robbery or jealousy. In a curious Kenya case, a man initially thought to have been the victim of bandits was found to have perished of something else entirely.

A Turkana tribesman named Abeya, working for Hunter, failed to return from hunting buffalo. His remains, mostly stripped to the bone by hyenas and vultures, were found next to a large tree. His rifle and ammunition were gone, and several ribs were smashed in, as if from a club. A cut across two of the ribs seemed to indicate the thrust of a spear. The inspector of the local police force had his men fan out into the bush, seeking clues. Hunter and his men joined the search, and eventually came upon a buffalo carcass, smothered with feeding safari ants. Hunter noticed a neat hole in one of the ribs, and dashed in through the ants to retrieve it. An 8 mm. bullet of the caliber Abeya had been carrying neatly matched the hole.

Once the man's rifle was found nearby, the violent event could be reconstructed. The Turkana had wounded the buffalo and followed it through the undergrowth. The animal had charged, breaking his ribs and thrusting him against a log where a broken stub had pierced him like a spear point, but not before Abeya had gotten off the shot which proved mortal to his assailant. The man, himself mortally wounded, had crawled back to the tree where he was found.

The buffalo's potential for violence notwithstanding, an unmolested animal is usually placid. Given the opportunity, most buffalo will retreat to a safe distance when man approaches. Hunter John Taylor once remarked that, "Men get queer ideas about buffalo. Most men without experience seem to think that buffalo will attack without any provocation. There is a belief that buffalo will invariably whip around on feeling the lead and make a savage and determined charge. Well, all I can say is that I have never experienced either of these things, and I have shot close to 1,200 buffalo . . . and have encountered a hundred times as many."

As with so many creatures, the buffalo is usually a terrifying beast only when we have made him so with our rifles.

River boating at night anywhere can result in some unpleasant surprises such as running onto a sandbar, a snag, or a barely submerged rock. Many African rivers contain additional hazards. Professional crocodile hunter Brian Dempster discovered this as he prowled the Zambezi River after dark, shooting saurians by flashlight. His skiff, powered with an outboard, once rammed a submerged hippo in the dimness and almost sank. On another occasion, he rounded a bend to find himself headed straight into a herd of hippos and only managed to weave his way through them without incident by dextrous maneuvering.

Early one predawn he and his two native assistants were returning to their camp when abruptly a huge hippo lunged up underneath their small craft, tossing it into the air and capsizing it. Dempster, treading the warm water, watched as the glistening, infuriated creature broke water to crush the boat in its massive teeth, biting and tearing until it sank. The hunter started to paddle gently toward shore, fighting panic, as he was now defenseless against the disturbed hippo as well as any crocodiles that might be in the vicinity. One of his helpers splashed wildly in the water close by, and cried out, "Help me! I cannot swim!"

The hippo turned from what splinters of the boat remained, submerged, and exploded from the water next to the floundering man. His scream stopped immediately as the yawning teeth snapped across his body. Dempster and his other helper managed to propel themselves quietly to shore, but their companion had made his last hunt.

In the spring of 1864, explorer Samuel Baker and his wife Florence were the first Europeans to lay eyes upon a thunderous 130-foot-high plunge of water on the upper Nile. Baker named it Murchison Falls; it is one of Africa's most magnificent natural features. Baker urged the natives paddling his canoe to pull as close to the base of the falls as possible. They were able to get no closer than some three hundred yards owing to the wild churn of current and whirlpools. The explorer, who was an avid hunter, noticed some crocodiles sunning upon the riverbank and shot one of them. The unexpected report caused the paddlers to drop into the bottom of the canoe. One of them, thoroughly frightened, dropped his paddle into the river. As Baker was to relate in his book, *Albert N'yanza,*

We were at the mercy of the powerful stream, and the canoe was whisked round by the eddy and carried against a thick bank of high reeds; hardly had we touched this obstruction when a tremendous commotion took place in the rushes, and in an instant a great bull hippopotamus charged the canoe, and with a severe shock striking the bottom he lifted us half out of the water. The natives who were in the bottom of the boat positively yelled with terror, not knowing whether the shock was in any way connected with the dreaded report of the rifle; the black women screamed; and the boy Saat handing me a spare rifle, and Richard being ready likewise, we looked out for a shot should the angry hippo again attack us.

A few kicks bestowed by my angry men upon the recumbent boatmen restored them to the perpendicular. The first thing necessary was to hunt for the lost paddle that was floating down the rapid current. The hippopotamus, proud of having disturbed us, but doubtless thinking us rather hard of texture, raised his head to take a last view of his enemy, but sank too rapidly to permit a shot.

It has been estimated that several hundred people are killed annually by African hippos. The water and mud-loving beasts, which resemble gigantic inflatable children's toys, are not known to be particularly aggressive (except bulls fighting over cows), but they are, after the elephant, the largest land creature, and are quite capable, if wounded or otherwise disturbed, of biting a man in two. The majority of fatal attacks occur when a hippo overturns a boat. In some cases, such as the incident in which Brian Dempster's assistant was killed, the hippo became enraged after an actual collision. In others, as was probably the case in which Samuel Baker's vessel was rammed, the hippo was defending a stretch of water it considered its territory. It is possible that a number of attacks upon canoes are made by mother hippos who mistake canoes for crocodiles. The mothers give birth to one-hundred-pound infants underwater, and for two years they vigilantly protect them from predators such as crocodiles and hyena or old belligerent bulls. Infant mortality is high, but if the youngsters survive, they may live for forty to fifty years.

In Greek, "hippopotamus" means river horse. By day, the huge rounded creatures like to submerge their bodies in still or slow-moving water with only the tops of their heads showing above the surface. Clumsy swimmers, they prefer shallow water, through which they can bounce with considerable agility under the surface as if performers in a ponderous ballet. After sundown the hippos heave themselves out of the water to graze ashore. During a given evening they may wander for miles to crop several hundred pounds of grass and other foliage. Back in the water, the daily excretions from their gargantuan midnight feasts provide nutrients for large populations of fish species such as the tilapia, a medium-sized bream-like fish.

Hippos lumber ashore on trails which are deeply incised both underwater and upon the riverbanks. A hippo may use the same trail for years, tramping it several feet deep into the earth. If a hippo is disturbed, it may decide to return to the water posthaste, thundering over anything in its path. A number of people have been killed by hippos simply because they were unable to get out of the way of panicked animals. Other land attacks merely point up the unpredictability of the hippo. In 1966 some Africans were frolicking upon a riverbank of the Limpopo River which forms the South Africa-Rhodesia border. A hippo, apparently irritated by the commotion, barreled out of the water with the yawning jaws with which bulls set upon each other during the mating battles, and bit completely through the torso of one of the revelers. In the same region, a man was walking along a riverbank with his wife, who carried their child upon her back. Spotting a bull hippo on the path, the man yelled at it, assuming it would dash back to the river. The animal charged, biting off the woman's leg at the hip and tearing away much of her side. She died instantly, although the child was uninjured.

Hippos have long been hunted for their meat, which is considered by Europeans as well as African natives as among the most flavorful on the continent. An average bull will yield over a thousand pounds of lean meat. Many tribes traditionally have killed hippo with pit traps or other comparatively safe devices. Certain tribes, however, such as the Bozo of the upper Niger, have inherited proud river cultures, and hunt the hippo in its own element, the water. This is a risky proposition, whether the hunt is conducted in the shallows or from canoes, and hunters are killed from time to time. Prior to a hippopotamus hunt, a ceremony is held to purify the hunters. The spears they will use are dipped in poison, and to test its strength a rooster is jabbed with a spear tip and tossed into the air. If the fowl is dead by the time that it hits the ground, the poison is believed to be strong enough for hippo. For protection, the warriors wear special brown tunics, amulets, and hollow belts of sewn goatskin. Live snakes are sealed inside of the belts to ward off danger; as long as the snake moves, its magic will repel the attack of a hippo, or so the Bozo believe.

Most hunters in the vicinity of a wounded hippo attempt to get out of the water as fast as possible. Roualeyn Gordon-Cumming, the flamboyant sportsman who blasted his way through South Africa around the middle of the last century, once reversed the process, charging into the water in a seemingly preposterous attempt to urge a wounded cow hippo weighing several thousand pounds toward shore where it could be dispatched. He described the venture in his book, *The Lion Hunter:*

> . . . she then kept continually splashing round and round in a circle in the middle of the river. I had great fear of the crocodiles, and did not know that the sea cow might not attack me. My anxiety to secure her, however, overcame all hesitation; so, divesting myself of my leathers, and armed with a sharp knife, I dashed into the water, which at first took me up to my arm-pits, but in the middle was shallower.
>
> As I approached Behemoth her eye looked very wicked. I halted for a moment, ready to dive under the water if she attacked me; but she was stunned, and did not know what she was doing; so, running in upon her, and seizing her short tail, I attempted to incline her course to land. It was extraordinary what enormous strength she still had in the water. I could not guide her in the slightest, and she continued to splash, and plunge, and blow, and make her circular course, carrying me along with her as if I was a fly on her tail. . . .

As in some implausible adventure cinema, Gordon-Cumming writes that he used his knife to cut hand holds in the thick hide of the animal's rump and, "after some desperate hard work, sometimes pushing and sometimes pulling, the sea cow continuing her circular course all the time, and I holding on at her rump like grim Death, eventually I succeeded in bringing this gigantic and most powerful animal to the bank." He then killed the hapless creature with another rifle shot.

The adventures of certain other hippo hunters, who possessed nerve but not luck, have ended badly for them. In the spring of 1959, a South African tribal administrator, Andries Steyn, stalked a rogue hippo which had been charging and overturning native Bantu dugouts on the Okavango River. Steyn sighted the glistening black animal and cautiously approached it. He carefully sighted his rifle and fired, killing it. At the explosion, a cow hippo suddenly exploded up from under Steyn's boat, capsizing it. As he floundered in the water, the hippo lunged at him, her great teeth chopping frenziedly at the water. She dragged him underwater and he was never seen again.

Even though the hippo can be a dangerous and unpredictable creature if agitated, the average African in the bush regards them with no more alarm than a Western motorist contemplates trucks. True, tractor-trailers occasionally do come hurtling across the middle line of a highway to crush a car, but the affair is impersonal, a matter of bad luck. A rogue hippo does not evoke feelings of evil and terror like a man-eating crocodile. Africans tend to think of hippos with equanimity and even fondness. A few years ago, hippos would occasionally graze upon the grass of the Jinja Golf Course close to Lake Victoria, Uganda. Rather than exterminating the intruders, officials made a rule that: "If the ball lands in a hippo's footprint it may be removed and dropped onto adjacent turf without penalty." Around Lake Edward, Uganda, residents recall with amusement the hippo which was observed to playfully nip the tail of a wading elephant. When the elephant whirled around in outrage, the hippo quietly submerged.

Some hippos even become folk heroes. The most celebrated was Hubert, who in the 1940s set off upon a thousand-mile ramble through drought-stricken South Africa. Hippos rarely venture more than a half-day's walk from their home stream, but Hubert was a true vagabond, wandering calmly along highways and even down city streets to graze calmly in parks. At the beginning of his trek, it was soon noticed by backcountry villagers that his arrival was usually followed by rain. He was soon welcomed and even worshipped as a spirit sent to bring relief to their parched fields. As he came into more settled regions, local radio stations noted his progress, and his strolls through various towns took on the aspects of a parade; children ran alongside and cheered while their parents held out vegetables and fruit. The entire country was saddened when Hubert was shot by a farmer who came upon him trampling through his crops.

In 1966 a two-ton hippo named Hugo captured the fancy of the citizens of Tanzania. The frolicsome beast would emerge from the milky waters of Kurasini Creek outside of Dar es Salaam to cavort with children and dogs on the bank, and solemnly follow herds of cattle as if compiling an investigative report upon their habits for the wild animal media. Like all hippos, he was possessed of a gargantuan appetite, which sometimes led him into the fields of nearby farmers, where pumpkins were his favorite fare. Although the farmers clamored for his hide, Hugo was saved by public sentiment, which was reflected in one of the most popular Tanzanian songs of the day.

> The hippo's name is Hugo
> He lives in Hippo Bay.
> He does not need finances,
> He does not smoke or drink,
> He only needs his chances
> To stay alive and sing.

With all beasts, including man, there are a handful of rogues and heroes, and all of the rest fall somewhere in between.

Tiger hunting from elephantback was once a popular, and occasionally dangerous, sport. This illustration, entitled "At Close Quarters," depicts an incident of the Duc D'Orleans hunting tour of India in the 1880's. Over the past four decades, the value of tiger skins and a rapidly dwindling habitat have threatened this magnificent beast with extinction. (From The Graphic, *June 1, 1889)*

During the early decades of this century, African elephants were frequently hunted from horseback. As evidenced here, the huge mammals sometimes regarded turnabout as fair play. (Courtesy of American Museum of Natural History)

*Boat capsized by a hippo robbed of her young. Although generally docile
unless provoked, hippopotami can be fearful adversaries when angered.
Numerous Africans are killed by the water-loving creatures every year.*
(Courtesy of American Museum of Natural History)

A missionary's escape from a lion. In 1845 missionary and explorer David Livingston was mauled by a lion in East Africa. Livingston survived the attack, which he described as causing "a sort of dreaminess in which there was no sense of pain nor feeling of terror." (Courtesy of American Museum of Natural History)

The outcome of this encounter is rightfully left to the imagination. Although most tigers take great care to avoid man, the victims of some notable man-eaters have numbered in the hundreds. (From Leslie's Magazine)

4
Man-Killing Cats

Matterhorn Peak, 12,281 feet high, is one of the most beautiful spikes in the Sierra Nevada of California. Some years ago a friend and I, behind schedule because of a late start and what proved to be a very long shortcut, finally reached the summit at sunset. The series of ledges we had easily ascended in daylight became increasingly difficult to descend as dusk tightened into full darkness. A shelf would pinch out. We would drop a pebble over the edge; sometimes we would hear it thunk upon an unseen ledge just below us, while at other times it would ricochet off a rock slab, or simply drop until finally we would hear a faint tick as it hit the bottom of a cliff hundreds of feet below us. At one point during this nightmarish descent, we were arrested by a high, prolonged shriek from the canyon below. In the haze of my exhaustion I thought it to be a woman screaming as she was attacked by a fellow camper.

Perhaps an hour later, finally off of the dangerous rock, I looked closely into the canyon for the glow of the campfire of the screaming woman. The rift, one of the few rarely visited areas of the Sierra Nevada, was a river of shadows; there was no spark of light. I decided I must have hallucinated the eerie sound.

Our base camp, to which we assumed we would return long before nightfall, was still several miles away. Shivering uncontrollably with the chill of the high elevation night and pushed to the edge of our physical stamina, we were delighted to discover and curl up in a bower of twisted lodgepole pines, which completely deflected the cutting winds. A thick layer of pine needles was splayed about, obviously by some animal. Shivering into sleep, I wondered if we had trespassed into a bear wallow. I was too exhausted to care.

Later, I abruptly awoke. An animal was softly circling the bower. For a period of time, terrified, I assumed it was the bear, irritated at our occupying his place. Then the circling animal coughed and I saw, against faint starlight, a twitching yellow tail.

We were sleeping in a cougar's den, the beast early American settlers called the catamount, panther, and mountain devil, fearing it greatly. The scream we had heard was that of the large cat—not of a woman.

We hurriedly left. For over four miles the cougar followed us with liquid grace as we stumbled our way down the faint path. Our fright was absolute. If the big cat decided to attack, we could not outrun it nor scale a tree to effect escape. Helplessness. I tried, unsuccessfully, to put out of my mind the story a logging friend had told me about a companion whose head had been chewed off by a cougar in the Fraser River country of British Columbia. But as is the case with the vast majority of people who have been trailed by cougars, our cat was merely curious and meant us no harm.

Cougars, like all of the great cats, are reclusive, nocturnal hunters of dawn, sundown, and the night. They are poems of powerful movement. The cougar ranges throughout North and South America, wherever it has space and game enough to survive. We tend to think of it as a creature of the wind-sculpted rocks and yellow grass clumps of the vast plateaus which stretch between the Rocky Mountains and the fertile farm valleys of the Pacific Coast, but it is equally at home in thick coniferous forests of Western Canada and swampy jungles of South America. A great many stories, like that of my lumberjack friend, have been told about unprovoked cougar attacks upon man.

Early accounts usually cannot be substantiated one way or another, but researchers have tracked down most reported modern attacks, and have found most of them to be fictional or exaggerations. There seems little doubt that a boy at Malott, Washington, was killed when he ran from a cougar which was probably following him out of curiosity. Within the last decade, a child in New Mexico was killed by an emaciated female cougar. There is strong evidence that the cat had been caged as a pet, and then released, prior to the attack. Other, nonfatal maulings which are authenticated have involved rabid or incapacitated animals, as well as a half-grown cub which had apparently been abandoned by its mother and was starving.

The other great cat of the New World, the jaguar, also seems to be feared by man out of all proportion to its aggressiveness toward us. Like the cougar, it has frequently been the victim of our rifles and spears. In Paraguay and Brazil, cattlemen hired jaguar hunters who, feeling rifles would be of little use against a charging cat in thick foliage, would provoke the jaguar to spring against a spear which they would set at such an angle as to impale it.

From the earliest times, man has hunted for food, yet has also killed the most powerful beasts to mystically acquire some of their presence. A number of the *tigereros,* who spearhunted the jaguar, lost out to their formidable adversaries.

The wild cats are a large and diverse family. Many of them are no larger than our domestic cats. The large-eared sand dune cat thrives in some of the most harsh desert environments in the world; the Pallas cat, chunky as a badger, feeds upon small rodents in the high mountains of southern Russia.

In the orchestration of the natural world, wild cats, large and small, have provided an essential function. The grazing animals would have literally chewed the world's grasses down to bedrock were it not for predators such as the great cats. They have evolved to astonishing grace and power. They may also, within a few decades, be extinct in the truly wild sense.

There are only three large cats which have actively hunted man, although man has always hunted most members of the cat family. I speak of the lion, the leopard, and the tiger.

The lion, as a symbol of strength and courage, has always held a powerful fascination for man in the regions it inhabits, or once inhabited. The emblem of Iran, where the lion is now extinct, was a lion holding a sword. Assyrians portrayed their kings as winged lions with human, bearded heads. Lion cults flourished in ancient Egypt, and in certain temples such as that of Amun-Ra at Heliopolis, priests bathed tame lions in perfumed water.

The lion of mythology is almost always the male with its spectacular mane and great roar, which explorer Thomas Baines likened to the bass of a cathedral organ. For centuries, we have nourished the image of the "King of Beasts" easily dragging down prey, no matter how large and dangerous, for its mate and cubs to feed upon. Cowardly, skulking hyenas would later move in to steal a few bits of the King's kill. Recent field studies have demonstrated that the killing is usually done by the female lions, or the hyenas themselves. The male lion, who dozes most of the time, but has excellent hearing and eyesight, will then charge up to scatter the hyenas or female lion and cubs, and contentedly feast his fill. In the lion world, the male would appear to be principally a sex object, whose major productive functions are mating, or roaring majestically to defend the territories of its pride from other males.

Most large cats are essentially loners, but lions form prides which range in size from two adults and their cubs to as many as thirty animals. As with wolf packs, the basis of the pride is kinship, although stray animals will often be absorbed. While most of its cousins, such as the tiger, jaguar, and leopard, favor forests with dense cover as a screen for their stalking, the lion prefers the open grassy vistas of the savannah, or scrub brush and thorn thickets. Lions have been observed in the Haud, a bone-dry expanse of land on the Somalia-Ethiopia border, more than fifty miles from the nearest known water. It has been postulated that these animals may go for weeks without water, quenching their thirst from the blood of their prey. Perhaps because it does usually live in regions providing little cover for stalking, lions are the only large cats who frequently hunt cooperatively, maneuvering prey to a spot where a concealed lion can spring out at it. Lions, like all of their family, have a poorer sense of smell than most of the herbivores they depend upon for food, yet are intelligent enough to allow for this, and stalk accordingly.

Lions are highly individualistic. It has been observed that while one lion might stroll down the suburban streets of Nairobi, all but oblivious to the honking of car horns, another will panic at the sight of a sheet flapping upon a clothesline. Their faces, at least to us, are highly expressive. If irritated, they wrinkle their foreheads and noses, baring their fangs. Angered, they lay back their ears and growl. A rapid twitching of the tail, as with domestic cats, indicates they are ready to spring. People who have done extensive field research with lions soon learn to recognize individual animals. Of course, this is also true with people who observe bear or eagles for any period of time. We probably have more trouble identifying individual snakes and sharks simply because their features are so removed from ours.

In captivity, lions and tigers have mated to produce offspring. They are known as "ligers" or "tigons" depending upon the sex of the male.

Man has hunted lions for a long, long time. European ice-age hunters depicted them upon the walls of caves. More than a thousand years before the birth of Christ, Egyptian pharaohs flushed lions from cover with a small army of beaters, and then tried to down them with arrows shot from a chariot. According to the records they left behind them in stone, they were quite successful at it. As we have not learned of royalty being mauled by wounded lions, it is probably safe to assume that they had a certain amount of backup in the form of bodyguards.

The hunting of African lions by affluent Europeans and Americans has been a vogue since before the turn of the century. In the 1920s, lions were often hunted from horseback, although in more recent times they are more usually stalked on foot. The modern counterpart of the pharaoh's bodyguards is the "white hunter," that legendary figure of iron nerves, a capacity for gin, and a sweetheart somewhere who has jilted him for a bank clerk. As well as guiding the safari and providing camp meat, the white hunter is expected to down a charging animal which the client has missed, as well as finishing off wounded game as it retreats into the brush. It is a dangerous occupation. White hunters, as well as a few of their clients, have been killed when charged by wounded lions. Professional hunter John Hunter once observed that several tombstones in the Nairobi cemetery bore the inscription, "killed by a lion," and that half of the professional lion hunters operating out of Nairobi had been mauled at one time or another.

Hunter himself experienced a number of tight situations. On one occasion, he heard the snore of a sleeping lion in high grass. His native assistant tossed stones in the direction of the sound to flush the lion. Two lions came rushing out of the grass, headed directly for Hunter. He killed the first one, but there was no time for a second shot. The second lion leaped completely over Hunter, skimming his head so closely that his hat was knocked off. Had the lion been attacking, rather than merely trying to get away, Hunter might well have wound up with one of those Nairobi tombstones.

Professional hunters work with a wide variety of clients, and not all of their most engaging stories have to do with the perils of the bush.

Hunter once served as guide to a German baron and his wife. The lady was lovely; the baron a fiercely jealous man. He employed an ex-major of the German army whose principal task was to act as chaperon for his wife. The white hunter, beautiful woman, and ex-major were searching for lion one morning. John Hunter and the woman wound up on one side of a ravine, the ex-major on the other. When the countess yelled for help, Hunter broke through the thick brush toward her, thinking she might have encountered a lion. He found her dancing about in her underpants, frantically trying to rid herself of huge safari ants which were crawling over her limbs and biting. Not wishing to afford the ants an opportunity to crawl up under his own clothing, Hunter shed them as he rushed to her rescue. He scraped the ants off the baroness with the back of his knife blade. She had just re-dressed when the ex-major burst into the clearing, avoiding what, to say the least, might have been a delicate situation.

Most seasoned white hunters have similar safari stories which have little or nothing to do with the hunt itself. Yet most of them have experienced close calls with wounded animals. Hunting lions which have been flushed into the open by beaters or waiting for them in a *machan,* tree shelter, is usually not very dangerous. Stalking a wounded animal back into cover can be very much so. The hunter often has only a vague idea where the lion is, while the lion probably knows exactly where he is. Lions have great speed for short bursts, but little stamina. Consequently, when stalking prey they usually approach it very closely, or in some instances, let it come very close to them. A wounded lion will usually remain motionless in concealing brush until the hunter is almost upon it.

White hunters traditionally stalk a lion which has been wounded by a client with a faithful gunbearer at their side, as there is rarely time to reload. When a man-eater charged John Kingsley-Heath, his first shot, although probably fatal, barely slowed it. As he was later to relate, "Kiebe [his gunbearer] was at my elbow, staunch as a rock, holding out the Purdey double. Dropping the .458 in a fraction of a second, I grabbed the Purdey and fired both barrels into the lion's head as he lifted off the ground in his final spring, six feet away. The two slugs whacked him down and he fell, kicking, at my feet."

Another hunter, in a similar situation, turned for his second rifle only to discover both gun and the gunbearer were up a tree. Fortunately for the hunter, the lion had been slowed enough so that the man was able to follow his gunbearer into the tree.

Peter Capstick, when charged by a man-eating lion, owes his life to his African companion, a man nicknamed Silent. Although Capstick's shot struck the lion, the impetus of its charge bowled him over. As Capstick was being mauled by the lion, Silent, armed only with a spear, shouted to divert the animal's attention. The lion whirled, springing onto Silent, cuffing the spear away, breaking the shaft off halfway. The lion began tearing at its new victim. Capstick's rifle had rolled off into the grass during the struggle. He could not find it. Finally, in desperation, he grabbed up the broken spear and plunged it into the lion's back, killing it. Both men recovered from their wounds.

Researchers in East Africa had noted a curious lack of struggle in the lions' normal prey once they have been brought down. Even if more stunned than seriously injured, most animals seem to accept their fate passively. Probably it is shock from the suddenness of the attack. Some of the few people who have survived a determined lion attack have remarked upon an odd detachment as they were being mauled. Capstick described it as an "almost dreamy sense of complacency . . . almost drugged." Another victim, Tony Fitzjohn, recalled the experience of being savagely bitten and clawed by a lion as being both soundless and painless.

Explorer and missionary David Livingstone left us a vivid account of a mauling which crushed his shoulder:

> . . . I heard a shout. Starting, and looking half around, I saw the lion just in the act of springing upon me. I was upon a little height; he caught my shoulder as he sprang, and we both came to the ground below together. Growling horribly close to my ear, he shook me as a terrier does a rat. The shock produced a stupor similar to that which seems to be felt by a mouse after the first shake of the cat. It caused a sort of dreaminess in which there was no sense of pain nor feeling terror, though quite conscious of all that was happening. It was like patients partially under the influence of chloroform describe, who see all the operation, but feel not the knife. This singular condition was not the result of any mental process. The shake annihilated fear, and allowed no sense of horror in looking round at the beast. This particular state is probably produced in all animals killed by the carnivora; and if so, is a merciful provision by our benevolent creator for lessening the pain of death.

The Masai, a proud and handsome East African tribe, are extraordinary lion hunters. Prior to British colonization, they were a fierce warlike people, frequently raiding neighboring tribes to obtain cattle, which provided both nourishment and status. Such raids have since been stopped, but the Masai continue to herd their cattle through the yellow grasses and scrub acacia of the savannah. Their diet still mostly comes from their cattle—meat, milk, and blood. The blood is usually taken from a small incision in the neck of an animal, and seems to cause them no more ill effect than that suffered by someone who occasionally donates a pint to the Red Cross.

When it can be demonstrated that a lion has been preying upon their cattle, the government usually gives the Masai permission to hunt down the offender. Several of the tall, lean warriors will set off to track the lion, carrying spears, shields, and knives. They try to encircle their prey, then slowly tighten the ring. Spears are hurled from close range; not infrequently the lion will spring upon one of its tormentors. His companions will then rush in with spears and knives, hoping to inflict a mortal wound or at least distract it, rather like dogs baiting a bear.

A number of Masai hunters wear hideous lion scars with pride. They are certainly more impressive than a lion's head mounted upon some rifleman's den wall.

No one is quite sure why a small proportion of lions become man-killers. Young, healthy animals have from time to time taken up the practice, as well as old or disabled lions that might have difficulty in obtaining their usual prey. When a lion has acquired a taste for humans, however, they sometimes will eat little else. Mother lions have been known to teach their cubs how to hunt man.

In 1898 an English engineer, Colonel J. H. Patterson, was engaged to oversee the building of a railroad through the scrub brush and thorn tangles in the vicinity of the Tsavo River in southern Kenya. Between two and three thousand men worked on the project, most of them African or Indian laborers. Upon arriving at the site, he dismissed, as unfounded, rumor accounts of two men who had been killed and carried away by lions. He soon had reason to change his mind. Hearing of yet another attack, he snatched up a rifle and rushed to the tent of the victim. There were lion tracks in front of it. One of the workmen who had been in the tent related how, fully awake, he had seen the lion stick its head into the entrance. With horror, he wondered if he would be its meal. Instead, the intruder seized one of the sleeping men and dragged him from the tent. Now completely awake, his companions listened to the sounds of the struggle, but did not interfere. As one of them remarked, "Was he not fighting with a lion?" the lion carried the man's body off into the brush. Patterson formed a tracking party which found little more than the larger bones of the victim, and the head, "with its fixed terrified stare."

It turned out there were two man-killers. The following night, as he sat with a rifle in a tree close to the scene of the tragedy, Patterson heard them roaring, but they took their victim from a nearby construction camp. Over the next few months, Patterson tried to shoot the lions from trees or *machans* by night; he searched the thick, thorny brush for them in daylight. He placed poison in dead donkeys. The lions ignored them, preferring live humans. Patterson even tried to lure the beasts into a trap baited with men. A cage was constructed out of wood and metal rails, divided into two sections, one for armed men and the other for the lions. It was hoped that one of the lions would enter the open door at one end of the cage, not realizing rails still separated it from the bait. Its tread would trigger a device to drop the door behind it. The men could then shoot it. Patterson himself sat in the cage several nights, attracting only voracious mosquitoes. Later, several *sepoys,* Indian soldiers, served as bait. This time one of the lions entered the cage and the door banged down. As the lion lashed about in its small prison, the *sepoys,* completely unnerved, fired at it wildly, missing the animal completely but finally shooting away one of the wooden bars, allowing it to escape.

The lions continued to claim victims with almost supernatural ease. The frightened construction crews surrounded their camps with fences of thornbushes. The man-killers leaped over them or broke through them, dragging their victims back out of the seemingly impenetrable barricades. Most of the workers considered Patterson's efforts to kill the man-eaters to be futile, as they believed them to be the spirits of two dead chieftains who were angered at the railroad's intrusion into their former territory. Approaching the camps after nightfall, the lions would roar before lapsing into the silence of their stalk. Men would then shout from camp to camp, *"Khabar dar, bhaieon, Shaitan ata"* ("Beware, brothers, the devil is coming"). The warnings were useless; eventually a shriek would be heard from one of the camps as another victim was claimed.

At first the lions were somewhat cautious, and several people escaped more or less intact after hair-raising encounters. One of them once sprang upon a man in a tent containing thirteen other people. As they shouted in terror, the lion, in confusion, released his victim and dragged off a sack of rice instead. One of the lions made off with a mattress upon which a Greek contractor had been sleeping, leaving the man unharmed. Patterson himself had more than one close call. One evening he and a tentmate heard something bumping against the guy ropes of their tent. Assuming it was a member of the work crew with a few drinks under his belt, they lighted a lantern and looked outside. Seeing no one, they returned to bed and slept soundly. The next morning they found lion tracks all around the tent. The animal had apparently been spooked off after blundering into the ropes.

While the man-eaters bungled some of their early attacks, they later became more bold, and neither thorn fences, rifle fire, shouting, nor fires could keep them away from a victim once they had selected him. At first, only one lion would make the actual kill. After a few months, sometimes both lions would take victims from the same camp in a single night.

Patterson had arrived at Tsavo in March. By December, most of the workers had had enough. Not unreasonably, they told him they had signed on to construct a railroad, not to provide food for lions or devils. After stopping a train by lying across the tracks, hundreds of them swarmed onto it and left. For three weeks all work on the railroad ceased as tree shelters or lion-proof dugouts were made by those workers who remained.

The lions became bolder. They had to, in order to secure the prey they had become so accustomed to. One of them chased the staff of the Tsavo station into the building and then leisurely wandered around the platform.

As far as Patterson, the hunter, was concerned, the lions continued to lead charmed lives. A clear shot at one of them was muffed when a companion stepped upon a rotten branch, and the animal fled into the brush. On another occasion his gun misfired, and the hunter was lucky to escape with his life. Patterson himself was stalked by one of the man-eaters as he perched upon a flimsy platform. On this occasion, however, his efforts were finally rewarded. He killed the lion. The jinx was apparently broken, as a few days later he shot the other man-eater. Both were large males, healthy and unusual only in their fondness for feeding upon people.

Between them, the two lions had devoured twenty-eight Indian workmen, as well as an unknown number of African natives.

Two years after the killing of the Tsavo man-eaters, a lion took to hanging around the vicinity of Kima, where it snatched off several victims. At one point, finding no footloose prey around the station, it leapt to the roof of the station, and tried to tear up the corrugated iron sheets in an effort to get inside. The telegrapher tapped out a unique plea for help: "Lion fighting with station. Send urgent succour."

The superintendent of the railway police, a Mr. Ryall, had his inspection carriage placed upon a siding at Kima. With two companions named Huebner and Parenti, he set out to hunt for the lion. Having no success, they returned to the carriage for the night. Huebner slept upon a high berth, Parenti upon the floor. The superintendent, proposing to keep watch for the lion should it appear outside of the coach, leaned against the door which led to the servants' quarters. He soon dozed.

The man-eater, which may well have been watching them for some time, lightly leaped up onto the platform at the end of the carriage. The door must have been slightly ajar, and the lion opened it with its paw. As the siding was still being constructed, the carriage was on a tilt. The weight of the lion caused it to lurch, the door slammed shut, and the three men were suddenly confined with the object of their hunt.

The lion sprang upon Ryall, stepping upon Parenti to do so. Huebner awoke in panic and scrambled toward the sliding door to the servants' quarters. To do so he had to cross the back of the lion, whose bulk filled the space beneath the bunk. Preoccupied with Ryall, the man-eater ignored him. On the other side of the door, the servants were desperately trying to hold it shut to keep the lion from adding them to its meal, but Huebner, whose adrenalin was no doubt pumping furiously, managed to wrench it open. The lion then sprang out through a window, shattering the glass, carrying the luckless Ryall in its mouth. Parenti, who had been unable to move up to that point as the lion's hind legs pressed him against the floor, fled to the safety of the station.

The lion that killed Ryall was later caught in a trap, placed on view for a few days, and finally shot.

Although not common, the depredations of these Kenya man-eaters is not isolated. A number of people were killed in the Ankole district of Uganda in the 1930s; in Zambia a man-eater ate fourteen people in one month. C. A. W. Guggisberg, an authority on large cats, has stated that, ". . . man-eating lions turn up more often than is sometimes assumed. It also cannot be said that man-eating is restricted to a few isolated areas, for in the course of a careful study of the subject I have come across records from practically all parts of the lion's African range of distribution. . . ."

Three or four small prides of man-eaters once terrorized the Njombe region of Tanzania. Between 1932 and 1947 it is estimated that they killed between one thousand and fifteen hundred people, or around a hundred people annually. Since the attacks occurred over fifteen years, there seems little doubt that mother lions taught their cubs to stalk and kill humans. Lions, at least those observed in captivity, have an average lifespan of thirteen years. On several occasions the Njombe lions charged through a herd of cattle, totally ignoring them, to attack the herdsman. The real fear for people in the scattered villages of the district came after sundown. It was not unusual for two or more lions to leap over thornbush enclosures and prowl for some time among the circular huts before attempting to steal into one of them for a victim. In the morning, the remains would be found out in the brush. Certain villages were abandoned after repeated attacks. No attempt was made to track the lions or kill them with what weapons the villagers possessed; the beasts were believed to be inhabited by the spirit of a "man–lion," the ghost of a powerful dead person who had been wronged and was seeking retribution.

When George Rushby, game warden for the region, finally killed one of the man-eaters and it was observed that he was not subsequently destroyed by the wrath of the "man–lion" spirit, African game scouts assisted him in killing seventeen other lions which were thought to have developed a taste for human flesh.

Certain people, for unknown reasons, seem to attract man-eaters more than others. In a number of instances lions have circled around or even stepped over sleeping people to get at their selected victim. A cyclist once pedaled down a hill, and was observed to pass between two partially concealed and motionless lions without being aware of them. They paid little attention to him, but sprang at and killed the cyclist who followed him. The selection of prey by perfectly normal lions seems to carry no predictability. A lion stalking a herd of wildebeest or zebras will often attack a young, healthy animal while completely ignoring an older, seemingly easier victim nearby.

Why do some lions become man-killers? A number of them, when finally shot, have been found to be old or injured in some way, making it difficult for them to capture more agile prey, as is usually the case with man-killing tigers. Lions often feed upon various kinds of carrion. Since epidemics and the burial habits of certain tribes result in human bodies which are readily accessible to lions, some may acquire the man-eating habit after scavenging upon them. Perhaps the major cause is that as game is killed off in an area and herds of cattle and goats move in to replace them, lions soon learn to prey upon these domestics, as well as an occasional herdsman.

Perhaps a more interesting question is why do so few lions become man-eaters. Even before the advent of modern guns, man has rarely been considered as potential food. Yet as a species we are neither fast, large, nor protected by armor or poison. The enthusiasm with which the occasional man-eater pursues its newly found game would argue against the old notion that we are unflavorful to other carnivorous species. While it is true that well-fed lions, like most predators, will usually respond with affection to human care and love, the idea that completely wild, yet hungry, lions will regard us chivalrously simply because we belong to the human race seems dubious.

Lions, like all large predators, are cautious. Their survival over a vast span of time has been dependent upon their intimate knowledge of the characteristics and habits of the creatures they seek as food. Mankind, since the earliest cave dwellers, has proved to be completely unpredictable and dangerous more often than not. Small wonder that unless molested, the majority of lions are content to simply gaze at man with languid curiosity.

Among people who have seen a number of large cats in the wild, there is a diversity of opinion as to which is the most beautiful. Many would opt for the tiger, with its great strength and bold stripes. Others would vote for the rare and magnificent snow leopard, which lives in the remote and sparsely populated mountains which sprawl across central Asia. The world of the snow leopard is one of pine forests, alpine meadows, and glaciers wedged between immense snow-plastered mountains. Still others feel the more common leopard which ranges across Africa and most of Asia to be the most striking of the great cats. The coat of the leopard is spotted with distinctive dark markings upon a background which ranges from pale yellow to chestnut. Throat, chest, and the inside of the limbs are white.

Although far from being the largest of the cat family—its weight rarely exceeds 175 pounds—the leopard combines strength and grace with superb agility. It can fluidly make leaps of over twenty feet and ascend a tree carrying a load of twice its weight. The leopard's stalking ability is extraordinary. C. A. W. Guggisberg, in his *Wild Cats of the World,* described a leopard's attack upon an impala: "It must have crept unnoticed to within almost touching distance of the impala, and there had been practically no rush at all. To me it certainly looked as if the leopard had suddenly materialized alongside the antelope." The leopard is an intelligent animal and its ability to move soundlessly, instantly freeze, and leave virtually no tracks is legendary. In India the leopard is said to sweep away traces of its passage with its tail.

Where hunted the leopard is usually a nocturnal creature, although in protected game preserves they sometimes move about quite freely in sunlight. They often live undetected for long periods of time in thickets or ravines which border cultivated fields. Such is the secrecy and stealth of the leopard that a number of people have spent years in the outback of Africa without ever seeing one. G. Schillings, a pioneer animal photographer around the turn of the century, once remarked that: "Vastly more numerous than the lion, the leopard is literally everywhere and nowhere." Leopard prints have been found in parks and gardens of Nairobi. Like the American cougar, leopards are able to adapt to a variety of settings—semiarid, rocky mountains, jungle swamp, savannah, scrub brush and hardwood forest. In 1926 the frozen carcass of a leopard was found at an 18,500-foot elevation, which Ernest Hemingway would later use as a haunting metaphor in his short story *The Snows of Kilamanjaro.*

Like most of the big cats, leopards feed mostly upon hoofed mammals such as wildebeest, gazelle, buffalo, and various kinds of deer, although their prey also may include birds, rodents, snakes, jackals, and monkeys, including baboons. While they seem to have little inclination for water, they have been known to catch fish or chase away eagles who have done so. There are strong indications that leopards will, on occasion, even attack mountain gorillas. When Ben Burbridge went into the region of the Virunga volcanoes on the Rwanda-Congo border to capture gorillas, he heard stories of leopards assaulting the great primates, including an account of a horrific battle which lasted all night long. The cat was killed. Some years later, biologist Dale Zimmerman was in the same region and observed a leopard stalking some gorillas close to where the bodies of two other gorillas had been found, apparently victims of life-or-death struggles with another animal.

Young leopards brought up by humans are usually affectionate and docile. Nobles of the Roman court sometimes kept leopards and cheetahs, which they thought were males and females of the same species. Duchess Margaret and King Louis XI of France were also known to have displayed captive leopards with great pomp and ceremony. The royal family of Dahomey in West Africa once worshipped the leopard. Important women of the clan were designated as "leopard wives," and wore clothes dyed to resemble the animal.

In a more sinister vein, a "Human Leopard Society" existed along the Sierra Leone coast of West Africa for a number of years. As initiation, new members of the society were required to eat a portion of human flesh. Then, wearing a leopard skin with sharp knives resembling claws which were fitted into the paws of the skin, the initiates would achieve full membership in the society by springing at a victim and killing him with the small, deadly knives. Fat from the victims was used in magical ceremonies.

While hunters over the last half century have sought the leopard with such fervor that they have threatened it with extermination, most leopards do everything in their power to avoid man. The great cats do have a fondness for the flesh of domestic dogs, and will frequently slip into a village to carry one away. People who have startled leopards, thus intent upon prey, have not infrequently been mauled or ended up as the prey instead of the dog, goat, or other domestic animal the leopard was stalking. Only a very small percentage of leopards ever become man-eaters. When they do, it is usually because they have suffered some incapacitating injury. Yet, when a leopard does turn man-eater, no beast in the natural world is more fearsome.

The *Madras Mail* of May 24, 1962, reported:

LEOPARD MENACE
IN BHAGALPUR
350 PERSONS KILLED
IN 3 YEARS

BHAGALPUR, MAY 23: The district authorities of Bhagalpur have launched an all-out drive to rid Banka sub-division of the menace of man-eating leopards which, according to local estimates, have claimed about 350 human lives in the last three years.

The District Magistrate, Mr. Srivatsava, told pressmen on Saturday that 82 persons were officially known to have been killed by leopards since 1959 in Karoria, Belhar, Bankan and Chanda in Banka subdivision. He said the number of victims may be higher.

He said eight batches of shikaris and hundreds of beaters had been deployed in a 20-square-mile area to liquidate the leopards. Provision had been made to use tear gas and also to dynamite caves, which were suspected to be the lairs of the man-eaters. A Deputy Magistrate was camping in the jungles of Banka, supervising the drive.

Kenneth Anderson, who like Jim Corbett, was a noted slayer of man-eaters, came to the Indian village of Gummalapur in response to a request from the district magistrate. Gummalapur, as well as a 250-square-mile region around it, was in a state of siege. A leopard had killed forty-two people. From sundown until well after dawn, villagers of the district stayed within their flimsy thatch huts, with crude barricades of rocks and boards sealing the entranceways. Even in full daylight, they only ventured about in large groups, carrying whatever antiquated firearms or objects capable of making a racket they possessed. Frustrated at finding no easy victims, the leopard clawed its way through the thatch wall of a hut one night, and dragged its screaming victim out into the night. Neighbors could only crouch in abject terror behind the feeble walls of their own shanties, powerless to assist the victim, knowing that friends, family, or themselves might be next.

Later, the leopard tunneled through another thatch wall to obtain a meal. Families began to reinforce the thatch with planking. The leopard, thwarted in attempts to burrow through the wall of one of these huts, leaped to the roof and tore off enough thatch so that it could drop inside. Finding it could neither drag a victim out through the walls, nor carry it back up through the hole in the roof, it killed the entire family—father, mother, and two children—in a rage before bounding back into the night through the roof.

Thinking that the clever beast which the villagers now referred to as a Devil might return to Gummalapur in its quest for food, Anderson seated himself against the walls of a stout building at nightfall. He had spread thornbushes over the roof, so that the leopard would not be able to spring down upon him. The scene, if you would picture it, must have an edge of surrealism to it. Here, in a lightless and apparently deserted village, a mustachioed man leans his chair against a wall. A loaded and cocked rifle lies across his lap. Close at hand, he has a blanket, a flashlight, some biscuits, and a flagon of hot tea. His pipe glows in the faint starlight, and he talks to himself both to keep awake and to attract the leopard. In the dark huts, where almost no one sleeps, villagers hear his voice and wonder if his mind has snapped with terror.

They were rather surprised to find him alive, albeit sleepy and stiff, the next morning. Anderson himself had experienced a touch of terror. In the early hours of the morning, clouds had obscured the sky. The hunter probably could not have seen the leopard if it were a yard away.

The next evening, Anderson rigged up a lifelike dummy which he placed inside a hut with its door ajar. He placed himself behind a barricade of boxes deeper within the hut. The outline was chiseled against an outline of bright starlight. Anderson smoked, sipped his tea. Around the witching hour he was brought to full alertness by a scratching noise across the roof. It was a rat, which plopped to the floor and scurried outside beneath the dummy.

On the following night, Anderson again sat behind his boxes, watching the mannikin and listening. A wind came up. Light dimmed and finally rain rattled upon the roof. Sure that no creature would be prowling about in such miserable weather, Anderson relaxed, then dozed. He awakened abruptly. The rain had stopped and it had lightened enough to clearly see the outline of the dummy. The dummy then moved, as in some weird dream. There was a low growl. The leopard had sprung upon the dummy and growled when it realized the ruse. Although Anderson rushed to the doorway, the street was empty and without movement. The Devil of Gummalapur had vanished.

Having a sense that the leopard would now be cautious about coming back into Gummalapur, Anderson decided to set up a vigil the following night at Devarabetta, a nearby village where the leopard had taken five victims. This time, as in his first night at Gummalapur, he sat against a building, after first covering its roof with thornbushes. By sundown, the people had secured their doors, and he was once again alone with his pipe, biscuits, and tea.

Devarabetta is fringed by jungle. Anderson heard the calling of jungle cocks and pea fowl. Later a simbar deer sounded its musical and distinctive cry of alarm, followed by the deep-throated moan of a tiger. Anderson relaxed. The tiger was merely going about its business of seeking prey under the dimness of great trees and thick foliage. Later, however, he spied an animal creeping down the rutted street. The leopard? He waited until it was only about thirty yards away before he switched on the flashlight he had clamped to his rifle.

It was a starving dog, which wagged its tail in a feeble effort at humble friendliness. Anderson fed it some biscuits and a sandwich. Satiated with what might have been the only proper meal of its life, the mangy mongrel curled up at the hunter's feet. After sleeping for some time, the dog suddenly awakened, growled, and pressed against Anderson's legs trembling uncontrollably. There seemed to be a shadow moving in the direction where the dog was staring, but it was gone before Anderson could be sure he had truly seen it.

After a few minutes, the hunter saw a long body spring effortlessly and without sound, as if it had been a ghost, to the roof of a building some twenty yards away. Moments later, there was a rustling overhead, as if the leopard were trying to make its way through the thornbushes which Anderson had placed on the roof of the building. Then silence. The hunter, now the hunted, tensed, having no way of knowing from which direction the leopard would spring.

The dog, which had been whining at Anderson's feet, suddenly rushed out into the middle of the street and began barking furiously at the corner of the hut against which the hunter had been leaning. Thus alerted, Anderson swung his rifle around and fired even as the leopard sprang upon him. His .405 bullet caught the leopard squarely. Two more quick shots finished it off.

The body of the Devil of Gummalapur, when skinned, was found to have two old broken-off porcupine quills in one of its toes, which not only must have caused it great suffering, but was probably the reason it became a man-eater.

The mongrel had undoubtedly saved the hunter from a quick death; the man undoubtedly saved the dog from a slow one of starvation. Their companionship was to last for years. Such a thing could only happen to a man who sits upon the starlit street of an Indian village, rifle across his lap, while smoking his pipe with biscuits and a flask of hot tea close at hand.

Over the years, Anderson killed several man-eaters, although most of them were tigers rather than leopards. The tiger is a magnificent beast; even a 400- or 500-pound animal can slip through forest almost noiselessly. They have been observed to bound a 20-foot-wide ravine and over 6-foot-high fences. Hunter Jim Corbett once followed the trail of one as it dragged a 600-pound cow for 2 miles through dense undergrowth and up a steep hillside. The stripes of a tiger, accenting its reddish coat, are as individual as a man's fingerprint—no two animals have exactly the same markings.

One tends to think of the tiger as a creature that prowls about the jungle-shrouded ruins of ancient temples, which indeed some of them do. Yet most of the zoologists now believe that the modern tiger originated in Siberia, stalking various members of the deer family through piny forests where snow might be several feet deep in the winter. Tigers pad through the steamy tropical rain forests of Sumatra, where temperatures are often over a hundred degrees; they have crossed frigid notches in the Himalaya, Hindu Kush, and Tien Shan Mountains which are well over 12,000 feet high. They are often great wanderers. Corbett speaks of a tigress that, over a period of 4½ years, prowled an area of some 1,500 miles. There is strong evidence that a Siberian tiger once paced 620 miles in 22 days.

Over the centuries, the most popular writers have generally portrayed wild animals in terms of human stereotypes. Thus we inherit the notion of the brave and noble lion, the beautiful and sinister tiger. Much of this difference in image has to do with visibility. The lion, essentially a creature of open country, is content to loll in the grass while tourists photograph it. The tiger, on the other hand, unless a man-eater, tries to avoid man if at all possible. As author Franklin Russell commented, "You can breakfast in New York on Monday and be looking at a wild African lion on Tuesday. But you can arrive in Bombay, as I did, and be told by natural history experts there that it might take you three or four weeks, if not months, to see a tiger."

Tigers have from time to time concluded that humans might be an appropriate meal. At Mohenjo-Daro, a five-thousand-year-old archaeological site on the Indus River, a bit of clay has been excavated that depicts a man peering fearfully at a tiger from the safety of a tree. Tigers usually become man-eaters because age, injury, or missing teeth cripple their usual hunting ability.

In 1904 a tigress, known to have killed 200 people in Nepal, crossed into the Kumaon province of India. An old gunshot wound had broken her canine teeth; unable to kill her natural prey, she survived by eating humans. Kumaon is in the foothills of the Himalaya Mountains, a beautiful, rugged country with small villages set back among stands of pine and oak. It was a land of terror. People were afraid to venture out of their homes. Unharvested crops were left to rot in the fields. In 4 years the tigress claimed 234 victims in Kumaon.

When Jim Corbett arrived to hunt the tigress, in 1907, frightened villagers told him about attacks. A large group of men were walking along a road, en route to a bazaar, when they heard agonized screams from the valley below. The tigress appeared, carrying a woman, its teeth locked into the small of her back. Unarmed and fearing the cat would turn upon them, the men did nothing as the woman was carried off into the brush, shrieking for God or man to save her.

The men later returned with guns and drums. They found the victim's clothes, and then her naked body upon a slab of rock. The tigress had licked away all the blood and as the men covered the young woman with loincloths, they averted their eyes, as it seemed she was merely sleeping and might awaken with shame to be discovered thus exposed.

In the same vicinity, the tigress leaped upon a woman who was cutting grass and started to drag her away. The victim's younger sister chased the tigress for a hundred yards, slashing at it with her sickle and screaming for the animal to release its bloody burden and take her instead. Finally, the tigress dropped its now dead victim, and turned, roaring with irritation, upon the courageous sister. The woman raced back to the village. Although her lips moved desperately in an effort to describe the incident which most of the villagers had seen, she was unable to make a sound.

When Corbett visited her a year after the attack, she was still speechless, although apparently normal in every other way.

The tigress dragged another woman from a lower branch of an oak tree where she had been cutting leaves as fodder for horses. Her companions fled in terror as she was carried off. Corbett tracked the blood trail to all that remained of the woman—some torn clothing and bones. Her family cremated the bones and scattered the ashes into a nearby stream so that they would be eventually carried into the Ganges River, sacred to the Hindu religion, and thence to the sea.

Corbett had been stalking the tigress for several days, without success, when a man charged up to him with the news of yet another killing. As Corbett was later to remark, "The man who had come for me was one of those exasperating individuals whose legs and tongue cannot function at the same time. When he opened his mouth he stopped dead, and when he started to run his mouth closed; so telling him to shut his mouth and lead the way, we ran in silence down the hill."

At the village, Corbett learned that the tigress had sprung upon and carried off a teen-age girl as she was gathering kindling. At the site of the attack, he found a pool of blood and a broken necklace of vivid blue beads. He tracked the tigress, who was carrying the body of the girl, through a thicket of blackthorn where strands of the girl's black hair had been caught by spurs of the plant, and through a dense stand of bamboo. The trail led to a watercourse where Corbett found a portion of the girl's leg. As he would later comment in his book, *Man-Eaters of Kumaon:* "In all the subsequent years I have hunted man-eaters I have not seen anything as pitiful as that comely leg—bitten off a little below the knee as clear as though severed by the stroke of an axe—out of which the warm blood was trickling."

As Corbett was musing over this grotesque object, stones suddenly rattled down the cut-bank in front of him. Instinctively he pointed his rifle at the top of the rise, and the tigress, which was apparently in the act of springing upon him, wheeled away. The trail led into a labyrinth of rocks where ferns and blackberry vines concealed deeply eroded cracks, a topography which was all but impossible for the hunter to make time over, but was so suited to the tigress that she frequently paused to feed upon her victim as she padded across it.

Corbett, realizing the futility of his pursuit, returned to the nearby village. He thought that if a great many men were to sweep the ridge, firing guns, banging drums or household pots, the tigress would be driven out of its rocky bastion, and try to escape through a narrow gap. By noon of the following day, 298 men were making their way through the rocks, making a great deal of noise, some of them firing rifles so antiquated that their barrels might well have split upon firing.

The tigress, upset by the pandemonium, broke for the narrow gap. Corbett shot twice, wounding her, but then she faced him, ears laid back and teeth bared as if preparing to charge. Corbett had no more bullets. Instead of making a spring at him, the tigress bounded away to a ledge of rock. Corbett plucked up the gun of one of the villagers, approached to within twenty feet of the wounded animal when he "found to my horror that there was a gap of about three-eighths of an inch between the barrels and the breech-lock. The gun had not burst when both barrels had been fired, and would probably not burst now, but there was danger of being blinded by a blow-back."

The hunter, having few alternatives at this point, took the chance. The gun did not blow back. He killed the most successful man-eater of all time.

Celebrations and a feast followed. Corbett brought the skin of the tigress to the woman who had not been able to speak since the death of her sister a year before. She ran about the village, calling out in a clear, strong voice to her family and friends that the tiger was dead.

There is no question that tigers and leopards have killed a great number of Indians. Certain tribes believe that man-eaters are actually people who have assumed the form of an animal. A native of the Satpura Range of central India, it was believed, discovered he was able to change himself into a leopard. His wife was unaware of it until the two of them came upon some nilgai, large antelope, one afternoon. In response to the woman's lament that they had no weapon to obtain some meat, the man handed her a root to hold, told her he was going to become a leopard, and that she must let him smell the root after he had killed a nilgai, as it would enable him to once again resume human form. Before her astonished eyes, he changed into a leopard, and pounced upon a nearby nilgai. When he returned with the prize in his mouth, the woman dropped the root and fled, screaming. In panic he searched in vain for the magical root and finally, his frustration turning to feline rage, chased down his wife and killed her. Unable to ever regain human form, he became the notorious man-eater of Kahani.

Man-eating tigers and leopards have paralyzed entire districts with fear until finally tracked down and shot by men like Corbett. On the other hand, the percentage of man-eaters is so small that most villagers pay little attention to the presence of roving tigers unless they are eating their cattle, or the poverty-stricken villager attempts to shoot them for their skins with antiquated weapons.

Some men on bicycles once encountered a tiger strolling down a country road. They dismounted, and watched the tiger amble by them. When later asked if he was frightened, one of them replied, "No, sahib, that tiger was deep in thought."

In his book *The Highlands of Central India,* Captain J. Forsyth remarked that "For the assurance of the timid I may as well say that I have never had my camp actually invaded by a tiger, though constantly pitched, with a slender following and without any sort of precaution, in the middle of their haunts." A number of other outdoorsmen have mentioned feeling the same security in tiger country. Like all of the great cats, tigers are often curious about man. A few years back, a Malayan policeman was sitting beside a moonlit stream. Something tickled his neck. He turned to find himself face to face with a large tiger. As the tiger sauntered off into the jungle, the policeman dashed to the cabin of a British forester, where he exclaimed with a great deal of agitation that he had been kissed by a tiger. Tracks confirmed his curious encounter.

While the average tiger is content to coexist peacefully with man, the reverse is not true. British colonial administrators and military men were enthusiastic hunters. Wearing Norfolk jackets and walking breeches, they trekked across the outback, lugging ten-pound express rifles. Camels carried tents, provisions, beds, canvas tubs, and other paraphernalia deemed indispensable for the hunt. Such men usually expended a great deal of effort in obtaining their trophies. Yet there were easier, safer ways to shoot tigers. Nobility, both Indian and English, had hundreds of beaters drive the animals from cover. They could then shoot them from the relative safety and comfort of an elephant's back. The party of King George V of England was loaned five hundred elephants for a hunt. They bagged thirty-nine tigers. The Maharajah of Udaipur killed over a thousand tigers during his lifetime.

Such aristocratic shoots, however, were expensive and not staged all that frequently. Between the turn of the century and the mid-1930s, the Indian tiger population may have actually risen. Yet in a little more than four decades, the tiger, like several species of large cats, is facing extinction. It is estimated that there were one hundred thousand tigers in the world at the turn of the century. There are now believed to be less than four thousand. Nearly all of the Siberian, Caspian, and Chinese tigers have been killed off, and the number remaining in India and Southeast Asia dwindles yearly.

The killing of tigers for their skins, which can be sold for what is a small fortune to the average Indian, has long been practiced. But they were mostly hunted with ineffectual old muzzle-loaders and tracked on foot or on the back of an elephant. Many of the famed man-eaters became so after being wounded by would-be poachers. But after World War II and India's independence, firearms became more available to the general populace, as did four-wheel-drive vehicles. Parties of gunners charged about the countryside in jeeps, shooting whatever wildlife they could run down or mesmerize in the beams of headlights or spotlights. People shot tigers for their skins and they killed tigers which threatened their domestic animals. Blackbucks, nilgai, and sanbar deer, and other tiger prey were now being shot to provide food for humans as distribution of antibiotics and food shipments caused India's population to almost double in twenty years. Zoologist George Schaller describes the post-independence period as one of "destruction that could almost be compared to the slaughter of the American prairies in the 1880s."

As the human population soared, wildlife habitat was swept away, forests cut for timber, and swamps drained, to create fields. It has been observed that everywhere in India there are now Indians. To supplement their crops, they diligently hunt game and gather plants. As the wild prey of both the tiger and the leopard disappears, they are forced to feed upon domestic cattle and buffalo to survive. To protect them, villagers shoot and poison big cats. It is the interlocking cycle of man and animals which has all but eradicated the wolf and grizzly bear from the United States, and threatens all of the most splendid wild creatures upon the earth. Pesticides have played a role in the decline of the tiger. Certain regions, such as the *terai* belt at the base of the Himalayas, were once excellent tiger habitat. Human settlers shunned the *terai* because of virulent malaria mosquitoes. After the use of DDT brought the mosquitoes under control in the 1950s, people moved down from the hills into this fertile country, clearing the forest and killing much of the wildlife.

Once again, progress in terms of human economics meant disaster for the wildlife. Yet in Chitawan National Park, a former royal Nepalese hunting preserve in the *terai,* tigers and other endangered species are making a comeback. The same is true in a number of Indian national parks. Money from the World Wildlife Fund and Operation Tiger have, over the last few years, allowed scientists to study tigers and the ecosystems in which they live. Although poaching and the continued sale of tiger skins are still a major problem, tigers are holding their own in some of the sanctuaries.

Sadly, the age when great cats such as the tiger, leopard, and lion roamed freely over large areas of the world is rapidly drawing to a close. Their survival now depends upon the determination of governments and individuals to create and maintain preserves so that we and our children may have an opportunity to enjoy the beauty of big cats in a natural setting. They have, admittedly, been dangerous to man on occasion. So have thunderstorms. Both are, in effect, powerful, elemental kinds of music. We need them.

5

Scaly Things that Shuffle and Lurk

Egypt's Valley of the Kings is best known for its temples and the elaborate monuments that cunningly concealed the tombs of ancient royalty. The nineteenth-century archaeologists who swarmed up the Nile discovered other curiosities. The caves of El Ma'abda were filled with thousands of mummified crocodiles. Some were wrapped in papyri, others placed in palm-leaf baskets, and still others were stacked like cordwood as if awaiting shipment on some barge. The mummies ranged in size from hatchlings to giants that would have been capable of biting a man in two. There were even quantities of crocodile eggs.

In Egyptian mythology, Menes, the first king of that land, was once attacked by his own hunting dogs. With the snarling beasts at his heels, he fled to the shore of Lake Moeris, where a crocodile was stretched out in the sun. The crocodile carried the king across the lake on his back, and on the opposite shore Menes founded the city of Crocodilopolis in gratitude. When Herodotus, the Greek historian, visited Crocodilopolis more than four hundred years before the birth of Christ, it was already centuries old. He was to remark upon the care that was given to the embalming of crocodiles. A few decades after the birth of Christ, a Roman geographer, Stabo, visited the city, which was now known as Arsinoë. He observed one priest open the jaws of a sacred crocodile, while another placed a portion of roast, a cake, and some honey-wine into its mouth.

The crocodile was thought to be the living manifestation of Sebek, the God of Water. Sebek himself was depicted in human form with a crocodile head. While the crocodile was honored in some parts of Egypt, it was passionately hunted in others. The inhabitants of Tentyra regarded crocodiles as evil entities, and were renowned for the ingenious ways in which they killed them. Pliny tells us they were given to chasing a crocodile across the water, leaping upon its back as it tired, and then thrusting a stick into its mouth. Using the stick as a bit, they would guide the humbled reptile to shore. While the Tentyrites may have displayed this feat with tame crocodiles in the Circus Flaminius, where they performed, one suspects that such a stunt in the wild would have resulted in some easy lunch for the croc.

By the middle of the last century most of the world had become known and mapped by Europeans. Yet one great geographical mystery remained: the source of the Nile. Ascent of the river from the Sudan was extremely difficult; the way was blocked by the Sudd, a labyrinth of floating vegetation which in the wet season was the size of England, a series of unnavigable cataracts, as well as by fierce tribes who had been provoked into desperation by the raids of slave traders. The equally hazardous route inland from the coast of East Africa eventually led to several large lakes whose relationships to each other and the river itself were for some time a formidable puzzle in itself.

All of the Nile explorers were colorful figures in their own way, but Samuel Baker and his beautiful young wife, Florence Ninian vos Sass, might have stepped out of the pages of fiction. We see Baker, bearded, resourceful, an ardent hunter, tramping into the heart of darkest Africa accompanied by a lovely woman whose golden hair reaches to her waist, whose Victorian skirts swish through the grasses and thornbush until she finally gives them up for more practical men's clothing. They survived all of the classic expedition calamities: mutinous porters, an attack with poisoned arrows, starvation, malaria, and the overturning of boats by an enraged hippo. In 1863, the Bakers were the first to ascend the Victoria Nile and followed it until their way was blocked by a thunderous plunge of water which they named Murchison Falls, as mentioned earlier, after the president of the Royal Geographical Society. There seemed to be crocodiles everywhere. As Baker was to remark in his book *The Albert N'yanza:*

> I never saw such an extraordinary show of crocodiles as were exposed on every sandbank on the sides of the river. They lay like logs of timber close together, and upon one bank we counted twenty-seven, of large size; every basking place was crowded in a similar manner . . . There was a sandbank on our left, which was literally covered with crocodiles lying parallel to each other like trunks of trees prepared for shipment; they had no fear of the canoe until we approached within about twenty yards of them, when they slowly crept into the water. All excepting one, an immense fellow who lazily lagged behind.

Seven years later Baker led a large Egyptian expedition up the Nile. This time the crocodiles were not content to merely bask in the sun. One of them seized an arm of a man who was gathering aquatic plants. Friends held on to him and wrestled him out of the jaws of the beast, but the arm had to be amputated. Another expedition member was pushing a boat off a sandbank when a crocodile caught him by the leg. Several soldiers were also shoving at the craft. They managed to drive the crocodile away, yet this man also lost a limb.

It was dangerous even out of the water. One day, a servant sat upon the edge of one of the boats, legs dangling well above the river's swirling brown current. A huge croc suddenly erupted from the water, plucked the astonished victim from his perch, and carried him back into the deeps before any of the numerous people standing or sitting close to him could do more than cry out.

In places, docks were built beside the river to accommodate the steamers of the expeditionary fleet. A channel some three feet deep and thirty yards long became a popular bathing spot, partially because it was so shallow and frequented that it was supposed few crocodiles would ever venture into it. The captain of one of the vessels was missing at muster one evening. Someone recalled that a short while earlier they had seen him headed toward the dock channel to wash away the grime of the day's work. The missing man's clothes were piled neatly on the bank next to his red fez. There was no sign of the captain himself. Fearing the worst, a number of people waded into the muddy, shallow slip, groping along the bottom. They soon came upon the body, one of whose legs had been crushed. Apparently the crocodile had held the victim under water to drown him, and had either been frightened away by the splashing or had planned to return later for its meal from the onset. As Baker was to write:

> Some months after this incident, a terrible calamity in the same canal was adjudged to have been occasioned by the same crocodile, although no actual proof could be adduced. About 7 P.M., Lady Baker and myself, together with Commander Julian Baker, R.N., were sitting in an open shed in the comparative cool of evening, when a man rushed past the sentries and threw himself upon the ground, clasping my legs in an agony of terrified excitement. The sentries immediately rushed forward and seized him by the back of the neck. Releasing him instantly by my order, the man gasped out, "Said, Said is gone! Taken away from my side by a crocodile, now, this minute." "Said! What Said?" I asked: "There are many Saids." "Said of the No. 10 steamer, the man you liked, is gone, we were wading together across the canal by the dock where Reis Mahomet was killed, the water is only waist deep, but a tremendous crocodile rushed like a steamer from the river, seized Said by the waist and disappeared. He's dragged into the river, and I've run here to tell you the bad news." We immediately hurried to the spot. The surface of the river was calm and unruffled in the stillness of a fine night. The canal was quiet, and appeared as though it had never been disturbed. The man who had lost his companion sat down and sniffed aloud. Said, who was one of my best men, was indeed gone for ever.

Henry M. Stanley, the American newspaperman who trekked across the interior of unexplored Africa in his search for missionary David Livingstone, was later on the Congo River in a small steamboat when a large crocodile made a determined lunge at the fragile paddlewheel. Possibly the croc took it to be some strange yet potentially edible creature. It tried to snap off one of the revolving blades, but was shot and killed in the nick of time.

Stanley, always on the alert for a good story, heard some curious crocodile tales from the natives. He was told that the chief of Ukerewe Island in Lake Victoria harbored a highly intelligent crocodile in his home. He fed it by hand, and the animal was as obedient as any human servant. When this chief became attracted to a harem girl belonging to the chief of a neighboring island, he dispatched the crocodile to obtain her. The crocodile dutifully swam the eight miles to the other island and caught the woman as she was bathing in some reeds. Cradling her gently in its jaws, the crocodile swam back to Ukerewe Island and delivered the uninjured prize to its master.

The Omo River snakes its way out of the Ethiopian highlands to empty into brackish Lake Turkana, a narrow finger of green water that stretches for 180 miles through the scorched desert and extinct volcanic cones of northern Kenya. On New Year's Day, 1897, English big-game hunter Arthur Neumann camped on the wild north shore of Lake Rudolf, as it was then called. Explorers Teleki and von Hoehnel had discovered the lake only ten years before. In late afternoon, Neumann went to the lake shore to bathe, accompanied by his Swahili servant, Shebane, who set up a camp chair and laid out towels. Then, as now, there were numerous crocodiles in the lake, but they seemed inoffensive, and Neumann had come to almost ignore their presence. In Neumann's own words:

> Having bathed and dried myself, I was sitting on my chair, after pulling on my clothes, by the water's edge, lacing up my boots. The sun was just about to set, its level rays shining full upon us, rendering us conspicuous from the water while preventing our seeing in that direction. Shebane had just gone a little way off along the brink and taken off his clothes to wash himself, a thing I had never known him to do before with me; but my attention being taken up with what I was doing, I took no notice of him. I was still looking down when I heard a cry of alarm, and, raising my head, got a glimpse of the most ghastly sight I ever witnessed. There was the head of a huge crocodile out of the water, just swinging over towards the deep with poor Shebane in its awful jaws, held across the middle of his body like a fish in the beak of a heron. He had ceased to cry out, and with one horrible wriggle, a swirl and a splash, all disappeared. One could do nothing. It was over: Shebane was gone. The dreadful incident had an insupportably depressing effect on me—a melancholy New Year's Day indeed.

Certain crocodiles, like lions, apparently become man-killers; that is to say, having taken one victim and finding it palatable but not dangerous, it may go after others. In the spring of 1966, a particularly bold crocodile killed a child in the Ethiopian village of Gambela, and later a full-grown woman. Both attacks took place in front of numerous other people. The croc had emerged from the Baro River, a leisurely, muddy flow which curls through Gambela. Villagers prudently began to approach the river with caution, and left off bathing in it altogether.

One hot afternoon of that same spring six youthful members of the

Peace Corps flew into Gambela from Addis Ababa for a short holiday. Despite warnings from townspeople and Karl Luthy, a professional hunter who was constructing a pontoon on the riverbank, the four boys and two girls swam across the waterway. After a bit, five of them swam back, but Bill Olsen, a Cornell graduate who was teaching science at an Ethiopian village, elected to linger in the water. Luthy was to record that:

> I recall seeing him on the far side of the river waist high in the water, his feet on a submerged rock. He was leaning into the current to keep his balance, a rippled vee of water trailing behind him; his arms were folded across his chest and he was staring ahead as if lost in thought. I continued working for a while and looked up again a few minutes later. Olsen had gone—vanished without a trace or a sound, and instinctively I glanced around, a prickle of apprehension spreading over me. But he was nowhere to be seen and I never saw him alive again, although we were to meet face to face much later when I fished his head out of the croc's belly.

> Give or take half an hour the croc took Olsen at 3:30 P.M. After that events followed in quick succession. Although I knew instinctively what had happened I had, as yet, no definite proof. At this point the other Peace Corps volunteers came back to the river shouting for Olsen to join them, little knowing that he had in fact left them forever. I continued to scan the river and eventually, a short distance downstream, a croc surfaced, with a large, white, partially submerged object in its jaws, whose identity was in no doubt.

> About 15 minutes had elapsed since Olsen disappeared. The croc then dived to resurface (still carrying the corpse) ten minutes later, now some distance downstream and difficult to see. The Peace Corps were at first incredulous at the news, stubbornly unwilling to believe what was obvious. Olsen had wandered off somewhere, they said, he would be back soon; they clutched at the silliest possibilities rather than accept the bitter facts. Eventually my binoculars arrived and they saw for themselves what was obviously the body of their companion in the jaws of a croc. They went to pieces then, crying, full of remorse and self-incrimination, and I confess that one of them received a sharp rebuke when he ran to me pleading for help.

> "Help who?" I shouted. "Help him? He's dead! Help you? I should hit you!"

> One does not care to see one's fellow man die such needless deaths. . . .

By now an excited crowd had gathered at the riverbank. Luthy's client, Colonel Dow, wanted to kill the crocodile immediately while it was in midstream, but the crusty professional hunter, wise to the ways of crocs, advised waiting until morning, when he predicted the predator would crawl out onto shore to doze in the sun. That way they could be sure they had killed the right one. Early the following morning, a crocodile was spotted on a sandbar not far from where Olsen had balanced upon the submerged rock. A strip of pale flesh hung from its jaws.

Luthy remarked that: "We were determined to destroy this croc, not only because it was a menace to the people on the river but also because an undeniable vengeance was in us. This was no circumstantial accident, but a deliberate and vicious attack in our midst. . . ."

Colonel Dow crossed the river upstream from the sandbar in a canoe, then carefully stalked his way back through the brush to a point behind the crocodile. He began to shoot. Four direct hits merely drove the reptile into the river, but a final bullet to its head had the effect of "sending the brute spinning crazily about its own axis." Luthy and other men dragged the dying animal out onto the sand, cut it open, and removed Olsen's

> . . . legs, intact from the knees down, still joined together at the pelvis. We found his head, crushed into small chunks, a barely recognisable mass of hair and flesh; and we found other chunks of unidentifiable tissue. The croc had evidently torn him to pieces to feed and abandoned what he could not swallow.

Over the decades of this century, as well as over countless past centuries, other African beasts such as lions, venomous snakes, and Cape buffalo, have killed as many, if not more, humans than crocodiles. (None of which has killed a fraction of as many humans as other humans.) For man, whose glorious visions of afterlife are infinitely more varied even than his languages, the idea that he might, even in an unguarded moment, become simply part of the natural food chain, is vexing if not absolutely unthinkable. A man-eating lion, at least, scatters a victim's bones under the stars and sun; the crocodile takes its prey to an underworld of mud and dank water.

As Alistair Graham commented in *Eyelids of Morning:* "To be eaten by a croc is to be consumed forever *by evil.* One forfeits all hope of immortality. One's soul is irrevocably Satan's, one's body is dung."

The belief that crocodiles, especially man-eating ones, are ambassadors of vile and sinister forces has caused many African tribes to regard them with fatalism. A Zulu was killed by a crocodile on St. Lucia Bay in South Africa, yet on the following day fellow tribesmen swam in the same croc-infested waters with apparent nonchalance. This is typical. The presence of a man-eating lion will cause a minor panic; tribesmen will generally strengthen the thornbush barricades around their villages and will try to be inside of them by sundown. A crocodile, however, is another matter. For a man or woman harboring some dark sin, or having offended someone well connected with a shaman, it is assumed to be only a matter of time before some crocodile exacts the ultimate penalty. On the other hand, a person with a clear conscience feels that he can fish waist deep in water seething with crocs and have nothing to fear.

Coptic priests of Ethiopia told travelers that Nile crocodiles were given to eating Moslems, but would never harm a baptized Christian. If accounts of alligator attacks originating in the deep South of the United States in the early decades of the last century are to be believed they would suggest that the reptiles were of great menace to blacks, but refrained from injuring whites, even if they were struggling helplessly in the water.

To ascertain if a crocodile has committed the unspeakable and devoured a man, it is necessary to kill it and then examine the stomach contents. This is known as paunching. When a suspect croc is killed in the vicinity of a recent attack, quite frequently portions of the victim are found. The odds in favor of finding human remains in a large crocodile shot at random are extremely small. Zoologist Hugh Cott, who shot hundreds of them to study their feeding habits, found parts of people in only four of them. Yet for numerous African adventurers the noisome business of paunching seems to have held a certain macabre fascination. A stuffed man-eater, after all, is bound to elicit more curiosity in one's den than the horns of a greater kudu which was merely nibbling grass at the time of its demise.

Robert Foran, in *A Breath of the Wilds,* reported the killing of a twelve-foot crocodile in which he found some beads, wire anklets and bangles, a woman's hand, a man's foot, the claws of a cheetah, the shell plates of a river turtle, a shinbone of a reedbuck, the hoof of a waterbuck, the horns of a goat, and a calf's hoof. Foran exulted in being the "executioner" of this carnivorous ark.

In an even less plausible story, an African adventure journal described a visit to an African village where, over several decades, a knobby patriarch of a crocodile had devoured a missionary, a colonial administrator, an animal photographer, and the sister of a local chief. The author killed this leviathan and claimed to have found in its stomach the missionary's cross, the watch of the administrator, the photographer's lens, and the copper bangles that had belonged to the woman. Delightful piffle, the like of which has been widely believed ever since Western man first turned to the Dark Continent for news of the exotic.

Pliny, the Roman naturalist, had his own notions.

> It [the croc] lives on land amongst the most odoriferous of flowers; hence it is that its intestines are so greatly in request, being filled as they are with a mass of agreeable perfumes. This substance is called *crocodilea,* and is looked upon as extremely beneficial for diseases of the eyes, and for the treatment of films and cataract, being applied with leek-juice in the form of an ointment. Applied with oil of cypress it removes blemishes growing upon the face; and employed with water, it is a cure for all those diseases the nature of which is to spread upon the face, while at the same time it restores the natural tints of the skin; an application of it makes freckles disappear as well as all kinds of spots and pimples.

Perfumes and human relics aside, scientific paunching has revealed that fish make up the bulk of crocodilian diet. Inexplicably, in some areas crocs feed almost exclusively upon a single species of fish. In Kenya's Lake Rudolf this is the tilipia, a medium-sized fish that resembles breem; in Zambia's Mweru Marsh the catfish is favored. Elsewhere, however, saurians will generally stalk anything that moves. Small crocodiles eat insects, frogs, turtles, and graduate to birds, rodents, and finally the larger mammals as they mature. Kermit Roosevelt found cheetah claws inside a crocodile he had shot. The salt water crocodiles of New Guinea have a fondness for the wild pigs that wander the fringes of stream and swamp. An entire porcupine was discovered inside an African croc.

Crocodiles have demonstrated a fondness for domestic animals. At Palau in the South Pacific, a submerged crocodile patiently waited while a party of people filed past on a shoreline trail, then lunged out to snatch away a trailing dog with such rapidity that the ambushed animal was unable to even get off a yelp. On another occasion, a man, woman, baby, and cat were sitting upon a Palau dock, anticipating the arrival of a launch. A crocodile heaved out of the water to snap up the cat, although the baby, which was brushed by the snout, was unharmed.

The popular image of the crocodile is that of a great drowsy log of a beast, soaking up the sun while birds clean the teeth of its gaping jaws. Nile crocodiles usually do haul out onto shore for a good portion of the daylight hours and will indulgently allow spur-winged plovers to pick parasites from their teeth and skin. Yet when hunting, most of which is done at twilight or in darkness, the crocodiles display speed as well as cunning. In the water, they carefully stalk larger prey before rushing it with powerful strokes of the legs and tail. Under a full head of steam, a croc can launch completely out of the water to snatch off prey which is more distant than the length of its body. Nile crocodiles will sometimes herd smaller fish towards shore with gentle swishes of their tails. When the fish are concentrated and swimming blindly in panic, the croc whirls around and chomps into them. Despite their ridiculously stumpy legs, crocodiles can move with surprising speed over a short distance of ground. Most land animals, however, are taken as they wade into a river or lake to quench their thirst. After seizing a larger animal, such as a reedbuck, the croc will attempt to drag it into deeper water where it can spin like an inverse bit to twist off a limb or other portion of the victim.

In the 1950s an Asian family visited Mzimi Springs, a verdant Eden in Kenya's Tsavo National Park. The clear pools formed by the springs are frequented by numerous species of wildlife, including hippopotami and crocodiles. Several members of the family were perched upon the side of a raft, feet dangling into the cool water. Suddenly, a crocodile clamped its jaws upon a leg of one of the men, and attempted to pull him off the raft. The men next to the victim grabbed him. After a desperate tug of war, they succeeded in pulling him back onto the raft, but in doing so had to drag the victim's leg back out through the croc's teeth. The man's leg was badly lacerated and he died from loss of blood.

Given the opportunity, crocodiles have little hesitation in making a meal of carrion. A naturalist once reported seeing two African saurians plodding across dry land, carrying the carcass of an antelope between them. It is far more likely that they had come across the dead animal rather than killing it out of the water. Human remains are occasionally found in the stomachs of Indian mugger crocodiles living in the Ganges. Since reliable accounts of mugger attacks upon living people are almost nonexistent, it is assumed that the remains were unburned portions of bodies which were cremated beside the river.

During the latter part of the last century, the village of Sesheke on the Zambezi River had a sinister reputation for man-eating crocodiles. They seem to have first acquired their taste for human flesh during the reign of Sepopo, a Barotse king. Sepopo, it would appear, had a great many enemies, both real and imagined. After executing a suspect for witchcraft or some other offense, he would have the bodies thrown into the river for the crocodiles. More recently, during Idi Amin's reign of terror in Uganda, entire truckloads of citizens slaughtered as "enemies of the state" were dumped into the Nile, on the not-always-correct belief that crocodiles would efficiently dispose of the evidence.

A semi-tame crocodile named Lutembe glided about Lake Victoria near Entebbe in the 1920s and 1930s. Lutembe, who was considered sacred, was regularly given offerings of fish, and assigned the dual roles of judge and executioner. A thief or other lawbreaker would be led to the lakeshore. Lutembe, or perhaps another crocodile assumed to be the Sacred One, would be lured to the spot by fish thrown into the water. The prisoner would then be prodded into the lake for judgment. If innocent, Lutembe would ignore him; if guilty, he would be eaten, thus shortening the judicial process by eliminating the possibility of appeals. It is said that a Catholic missionary, incensed at this pagan jurisprudence, marched to the lakeshore carrying a rifle while leading a band of his converts in a rousing rendition of "Onward Christian Soldiers." When a bullet merely bounced off of the reptile's thick hide and it submerged, Lutembe's stock among the recent converts rose appreciably while that of Christianity faltered.

Madagascar, lying off the east coast of Africa, is the fourth largest island in the world, a region which combines desert, highlands, and tropical rain forests. Most of the animals which are feared by man on the African mainland, such as lions, leopards, hyenas, and wild dogs do not exist upon Madagascar, and there are virtually no venomous snakes. Crocodiles do live on the island, and they have had an important role in the mythology and customs of certain island tribes for centuries.

Legend has it that a ragged stranger once entered a thriving village in a dry, dusty valley in northern Madagascar, humbly requesting a glass of water. Most of the inhabitants, arrogant and suspicious of strangers, turned him away. Finally an old woman, wrinkled with kindness, gave him a drink in her best glass. The powerful wizard, for such the stranger was, advised his benefactress to gather her family and possessions immediately and head for high ground. Once they were well out of the valley, the wizard caused the niggardly springs and wells of the vicinity to gush out so much water that Lake Anivorano was formed, drowning the village and the lands around it. The inhospitable villagers, as the waters filled their mouths and bodies, became crocodiles, and the reptilian descendants of them have lived in the lake ever since.

In another part of Madagascar a live woman is said to have been discovered in a fish trap. She remained on land long enough to give birth to two sons before returning to the water and her crocodile husband. The boys grew into men, married, and their descendants became members of the clan of Zafandravoay. People belonging to this widespread clan regard the saurians as benign protectors and exhibit no fear of them. At a Zafandravoay funeral, a nail is pounded into the deceased's forehead to keep him from drifting away into the forest as a spirit before the body can be sealed in a tomb. Once the tomb is closed, the dead person is believed to change into a crocodile and enter a new abode in the water.

In parts of Madagascar, sacrifices were once regularly made to crocodiles. A chicken, goat, or ox was generally thought to be a suitable offering to one's saurian ancestor, although human sacrifice was not unknown. Over a century and a half ago a French naturalist reported that a tribal chief at the Bay of Antongil annually sacrificed a girl and a young man. An immense crocodile lived in a nearby pool. The youths, weighted down with jewelry and clothed in elegant garments, would be suspended just over the pool on a forked branch until the crocodile saw fit to take them.

Sacred though a croc might be to some African villages, greediness on the part of the reptiles was usually frowned upon. An early-day traveler to Liberia saw a shaman call a crocodile out of the water. It was ceremoniously fed a chicken. The croc, as well it might, apparently welcomed these tidbits. The arrangement was satisfactory to all concerned until the saurian attempted to make an entrée out of an unoffered heifer. The shaman soundly drubbed the animal for its enterprise.

In parts of the world it is believed that when a crocodile is killed, another crocodile will seek revenge by taking a human. Conversely, man-eaters are often expected to atone for their sins. In the summer of 1967, two natives quietly poled their bamboo raft through the Airai mangrove swamp of the Palau Islands in the South Pacific. It was a couple of hours before dawn, a tranquil time. Pale moonlight penetrated the low, tangled foliage. A good time to be spearfishing. One of the men, goggled, slipped overboard into the tepid water, dove under the surface, and snapped on his waterproof flashlight. After a minute or two, his companion noticed something strange about the underwater light; it seemed to be moving erratically, rapidly, from one side of the raft to the other. Abruptly, it began to charge swiftly toward deeper water. The raftsman poled in pursuit, soon realizing no man could swim that fast, and wondering if his friend had speared a large fish and was now being towed.

A dark form burst above the surface of the water some twenty feet in front of the raft. In the faint moonlight it appeared to be a crocodile with a man in its jaws. The beast was at least twice the length of the man. As the raftsman froze, the figures seemed to vanish as if they had been apparitions. The flashlight had winked out. The surface of the water was calm and empty.

After hastily poling his way to the nearby island of Koror, the raftsman enlisted the aid of police. A search began immediately, but it was well after sunup before the ravaged corpse was found about half a mile from where the fisherman had disappeared. An entire shoulder and arm were missing, as well as other chunks of the body. The nature of the wounds confirmed that the attacker had been a large crocodile. Natives of Koror insisted that the reptile should be hunted down and killed, but another islander, scientist Robert Owen, had a different idea. If the man-eater could be captured, he reasoned, a zoo might pay up to $2,000 for it. The proceeds could then go to the man's widow. Owen baited a steel trap with a live dog close to the scene of the tragedy. For several days nothing happened except that the hapless dog drowned in an unusually high tide. Then, on the tenth day, a twelve-foot crocodile was found thrashing mightily inside the cage.

Normally, a crocodile suspected of killing a man would be cut open to see if the stomach contained evidence, but as Owen wanted to keep the croc alive, he somehow talked the staff of the local hospital into strapping it to a table and taking an X-ray. Human bones, unmistakably, were inside the croc's belly.

While trying to negotiate for a zoo sale, Owen put the crocodile on exhibit in its cage: twenty-five cents a look. Meanwhile, the Koror village elders held court and decreed the man-killer should die. Owen found himself in the position of an Old West sheriff attempting to protect an unpopular prisoner from a hanging mob. As he was to recall: "For a couple of days it was really hectic trying to keep that killer alive. We took knives away from three Palauans who had come to the cage where we put the croc on display. . . . One time, I caught a little old woman jumping up and down on the crocodile's head."

Several days later someone managed to poison the captive fatally, finally avenging the fisherman's death.

Attacks upon men in canoes are rare, yet have occurred. The men of some Palauan tribes spear fish and turtles in tidal swamps from dugouts. Naturalist Wilfred Neill once observed two such hunters slowly work their way through a thick mat of lily pads in a lake adjacent to a salt water swamp. The boatmen were some distance from Neill, and probably unaware of his presence. The man in the bow was peering intently at the water ahead of him while his companion concentrated on stroking his paddle quietly. Neither saw a crocodile rise from the lily pads at the side of the canoe until it clamped onto the bowman's ankle, overturning the craft. It began to whirl with its victim. The man who had been paddling started to swim to shore, somewhat hampered by the spear he had grabbed as the canoe turned turtle. He looked back and saw his companion in the jaws of the saurian. Without hesitation, he swam back and plunged the spear into the crocodile. It released the victim and, as Neill approached in his canoe, it dove beneath the cover of aquatic vegetation. Although the man's foot was badly mutilated, he seemed to feel that stopping the flow of blood with mud and grass would be treatment enough. Neill talked him into going to a doctor, where the wound was found to be so severe that the foot had to be amputated.

A couple of weeks later Neill again saw the same man, who seemed in high spirits as he hobbled about on a crutch he had improvised from a tree branch.

On the Omo River of Ethiopia some large crocodiles once charged a boat in which Richard Leakey was riding. Fortunately for the famed paleontologist, the boat remained upright, even though the crocs had bitten into its side. "They either considered our boat to be a menace to their society, or the source of a tasty meal," Leakey was later to muse.

A chilling attack was witnessed some time ago by passengers on a Congo River steamer. A boatman was crossing the river, oblivious to the fact that a crocodile trailed in his wake. As the crocodile began to gain upon him, he looked back, suddenly aware of his danger. The youth paddled wildly toward a small island, as the croc steadily closed the gap. With relief, the steamer passengers watched as he reached a small island, little more than a sandspit, just ahead of his pursuer. He jumped out of his boat and ran down the sand. The crocodile padded out of the water and swiftly moved after him on raised legs. The young man reached the end of the spit and turned, horror-stricken. He started to run back toward the canoe. The crocodile cut him off, knocked him down with a sweep of its tail, scooped him up with its jaws, and plunged into the river. No one on the steamer had a gun; all they could do was watch the grisly drama.

Not all crocodile attacks have such a doleful ending. Explorer Mary Kingsley, a spirited and observant woman who prowled Africa in the 1890s, was once canoeing a tidal lagoon when an eight-foot crocodile lunged out of the water as if trying to capsize the craft or climb aboard it. Momentarily, the creature's forelegs rested upon the stern. As Kingsley was later to relate:

> I had to retire to the bow to keep the balance—it is no use saying because I was frightened, for this miserably understates the case—and fetch him a clip on the snout with the paddle, when he withdrew, and I paddled into the middle of the lagoon, hoping the water there was too deep for him or any of his friends to repeat the performance.

Trapper Noel Monkman, who collected crocodiles for zoos in northern Australia, had his share of close calls. On one occasion, his skiff rammed a submerged log. As he was in the water, repairing the damage, the current billowed out his shirt. A passing saurian snapped at it, dragging Monkman to the bottom of the river. Struggling frantically, he was finally able to tear free of the shirt and swim to shore, expecting that at any second the croc would seize his legs.

P. J. Darlington, an American entomologist, was stationed in New Guinea during World War II. One day he made his way along a submerged log seeking mosquito larvae. He had squatted to dip up a test tube of swamp water when he noticed a ten-foot saltwater crocodile rising toward him. As he scrambled along the slippery log toward solid ground he slipped, and fell into the water. The crocodile clamped its jaws around Darlington's arms and dragged him down into the water, spinning him around and around. Darlington kicked and struggled until the croc, apparently interested in less lively prey, abruptly released him.

Arnhem Land, in northern Australia, is a vast roadless region where waterfalls plunge over towering red cliffs to a marshy country where parrots and black cockatoos flap above meandering waterways. Arnhem Land is an aboriginal preserve—a region of sacred rocks, trees, and streams. To know these places in a deeply spiritual way, aboriginal males occasionally set out upon a walkabout, a nomadic pilgrimage. A man named Micky and three companions were on a walkabout in the 1950s when they came to a tributary of the King River. They began to swim across it. Micky, a strong swimmer, was in the lead. Suddenly, fifteen yards ahead of him, a crocodile raised its head above the water. Micky shouted warning to his friends, drew a great chunk of air into his lungs, and attempted to frog-kick his way underwater to the opposite shore. It was farther than he had thought; he had to surface for air before his hands or feet scratched bottom. He broke water within inches of the croc.

The crocodile came at him, clawing and snapping. It dragged him underwater. Micky fought, writhing and jabbing his fingers at its eyes. The croc momentarily released him, then dragged him underwater once again as he struggled toward shore. One of his companions, a man named Horace, jumped into the water, shouting and beating upon the surface. He pulled his friend to shore as the crocodile, frustrated in its meal, lashed about them. Miraculously, although the crocodile had severed most of the major blood vessels and tendons in Micky's legs, he was still alive. Horace slapped mud, and then more mud, over the pulsing wounds, and when the bleeding was finally stopped, he carried his friend for five days upon his shoulders—walking for half an hour, resting for half an hour—until he staggered into the village of Goulburn Island, where there was an airstrip. Micky was flown to a hospital and somehow survived, a testimony to the endurance of a man who refused to believe a crocodile could kill him on that day, for there had been no dreams or other omens.

Micky's assailant, the saltwater crocodile, ranges throughout southwest Asia, Indonesia, the Philippines, New Guinea, Borneo, and northern Australia. Other than the Nile crocodile, it is the only notable man-killer in the saurian family, although a handful of attacks have been laid to the American alligator. The caiman of South America is certainly large enough to take human prey; it apparently chooses not to do so. It is, however, the subject of some wonderfully scary and totally unauthenticated stories. Other saurians, such as the mugger crocodile and the rare, narrow-snouted gharial of India, the Chinese alligator, and the American crocodile, have apparently never regarded people as offering much potential as a meal. Perhaps the most terrifying true crocodile story, or wild beast story of any kind, features the saltwater crocodile as villain.

Ramree Island lies off the west coast of Burma, a large oval of thick jungle growth which at its southern end is connected to the land by an eighteen-mile neck of mangrove swamp. During World War II it was the site of fierce fighting. British troops had pushed Ramree's Japanese defenders across the island until they were at the edge of the swamp. Ships of the Japanese Imperial fleet, steaming to the rescue, were intercepted by vessels of the Royal Navy. The British commanders expected the trapped Japanese forces to surrender; instead, by the tens and then by the hundreds, they slipped into the swamp and began to slog through the waist-deep water of the interminable, trackless ooze. British soldiers prowled the open leads in canvas boats with mortars and machine guns mounted on railroad ties. The British forces managed to secure the few routes by which a man on foot might make his way to the mainland. Now that there was no escape from the swamp they anticipated a mass surrender at any time. Instead, the Japanese responded with gunfire, which the British troops returned. Bruce Wright, a naturalist, was at Ramree Island, and in his book *Wildlife Sketches, Near and Far,* he described the gathering horror:

> The din of the barrage had caused all crocodiles within miles to slide into the water and lie with only their eyes above, watchfully alert. When it subsided the ebbing tide brought to them more strongly and in greater volume than they had ever known before it the scent and

taste that aroused them as nothing else could—the smell of blood. Silently each snout turned into the current, and the great tails began to weave from side to side.

By sundown, the tide was in full retreat. Corpses floated on the shallow water or caught in mangrove tangles. Living soldiers, wounded and unwounded, became mired in clutching mud. At twilight, the crocodiles began to feed. Throughout the long night, men aboard boats anchored at the edges of the swamp heard the ponderous splashing of the crocodiles, the lighter, frenzied splashing of their victims, and screams of men attempting to thrash out of a nightmare come true.

One thousand men had waded into the swamp separating Ramree Island from the mainland. Only twenty survived.

One of the most curious bits of saurian lore has it that crocodiles shed hypocritical tears over their victims. The origin of the myth is unknown, but it was mentioned in a natural history encyclopedia written in 1225 by Bartholomaeus Anglicus, a Franciscan teacher: "If the crocodile findeth a man by the brim of the water, or by the cliff, he slayeth him if he may, and then he weepeth upon him and swalloweth him at last." William Shakespeare, who delighted in such obscurities, used the image, as did a number of poets.

While there is not a shred of evidence that a crocodile has ever wept after eating someone, it is equally true that people have not been prone to inconsolable grief after killing a croc. Crocodiles, in their businesslike quest for food, undoubtedly have killed a great many people. A recent estimate pegged the number of Nile crocodile victims at three thousand per year, but no one really knows for sure. On the other hand, natives living in the vicinity of crocodiles, possessing an interest of their own in available protein, have killed a vast number of crocodiles, often baiting ingenious devices of sharpened wood designed to turn sideways in the reptile's stomach, thus impaling it.

Early explorers found the bayous, swamps, lakes, and placid rivers of America's deep South to be teeming with alligators. Traveler William Bartram described an encounter with some of them in his *Travels*, published in 1791:

But ere I had halfway reached the place, I was attacked on all sides, several endeavouring to overset the canoe. My situation now became precarious to the last degree; two very large ones attacked me closely, at the same instant, rushing up with their heads and part of their bodies above the water, roaring terribly and belching floods of water over us. They struck their jaws together so close to my ears, as almost to stun me, and I expected every moment to be dragged out of the boat and instantly devoured. But I plied my weapons so effectually about me, though at random, that I was so successful as to beat them off a little. When, finding that they desired to renew the battle, I made for the shore. . . .

Bartram was writing of the St. Johns River of Florida, upstream from where, a decade before, William Stork had observed that "alligators are here in great numbers, they never attack men either in the water or upon land; all the mischief they do is carrying off young pigs from the plantations near the rivers." With the exception of some suspiciously lurid accounts of gator treachery, most eighteenth- and nineteenth-century writers advised, like Stork, that while alligators demonstrated a fondness for the flesh of dogs and smaller livestock, they were shy around people, who even swam in their vicinity without fear.

When it was discovered that gator hides could be made into shoes, wallets, luggage, belts, watchstraps, and other salable items, people began to stalk the reptiles with as much zeal as elsewhere they killed buffalo or trapped beaver. Between 1800 and 1940 an estimated ten million alligators were slaughtered, at first in the places that were easy to get to, and finally in trackless swamps which were difficult to get in or out of. Ninety percent of the alligator populations of Louisiana and Florida were killed off in just two decades, the 1930s and 1940s. State and federal wildlife officials began to view the situation with alarm, and sportsmen, as well as the general public, began to listen seriously to conservationists who had long maintained that gators help to maintain populations of wading birds by gobbling up the raccoons and opossums which swim out to raid nests, as well as by consuming rough fish and wallowing out depressions which hold water in time of drought.

By the 1970s, states began to prohibit alligator hunting; edicts were made which had as much effect upon many local hunters as laws concerning whiskey taxes had had upon generations of their families. Some rural judges, dubious as to the applicability of distantly conceived laws to their own communities, merely issued token fines to apprehended poachers.

Then, in the early 1970s, alligators were declared an endangered species and interstate commerce in hides became a federal crime. New York, the fashion market, prohibited sales of alligator-hide products, and other states soon followed their example. Since then, alligators have made a steady comeback. As well as repopulating the backcountry, they are increasingly coming into contact with people. City officials in New Orleans complain that gators occasionally slip into the waters of park ponds to pick off ducks. Alligators have begun to turn up in people's gardens and swimming pools, on golf courses, and in sewers and schoolyards. An eight-foot gator waddled into a busy Miami intersection, holding up traffic until a game officer arrived to capture it. The delayed motorists were highly entertained, the game officer was mildly bitten, while the reactions of the gator were, true to its ancient saurian nature, properly inscrutable.

Such incidents are probably due less to the resurgence of gators than to the fact that suburbs are springing up in places which were wild, roadless marshes a decade or so ago. The shy gator, in many cases, has no option but to live in proximity to humans. The people, for their part, respond to alligators slipping around the corner of their verandas either with hysteria, or by courting them as they would an exotic pet, feeding them fish, marshmallows, or the sort of bones the butcher saves for their dogs.

Both responses have created problems. The people who fear the gators would have them exterminated, or at least banished to some distant, wild places, of which precious few are left. The people who accept the saurians as friendly creatures of the wild are traumatized when one of them, having lost fear of man through offerings of marshmallows, forgets itself and reacts like the 200-million-year-old predator and survivor that he is. In 1975 Thomas Chickene brushed against what he figured to be a submerged log in a flooded mining pit. The log was a twelve-foot alligator which pulled him underwater with its jaws clamped around his chest. Chickene finally managed to struggle free after jamming his arm down the saurian's throat. In 1973 a sixteen-year-old girl was fatally mauled by an alligator as she swam in a lake after dark. The alligator later identified as the killer had been fondly regarded by lakeshore residents; some of them fed it tidbits regularly.

Such incidents underscore a dilemma faced by wildlife managers, especially in the National Parks—when a wild animal loses its fear of man and becomes accustomed to accepting handouts and being around them, an occasional attack is bound to happen. Countless people are bitten by domestic dogs and scratched by cats every day, and these flare-ups are accepted as a matter of course; yet when the rare person suffers aggression from a gator it becomes front page news.

Such attacks are so rare as to literally hold less potential danger to a man in a swamp than a stroke of lightning. The lightning, of course, is impersonal; it will not try to eat us, and therein lies the source of our shudders with regard to all saurians. Thousands of people, including myself, have paddled canoes through the Okefenokee Swamp, where there are a great many alligators, without incident.

The repopulation of the alligator has been so successful that three Louisiana parishes, with permission from the federal government, now permit a limited and controlled harvest of alligator hides. The experiment is being watched closely, not just by those who are commercially concerned with the expensive trivia which can be manufactured from the hides, but by those concerned with the survival of the alligator outside of what few preserves exist. If there were economic reasons to do so, would controlled hunts provide incentive for private landowners to attempt to maintain alligator populations, as they do with deer? No one, as yet, can say.

The alligator, along with Johnson's crocodile of northern Australia and the New Guinea crocodile, are the only saurians not in grave danger of extinction by the end of this century. Long ago, man began hunting members of the crocodile family for reasons other than obtaining meat or erasing the relatively small danger they have posed to him. It is not surprising that crocodiles, considered to be exotic and diabolical, have long been extolled for their esoteric products. Ancient Egyptians compounded a paste for hair restoration from the fat of crocodiles, snakes, gazelles, and hippo. A medieval bestiary remarked that "Crocodile dung is made into an ointment, with which wrinkled old women of pleasure anoint their faces and become beautiful again, till the sweat flowing down washes it off." In the Sudan during comparatively recent times, musk glands sold for as much as two heifers. They were used as ingredients in an ointment which was highly prized by Nubian beauties. Parts of the Chinese alligator have traditionally been sought for medicines and aphrodisiacs. Fashionable European hotels presumably wishing to put flourish into their menus have served alligator feet.

Crocodilians coexisted with dinosaurs, and have survived several ice ages. One of the reasons for their longevity as a species is their tough, flexible hides, which mankind has so desired that he has hunted them to the brink of extinction over the past century. When alligator hides were relatively inexpensive, some people upholstered their automobiles with them. Prices have gone up, but the trade still flourishes. Hermés, a French firm, points with pride to its $300 wallets and $2,000 handbags. Recently, an American paid $7,500 for a portable bar covered with saltwater crocodile skin.

It is only now, in what may be the twilight years of an impressively long existence for the saurians, that we are beginning to learn that there is more to the crocodile than a symbol of evil, an eating machine, a potential for purses. Crocodile brains are much more advanced than those of other reptiles, and they learn quickly. Curious as it sounds, the closest living relative of the crocodiles are warm-blooded birds. Many species of crocodiles build nests for their eggs. Crocodiles engage in courtship and are attentive parents. Nile crocodiles, for example, become sexually active once a year. They flirt, moving their massive heads up and down, rubbing jaws. When the female is ready for mating, usually after two or three days, she drowsily opens her jaws and leaves them open. The two crocs, who are monogamous, then slide into the water for coupling. After five months, the female prepares a nest and lays her eggs, covering them with dirt and aquatic vegetation. For three months, fasting, she guards the nest. The male, although he does occasionally take food, prowls the vicinity to keep away other males as well as small mammals given to raiding nests.

Finally, the babies break through their shells and begin to make chirping sounds. The mother digs them out, and then gently, with jaws which can crush a leg bone of an antelope as a person might snap a pretzel, she carries the tiny newborns to the water where she washes and releases them.

The crocodile, as we have seen, is no imaginary beast beyond the fire; it has consumed spiritual man with as little remorse as a shark, or as a man sitting down to carve a roast of beef. Yet in the overall context of the world we live in today, it is infinitely less dangerous to man than a disease-bearing mosquito or even rickety stepladders.

A crocodile is, after all, simply a crocodile, which is worthy of celebration in and of itself.

6

Killer Bees

In 1962 a man named Leonardo de Matos was working on a tractor in an open field near the small village of Itabira, Brazil. Suddenly, a thick swarm of bees hummed out of the forest and veered toward him. Before the startled farmhand could decide what to do, the bees were upon him, stinging repeatedly. They covered his entire body. As numerous bees jabbed their stingers through his light shirt, de Matos grabbed wildly at a can of kerosene that lay next to the tractor and sloshed it over the bees that crusted his chest and back. Bees continued to sting him. Desperate and berserk with pain, he struck a match and ignited his shirt. He ran, aflame and screaming, as more bees pressed the attack.

A visitor to the farm, at first dumbfounded by the swift horror of events, snatched up a fire extinguisher and attempted to put out the flames and rout the bees. The swarm turned upon him. As the visitor ran for his life, de Matos stumbled, fell to his knees, and died. He had been stung more than a thousand times.

The swarm became even more agitated. The enraged bees killed two cows, a horse, and some pigs before attacking a bus bound for Rio de Janeiro. Passengers yelled in pain as bees in the forefront of the swarm flew in through open windows, stinging them. The bus driver, who was also stung, pressed the accelerator to the floor. The lumbering vehicle picked up enough speed to outrun the dark roiling mass of the swarm.

A related incident involved a Brazilian who started for home after an evening of drink and talk at a rural tavern. He lurched off in the direction of his house tossing pebbles at imaginary objects as he sang to himself. It was late; the forest was hushed. Without warning a swarm of bees swooped out of the darkened trees toward him. Possibly one of his pebbles had struck their nest. In any case, buzzing angrily, they overtook him and attacked. He ran, agonized, to a small pond and dove into it. He swam underwater for as long as he could hold his breath. The bees, hovering over the pond, dove at his head as soon as he broke the surface. He screamed and sputtered, splashing in panic. Bees flew into his mouth and ears.

The attack was witnessed by a fear-stricken bystander who did not move for fear of drawing the bees' attention to himself. The body of the victim, floating face down, was pulled from the pond the following morning. The head was swollen to the size of a watermelon, the eyes were mere slits, and there were dead bees in its stomach.

Suzano is a suburb of São Paulo, Brazil, that boasts a busy shopping district. One morning, as two workers were repairing the old, rotting roof of one of the shops, some bees flew out and stung them. The roofers hastily retreated down their ladder. As they left, more bees emerged from crannies and cracks in the roof. They began to swarm and soon a cloud of them hovered over the area.

A ragpicker, passing by the building, was abruptly attacked. He fell, writhing. A police car was cruising in the vicinity and the patrolmen jumped out, flailing at the bees, and pulled the ragpicker into the car. They rushed him to a hospital for treatment. By now, bees were stinging shoppers at random. A panic set in. Most of the terrified shoppers who were outside when the attack began had no place to go since tradesmen had reacted promptly to the turmoil by locking their doors. People dashed madly about, screaming and slapping at the bees.

Police, firemen, and three trucks of military personnel arrived to evacuate the injured and cordon off the area, which had begun to resemble the set of a science-fiction movie: Shrieking men and women were dashing about or lay sprawled next to buildings that were quite intact while pigeons hopped and fluttered as if nothing was amiss. Would-be rescuers became victims; victims revived to drive them to hospitals.

In a very real sense, the business district of Suzano had been temporarily conquered by a swarm of bees.

Eventually, Mogi das Cruzes, a nearby town, sent a trained squad of bee fighters to the area. Five men wearing protective boots, gloves, and coveralls with wire veils and helmets arrived. They were equipped with flame-throwers and highly potent spray guns of insecticide. Confusion and terror were rampant. The state police had attempted to use tear gas, which had a marked effect upon the milling people, but none whatsoever upon the bees.

It took almost twenty-four hours to drive all of the bees from the shopping district. In all, twenty-six people were hospitalized, dozens of others were badly stung, and an entire town had been terrorized. The streets were covered with debris and bee corpses. The two workers who had been initially attacked, and then left to treat their stings at home, read about the carnage with astonishment in the newspaper the following morning.

Prior to 1956, Brazilian bees were no more aggressive than their American counterparts. The change came about when Dr. Warwick Kerr, a noted Brazilian geneticist, attempted to increase the honey output of the local bee population. The bees in Brazil were of the European variety. They did not sting and were exceptionally gentle. These bees were primarily Italian bees. It was known that African honeybees, while exceptionally aggressive, produced almost twice as much honey as the Italian bees. Dr. Kerr wanted to breed a bee with the temperament of the Italian bees but the productivity of the African ones.

In 1956, using monies awarded to him for his prior research, Dr. Kerr went to Africa to get some African queen bees with which to begin his new experiments. He carefully selected queens, screening out the more aggressive ones. The bees were shipped to Brazil, but were killed in transit by an inspector's insecticide. Frustrated, Dr. Kerr then shipped some new queens, omitting the time-consuming screening process. The actual queens that became the breeding stock were selected at random.

The experiment began. The bees were quarantined, due to their excessive aggressiveness, in a forest in the state of São Paulo. Dr. Kerr originally intended to distribute the queens directly to the beekeepers, but when he saw how aggressive they were, he decided to genetically improve the bees first. He intended to mate the African queens with the passive Italian drone bees and then, taking the hybrid queens, breed them back to the Italian drones and thus remove the genetic aggressiveness.

As a safeguard, Dr. Kerr placed queen excluders around all of the African colonies. These excluders are designed with slits in them to permit the smaller worker bees to pass through unharmed, but to keep the larger breeding queens and drones confined. To make certain of this, he placed double excluders on all hives and then surrounded the hives with fencing.

A visiting beekeeper, apparently unaware that the apiary contained the exotic African queens, removed the screens. The identity of the man who opened this genetic Pandora's box remains a mystery, as does his reason for doing so. Obviously, he must have been aware that the excluders had been placed there for a purpose. By the time it was discovered that the screens had been removed, twenty-six queens had swarmed with numerous drones to establish new colonies in the forest. All honeybees form new colonies by swarming. Before flying away, the old queen and drones feed royal jelly to larvae, out of which emerge new queens. The strongest new queen kills her rivals, and then sets off to form a colony of her own.

As the twenty-six aggressive African queens and their drones fanned out through the forest, they began to cross-breed with the calmer local bees, producing a vicious yet productive hybrid. African bees raided hives of local bees, stealing honey and often killing the occupants and taking over the hives. Many farmers in southern Brazil had hives close to their homes. They were at first puzzled as bee attacks on children and animals increased alarmingly. The violence as well as the frequency of the attacks accelerated. A man in the village of Aguas de Lindoia was stung repeatedly about his head. Unable to escape or withstand the agony, he pulled out a pistol and shot himself in the head. Joaquin da Silva, an elderly man of the same village, encountered a swarm of African bees while on horseback. The horse bucked him off. He broke his leg in the fall, yet considered himself lucky. The bees pursued the hapless horse, which died of its stings three days later.

The new strain of Brazilian bee, with its African genes, spread like wildfire. People began to call it the "killer bee."

What makes the Brazilian bee so different from all other bees in South America? Physiologically the Brazilian bee is similar to its relatives of Europe. It collects pollen in the same way and produces honey in the same way. If anything, the Brazilian bee is somewhat smaller than the Italian bee and the German bee, the bees most common to North and South America prior to the influx of the African bee. The comb cell size of the new hybrids is also somewhat smaller than that of the European strains. Physically there are slight changes in various features of different types of bees, but these are variable even within the particular species.

Behaviorally, there are a number of differences between African bees and their hybrids on the one hand, and domesticated European honeybees on the other. In general, all the differences are related to a type of aggressiveness that is peculiar to the African/Brazilian bee and its fierce adaptability. Brazilian bees work longer hours, sometimes as much as two hours earlier and two hours later than European bees. They work farther from the hive in the search for pollen and at lower temperatures. At times they even go out in light rain. All bees do a curious little mid-air dance called the "waggle dance." This dance indicates the direction to food sources to those remaining in the hive. The new Brazilian bee's dance is more precise, covers greater distances and goes to within a closer range to the hive than that of the European bee.

There are other points, aside from the aggressiveness shown by stinging, that indicate how high-strung this new bee is. Its flight is nervous and jerky. Instead of landing on entrance boards and walking neatly into the hive, the Brazilian bee is often known to fly right in, almost as if, were there a door, it would kick it down to announce an entrance.

Being high-strung also causes other behavioral traits. The new Brazilian bee feels fear and threats from more places and in more ways than researchers have been able to understand. If bees have psyches, then this hybrid's psyche is paranoid and it feels threats to its dominance and safety at times when there are none. Most bees will travel well. A full hive can be carried from place to place, even in motorized vehicles. The Brazilian bee, in its fear of attack, will crowd around its queen and form a tight ball for her protection. The balling is so extensive that occasionally the queen is smothered. Without a new queen, the entire hive will die.

Most professional beekeepers who prefer the new Brazilian bee in spite of its difficulties will cite its hard work and increased productivity as the chief advantages. They say that this bee produces up to twice as much honey per hive as their old bees and that this increase is worth the dangers. Scientists, however, are divided on the reasons for this. It is true that the hybrids carry considerably more pollen and nectar per load than other bees, in spite of their size. They weigh ⅔ the weight of the Italian bee but carry almost twice as much nectar. Under the same set of circumstances, it has been reported that the hybrid produces from 1¼ to 2 times as much honey as the Italian bee.

It is also true that the new Brazilian bee has no qualms about robbing the food stores of other colonies. This occurs most frequently just after someone has opened the hive for collection or has cared for the bees in some direct way. The fear returns and immediately the African bee and its descendant, the Brazilian, go off looking for a quick, sure food source. With no time for new foraging, robbery of other hives is the obvious recourse. This throws off the calculation of actual production because, even though the new Brazilian is consistently giving more honey per hive, it is somewhat like juggling apples from one's right hand to one's left. There has been no accurate study of the bee's production without robbing.

It is not difficult to understand the evolutionary changes that account for the genetic development of the African bee and its acquired characteristics. Bees originally were native only to Asia. When they migrated to Europe they found lush foliage and easily available food sources. There was no need to worry or protection. If the hive were robbed by animals or men, more nectar was to be had. European bees had security. In Africa, however, food sources were much harder to come by. The bees had to become more aggressive in order to obtain their food and then to keep it. Robbery could mean extinction of the entire colony. The bees "learned" to go farther, longer, and to be more protective. They adapted.

This adaptation is further evidenced by the African bees' breeding habits. They lay more eggs, the eggs hatch sooner, and the new queens start laying earlier. They have a continual population explosion to compensate for the higher mortality rate of their harsher life. This causes overcrowding and a propensity to swarm and abscond. Absconding is the relocation of a new hive in a new location away from the still functional mother hive. New Brazilian hybrids swarm and abscond continually.

When a bee stings, its stinger, well barbed, settles into the skin and a toxin is released, pumped by muscles through the stinger and into the flesh. When the bee flies away, the stinger and attached muscles are yanked out of the bee's body. This disembowels the bee and it dies very shortly thereafter. The muscles, still attached to the stinger, continue to pump toxin into the flesh and at the same time continue to drive the stinger further into the flesh. Thus, a sting is more than the initial attack. It continues even after the bee is gone.

In tests conducted by the United States Navy at the Naval Underseas Center in San Diego and in the Army's tests at the Chemical-Biological Warfare Center at Edgewood Arsenal, Maryland, it was concluded that there are substantial differences in the new Brazilian bee's venom that set it apart from other bees.

There are two primary and vital differences between the Africanized hybrid's venom and that of other bees. The first is that the hybrid's venom is approximately twice as strong as that of the bees commonly found in the United States. This means that half as many stings from these bees would be lethal compared to the normal lethal dosage of venom from European bees. In light of the hybrid's increased aggressiveness and tendency to sting, this becomes a vital fact. The second is that chemically, the hybrid's venom contains a neurotoxin, a substance that attacks the nervous system and causes nerve damage and eventually breathing stoppage. In addition, it is now believed that the muscles surrounding the stinger of the Africanized bee continue to pump longer and harder after being ripped away from the bee. For all of these reasons, the new Brazilian bee has a formidable weapon.

To fully understand how potent a weapon these bees have, one must understand how bees use them. In this, too, the Brazilian bee excels. When faced with danger, all bees release alarm pheromones, chemicals that respond to a threat by a call to attack. It appears from studies that Brazilian bees release more pheromones sooner, respond quicker and in greater number to their call, are more sensitive to the smell, release the pheromones both at the hive entrance and in the air for more immediate communication, and have an increased ability to use visual and auditory signals around the intended victim. This is their heightened nervous/aggressive system at its apex of ability.

The bees respond to this call with great numbers of defenders. As stated earlier, new Brazilian bees reproduce more often and more prolifically than other bees. A hive can contain between 40 thousand and 60 thousand bees. It is not uncommon to have 10 thousand bees respond to a believed assault on the hive. The army/navy tests have shown that it takes only thirty to fifty stings to cause respiratory failure in a normal full-grown male and consequently death. The odds of getting those fifty stings from 10 thousand swarming bees are highly in favor of the bees. They have been known and documented to have stung a test target ninety-two times in five seconds.

Compounding this is their viciousness and aggressiveness as evidenced by their ability to pursue and continue an attack. Once provoked, the new Brazilian bee goes berserk. It will pursue a victim for over a mile, over water, through jungle and city alike until its fury is spent either in massive death to the swarm, smoke or fire control, or its own abandoning of the assault. Once provoked, they will continue to attack anything and everything far longer and farther than European bees. A killer-bee attack can go on for close to twenty-four hours.

The descendants of the twenty-six African queen bees that were released in the state of São Paulo in 1956 proliferated, cross-bred with the local bees, and began to expand their territory at an alarming and astonishing rate. By 1963 the aggressive new hybrid bees had advanced over three hundred miles from their remote forest apiary to the vicinity of Rio de Janeiro. Thus established, they began to expand inland and up and down the coasts at a rate of about two hundred miles a year. By 1965 they had reached the capital city of Brasilia. As the bees came into contact with more populated areas, confrontations increased. Swarms of them disrupted soccer matches and parades. One swarm colonized the ear of a statue in downtown Recife. Vehicles seemed to anger them. Natanael Fereira, a farmer, was plowing with his tractor when he apparently ran over a nest. A few bees stung his legs; then he looked up to see that "the sky was dark with bees." Fereira bailed out of his tractor and the bees continued to pursue the driverless machine as it lurched off across the field. People besieged by bees turned to the local *bombeiros,* or firemen, for help. Some fire stations received as many as twenty calls a day to drive away attacking bees.

The northeastern states of Brazil—forming the continental nose that points across the Atlantic Ocean toward Africa—are hot and dry. Prior to the arrival of the killer bees in 1967, honeybees were rare in the region. They are now both numerous and feared. One morning Dr. Eglantina Portugal was stung by a bee as she arrived at her school in the city of Aracaju. She slapped at the bee, which apparently released its alarm pheromones. Dozens, then hundreds, then thousands of bees swarmed out of nearby trees. Dr. Portugal tried to run but was hampered by a lame leg. She tripped, falling into a ditch. As the bees covered her, people from nearby houses rushed out with water, but were driven away by the bees, as were the firemen who arrived shortly thereafter. Dr. Portugal died of the stings, adding to a growing list of bee fatalities.

By 1975 Africanized bees had been reported as far north as British Guyana and as far south as Buenos Aires, Argentina. Specimens were turning up on the slopes of the Andes Mountains.

Passo de los Libres, Argentina, is a border town near an international bridge that spans the Rio Uruguay to Brazil. The town's latitude is something between that of New Orleans and Los Angeles. It is definitely not tropical and its bees were believed to be passive and calm.

It was midmorning and the bridge was crowded with tourists, travelers going back and forth to work, customs men, and some fruit trucks going from Argentina north to the town of Uruguaiana to market. The produce was fresh. Suddenly bees, attracted by the smell of the fruit, attacked the bridge. People panicked. Some fainted, others jumped off the bridge. Customs men locked themselves in their booths, people hid under coats, cars, and anything else they could find. It was a small war zone and the people were trapped and hysterical. This only further aroused the wrath of the bees. By the time they covered the produce trucks in a huge swarm, people were lying everywhere screaming and moaning in pain. The attack went on for hours until five fire departments fought them off.

There had been about 1,500 people on the bridge. Of these, 1,019 were stung badly enough to require hospital treatment in Passo de los Libres. Another 140 people were treated in Uruguaiana. Dozens were in either serious or critical condition.

In the United States, where we tend to look at the honeybee as an industrious, friendly insect which harmlessly buzzes an occasional chocolate cake at a picnic, scenes such as the mayhem at Passo de los Libres are hard to visualize. Yet the Africanized Brazilian bees are slowly, steadily, heading toward the United States, and some experts predict they will arrive by the early 1990s. The bees fly very high over the land, at times thirty meters in the air, crossing over water and cities. A swarm was reported landing on a boat over twelve miles from land. As a 1972 report made by the United States National Academy of Sciences stated: "The present Brazilian bee is a highly variable creature, acting in a wide variety of ways and changing constantly." The report went on to recommend that "efforts be made to minimize the likelihood of this bee and its hybrids moving into North America."

Should the Brazilian bee reach the United States, the threat to the safety of people and livestock is not the only problem. Fear could lead to legislation that might strictly control the beekeeping industry. Beekeepers themselves will run greater risks and will have to adopt new and more expensive safety measures. All this will add up to increased costs that will no doubt be reflected in higher prices for honey.

The dangers will also all but close down the hobby beekeepers. This has already happened in Brazil and if the unchanged Brazilian bee enters North America there is no reason to believe the situation would be any different here.

An additional problem is that, because of the increased danger of colonies going completely out of control when disturbed, hives should be kept at a safe distance from people, especially children and livestock. Yet bees must be near to crops in order to pollinate them, collect pollen, and store nectar. Crops require people and the kinds of noisy machinery which seem to agitate the bees.

These are not the greatest economic effects of the Brazilian bee. As the National Research Council's report stated: "The greatest economic impact of Brazilian bees, should they reach North America, could be expected in connection with pollination. Many species of plants would become extinct or, at best, relatively nonproductive without insect pollination. Honeybees account for an estimated 80 percent of the total pollination activity by all insect species in the United States. Approximately fifty *major* agricultural crops are benefited substantially by bee pollination. The value of honeybee pollination to agriculture has been estimated at one to six *billion* dollars annually in the United States." If Americans are not affected by the physical dangers, they most certainly will be jostled by the economic ones. No amount of possible increased honey production can come close to the risks to the entire agricultural community if bees have to be kept away from people. And, as stated earlier, it is not even certain that net honey production would increase.

Moving hives from field to field for pollination would most likely be impossible with Brazilian bees, because of their tendency to kill the queen when moved. Even if the queen were to survive, the bees' increased agitation and aggression, due to the travel, would make it inadvisable to move them so often.

Another negative effect of this new hybrid is a loss of wildlife due to the same loss of pollination of wild crops. Less food leads to less population. In cities honeybees are one of the few beneficial insects. They cross-pollinate trees, fruit, and berries in parks, and these, in turn, attract flocks of birds into the cities. If the bees were vicious, they would have to be completely exterminated in urban areas and the life that goes on around man would be severely strained to survive in cities.

In short, the entire ecological balance of a continent, both rural and urban, could be completely thrown out of whack, seriously upset by a threat to life-support systems and the safety of life.

Are there any solutions? Are there any ways to stop the bees from migrating both physically and genetically across this continent as they have in South America? There are ideas but none of them is guaranteed and none of them is without its weak points.

The simplest solution would be if the climate of the North American continent would naturally keep the bees in South America. This is highly unlikely. Even if they somehow did not enter the United States, whose southern states have climates comparable to those where the bee is already found, they would most definitely enter Central America and Mexico, the leading producers of honey in the world. Their appetites and foraging distances make it likely that they could not be contained once they passed through the narrowest parts of Central America.

If the Brazilian bee were to find its way into the temperate zone, it is likely that it would die in the winter. What enables it to work longer hours is that, due to the warmth of Africa where the African bee originally developed, these bees are light-sensitive, not heat-sensitive. Where a European bee will wait until the air temperature reaches a certain warmth, a Brazilian bee, not worrying about the heat, will wait only until it is light and will then begin to forage. This comes from the inbred "knowledge" that it will be warm, a trait learned by its African forebears. In the winter, a Brazilian bee will forage even when temperatures are subfreezing. When this happens they die while they are away from the hive. They disappear.

In temperate climes apiaries constantly need to be restocked in the spring. The package bee industry ships millions of bees, queens, and others, all over North America and especially to Canada. Most of the breeding farms are in the southeastern United States. This implies that, should a breeding farm by chance or intent begin to breed African or Brazilian hybrids, they would spread over the continent almost overnight. It is true that they would die every winter in the northern states, but that is small consolation.

There is a possibility that Central America can be looked at as a potential human/bee battleground. Three types of barriers can be set up where the land is narrow to try to block the bees. It must be remembered that it is possible that they will come to North America by sea, from island to island through the Caribbean. This is not likely, but it is possible. If they do come by land, they must do it over a narrow, workable area.

The first possible barriers would be the introduction of disease organisms and/or other natural enemies affecting the bee population. This presents problems. The primary one is the problem of containment. The "war zone" must be wide enough so that bees cannot go out to sea, thus bypassing the disease organisms or natural enemies, yet the zone must also be narrow enough so that it is a workable area. If the bees can be contained in the affected area for a long enough time, it should slow or halt the migration. There are other problems, however. There are no diseases or enemies that are common solely to the African bee and its offspring. All bees will be affected. The entire bee population of the isthmus could be exterminated, eradicating the essential benefits of pollination along with the bee. The entire ecological balance of Central America could be gravely affected.

Another suggested solution would be to effect a reversal of that initial genetic experiment. This calls for a genetic barrier of a zone supersaturated with gentle Italian drone bees so that the odds for Italian drone-Brazilian queen matings skyrocket. Theoretically, if enough of these breedings occur the desired effect could be accomplished. Yet it is hard to say at what point there would be enough matings, and even whether or not those matings would work. How dominant are the African bee genes? There is no way of knowing, and the time for testing is running out.

It appears that the problem is serious and immediate. The problem is new. The bees are new and the threat is new. Genetic tampering for improvement or destruction was once encountered only in the realm of fiction—science fiction. Science fiction is becoming science fact. A whole series of questions, both scientific and moral/philosophical, have arrived by way of a honeybee messenger, and they may no longer be avoided. The answers must be decided in the very near future, but at the present there is only a very large question mark looming over all of us and the future of man. It's ready to fall on our heads. And it's much bigger than a bee.

7
Behold the Serpent

It is generally accepted that snakes are long, tubular reptiles with forked tongues. Most people accept that they are cold-blooded, have teeth or fangs, and crawl about on the ground or in tree branches. Some of them lay eggs.

As well as these basic facts, herpetologists agree upon numerous fascinating details of snake evolution, structure, and life styles.

Other than these basic facts, since before recorded history and on a worldwide basis, mankind has found little to agree upon when it comes to the nature of snakes. While naturalists would have us believe that snakes are basically unaggressive creatures, only too happy to flee at the approach of man, a vast number of people throughout history have believed the snake enjoys nothing as much as biting or crushing a human being to death. Various societies have seen the snake as a God, Protector, Devil, Corrupter, Ghost, Divine Messenger, Seducer, Trickster, and Oracle, and have used it as an executioner, a symbol of tribal friendship, and for virtually every role in between.

One of the most persistent folk beliefs about snakes is that they mesmerize their prey. This is an ancient notion and perhaps originated when it was observed that mice, rabbits, and other creatures relished by snakes tend to freeze at the approach of a predator, hoping it will fail to notice them. There is little doubt that a person staring into the lidless, unblinking gaze of a snake could induce a state of self-hypnosis, but extended eye contact with an eagle feather, a clock's pendulum, or the twitching tuft at the end of a lion's tail could have the same effect.

It has also been widely accepted that snakes will cut down their prey with a gust of vile breath. When a large snake is in the process of digesting a victim, its breath may be less than floral, yet there is absolutely no scientific evidence that snakes attack with their exhalations.

Pepys's *Diary,* in the entry for February 4, 1661, mentions a dinner party he attended at which a Mr. Templar, "a man of honour," discoursed upon large snakes which lived in little-traveled regions of northern England.

> They observe when the lark is soared to the highest, and do crawl till they come to be just underneath them; and there they place themselves with their mouths uppermost, and there, as is conceived, they do inject poison upon the bird; for the bird do suddenly come down again in its course of a circle, and falls directly into the mouth of the serpent, which is very strange.

Pepys marveled at how travel could enrich both the mind and the imagination.

In medieval Europe it was thought that snakes had a fondness for wine, and soon became drunkards if given the opportunity. In the absence of wine, they were believed to have such a craving for milk that they would contrive to suckle sheep, cows, and goats, and even human mothers with unweaned infants. Similar beliefs persist in various parts of the world. The Hottentot of South Africa tell of the serpents which creep into huts at night. If a woman will not allow one of them to suckle, it will bite her. The Tarahumara Indians of Mexico subscribe to a similar notion, except that their snake is harmless and fools the nursing infant by offering its tail as a substitute. The vision of Aberico, a ten-year-old boy, has him escorted through Hell by St. Peter and two angels. They enter a "fearful wood" where women hang from gigantic thorny trees, snakes nursing at their breasts. This, the boy is told, is the punishment for heartless women who have refused to nurse motherless babies.

In actuality, snakes find both wine and milk repugnant. Their teeth would make the suckling of any mammal quite painful, and it is difficult to imagine woman or beast who would put up with it or not be rudely awakened if asleep. In India, milk is sometimes put out for cobras at night and the donor is usually gratified to find the bowl polished clean in the morning. Although snakes may not be partial to milk, there are many prowling creatures that are.

Many species of snakes lay eggs; others give live birth. Perhaps in some remote time, a hunter cut open a snake on the verge of giving birth and, finding squirming babies instead of eggs, began the legend of mother snakes swallowing their young in time of danger. Whatever the origins, the story has been widely accepted for centuries. Egyptians wrote of this maternal act in 2500 B.C. Sensing a threat, the mother hisses softly, yawns her jaws, and the young snakes slither inside, remaining in her stomach until the coast is clear. Scientists are skeptical, pointing out that this has never been observed in captive snakes. They also point out the difficulties of sliding across the mother's teeth without injury, her powerful digestive juices, and the fact that most snakes evidence little interest in their offspring anyway.

No matter. Bring up the subject in any winterbound country store in America where folks are crowded up against a stove for heat and there is bound to be someone who knows a fellow who has seen a snake swallow her young.

Whole libraries of books could be written about reasons that some places have snakes or certain kinds of snakes, while others do not. Naturally the Irish, being great talkers, have a foot in this door. There are, for a fact, no wild snakes in Ireland. Although a herpetologist might lay this to the climate being too cool and damp for their liking, most Irishmen explain that snakes cannot survive in the pure air of the Emerald Isle, or that St. Patrick drove them out in the fourth century. According to tradition, Ireland was controlled by snake-worshiping Druids when St. Patrick arrived. The pagan excesses of the Druids were enough to tax the patience of a saint, especially one with the forthright faith and power of St. Patrick. He vanquished the Druids and then beat upon a sacred drum, which so demoralized the serpents that they began to flee the island, squirming into the sea. A Christian victory was all but secured when the drumhead broke. Providentially, an angel floated down to repair it, and the last of the reptiles was driven into the churning surf.

Despite the climate, herpetologists see no reason why some species of hardy snakes could not survive in Ireland. James Cleland, an Irish landowner, once purchased six nonvenomous snakes at London's Covent Garden Market in 1831. He released them on his grounds and they wandered. A man killed one of them about three miles from Cleland's home, thinking it to be a sort of eel. It was later examined by a naturalist. He concluded that the creature was, beyond the pale of a doubt, a snake. Since the mysterious serpent had been found close to St. Patrick's grave, the affair created quite a stir. A minister predicted the end of the world while another clergyman insisted the snakes were signaling an impending cholera epidemic.

Cleland retained a low profile throughout the furor, and privately resolved to import no more snakes.

As with truly large fish, most giant snakes seem to evade capture and the tape measure. Indians of Guyana relate how a hunting party came upon a strange, high wall when they ventured into a region which was unknown to them. It was smooth and they could not climb over it. After following the wall for two days, they came to its terminus—the head of a monstrous anaconda. They fled in such haste that no one noted landmarks, but the creature is surely still there, dozing away its days far back in the jungle which has never since been walked by man.

Pliny, the Roman naturalist whose observations of animal life are in many cases only exceeded in whimsy by those of Mark Twain, described in some detail the ways in which giant serpents would bedevil other large creatures, including elephants. It seems that the snakes craved cool and refreshing elephant blood, especially during the swelter of summer. The serpents' methods of attack were downright diabolical. Sometimes they would lunge at an elephant from concealment, seizing it behind an ear to avoid the dangerous, flailing trunk. Another ploy was to drop from a tree onto an elephant's back. The wily snake would then truss the pachyderm's ponderous legs with its coils while suffocating the mammal by thrusting its head up the trunk. The serpent's greed was often its undoing, for the elephant, drained of blood, frequently collapsed upon the attacker, mashing it.

During the Punic War, the Roman army came across a 120-foot-long snake on the banks of the Bagrada River. The monster was captured, but not before numerous valiant soldiers had been killed and the beast had been assaulted as if it were a fortress. Or so the official account went. It was apparently believed in Rome, for Regulus, leader of the army, was presented with high military honors for his leadership in the epic struggle.

It is a soft, warm tropical night. At the edge of a thatch-roof village, a man sprawls, snoring gently having passed out after a monumental toot. There is a slither in the grass next to him and a huge python, sensing the sleeper by the heat he gives off, slowly and gently begins to swallow one of the man's feet. While the man remains poleaxed from the effects of his celebration, the snake gradually, with powerful contractions, swallows his leg all the way up to the trunk. Here the great serpent is stymied, but lingers, unwilling to withdraw. At dawn the celebrant wakens. Seeing his entire leg inside the dreaded python, he screams. Friends rush quickly to his aid and remove him from the snake, finding, to their horror, that the leg has been gently digested during the night. Amputation saves the man's life.

This story is but one of many widely circulated and believed tales concerning the constrictors—pythons, boa constrictors, and anacondas. We hear of the anaconda which drops from a tree branch onto the unsuspecting traveler in the Amazon jungle, entrapping him in massive coils which tighten until his very bones begin to snap and turn to mush.

In point of fact, while a python could (and may well have) swallowed a recumbent man's leg somewhere, it is doubtful that the digestive juices, powerful though they are, would do little more than begin the process in a few short hours. Contrary to popular belief, constrictors do not crush the bones of their prey, rendering them easier to digest, but gradually squeeze them into suffocation. While a large snake is capable of ingesting a child or even an average-sized man, they almost never do so, even though constrictors are not just inhabitants of the sparsely inhabited South American rain forest, but live on the outskirts of cities like Bangkok. Still, the giant snakes are almost as feared as the much more potentially dangerous, but smaller, venomous snakes.

Lacking authentic dragons, we take what we can get.

In 1907, while surveying in the Amazon for the Royal Geographical Society, Major Percy Fawcett noted in his diary that he had shot a sixty-five-foot-long snake. He commented that: "A penetrating foetid odour emanated from the snake, probably its breath which is believed to have a stupefying effect, first attacking and later paralysing the prey." No one doubts that Fawcett shot a very large snake, but since snakes are odorless, one is tempted to think his imagination may have been stimulated in the excitement with regard to size as well as scent.

Nevertheless, constrictors do grow to gratifying immensities, and to see one of them in the wild, slipping through foliage like a slender, boldly patterned tree trunk bewitched to life is an awesome experience. Few people do, for the giant snakes are reclusive and wizards of concealment. A 37½-foot-long anaconda shot on the upper reaches of the Oronoco River in eastern Colombia is accepted as the largest reliably reported snake to date. The reticulate python in southeastern Asia may be as long as 33 feet. The boa constrictor, smallest of the giant constrictors, grows to 18 feet in length, while maximum length of the other pythons—African, Indian, and amethystine—range between 20 and 32 feet long.

Most of the few plausible accounts of giant constrictors fatally attacking men are second or third hand, and there is no way of separating the factual from the fanciful. It is, however, generally accepted that a fourteen-year-old Malaysian boy fell prey to a seventeen-foot python. The snake was seen to have a curiously elongated bulge in its middle. When killed, the body of the boy was found. In the February, 1956, issue of *Natural History,* a fatal anaconda attack was reported. Some children were splashing about in the Yasuní River of Ecuador when a thirteen-year-old boy disappeared. His friends saw some bubbles rising near the shore. One of them dived underwater at the spot. Groping in the murky water, his hands came in contact with the trunk of a huge snake. He quickly swam ashore. Throughout the rest of the day and all through the night the missing boy's father, Winchester rifle in hand, searched for the snake. The next day he killed an anaconda. It was lying half in and half out of the water, next to the body of the boy, which it had regurgitated.

The Txukuhameis Indians live on a remote stretch of the Xingu River, a major tributary of the Amazon. They are one of the few Brazilian Stone-Age tribes which have neither been exterminated nor had their culture substantially diluted by outsiders. Txukuhameis hunters occasionally capture huge anacondas. The snakes are killed, but taboo forbids participation by fathers of small children or expectant mothers, out of fear that other anacondas might harm their offspring in retaliation.

A young woman was once found dead in the coils of an African python on an island in Lake Victoria. Although the snake undoubtedly killed her, it could not possibly have swallowed her. Herpetologist Clifford Pope has noted that:

> The answer may lie in the size and intelligence of man. Human shoulders are probably too wide for boas and pythons of average size whereas clothes and other apparel cause a man to look even larger than he is. Alertness, incessant activity, and social habits make him anything but an easy victim. His ability to learn about snakes allows him not only to avoid them but to turn the tables by becoming the aggressor.

Outside of the domain of fiction, where the giant constrictors are stock villains, attacks upon man by giant snakes are extremely rare.

The giant snakes are known for their lengthy voyages upon clumps of vegetation that accidentally become water-borne. A boa constrictor, in good condition, crawled from such a raft of vegetation when it beached on St. Vincent, one of the Windward Islands. A scientist who examined the plant life of the natural raft concluded the snake had drifted 200 miles from the shore of South America. The volcano of Krakatoa, in the East Indies, violently erupted in 1883. The sound carried for 3,000 miles and 130-foot-high waves drowned an estimated 36,000 people on neighboring islands. All animal life on Krakatoa itself was wiped out, yet by 1908 reticulate pythons, having somehow crossed the waters of Sunda Strait, were once again inhabiting the island.

Mobile as they may be, time may be running out for the giant constrictors. The tropical rain forests of South America, Africa, and Southeast Asia are being peeled back by loggers and farmers. There is a flourishing trade in snakeskins and live snakes for zoos, collectors, pet stores, and oriental apothecaries. As with many of the most spectacular creatures, they are frequently killed simply because they are large and beautiful.

During the eighteenth and nineteenth centuries pythons were worshiped on the west coast of Africa. Traders and travelers reported that villages of any importance had a circular clay temple which housed a large python, a living deity. Kings sent gifts to the python gods; if one of them strayed from its hut, commoners prostrated themselves upon the ground upon catching a glimpse of it. A python was addressed as "master, father, mother, benefactor."

William Bosman, a Dutch trader, wrote at the turn of the nineteenth century that the lesser pythons were ruled by a "huge chief monster, uppermost and greatest, and as if it were grandfather of all, who dwelt in his snake house beneath a lofty tree and there received the royal offerings of meat and drink, cattle, money and stuffs."

Killing or even molesting a python was a serious offense. Bosman wrote: "A long time past, when the English first began to trade here, there happened a very remarkable and tragical event. An English captain being landed, some of his men and part of his cargo, they found a snake in their house which they immediately killed and without the least scruple, threw the dead snake out the door; where being found by the Negroes in the morning . . . they furiously fell upon the English, killed them all and burned their house and goods."

Punishment, it seems, could be meted out to any creature which had the audacity to tangle with one of the sacred pythons. Bosman tells us that:

> . . . a hog, being bitten by a snake, in revenge seized and devoured him in sight of the Negros who were not near enough to prevent him. Upon this the priests all complained to the King; but the hog could not defend himself and had no advocate and the priests begged of the King to publish a royal order that all the hogs in his kingdom should forthwith be killed . . . the King's command was published all over the country, and it was not a little diverting to see thousands of Blacks armed with swords and clubs to execute the order. . . . The slaughter went on . . . which cost many an honest hog his life. And doubtless the whole race had been utterly extirpated if the King, perhaps moved to it by some lovers of bacon, had not recalled the order. (From John Pinkerton, ed., *Voyages and Travels*, "Willem Bosman's Guinea . . . the Gold, the Slave and the Ivory Coasts" [London: Longman, Hurst, Rees and Orme, 1808–14].)

According to Bosman, people of Dahomey referred to their python god, Danh-gbi, as "their extreme bliss and general good." Danh-gbi was worshiped as the god of rain and fertility. Young women served the snake by dancing for him and singing, especially when there was need of rainfall. When millet and other crops began to push up from the soil, old snake priestesses would select several girls between the ages of eight and twelve to live in the snake's house as his brides. After a period of ceremonial instruction, the "brides" performed erotic fertility rites with the priests to symbolize sexual union with the snake. Eventually, under the direction of the snake god, they dispensed sexual favors to men whose crops were germinating. In return, the farmers would present a portion of their harvested crops to the snake as well as other gifts, thus supporting the priest class. There was no stigma attached to this form of prostitution since the whole community benefited from a rich harvest. Members of the snake's harem could marry mortals if they chose, but the resultant offspring, as with those of other encounters, were thought to be children of the god.

When West Africans were uprooted and carried to the West Indies as slaves, they brought their beliefs in the snake god with them. Worship of serpents was at the core of voodoo for many years in Haiti, although the penalties for slaves who participated were severe: torture and branding. Voodoo priests looked after snakes in small temples which were hidden away in the thick rain forests of the mountains. By the nineteenth century snake worship had begun to wane on Haiti, becoming only one of several elements of the greater voodoo.

Snake charming is an ancient form of worship which has been practiced in North Africa and Southern Asia for centuries. In early Egypt priests who participated in such displays were thought to be under the protection of Ra, the Sun God. Some modern snake charmers of India and Pakistan observe rituals which date back to prehistoric times. A number of snake-charming sects do not alter the venomous snakes they work with and later release them unharmed. More frequently the venom is "milked" before a performance or the fangs removed. The presentations of snake charmers may range from ancient mystic entertainments to pure carnival flimflam.

Although puff adders, vipers, and even nonpoisonous snakes are occasionally displayed by charmers, it is the cobra which has become the symbol of their trade. Cobras are large—the king cobra may grow to more than eighteen feet long—beautifully patterned, alert, given to raising their hooded heads high in the air if aroused and, very importantly from the charmer's point of view, not particularly fast when striking. From Morocco to Indonesia the cobra evokes a mythology of old serpent gods.

The Jogi tribe of Pakistan is rather like the European and American Gypsy of a century ago. They are a restless people who intermarry within the tribe and generally keep to themselves except when relieving the general public of a few extra rupees at every opportunity. Their women wear bright, loose clothing ornamented with mirrors and decorative stitchery, blue and red block-printed scarves, gold nose rings, and as many silver anklets, earrings, and necklaces as they can afford. Jogis are said to possess a considerable store of magic, and some of their income is derived from the selling of charms. They deal in love potions, amulets for protection against snakes and demons, as well as concoctions to make men more virile and women fertile. A Jogi customer once showed up at a hospital in great distress. It seems she had bought some snake eggs as a surefire cure for her barrenness. She had dutifully swallowed the eggs as instructed, but then felt her stomach churn wildly. The poor woman was convinced that the eggs had hatched and that her stomach was filled with snakes.

Jogi tribesmen are flamboyant showmen. They specialize in snake charming. The performer will amble down a street or stand upon a busy corner playing *ragas* on a *bheen,* an instrument made of twin flutes and a gourd. When a crowd has gathered, the lid of the clay pot or woven basket which contains the snake is removed. The cobra is induced to rear up from the vessel and spread its hood. It watches the Jogi charmer alertly, swaying as he sways in rhythm to the *bheen.* The music is rich and eerie, resonant yet piercing. The cobra responds only to the motion, not the music, as it is stone deaf like all snakes. The larger cobras are often defanged or have their mouths sewn shut; even so, the snake charmers are occasionally fatally bitten when catching or handling the reptiles.

Ancient tradition has it that king cobras guard the shrines of two powerful spirits on Burma's Mt. Popa. Be this as it may, the forests which cover the lower slopes of the volcano are uncommonly well populated with king cobras. From time to time snake charmers come to Mt. Popa in hopes of capturing large specimens for their shows. When a suitably lethal-looking cobra is secured—say a twelve-foot-long reptile—the charmers assure the spirits that the snake will be released unharmed on an appointed day. If a Burmese charmer is bitten and dies, it is assumed that one of these vows has been broken. Author Frank Outram witnessed an impressive performance that was conducted by a woman assisted by her husband. It was, in fact, her third husband, the first two having been fatally bitten by their charges.

The king cobras are usually subjected to a ten-day fast in order to calm them and observe their mannerisms. Snakes which are overly aggressive or retiring spell potential trouble for the charmer. The basket is set up at a village bazaar, and often a small band with flutes, gongs, and drums will produce somber music to attract a crowd. After some preliminary feints which arouse the cobra and provoke it into raising out of the basket and spreading its hood, the principal performer teases it, causing the serpent to strike repeatedly. Since most of these snakes have not had their fangs or venom removed, the charmer's life depends upon his (or her) skill and agility. Compared to many other kinds of snakes, the king cobra is not fast, and an alert charmer can usually dodge its strikes with ease. Some of the more intrepid performers bring their act to a close by kissing the cobra upon the head.

A well-known snake charmer and juggler of Madras once captured an exceptionally large cobra. It was later speculated that he planned to remove the fangs of the snake before using it in a public performance. On the way home, however, he encountered some friends, and passed the day in conversation and drinking. That evening, while still in his cups, he amused his friends by giving an impromptu show with his snakes. The new cobra struck him lightly upon the chin. Droplets of blood appeared on what might have been a pair of pinpricks. The man sobered immediately. "I am a dead man," he stated. "Nothing can save me." Within two hours he appeared to be dead, although his friends who had seen him perform astonishing feats and outrageous stunts, waited around for seven days before they were convinced it was so.

Quite properly, the law pays little attention to the snake handler who is careless or unlucky and is bitten. On the other hand, concern has been expressed when a snake charmer persuades some novice to allow himself to be struck by a venomous snake. In India some professional cobra showmen conducted a school in which the students were advised that the best way to develop an immunity to venom quickly was to let the snakes bite them. If they had trust and were in tune with the powers of the instructors, no harm could come to them. Unfortunately, a few students apparently suffered a shallowness of faith. In one class of ten, three neophytes expired. Although the teachers swore that, given time, they could bring their pupils back to life, the British Colonial authorities took a jaundiced view of the whole affair and sentenced the instructors to five years in prison.

On the Gold Coast of Africa, now the nation of Ghana, some snake charmers once set up shop to vend talismans and potions which would protect a man from the most venomous of serpents. To illustrate the power of their medicine, they had a blacklipped cobra and two Gaboon vipers at hand. They stirred up a considerable amount of interest, but business at first was predictably slow, in fact nonexistent. Finally a brave soul plunked down a shilling. A ring of twisted copper wire was placed upon his finger, and he was given a draught of liquid to drink. The cobra was handed to him while the snake charmers conducted a ceremony designed to assure the good will of the snake. At its completion the cobra bit the customer upon the cheek. He perished within the hour. The head snake charmer's industry was rewarded by three years in jail for manslaughter.

The law is not always sympathetic to the unsuspecting victim of snakebite. In October, 1974, Gerald Overstreet of Del Rio, Texas, was reaching for a jar of jelly in a Gibson's department store when a four-foot, eight-inch rattler lunged out from a display and struck him upon the leg. A clerk brained the snake with a shovel. Overstreet was laid up for ten days in a San Antonio hospital. He sued, but the Texas State Supreme Court upheld a lower court decision that the store was not required to take precautions against snakes.

Texas is, after all, still a frontier and a man ought to be able to look after himself when he comes to town.

From time to time Americans living in India hire snake charmers to capture cobras that have taken up residency in their gardens. The United States Embassy in New Delhi used to have a snake charmer on retainer who could be called in when the presence of cobras was suspected on Embassy grounds. He was paid by the snake. When summoned, his attention was usually focused upon an outcropping of rock which employees dubbed Cobra Hill since the professional, after poking about the shrubbery of the mound, never failed to capture at least one specimen, which he would draw out of his gunny sack to display to the suitably awed Embassy staff. In 1963 the minister counsellor, Benson Timmons III, after witnessing several such catches, was impressed not only with the man's perfect record, but that in the interests of safety he always requested the staff observe the operation at some remove. Timmons, a prudent man, began to suspect they were paying for the same snakes over and over again. At subsequent alarms, he examined the gunny sack before the snake charmer headed for Cobra Hill, and that unfortunate's record immediately fell from 100 percent success to zero.

Cretan Nearchus, an admiral of Alexander the Great, had this to say about snakes in the Punjab in 320 B.C.: "They retreat from the

Crocodiles had a prominent place in Egyptian mythology, and were frequently mummified. In this ceiling painting from the tomb of Pharaoh Sethos I, a crocodile accompanies Hetsamut, the hippo goddess.

This illustration accompanied a doleful account of crocodile attack that appeared in The Sunday School Advocate *in 1888. While pointing out that such monsters do not live in northern climates, the author informed his readers that an even more terrible dragon, Sin, was ever on the ready to devour them.*

Although other African animals such as lions and venomous snakes have killed as many people, the crocodile is more feared by African tribesmen, as they believe it to be an ambassador of vile and sinister forces. Accounts of real or fancied crocodile attacks, vividly illustrated, were a favorite subject of various English publications around the turn of the century. (From Alistair Graham, Eyelids of Morning)

On New Year's Day of 1897, English big-game hunter Arthur Newman bathed on the shore of Kenya's Lake Tarkana. His Swahili servant, Shebane, was washing himself a short distance down the shore. Newman heard a cry of alarm and looked up to see "the head of a huge crocodile out of the water, just swinging over toward the deep with poor Shebane in its awful jaws. . . ."

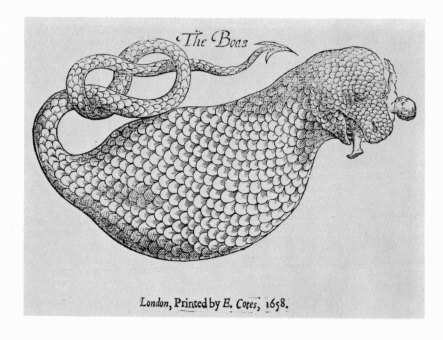

The Boas

London, Printed by E. Cotes, 1658.

This fanciful, tragic encounter between a boa and a baby is from E. Topsell's The History of Serpents, *published in London in 1658. Contrary to popular belief, the giant constricters—boas, pythons, and anacondas—almost never molest man.* (Courtesy of American Museum of Natural History)

The anaconda, like most of the larger constricters, is capable of killing a man, although it rarely does so, despite its prominence as a terrifying villain as portrayed in dubious adventure books.

"A gardener who wanted to make a close study of how to raise bees!" by Daumier.
(BETTMANN ARCHIVE)

plains to the villages that do not disappear under water at the time of the inundations and fill the houses. . . . On this account, the people raise their beds to a great height from the ground and are sometimes compelled to abandon their homes. . . ."

Now as then, the people of southeastern Asia suffer more fatal snakebites than those of any other part of the Earth, and the majority of the snakebites occur during the monsoon months. Some ten to fifteen thousand deaths annually are reported in India alone. Although several species of venomous snakes contribute to this statistic, the cobra is probably the chief villain. It is an odd villain. The sea snake usually attacks without the victim even knowing it. Both Russell's viper and the saw-scaled viper are said to be easily irritated, pugnacious. The krait fatally bites many people while they sleep. Cobras, on the other hand, are generally shy creatures who try to avoid man in the wild and are rather docile in captivity. The problem lies in the fact that cobras and Indians occupy much the same territory; the snakes are drawn to cultivated fields by the vast number of rodents which feed upon the grains, and accidental yet fatal encounters with barefooted and barelegged farmers are inevitable. Still, were it not for cobras, India's grain crops would be overrun with rats and the resulting famine would be far more disastrous than the snakebite fatalities.

Cobras are worshipped in many parts of India. The *Nagas,* serpent deities, are associated with fertility, hot springs, volcanos, and lightning. Tradition has it that when Buddha was meditating under a searing desert sun, a cobra named Muchilinda spread its umbrellalike hood over the sage to shade him. When he was finished, Buddha laid his hand upon the back of the serpent's hood, blessing him. The distinctive marks remain to this day.

Each year thousands of people come to the village of Shirala in west central India to celebrate the festival of *Naga Panchami.* In ancient times, villagers believe, the great god Shiva granted them protection from cobras; since then they have revered the sacred snakes in annual rites. Prior to the *Naga Panchami,* which occurs in July, the local populace gathers numerous cobras, placing them in clay pots. Just before dawn on the appointed day, villagers take ceremonial baths. At sunrise, they parade through the streets to a small shrine. Behind the blaring tubas and trumpets of ragtag brass bands are marchers bearing snake pots and large monitor lizards lashed loosely to poles. The lizards are alive and decorated with red pigments. According to legend, Shivaji, a seventeenth-century king, tied a rope to the tail of a monitor lizard at the base of a besieged enemy fortress. The glue-footed creature easily scaled the wall and the king's soldiers swarmed up the rope and routed the defenders.

At the shrine and later in private homes, the cobras are taken out of the pots. Offerings of food are laid out, and worshipers pray before the snakes, often within striking distance. In the course of the festival the cobras are handled repeatedly without incident. Yet these are snakes whose fangs and venom glands have often been examined by outsiders and found to be intact. At dusk the snakes are returned to the earthen pots.

Feasting, drinking, dancing, and general merriment follow. The next morning the cobras are released back into the fields.

Cobras are not always as well behaved as those participating in the *Naga Panchami* or other Indian snake festivals. African cobras, like their Indian cousins, can be lethal if abruptly disturbed. Kumasi is a bustling city of fifty-nine thousand population in central Ghana. A few years ago, a hospital annex was being constructed there. As a bulldozer was butting its way into a thick patch of undergrowth, a large cobra dropped from an overhanging branch onto the driver's seat. The driver, whose reflexes were superb, grabbed the snake just behind its head. A nine-foot cobra is not only muscular, but generally full of fight if in the process of being strangled. The snake lashed its body back and forth, finally coiling it around its tormentor. The catskinner could not let go of his captive without risking an almost certain bite. With extraordinary dexterity he managed to one-handedly turn the bulldozer around and jockey it to the nearby hospital, all the while clutching the writhing cobra in the other hand. He stopped in front of the building where a small crowd excitedly surrounded the machine. A man produced a pistol and offered to shoot the cobra's head off. The driver politely declined the offer, prizing his hand and dubious of the man's marksmanship. The crowd hushed and for a few strained minutes both snake and catskinner were stalemated, almost motionless, as if figures in a symbolic tableau.

Finally, someone emerged from the hospital with a gauze muzzle soaked in chloroform. With this, the cobra was knocked out as cleanly as if it were being prepared for surgery.

Although there are a number of venomous snakes in Africa, the mamba is the most feared. The very name, black mamba, has a sinister edge to it. (Other mambas—green, West African, and Jameson's —are also venomous, but smaller than the black, and lack its villainous charisma.) Among many Africans, there is a widespread belief that aggravated mambas, once they have selected a victim, can chase down and kill a walking or running man, or even a person fleeing on horseback.

In South Africa it is said that a Boer farmer was turning a field with a team of oxen a few years back when his plough sliced through an underground mamba den. One of the enraged snakes pursued the unsuspecting farmer. When he paused to adjust the traces, the mamba, well over ten feet long, coiled and then struck the hapless man in the neck. It then bit both oxen in the flanks. The oxen and the farmer were found dead in the field.

The mamba is a large snake. Black mambas of fourteen feet in length have been taken. They are quick, agile, and quite capable of killing a man with their venom. Since numerous Africans share territory with mambas, and wander about barefooted, a fair number of them are fatally bitten each year. Yet as C. J. P. Ionides, who was senior game ranger of Tanganyika when it was a British colony, commented:

> . . . The mamba is not an aggressive snake, being rather timid and anxious to avoid an encounter. If concerned, it will strike out in self defence, but prefers to get away if it can. I have caught scores during the last few years and consider them quite gentle but very nervous snakes.

At least part of the mamba's diabolic reputation comes from its habit of often gliding well off the ground in the thick foliage of the rain forest. It is disconcerting enough to see a large venomous snake next to one's feet; it is even more unsettling when such a snake suddenly appears at eye level. Like its close relative, the cobra, the mamba may erect its head and neck when provoked or frightened. In Nyasaland, a district officer reported that a mamba struck his windshield. Another official was driving slowly through the backcountry when a mamba reared up and lunged at the door of his open touring car. Judging from newspaper accounts, these attacks were expressions of violent, reckless aggression. In reality, they were more likely no more than defense reactions to the large and noisy creatures which were powering toward them so rapidly that they were unable to flee.

Eventually, most discussions about snakes will stop nibbling around the edges and get down to the core of our curiosity, namely, what is the most deadly snake? And, of course, there is no easy, simple answer. In his thorough study *Dangerous to Man,* Roger Caras commented that, "Snakes almost certainly kill more people in a year than sharks do in a century, more people in a month than man-eating cats do in a hundred years, and more people in a day than rogue elephants have since time began." Yet, as almost all field naturalists have stressed, venomous snakes demonstrate little or no aggressiveness toward man, usually striking only when threatened. The danger of venomous snakes in general is that millions of people and snakes live in the same areas, and, perhaps more importantly, most victims are completely unaware that a reptile is in the vicinity until they place a hand or foot upon or next to it. *Snake in the grass, alas!*

As a child I checked out every book in each of the various small town libraries where I lived that had anything remotely to do with Adventure in Distant Places. From these sources, I came away with the notion that, hands down, the most notable man-killing snakes were the black mamba, fer-de-lance, and bushmaster. Somehow cobras were too closely associated with snake charmers and civilization to be suitably lethal in my imagination, and rattlesnakes too familiar. I, like most of my playmates, had seen a rattler or two in my time and was blasé.

I was later to learn that all of these snakes do indeed have formidable reputations, as do several other species. While the mambas are highly venomous, alert, and one of the fastest snakes, they are more apt to use their speed in getting away from someone rather than attacking. The slower puff adder may well cause more fatalities as it is less likely to move off at the approach of a human. Other African exotics include the spitting cobra, that blinds prey by ejecting its venom; the boomslang, a tree-dweller that tries to frighten potential foes away by swelling the forepart of its body to twice as much as normal size; and the Gaboon vipers, possessors of the longest fangs of any snake, up to two inches long.

The Gaboon viper and the puff adder are members of the viper family, whose most dangerous members include Russell's viper of southeastern Asia, and the saw-scaled viper, and the horned viper that inhabits the desert country of North Africa and the Middle East.

The horned viper is extremely venomous and dangerous in that it often curls up on paths over which people walk with little or no footwear. Many nomadic Bedouins carry snake stones, usually carnelian or onyx pebbles which have been rubbed smooth by the thumb of the owner, believing not only in the protection such a stone can provide against snakebite, but in its curative powers. It is thought that certain litanies, recited over a victim, will assist in the cure, and that an antidote exists in one of the "horns." In his *Travels in Arabia Deserta,* published in 1888, Charles Doughty describes an incident in which he and some Arab companions encountered a horned viper. "The lad Mohammed divided the head with a cutlass stroke . . . the old Moor would have her horns. 'Wot ye, in the left horn lies the venom and the antidote is in the other, if it be drunken with milk—or said I amiss, let me think in which of them. Well lads let her be, for I have not this thing certainly in my mind.' "

Like the vipers, the pit vipers generally have a broad, triangular head. They are characterized by two heat-sensitive pits located between the eyes and nostrils. The eastern and western diamondback rattlesnakes are pit vipers and considered the most dangerous snakes in North America. The fer-de-lance is a long, slender pit viper of Central America. Annually it causes numerous fatalities, especially among workers in banana plantations. The bushmaster is the largest of the pit vipers, frequenting the lowlands of Central America and upper South America. Specimens more than twelve feet long have been reported, but a length of nine to ten feet is more common.

In the summer of 1949 a team with the Inter-American Geodetic Survey was working in the jungle hill country of the Canal Zone. The crew slept out in the open under canvas rain shields. A little before midnight one evening, Al Pimental, a surveyor, was just beginning to drop off to sleep when he heard a faint rustle close to his head. Moments later a large snake slithered across his cheek. Pimental froze, suspecting his visitor was a bushmaster. The snake crawled inside his sleeping bag and down his body to his stomach, where it coiled in repose.

Throughout the endless hours of darkness Pimental somehow managed to will his body to remain motionless. Well after dawn, his companions came to waken him, thinking he had overslept. They drew up abruptly when they saw Pimental's wild eyes, drawn face, and the pronounced bulge in his sleeping bag. A local Indian who was with the party, thinking a smoke might comfort the trapped man, asked *"Cigarillo?"*

The snake stirred.

Pimental closed his eyes. No one else moved. The snake settled itself again.

The Indian pantomimed blowing smoke. The others understood and Pimental signaled yes by moving his eyes up and down. Semidamp grass was burned in a supply bag. A slit was made in the bottom of the sleeping bag and smoke forced into it. The snake writhed. Smoke drifted out of the neck of the sleeping bag. Pimental's face teared as he fought against coughing. The snake once more relaxed upon his stomach.

The anxious surveying crew pantomimed trying more smoke. Pimental signaled no by moving his eyes back and forth. The snake had now been in his bag for almost twelve hours; in all that time the man had not moved. It was by now a hot, brassy day, and even under the shade of the rain shield it was almost unendurably hot in the sleeping bag. Pimental often shut his eyes to keep out the stinging sweat. His friends stood by hopelessly, unable to help; they might as well have been on another planet.

The crew boss was beginning to think Pimental would pass out from the heat when a desperate idea came to him. Stealthily, gently, so as not to disturb the snake, he removed the rain shield. The tropical sun now beat directly upon the sleeping bag. They waited. The cold-blooded snake should not have been able to endure the rising heat inside the bag, but it remained loosely coiled, limp against the man's stomach. For the man, cramped in every muscle and almost delirious from the heat, the torture mounted. One of his companions later remarked that he "looked like a drenched corpse, his eyes closed tight against the glare. The heat was like a blast furnace. . . ."

Just as it seemed he was on the verge of breaking, of moving or passing out, the lump in the sleeping bag made a slight movement, then slid out across his body and past his cheek into the glare outside. It was a bushmaster. The snake was heading for shade when one of the men killed it. The ordeal was over.

In his book *The Rivers Ran East,* Leonard Clark commented that the bushmaster can be "fatal to a man in five minutes," and "will continually strike until the victim is dead." Because of its size and the potency of its venom, the bushmaster must be considered among the most lethal snakes of the world. Yet it would appear that the South American rattlesnake and the fer-de-lance claim more victims. Possibly this is because the bushmaster is less frequently encountered. In addition, it has turned out to be remarkably docile on occasion.

An amateur snake collector in Panama, armed with a butterfly net, charged after what he took to be a boa constrictor. As the reptile was attempting to escape into the brush his pursuer grabbed it by the tail and entangled its head in his net to keep it from striking. He dropped it into a small box. When the bushmaster, for such it was, attempted to crawl out, the collector gently and reprovingly slapped it upon the snout. Surprised, the highly venomous snake slipped meekly back into the box. Fortunately, someone noted the mistaken identity before the collector attempted any more casual handling of his captive.

An employee of a Colombian rubber station also mistook a bushmaster for a boa. Presumably lacking a butterfly net, his method of securing his prize was to tie a shoestring around the nine-foot-long, cinnamon-colored snake's neck. He then attempted to lead it, as in some bizarre fable, down the jungle path. The snake balked, breaking the string. The man patiently retied it and eventually delivered the bushmaster to an astonished herpetologist.

The world's highly venomous snakes belong to two large families, the vipers and the elapids. The elapid family includes cobras, mambas, kraits, sea snakes, and the Australian tiger snake. The small and usually inoffensive tiger snake causes a number of deaths every year as its venom is extremely powerful.

"As we sailed along we saw multitudes of grampuses every day; also water snakes of divers colours. Both the Spaniards and Indians are very fearful of these snakes, believing there is no cure for their bitings." When the English pirate, Basil Ringrose, described the sea snakes he saw off the coast of Ecuador in 1679, there was indeed no antidote for their venom. Nor is there any today.

Late on an autumn afternoon in 1954, a Chinese boy was paddling around in low surf off Penang Island, Malaysia. He felt something brush his foot. Glancing down, he was astonished to see a sea snake clamped to his ankle. On the beach, the boy showed the bite to his father. As there was no pain, the child was allowed to return to his play in the water. An hour after the bite he complained of being weak and stiff. By midnight he was passing blood, and he died shortly after dawn. That same day, not far from where the boy had been bitten, a twenty-six year old man was also attacked by a sea snake. He managed to hang onto life for seventy-seven hours.

There are some fifty varieties of sea snakes, many of them beautifully mottled. As with land snakes, the toxicity of their venom appears to vary widely depending upon the species and the locale. It has been reported that fishermen in the vicinity of Karachi, Pakistan, consider them to be virtually harmless. On the other hand, Malcolm Smith, a doctor and herpetologist who served as court physician to the King of Siam, wrote that, "I have travelled considerably among the fisherfolk who live along the Gulf of Siam where sea-snakes abound, and there is hardly a village that cannot tell you of its fatalities." Experiments have been conducted in which the venom of sea snakes, tiger snakes, death adders, and cobras were injected into rats and rabbits. The results indicated that sea snake venom is from two to ten times as powerful as that of their terrestrial cousins. Another researcher, Dr. Bruce Halsted, concluded that the venom of one species of sea snake is fifty times more potent than that of the king cobra.

Victims of sea snake bite seldom feel more than the equivalent of a pinprick. For a period of a half hour to eight hours there are no other symptoms. Then the muscles become weak and stiffen, eyelids droop, and the jaws lock. The heart and kidneys become progressively more damaged. Death may occur after twelve hours, or take several days.

Fortunately for divers and bathers, sea snakes carry a smaller amount of venom than cobras and many other dangerous land species. When biting, they may release only some of their deadly venom, or, quite frequently, none at all. Like all serpents, they usually show little aggression toward man unless molested. In the April, 1972, issue of *National Geographic,* Kenneth MacLeish described how he and a team of divers swam among sea snakes off Australia's Great Barrier Reef, observing and photographing them, as well as taking specimens. Wet suits were worn not only for warmth, but as protection from snakebite. With one exception, the snakes attacked the divers only as they were in the process of catching them with snake sticks or by hand. The exception came when MacLeish approached a pair of snakes who may have been mating. One of them, angered at the intrusion, headed directly for him. The long orange-yellow snake bit him repeatedly on an arm, then snapped at a swim fin and one of his legs before swimming off into deeper water. Had MacLeish not been wearing a wet suit, he probably would have been killed by the bites.

Most species of sea snakes live in shallow waters off islands of the

South Pacific, Australia, and southeastern Asia. The yellow-bellied sea snake, however, is also distributed throughout the Indian Ocean, and is found on the west coasts of South and Central America, as well as Mexico. As yet, there are no sea snakes in the Atlantic Ocean, but biologists fear the proposed sea-level canal across Central America, if built, would introduce them.

Sea snakes, like the shark and grizzly bear, belong to that small and elite fraternity of creatures who have almost no natural enemies. Large fish such as red snapper, grouper, and sharks living in the habitat of the sea snakes—the Pacific and Indian Oceans—shun them as food. Yet in a fascinating research experiment, it was found that Atlantic Ocean fish, who are unfamiliar with sea snakes, will eat them with gusto, at least until the odds catch up with them and they are bitten and die.

Only the venom, not the flesh, of the sea snake is poisonous. Consequently, the people of Southeast Asia prize them as food, especially when smoked. Probably the greatest number of sea-snake bite fatalities are suffered by fishermen when disengaging them from their nets or otherwise handling the lethal delicacies. The sea snake's only other enemy is the sea eagle, which snatches them up with its talons when they surface to breathe, flaps to the nearest shore and then drops them to their death upon rocks.

In their adaptation from land reptiles to creatures of the water, sea snakes have evolved some interesting characteristics. Their tails are usually flattened and rudderlike to give them more power and maneuverability in swimming. The sea snake's single lung runs all the way to the end of its tail, enabling some species to dive for up to two hours without surfacing. Like other terrestrial reptiles which have returned to the ocean, such as the marine iguana and sea turtle, the sea snake has developed a salt gland which removes salinity from the water they ingest. Sea snakes are occasionally seen floating upon the surface of the ocean with little more animation than sections of slender driftwood. Where two currents of water converge, floating objects, both inanimate and animate, are sometimes drawn together at the seam. In his book, *The Trail That Is Always New,* W. P. Lowe recollected steaming through the strait of Malacca when:

> I saw a long line running parallel with our course. None of us could imagine what it could be. It must have been four or five miles off. We smoked and chatted, had a siesta, and went down to tea. On re-

turning to the deck we still saw the curious line along which we had been steaming for four hours, but now it lay across our course, and we were still very curious as to what it was. As we drew nearer we were amazed to find that it was composed of a solid mass of sea-snakes, twisted thickly together. They were orange-red and black, a very poisonous and rare variety known as *Astrotia stokesii*. Some were paler in colour and as thick as one's wrist, but the most conspicuous were as thick as a man's leg above the knee. Along this line there must have been millions; when I say millions I consider it no exaggeration, for the line was quite ten feet wide and we followed its course for some sixty miles. I can only presume it was either a migration or the breeding season. I have on various occasions looked in vain in these same waters, and also enquired from officers of ships navigating this region, but have failed to hear of a similar occurrence. Many people have seen snakes of this description but never in such massed formation. It certainly was a wonderful sight. As the ship cut the line in two, we still watched the extending file of foam and snakes until it was eventually lost to sight.

Snakes, always a wonder and rather mysterious, lost none of their charisma when they returned to the sea.

Throughout history the majority of people have feared snakes in varying degrees. Since fright is a desired reaction to the hoary practice of practical jokes, snakes have often been the principal, or only, prop. The prankster places the reptile in someone's house, bed, tent, sleeping bag, boot or shoe and then lingers to watch the ensuing consternation. Such jokes have badly backfired on occasion when the "dead" animal has turned out to be very much alive. There have been cases where the practical joker, in the interests of verisimilitude, has sewn shut the mouth of a poisonous snake. A Texas cowhand, finding such a rattlesnake in his boot, became so enraged that he killed the companion who had placed it there.

At times, the "joke" slides into more sinister implications. Some civil rights workers who came to Mississippi during the summers of 1964 and 1965 came upon live cottonmouth moccasins that had been dropped into their cars. At the entrance to one voter registration office, a dead cottonmouth was placed upon an oil drum as a warning to blacks. Ancient Hindu and Mohammedan law took a dim view of similar antics. The *Code of Gentoo Laws* states that: "If a man, by violence, throws into another's house a snake or any other animal of that kind, whose bite or sting is mortal, this is Shahesh, i.e., Violence. The magistrate shall fine him five hundred puns of cowries, and make him throw away the snake with his own hand."

The warriors of at least two cultures apparently used snake venom in battle. Hill tribes of India are said to have dipped their arrows and spears in cobra venom, while the Tartars probably used viper venom for the same purpose.

In the third century B.C., a Roman expeditionary force was turned back by Carthaginians who catapulted earthen pots filled with snakes into their boats. As the pots shattered, the snakes slithered in all directions. Most of the Roman seamen dropped their oars, stumbling about in panic, and their officers soon surrendered. Although this seems to be the only battle in which snakes played a decisive part, during the Middle Ages small casks of snakes and spiders were occasionally lofted over the walls of a besieged city or fort to terrorize the occupants.

The sporadic use of snakes in warfare seems to have fizzled out for good with the invention of gunpowder. Yet from earliest recorded times to the present, they have dramatically, if sparingly, been assigned the roles of executioner, besides being used as instruments of suicide and murder.

During the heyday of the Roman Empire, it was believed that infant vipers, as a matter of course, would kill their mothers shortly after birth. The Roman punishment for a child convicted of matricide was that he be put into a sack with vipers, and then both child and snakes would be drowned together.

In 1615 England sent an ambassador to Jahangir, ruler of the Mogul Empire, which at that time sprawled across most of what is now India. The ambassador's chaplain, Edward Terry, later described an execution by snakebite he had witnessed, adding that:

> There was another condemned to die by the Mogul himself . . . for killing his own mother, and at this the king was much troubled to think of a death suitable for so horrid a crime; but upon a little pause, he adjudged him to be stung to death by snakes, which was accordingly done. . . . There are some mountebanks there which kept great snakes to show tricks with them; one of those fellows was presently called for to bring his snakes to do that execution, who came to the place where the wretched creature was appointed to die, and found him there all naked (except a little covering before) and trembling. Then suddenly, the mountebank (having first angered

and provoked the venomous creatures) put one of them to his thigh, which presently twined itself about that part, till it came near to his groin, and there bit him till the blood flowed; the other was fastened to the outside of his other thigh, twining about it (for those snakes thus kept are long and slender) and there bit him likewise. Notwithstanding, the wretch kept upon his feet near a quarter of an hour, before which time the snakes were taken from him; but he complained exceedingly of a fire that with much torment had possessed all his limbs, and his whole body began to swell exceedingly. . . . About half an hour after they were taken from him, the soul of the unnatural monster left his growing carcass, and so went to its place.

Death from the bite of a venomous snake can be prolonged and excruciatingly painful. In consequence, it has never been a popular form of suicide. Nevertheless, from time to time people have made the Grand Gesture with the assistance of a poisonous snake, the most famous, of course, being Cleopatra. The ambitious queen, while successful in retaining her power by seducing Julius Caesar and Mark Antony, failed to impress Octavian amorously after he conquered Egypt. Rather than absorbing the humiliation of being carted off to Rome as a captive, tradition has it that she connived to have an asp brought to her concealed in a basket of figs. She placed the asp upon her arm, it bit her, and she died. Herpetologists have since speculated that the asp was probably a horned viper or cobra, a nuance which in any event would have been of little concern to the unfortunate queen.

Suicides in recent times have included a Florida collector who deliberately nettled one of his cobras into striking him, as well as a southern California man who jumped into a snake pit and provoked the occupants, hoping they would bite him. The snakes obliged by striking him eighty-five times. As the facility was closed, there was no one to stop the mayhem. Somehow the man managed to stagger home to die. A bacteriology professor used a more direct method of suicide, injecting himself with venom.

People who fantasize the perfect crime have long pondered the possibilities of venomous snakes. The victim, say an elderly but durable miser who lives in the country, plops onto her porch swing one morning. She has barely tasted her lemonade before the rattlesnake she has almost sat upon buzzes a warning and then strikes her repeatedly. Her only son, a reckless and unlucky gambler when not attending to her needs, assists her to the car, which simply will not start. He weeps convincingly at the funeral and mutters that he warned her not to move to Arizona.

In real life, snakes are less than the ideal weapon for homicide. There are cases where the would-be murderer has been bitten himself. Snakes are by nature shy. Nevertheless, in areas where a sizeable number of people do die of snakebite, magistrates have voiced opinions that numerous supposed victims of snakebite were actually homicides that could never be legally proven. Killers have been known to plant mambas on the paths leading to Africans' huts. Indian cobras have been deliberately released in homes of intended victims.

A Los Angeles man once attempted to murder his wife with a rattlesnake. Although the snake bit the woman, she did not die and the husband completed the grisly business by drowning her.

In 1978 a young attorney named Paul Morantz won a $300,000 damage suit for a client who claimed the Synanon Foundation, a drug rehabilitation organization, had abducted and brainwashed her. After his courtroom victory, Morantz feared Synanon members might seek vengeance, and requested police protection. Three weeks later the lawyer reached into his mailbox and felt a swift jab of pain. The fangs of a 4½-foot diamondback rattler were buried in his hand. He was rushed to a Santa Monica hospital where eight vials of anti-snakebite serum were administered. Although Morantz's arm was swollen to three times its normal size, he recovered.

"It was a granddaddy of a rattler," one of his doctors commented. "If he hadn't received treatment so quickly, it could have killed him."

Neighbors had noted two men shoving something into Morantz's mailbox, remembered the car, and the license was traced to a Synanon commune 275 miles north of Los Angeles. Two men were arrested on charges of assault with a deadly weapon. One of them was Lance Kenton, son of the bandleader. As a youth, he had collected rattlesnakes.

The Devil in Miss Jones, one of the few truly erotic films ever made, features a sensuous scene between the languid, unclothed heroine and what appears to be an attentive snake. Although much of the film is graphically sexual, the scene in which Miss Jones fondles the serpent and it slithers across her stomach en route from breasts to thighs is merely suggestive, mysterious.

The notion of women and snakes having intimate contacts that men can never properly understand is an ancient one. Plutarch tells us that Olympias, the mother of Alexander the Great, was discovered by her husband, Philip of Macedon, to be sharing her bed with a serpent. From that time on he slept in a separate chamber, fearing to interrupt his wife's consort with what might well have been a god.

E. Topsell wrote:

We read in Plutarch of certain serpents, lovers of young virgins, who after they were taken and ensnared, showed all manner of lustful, vicious, and amorous gestures of uncleanness and carnality. This accusation is illustrated by a tale about a virgin called Aetolia, who had a serpent lover. He visited her every night, "sliding gently over her body and never hurting her." This charming idyll was cut short when the girl's guardians saw what was going on. They promptly removed her to another town. The grief-stricken serpent sought his inamorata high and low and eventually discovered her quite by chance. Presumably feeling slighted, he "saluted her not as normal with fawning and gentle sliding but fierce assaulted her with grim and austere countenance, flying to her hands and, binding them with the spires of his body fast to her sides, did softly with his tail beat her backer parts."

The Warrau and Akawai tribes of the Pomeroon River Basin in Guyana have a legend that Alligator once promised to give the Sun his daughter as a bride. Alligator was a notorious wheeler and dealer and, in fact, had no daughter. The Sun, he reasoned, had a distant vision of the world and could be easily fooled. He carved a lovely woman from the wood of a wild plum tree. In his haste to complete the project, he neglected only one detail, the woman's corner of creativity. The Sun angrily rejected his incomplete bride-to-be. In exchange for being fed grain from her hand, a woodpecker created the maiden's missing anatomical detail. To demonstrate that she was now ready for reproduction, Alligator gently pulled a snake from her newly created organ. The Sun was pleased, took her as a bride, and has had close ties with mankind ever since.

In ancient Greece, Dionysus was the divine patron of crops and vineyards. Women who worshiped at his shrines sometimes wove serpents into their hair and held them ecstatically next to their bodies. To be initiated into the Dionysian mysteries, a woman guided a snake's head down between her breasts and retrieved it after it had slid between her thighs, symbolizing sexual and mystic union with the god.

For more than a century and a half after the first African slaves were landed in Haiti, snakes were worshiped as personifications of a powerful god. At some nocturnal ceremonies, communicants were encouraged to ask the temple snake for advice and favors. A priestess then withdrew with the snake. After real or simulated intercourse with the serpent, she would speak to the congregation from a trance. Her oracular messages were thought to be the words of the god himself. The snake was then placed upon an altar and a sacrifice, usually a goat or a fowl, would be made.

Mederic Saint-Mery described the conclusion of such a ceremony in the latter part of the eighteenth century:

> Some are subject to fainting fits, others to a sort of fury; but with all there is a nervous trembling which apparently cannot be controlled. They turn round and round. And while there are some who tear their clothes in this bacchanal and even bite their own flesh, others merely lose consciousness and falling down are carried into a neighbouring room where in the darkness a disgusting form of prostitution holds hideous sway.

Saint-Mery's rather lurid account of a voodoo ceremony has provided the basis for many a cinema shocker. Interludes of uninhibited sex within a religious framework have cropped up in many societies, including our own, as with the Roman revels in celebration of Bacchus and the practices of several American splinter sects. Much of the sinister glamour of the early Haitian voodoo rituals had to do with the fact that they were outlawed by authorities, carried out in secrecy, and featured the age-old notion that communication with a deity could be achieved by the sexual union of a woman and a serpent. In modern voodoo the snake is but one of many spiritual powers that are addressed, and ceremonies are a good deal more restrained.

In our own legends, the snake is both life-giver and usher of death. At the Biblical Garden of Eden, of course, it was the wily serpent who soft-talked Eve into eating of the forbidden Tree of Knowledge, which prompted God to expel both her and Adam into the harsh realities of the world outside, where they would be deprived of eternal life. Hermes, the Greek messenger of the gods, was originally a snake spirit of fertility, then evolved into a complex deity who could not only guide the dead to Hades, but bring Persephone back from the underworld. Athena, envious of Medusa's beauty, transformed her into a fanged creature whose hair became a writhing mass of snakes. After Perseus decapitated her, venomous snakes arose, as if in birth, from the blood which dripped from her neck. The blood from the right side of Medusa's body could heal and even resurrect the dead, while that of the left side was fatal poison.

Traditionally, the Australian aboriginals believe that creation took place in the stomach of a giant snake, where there were rivers, rainbows, and lightning.

Throughout the long span of mankind, the snake has been seen as a deadly threat or powerful protector, a demon or a god, the personification of life and death, rather than merely a reptile, sometimes large, sometimes venomous, always beautiful, concerned chiefly with the business of survival, just like the rest of us.

8
The Belled Vipers

When Europeans first came to the Americas they soon became aware of a snake that some Indian tribes held in reverence and often feared. Pedro de Cieca de Leon described it in *La Chronica del Peru,* published in 1554: "There are other snakes . . . which make a noise when they walk like the sound of bells. If these snakes bite a man they kill him." Since the time of this matter-of-fact statement, the rattlesnake has been subject of as many legends, folk beliefs, and myths as any creature on earth.

The rattlesnake has been regarded as an exceptional beast long before the Spaniards arrived at the shores of the New World. The Tewa Indians of what is now southwestern United States regarded it as a benign yet powerful entity, calling it "Grandfather." The Mayas, on the other hand, referred to rattlers as "little sharks of the woods." They believed that a man who dreamed of snakes would have a quarrel with his wife, and that if he dreamed of a naked woman he would encounter a rattlesnake on the following day.

Bernal Diaz del Castillo, in his description of Cortez's conquest of Mexico, remarked upon the zoo of Aztec emperor Montezuma: "In this accursed place were many vipers, and poisonous serpents which have at their tails somewhat [*sic*] that sounds like castanets; these were the most dangerous of all, and were kept in vessels filled with feathers, where they reared their young, and were fed the flesh of human beings and dogs."

The maximum size of rattlers has long been a matter of lively conjecture. A snake with a head as big as a water bucket and rattles the size of coffee cups was reported in Arkansas, while a rancher's wife in Baja California claimed to have seen a rattlesnake between twenty-five and thirty feet long which "hissed with such force it sounded like a bull." In actuality, specimens of the eastern and western diamondbacks, largest members of the family, are rarely over six feet long, although the measurement of a rattler slightly over eight feet long has been accepted by herpetologists.

For some time, it was believed that the snake's unique appendage —horny, segmented rattles—could be counted to determine age, a segment for each year of its life. Not so: rattles have different rates of growth and often break off. It has, from time to time, been thought that the distinctive buzzing of rattles was used to attract prey as well as potential mates, but is now accepted that rattling has but one purpose, which is best summed up in the motto: "Don't Tread On Me."

Rattlesnake venom, which is stored in glands on either side of the rattlesnake's head, can be remarkably potent—as much as forty times as toxic as sodium cyanide and seven times as toxic as the amanita mushroom. Injected into prey, the venom attacks both the neurological and the circulatory systems. After an initial strike, say upon a mouse, the snake waits for a time before cautiously approaching the victim. In the meanwhile, complex enzymes are acting, in effect, as a meat tenderizer. The venom is delivered through hollow fangs which fold up against the roof of the snake's mouth when it is not striking. The fangs are quite brittle and frequently break off. This poses little problem for the snake since there are rows of fangs forming behind the set currently in use. The fangs may be replaced every two or three weeks in some species. These curved, hollow needles are essential to the rattlesnake's predation, as the venom must be injected to be effective. A person without cuts in the mouth or ulcers can hook down a jigger of rattlesnake venom with as little effect as if it were egg white. Researchers who have done so report the venom has a slightly sweet taste and may faintly tingle upon the lips.

The eastern and western diamondbacks, because of their size and the quality of their venom, are considered the most dangerous of the rattlesnakes in the United States. Western diamondbacks frequently hang around farm buildings where there is good rodent hunting. It puts them in the vicinity of people and defensive strikes often result. People bitten by rattlesnakes suffer hemorrhaging, swelling, and allergic shock. The effects are intensified by quickened circulation: the worst thing the victim of a rattlesnake bite can do is to panic and run. Since the venom destroys tissue around the area of the bite, gangrene may be a nasty side effect.

In some regions the tropical rattlesnake of Latin America is greatly feared—it is said to be able to break a man's neck with a single bite to any part of the body. The venom contains crotamine, a neurotoxin which causes a man's neck muscles to completely relax and the head to loll uncontrollably.

Rattlesnake venom is not to be trifled with. There is a cherished, erroneous belief that a snakebit mother's milk will be poisonous to her baby. Some folks hold that rattlesnakes can inject venom into a spring, and that animals or people who drink from it will topple over in a stupor, thus providing easy prey. It is said that Ethan Allen was once struck several times by a rattler when on a memorable bender. The snake's eyes crossed. It became very drunk. When he sobered up, Allen thought he had been bitten by mosquitoes.

Early on, American settlers began to describe various substances that would protect one from rattlesnake venom or provide cures for it. The Reverend Francis Higgeson of New England wrote in 1630 that: "Yea, there are some serpents called Rattle Snakes that have Rattles in their Tayles, that will not flye from a man as others will, but will flye upon him and sting him so mortally that hee will dye within a quarter of an houre, except the partie stinged have about him some of the root of an Herbe called Snakeweed to bite on, and then he shall receive no harme."

In addition to a wide variety of plants, snakebite remedies used over the years have included opium, kerosene, garlic, eggs, toad urine, mud, gunpowder, tobacco, salt, iodine, enemas, and prayer. In some parts of the country, even today, the splitting open of a chicken and pressing it against the puncture wounds of a bite is deemed a highly effective treatment, as it is thought the venom will thus be drawn out. Deer liver is thought to act in the same way. Madstones—which may be semiprecious stones, bits of calcinated deer horn, or bezoars, concretions which build up in the stomachs of deer, cattle and goats—have been considered to have miraculous curative effects, not only for rattlesnake wounds, but for the bites of rabid dogs and scorpion stings.

One of the classic yarns of the West concerns a frontiersman who, bitten upon a finger and far from help, saved himself by lopping off the stricken appendage with a bowie knife or blasting it away with a six-gun. Although this may have actually been the case upon rare occasions, the medical profession has never expressed enthusiasm for the treatment.

Whiskey, usually in liberal doses, has been far and away the most popular folk cure for rattlesnake bite. Laurence M. Klauber, whose *Rattlesnakes, Their Habits, Life Histories, and Influence on Mankind* is the definitive study of the reptile, commented that: "The rattler, more than any other cause, made the High Plains country a hard-liquor area. . . . One who had applied the precepts of safety first by imbibing freely was immune to rattlesnake bite until the effects had worn off. So the cure was taken as a safety measure against a possible encounter with the affliction."

It has been estimated that prior to the turn of the century some ten percent of the deaths attributed to snakebite were actually due to alcohol poisoning.

There had always been some American doctors who prescribed booze as the best antidote for snakebite, but between 1830 and 1870 the treatment gained its greatest popularity. It was held that a man thus treated could not become intoxicated until the venom had been neutralized. When a man failed to show signs of recovery after the prescribed amount of alcohol had been taken, additional dosage was then usually advised. Recommended dosages included two quarts of corn whiskey in twelve hours as well as 104 ounces of applejack in four hours. One doctor gave a victim a quart of brandy and a gallon and a half of whiskey over a 36-hour period. He later wryly commented in a medical journal that his patient not only completely recovered but was then seen searching for another rattlesnake to bite him.

By the 1880s the medical profession had begun to take a dim view of alcohol as an antidote, finally realizing that its effect on the circulatory system only compounded the victim's woes. About this time the use of potassium permanganate came into vogue. Once it was demonstrated that the compound would destroy snake venom in a test tube, permanganate was included in most snakebite kits. Half a century later it too was discarded as an antidote when it was discovered that permanganate had no effect whatsoever on venom once it was in the body tissues.

Why should so many apparently worthless and even destructive antidotes have been used over and over? Part of the reason, of course, is something known to field anthropologists: the mind, through absolute belief in ceremony or objects, can have a much greater role in healing than most of the medical profession in Western countries cares to admit. Then, too, the amount of venom delivered by a striking snake is a major factor. When killing prey, a rattler is sparing of its venom and only injects enough to get the job done. When something as large and potentially threatening as a man clomps close to it, the snake usually strikes in panic. A small amount of venom may be released, or a great deal. Research at the University of Southern California Medical School has indicated that in perhaps a third of all rattler strikes at man, no venom at all is injected. In such cases, a split chicken, a moonstone, or healthy slugs of John Barleycorn are all going to produce cures that are nothing short of miraculous.

Rattlesnakes, like other pit vipers, prey upon a variety of rodents and other small mammals, lizards, birds, amphibians, and even fish or other snakes on occasion. In turn, rattlesnakes provide dinner for a number of other creatures, most notably the red-tailed hawk. Pigs, both wild and domestic, enthusiastically trample rattlers to death and eat them. Their layers of fat usually protect them from the venom.

I spent part of my childhood in California's Imperial Valley, living in a wonderfully ramshackle house which had once been occupied by the stationmaster of the Butterfield Stage. One wall was partially made out of whiskey bottles to conserve cement. There was a dinosaur footprint upon a rock of the hearth. My greatest pride in the house, however, had to do with the king snake which had taken up residence underneath it. The snake, I was told and believed, was the guardian that kept rattlesnakes away. Actually the storied animosity between these two reptiles has been scientifically questioned, but if a king snake happens upon a smaller rattlesnake he will often kill and eat it.

Be that as it may, in parts of Texas people still talk about the rattlesnake who was fleeing from a king snake with such speed that the friction set the grass afire. The pursuer, hard pressed to keep up, put out the flames with its perspiration. No one knows how the chase turned out, but the route was marked by a narrow swath of charred grass. Other folks recall the time a rattler and a king snake swallowed and began to digest each other's tails. They were greedy and neither would give up. The circle formed by their bodies got smaller and smaller until there was little more than a dot and finally nothing at all.

The roadrunner of the Sonora Desert, one of the most cheeky birds anywhere, is said to occasionally encircle a dozing rattlesnake with a corral of cholla cactus stems. The snake, in trying to escape, pierces itself upon the spines and bites itself to death in frustration.

John Brickell's *The Natural History of North Carolina*, published in 1737, contains an observation that: "Tortoises are mortal enemies to the rattlesnakes, killing them whenever they meet, which they do by catching the Snake a little below the Neck, and so draw his Head into their Shell, which makes the Snake beat his Tail, and twist about with all the strength and violence imaginable to get away, but the Terebin soon dispatches him, by pressing him to Death between his Shells, and there leaves him." As no scientists since Brickell have reported witnessing a similar event, it is probably safe to consign the tale to folklore.

Rattlesnakes are generally credited with good sense. If one of them sees a herd of cattle loping its way, it will make for the nearest hole in the ground. If the aperture leads to a prairie dog den, the rattler can attain both deliverance and a good dinner. He will then doze, after the fashion of his kind, while digesting. There are certain cattlemen who maintain that other prairie dogs will avenge their devoured comrade by scratching dirt onto the entrance of the hole until it is blocked, and then sealing the rattler's grave by tamping the earth hard with their noses.

The persistence of rattlers is legendary. In 1853, a family was creaking across the Kansas grasslands in a prairie schooner when they came upon a large female rattlesnake and killed it. When they moved on, one of them tied the dead snake to the tailgate. The family made fifty miles that day with the snake's head sliding along behind the wagon. More than once, the father or the eldest son, flanking the wagon on horseback, had a notion they were being followed. Yet when they looked back, all they could see was the seemingly endless stretch of grass with the wagon tracks cutting through it. They camped. The next morning a large male rattler mortally struck a child who was sleeping in a bedroll beside the wagon. It was only then that they realized the vengeful mate of the snake they were dragging westward for luck had followed them all that distance. Or so the story goes.

In New Mexico they tell of a sodbuster who was struck so violently by a diamondback that the fangs punched right through the leather of the unfortunate man's boot. The family was poor, just getting by, and a week after the funeral the son pulled on his father's boots one morning, as his were so old and battered they were letting in daylight. He had scarcely finished the barnyard chores before he felt excruciating pain in his leg. The leg began to swell immediately; he could barely get his boot off. The lad passed away from his mysterious ailment before a doctor could be summoned.

For some time a local cattle baron had coveted the homestead, for it contained a cool, steady spring. With no menfolk left to stand up to the rancher and his wranglers, the woman moved off the land and took a job as cook at a stage stop.

As he was looking over the sodbuster's shack with an eye to using it for a line camp, the cattle baron noticed a pair of boots in tolerable condition which had been left behind. He tried them on, suddenly stiffened with shock, then keeled over dead. When his foreman pulled off the boots, it was found that there was a rattlesnake fang inside one of them, broken off and still coated with venom. The cattle baron was buried next to the spring, boots beside the headstone.

One of the more curious rattlesnake tales concerns a youth who had just become the proud owner of a Model A Ford. A professional driver challenged him to a race around California's Salton Sea, giving him a handicap head start. Close to the finish line the sleek racing car caught up to the flivver, whose pistons were all but flying out of their cylinders. Both contestants were so intent on gaining a few inches on each other that they failed to notice a patch of cholla cactus and plowed into it. All their tires, punctured by innumerable spines, deflated immediately. The local youth, spotting a nest of sidewinders, pushed directly through them. Naturally, they struck viciously at the flapping rubber. The tires swelled back to normal size. The youth leisurely chugged home to victory.

On another occasion, a big, vividly-patterned diamondback reportedly sank his fangs into a massive, overinflated rear tire of a John Deere tractor. The released air pressure blew the snake up like a balloon until its belly scales lost contact with the dirt and it drifted upward. Folks at a nearby ranch house saw it floating high overhead and thought it was some sort of Chinese kite.

Rattlesnakes try to avoid men, and are usually quite good at it. Although millions of people—hikers, hunters, surveyors, ranchers, snake catchers—amble through their domain every year, only a small percentage ever see a rattler, let alone get bitten. It is estimated that around thirty-two hundred people are bitten each year and that, on the average, perhaps only a dozen of these victims die. In recent years, prompt medical attention has held down the number of fatalities. Approximately one out of four rattlesnake bites is the result of people trying to handle rattlesnakes. A great many bites occur when someone inadvertently steps next to or upon a snake. Fear of rattlesnakes has caused people to abandon buildings, make drastic changes in their travel or camping plans, or set up time-honored defenses such as laying a loop of lariat around their bedrolls in the mythical belief that no snake will crawl over a rope. In 1952 a Mexican wetback refused to sleep with his companions in a railroad culvert near San Diego, erroneously believing it contained rattlers. He slept between the rails up above, convinced none of the dreaded snakes would cross them. He was killed by a train.

As a child, I used to spend summers on my uncle's cattle ranch in southern California. The property embraced a canyon and the surrounding sidehills. A deeply eroded ravine ran down the middle of the canyon, so narrow in places that brush met overhead, creating a tunnel of sorts. One morning, while my uncle and cousin were repairing a pipeline that ran from a spring to a watering trough, I wandered down a cowpath that bisected the ravine. In the bottom of the ravine I heard a dry buzzing. Looking into the mouth of one of the "tunnels" I could make out a large, coiled diamondback rattler a few feet away. With great excitement I charged breathlessly back up the path to tell my uncle. He was justifiably skeptical, as all summer I had been reporting "rattlers" that invariably turned out to be bull or garter snakes. Leading the way, I raced back down the sandy path and jumped down the small drop-off at the bottom of the ravine. The snake had uncoiled and was sliding its way across the path. One of my boots landed squarely upon its back. For a moment, paralyzed, I stared down at the triangular, flat head as it attempted to strike upwards at my ankle. Fortunately, my boot was so close to the head that the creature simply did not have enough swing for a strike.

With a terrified yelp, I sprang up and around and my legs were churning up the path the minute they touched it. A whirling dervish could not have put on a more impressive performance. My uncle dispatched the snake with a shotgun. I still have the rattles in my desk drawer and finger them once in a while for luck.

Although most rattlesnakes tend to be scattered about their various habitats, occasionally, for reasons not completely understood, a relatively small patch of land will be filled with them. Traditionally, such nests guard lost mines, buried Spanish gold, and Wells Fargo strongboxes. In 1954, when George and Caroline Mol bought a farm on Wabasis Lake, twenty-five miles northeast of Grand Rapids, Michigan, they had no anticipation of stumbling across lost treasure; nor did they expect to encounter many rattlesnakes. The first summer they captured a massasauga rattlesnake, the only species of poisonous reptile found in the state. They found another one that had been run over on the road. Over the next ten years, they encountered and caught a few of the small rattlesnakes each year, donating most of them to the John Ball Park Zoo in Grand Rapids.

In 1964 the Mols decided to move to a house on the shore of the lake, and started to cut and grade a road through the thick growth of poison sumac and tamarisk. They found the brushy marsh to be alive with rattlesnakes, capturing thirty the first year of roadwork and thirty-two the second. The Mols, level-headed folk, were not unduly alarmed at the quantity of their venomous neighbors, although they exercised care and warned their three children to be on the alert. Still, there was the occasional close call. Mrs. Mol was scattering grass seed on her lawn when she happened to look down and see a large, coiled rattlesnake only a step away. It had not buzzed. Her daughter, when she was six, once stepped right over a rattler before seeing it. A boy who was visiting saw what he took to be a thick strand of rope, and was preparing to kick it when it gave a warning rattle.

These incidents would seem to accent the rattlesnake's lack of aggression if left alone.

Twenty-one years after the Mols had moved to Wabasis Lake, Mrs. Mol went out to weed her yard. It was late in September and there had already been frost. She did not exercise her usual caution in looking for rattlers, by now an automatic reflex, as she felt they would all have gone into hibernation. Suddenly, her leg was struck by a thirty-inch rattlesnake. It had sounded no warning. As her husband applied a tourniquet and then drove her to a hospital, the initial stinging, numbing sensation became an almost unendurable pain. The leg began to become discolored and swelled almost immediately. Although she was able to walk to her car and into the hospital, she later remarked that she could not have walked an additional 100 yards.

She recovered, but not until after an ordeal of eleven days in the hospital and weeks of recuperation at home. The rattlesnake, which her husband promptly captured, proved to be a pregnant female, which may have accounted for its testiness.

Rattlesnakes are good swimmers. My wife and I and her brother once camped beside a mountain lake in southern Colorado. I had just started to build a campfire when I heard a shout from the brother, who was fishing at the shore. His rod was whipping and I assumed he was on the verge of landing a trophy trout. As he reeled his catch close into the pebbles on the beach, we were both astonished to see that his three-pronged lure had snagged a fair-sized timber rattle-snake at midsection. Just as he swung it over dry land, perplexed as to what to do next, it writhed off the hook and started to slither up the beach. In the backcountry, I try to avoid killing snakes of any kind. Yet this was a popular lake on a holiday weekend. Children were running about everywhere. I brained the rattler with a rock, no easy thing, as a snake is about as hard to kill as a garden hose. I skinned it, cut it up and marinated the meat overnight in red wine and cooking oil. Breakfast was a delectable omelette of rattlesnake, eggs, fresh mushrooms, and green chili.

Old Timers in the Salmon River country of Idaho remember "Hacksaw" Tom Christensen, who lived on one of the few level benches beside the River of No Return for a good many years and had an uncommon fondness for rattlers. Before coming to the Salmon River country, Hacksaw had been something of a wanderer. He acquired his nickname by sawing his way out of a Montana jail and his interest in rattlesnakes by once settling into an abandoned house in Utah that was filled with them. While most men would have promptly decamped or attempted to exterminate them, Hacksaw took it upon himself to study the creatures and learn their ways. By the time he came to live in Idaho he was so comfortable with them and they with him that he would often carry a snake or two with him when he went to the town of North Fork. More than once he was observed to pick up a snake beside a trail, calm it, and end up giving it a ride in his shirt. Hacksaw's rattlesnakes, when he would remove them from his shirt at one of North Fork's watering places, would create quite a stir. Folks would generally set him up with rounds of drinks but were understandably edgy about occupying stools next to him.

> And these signs shall follow them that believe: In my name shall they cast out devils; they shall speak with new tongues; they shall take up serpents; and if they drink any deadly thing, it shall not hurt them; they shall lay hands on the sick, and they shall recover. (Mark 16: 17–18.)

On a blazing southern summer day in 1909, a short, stocky man named George Hensley reread Mark 16 in the Bible, and for him, pieces of the eternal puzzle of life and death began to come together. It had to do with literal faith in the scripture as written. He walked from his home in Grasshopper Valley, Tennessee, up onto White Oak Mountain, and there he found and picked up a rattlesnake.

Although he would later claim to have been bitten by rattlers over four hundred times, and would finally die from the venom of the last one, Hensley picked up the White Mountain serpent as gently as if it had been a bird, and it was gentle in his hands.

A new American religion was in the making.

Not long after, Hensley brought his snake to an evangelical service at the Sale Creek Church in Grasshopper Valley. He read the text from the Book of Mark. Serpents were a manifestation of the Devil; anyone with true faith in the Lord could not be bitten. He held out the snake for members of the congregation to touch. Slowly, hesitantly, they placed their fingers upon it and then, seeing that it remained calm, some of them handled it. Hensley soon had a number of converts, mostly hardscrabble farmers whose stern religious codes prohibited drinking, dancing, smoking, movie going, or the use of cosmetics. The church was the core of their social activity. Services were intense and fervent. The faithful warmed up with revival songs like "The Devil in a Box," and "Jesus Is Getting Us Ready for the Great Day." Folks prayed and shouted praises to Jesus and the Lord. Some would speak in tongues. The climax of the meetings would come as rattlesnakes and copperheads were withdrawn from a wooden box and the worshipers would mill about while holding them.

The fangs of the snakes, according to people who examined them, were not tampered with; nor was the venom milked. Rather incredibly, the Grasshopper Valley snake services had been going on for almost ten years before one Garland Defriese was struck by a rattler.

He fell to the ground, but recovered after a few weeks. While some of the congregation took this as a sign that snake handling had lost favor in the eyes of the Lord, others felt it merely meant Defriese had been backsliding.

Because of isolation rather than deliberate secrecy, the Grasshopper Valley meetings had gone virtually unnoticed by the outside world. The use of rattlesnakes in worship spread into the Kentucky hill country in the 1930s. A farmer in Harlan County who had little use for poisonous snakes in any setting, expressed his irritation at his wife's participation in the ritual by suing three church members for breach of peace. The charge was dismissed, but an Associated Press release on the trial was noticed by an editor of the *St. Louis Post-Dispatch*. A reporter and a photographer were sent to cover a meeting at the Pine Mountain church in Harlan County.

In his book, *They Shall Take Up Serpents,* Weston La Barre wrote an account of the meeting based on the story filed by the *Post-Dispatch* reporter.

> Cymbals, tambourines, foot-stamping, and hand-clapping provided the rhythm for the worshipers who, men and women both, passed serpents from hand to hand while jerking violently all over their bodies. One man thrust a snake before a seated woman holding a baby; the woman smiled, and the baby gravely reached forward and touched the snake. A dark-haired timberman opened the mouth of one rattler to show its intact fangs to the visitors; another man showed the scars of at least three bites on his hand and arm. . . .

> The snake-handling lasted about half an hour, but the service went on for an hour more. To the singing of such songs as "Jesus Is Getting Us Ready for the Great Day," several female communicants, eyes shut, hands waving . . . moved their feet in a rhythmic step and wheeled slowly in backward circles. Frequently their bodies would jerk as if the spine were being snapped like a whip. Some of the men also performed this jerk. Firehandling by male saints was also performed: their hands, held in the flames of a kerosene torch and a miner's acetylene lamp, were blackened by smoke but otherwise appeared unhurt. (From Weston La Barre, *They Shall Take Up Serpents* [Minneapolis: University of Minnesota Press, 1962].)

Many members of the snake-handling churches have professed to be terrified of snakes unless "filled with the power" that comes to them at their services. Some churches employ only nonbelievers, or "sinner men," to provide snakes for them. Snakes are delicate creatures in certain ways; their health seems to suffer from repeated handlings, and usually they are released after a few weeks and new snakes are obtained. Having triumphed over snakes, some congregations tested the spirit of the Lord to protect them in other ways. During a service of the Dolley Pond Church of God With Signs Following, a visiting Baptist minister shoved an ignited blow torch into the hands of a believer. "Try this," he said, much to the amusement of the other nonbelievers. As expected, the snake cultist merely stared at the roaring torch which had been pressed into his hands. Then a grandmotherly type in a sunbonnet stepped forward, fixed the Baptist minister with her eyes, and thrust a hand into the tongue of the flame. She removed it unharmed. As every carnival fire-eater knows, there are relatively cool pockets within the flame jetted from a blow torch. Yet there is no doubt that this woman was acting purely upon blind faith rather than any sort of knowledge of this phenomenon. From time to time blow torches have been used in meetings ever since.

. . . *and if they drink any deadly thing, it shall not hurt them.*

At the Dolley Pond Church, as with other snake-handling churches, a glass of liquid laced with strychnine was kept on hand in case a member felt a particularly powerful surge of faith and wished to test it. Few snake handlers, even in their most ecstatic moments, have felt up to this test, although members of the Dolley Pond Church asserted that on rare occasions worshipers had tossed down, without ill effect, a strychnine solution which was "strong enough that one drop on a grain of corn will kill a chicken." This has not been reliably verified. At a meeting held at Summerville, Georgia, in 1947, a farmer named Ernest Davis swallowed the better part of a "salvation cocktail" that contained strychnine. He was buried five days later. At the funeral his wife remarked that "Ernest just had too much faith."

In 1945, Lewis Ford, a sturdy man in his midthirties, was fatally bitten by a rattlesnake at the Dolley Pond Church. The snake that had struck Ford was handled by grieving members of the church at his funeral.

The circumstances around Ford's death were picked up by newspapers around the country. Tom Harden, pastor of the Dolley Pond Church, was an intense young man of unshakable faith. He had once been struck by a rattlesnake during a service and was close to death for four hours. The prayers of his followers were credited with his recovery. Now that his church was in the public eye, he saw an opportunity for gaining converts within the city limits of Chattanooga, which to the pious hill people was a fortress filled with all kinds of wickedness. Harden, accompanied by cult founder Hensley, set up in a tent with an oil drum altar. Word got around. A curious crowd gathered and traffic was blocked. Harden and Hensley, to their delight, were taken to the city lockup. They likened their persecution to that suffered by the Biblical prophets. While church members gathered outside of the jail to pray for the policemen who had been unwitting tools of the Devil by making the arrest, the two incarcerated leaders sang resonantly until well into the night. They refused to pay a fine for disorderly conduct on principle, served several days on a road gang, and were released.

While snake cultists regarded the release as Divine Intervention, the powers that be were beginning to feel things were getting out of hand. The Tennessee legislature unanimously approved a bill prohibiting the handling of venomous snakes. Other states would follow suit. Activities of the Dolley Pond Church and similar congregations continued, but more surreptitiously.

Hamilton County sheriff Grady Head raided the Dolley Pond Church in midsummer of 1947, with newsmen from Chattanooga trailing in his wake. The sheriff, hat clapped firmly atop his head and cigar in mouth, strode into the tamped-earth floor of the frame building. The confrontation was pure theater.

SHERIFF (*blustering*): You's in charge?

HARDEN (*very much at ease*): Well, now, I guess I am.

SHERIFF: Where's your snakes?

HARDEN: We ain't got none here. As a matter of fact, I didn't know there was to be any services tonight. I just came down to see what the trouble was.

REPORTER (*interrupting*): You might as well go ahead and get your snakes and handle them tonight. You are going to be arrested sooner or later, and you might as well get it over with. [Pause] Look, there are a lot of us reporters here and we're all set for a big show. Get out the snakes and let's get it over with.

HARDEN (*drawls*): Well, now, I reckon I sure do appreciate all that, mister, but before I handle those snakes I believe I'll still wait on the Lord. (Sheriff's party searches building. They find no snakes and begin to leave.)

MEMBER OF CONGREGATION (*mounts rough wooden pulpit*): You folks be back Sunday. We'll have some serpents if it's God's will.

Sheriff Head did return to Dolley Pond Church on the following Sunday to find a lively service in progress. But no snakes. The will of the Lord was, apparently, that they be handled the night before. The sheriff, whose frustrations were occasioning a certain amount of levity around the county, finally arrested the snake handlers with the assistance of plainclothesmen. The irrepressible congregation, still singing, was escorted to jail. Several snakes were confiscated. They were killed with a piece of sheet iron, as it was feared the sound of gunshots might incite the prisoners to God-knows-what manner of religious enthusiasm.

The good sheriff of Hamilton County was not the only lawman to experience difficulty in closing down a snake service with any degree of dignity. At a well-publicized "Interstate Convention" held in Durham, North Carolina, during the autumn of 1948, a squad of policemen entered the Zion tabernacle armed with long-handled forceps. One of the pastors greeted them with two copperheads and a rattlesnake in one hand and a Bible in the other. The accordion player also possessed a copperhead, as did a young girl. Even with the forceps, the officers had a hard time rounding up the snakes. Reverend Colonel Hartman Bunn, a balding man in a conservative suit, solicitously asked one of the harried officers if he might help. A woman screamed, "Leave us alone! You are stopping the work of God!" Bunn, all smiles and good will, touched the policeman's shoulders fraternally, saying, "I love all the police, I feel so good I could kiss them all!" The officers managed to withdraw with the captured snakes in a hinged box before this gesture of friendship could be consummated.

The snakes' passivity during service has been astonishing. Prior to actual handling, the box containing the snakes may be kicked repeatedly by cavorting zealots to "stir up the Devil." Snakes are held by the devout in various ways, most of which afford them ample opportunity to strike the holder. In considering this, La Barre described a meeting at the Dolley Pond Church:

There may be some jostling to get snakes, but good manners of a sort are usually preserved even in this. However, shaking violently from head to foot, a believer with the spirit in him may grab a snake from a quieter or less aggressive member or from one whose interest in the snake is visibly flagging. The snake may be held in various ways. Sister Harden, the preacher's sister, was observed to hold a large snake before her in both hands at about waist level, eyes closed, body bent tensely forward in an arc, lips stretched into a tight oval open-jawed scream, while two other sisters stood behind her, one clapping, the other with the left hand clasped over the right fist, and both of them shouting also. Sister Minnie Parker, a buxom elderly gap-toothed woman—who walked barefoot among seventeen buzzing rattlesnakes in a homecoming service in the summer of 1946—held a beautiful large timber rattler around her neck like a necklace . . . while cooing with closed eyes and a delighted expression on her face. A young woman in a store-bought dress held the thick middle of a very large rattler across her forehead with both hands like a coronet, the head of the snake over her right shoulder and behind her back, with the rattle reposing between her breasts. . . .

Preacher George Hensley allowed Brother Lewis Ford (who, it is to be recalled, later died of a bite) and another man to drape a crown of snakes on the top of his head; but such decorations do not stay long in position and the snakes may drop heavily to the floor. . . .

A particularly admired gambit is to grasp the snake about midbody and then raise it slowly until the flickering tongue touches the nose of the worshiper, who meanwhile stares intently into the snake's eyes. This is to taunt and to overpower evil with the "spirit" in the worshiper.

The snakes are not doctored, nor are they trained. Bites are rarely suffered by the worshipers and most of these are not fatal. Pastor Tom Harden of Dolley Pond Church almost died from his first bite, yet scarcely noticed three subsequent later strikes. He described one of them as feeling "like I'd hit the crazy bone in my elbow." A number of snake handlers claim to have been bitten over thirty times without serious consequence. Professional herpetologists, of course, handle innumerable venomous snakes during their careers and rarely have trouble with them, although a few have been fatally bitten. Herpetologists, however, whether in the field, zoo, or laboratory, customarily do not drape specimens around themselves while convulsively moving with religious ecstasy, nor casually pass them to other scientists. Cult members who are struck almost always refuse any treatment except prayer, feeling that other remedies would thwart God's will.

Still, with rural snake-handling congregations scattered throughout the southern Appalachians, there were fatalities. Middle-aged Ruth Craig held a small service at her farm near New Hope, Alabama, in 1951. She displayed a rattler contained in a glass jar and told her fellow worshipers that "I'm going to handle the snake and anyone who doesn't believe had better leave." The snake refused to emerge from the jar when opened. Mrs. Craig broke it. The rattler headed for the door and when Mrs. Craig attempted to grab it, the snake bit her four times in rapid succession on the arms and shoulder. She soon collapsed into a coma from which she did not emerge.

Three years later, an elderly snake cultist of twenty years, Reece Ramsey, attended an open-air service near Rising Fawn, Georgia. He was struck on the side of the head by a "satinback" rattlesnake. Refusing offers to take him to a doctor, he requested that the preacher's daughter sing, "Only a Rose Will Do." Ramsey seemed pleased, walked toward the preacher, staggered, and then collapsed, writhing. The minister lifted his head off the ground, resting it in the crook of his arm. While the congregation sang, "I'm Getting Ready To Leave This World," Ramsey died.

Forty-six years after he had pondered scripture and picked up a rattlesnake on White Oak Mountain in Tennessee, George Hensley attended a service at Lester's Shed near Altha, Florida. By his own reckoning, the seventy-year-old founder and prophet of the snake-handling cults had been bitten over four hundred times until he was, in his own words, "speckled all over like a guinea hen." As he had so many times in his life, Hensley serenely handled a diamondback rattlesnake. The dry, smooth scales in his hands, the snake's steady lidless stare, and the feel of it sliding across the back of his neck, were the old familiar touchstones by which he transcended the trials and uncertainties of daily life, by which he affirmed, by the power of his faith, his right to go to a new life.

After fifteen minutes, he started to put the snake back into the box. The diamondback struck him upon the wrist. His arm soon became swollen, purpled. He died the following morning.

By 1961, the beginning of what was in many ways to be one of

America's most violent eras, when liquor stores in Watts were torched from simple flames and Vietnamese civilians burned after being splattered with the more complicated napalm, nineteen followers of George Hensley had succumbed to the bites of serpents that had been placed upon the earth to test their faith. Only nineteen. Remarkable. But it was more than enough for authorities in several states to lean heavily upon the cultists. They went underground. Then, as now, meetings were conducted in the open, in farmhouses, and in seedy rented halls close to the railroad tracks of mill towns. In the fall of 1961 a young woman was fatally bitten while handling a snake at a meeting in a coal-mining region of West Virginia. After the funeral, her mother heard that the tragedy had prompted members of the state legislature to come out for a bill prohibiting snake handling.

"I'm letting God fight my battle," she said. "You think I'm going to let some of these little judges and lawyers make me back up on my salvation? No!"

The curious cult which started on a summer's day in Grasshopper Valley has raised some interesting questions about the relation of man to animals, and man to himself.

The principal villages of the Hopi Indians cluster on top of three slab-sided mesas in north-central Arizona. This is dry, beautiful country, where arroyos cut their way down through wildly eroded layers of sandstone, and there is a sense of immensity to the sky and land as well as an almost infinite variety of detail—plant and rock form. As they have for centuries, the Hopi grow corn and other crops on plots below the mesas. The Hopi culture is subtle, complex, and draws strength from a rich spiritual tradition. Like most of their religious rites, the biennial snake dance of late summer is an ancient ceremony. The dance itself, in which participants hold live rattlers and other snakes in their mouths, is the culmination of a sixteen-day ceremony, or extended prayer, in which the gods are asked for rain. The snakes, when released, carry this message to the spirit world.

Long ago, according to legend, a restless Hopi youth, Tiyo, marveled at the great river and canyon that passed through Hopi lands. Seeking its mysterious destination, he built a crude boat and passed through what we now call the Grand Canyon. At the end of his voyage he came to the abode of Spider Woman, who gave him food and crawled behind his ear to offer advice as he ventured into the spirit world. His way was blocked in turn by a mountain lion, a bear, a wildcat, and a rattlesnake. Spider Woman placated each of them with a prayer stick.

He finally reached the kiva of the snake people and descended into it on a pole ladder. The kiva was filled with men and women. Their chief gave Tiyo a pipe, instructing him to swallow the smoke. This seemed impossible, but Spider Woman, still nestled behind his ear, drew the smoke away. The people in the kiva then clothed themselves in snakeskins and were instantly transformed into serpents.

A beautiful woman had become a rattlesnake. Spider Woman told Tiyo to catch her. She reacted with fury. Rattles buzzing, she made as if to strike, but the young Hopi spat a potion at her which Spider Woman had given him. She calmed, allowed him to touch her, and then brought him peaches, melons, and *piki,* the paper-thin traditional bread of the Hopis. After the snake people taught him their ceremonies, Tiyo returned to Hopi country with the rattlesnake woman as his bride. His people were overjoyed at his return and welcomed his wife.

Time passed. Tiyo's wife became pregnant and gave birth to snakes. This was accepted, but as the snakes matured, some of the Hopi children were bitten, and finally Tiyo and his family were driven from the village. Gradually, the rains became less frequent; young corn was choked by drifting dust, and a relentless, blazing sun sucked at the springs and waterholes until they dried to ovals of cracked mud. Horizons of grass became the scorched expanse of the Painted Desert.

In this time of desperation, the people turned to Tiyo for advice, as he had been to the spirit world and returned. Tiyo told them the gods were angry that the snake children had been sent away from the villages. They could be appeased only by a ceremony. He taught them the songs and other rituals he had learned in the snake kiva. Over a period of four days Hopi men fanned out across the rimrock and bottomlands, catching snakes. The snakes were ritually bathed, prayers given. On the last day, men danced with the snakes held gently in their mouths, and then released them out in places of rock and wind so that they might carry a message of repentance to the gods, and ask them for rain.

Today, members of both the Antelope and Snake societies participate in the ceremony. On the altar in the Antelope society kiva is a painting of snakes as lightning. Bean and melon vines dangle from it.

During the final four days before the dance, priests lead hunts for snakes. Small children often accompany them, stroking rattlesnakes with a stick to which two eagle feathers are lashed, until they uncoil and can be grabbed behind the head. Hopi children have been taught to respect snakes, but not to fear them. On the four final mornings, priests go to each of the springs in the area to sprinkle sacred corn meal upon the water. In the kiva, the snakes are ceremonially washed.

The day of the snake dance draws many outsiders—Navajo men on horseback, ranchers whose pick-ups kick out plumes of dust from the dusty roads that radiate out from the Hopi mesas, dedicated Indian watchers in cowhide boots and sunglasses. Chants and dancing. Then, a snake-priest picks up a serpent from the *kisi,* the wooden snake shrine, places it in his mouth, and begins to dance in steps which are as old and intricate as any piece of music. He is accompanied by a man with an eagle feather snake whip. Should a rattlesnake begin to coil, as if to strike, he strokes it, calms it, with strokes of the feathers. Soon the square is filled with dancers and snakes—rattlers, bullsnakes, whipsnakes. After circling the square, the dancers set their snakes down and pluck up others. Finally, sacred corn meal is scattered and snake priests gather up wriggling tangles of snakes, venomous and nonvenomous, and rush off to the four directions which are symbolized by the oriole of the north, the bluebird of the west, the magpie of the east, and the parrot of the south. The snakes are released out in the places of rock and wind.

Rain has always then come to the parched Hopi mesas within hours.

9

Wolves

While a teenager, I once camped with two companions on a remote crook of the Yukon River where a pack of wolves back up in the darkness howled with a glorious wildness. It was a wonderful sound; also rather scary. We had the better part of a quartered moose one of us had shot, stored upon a crude raft snubbed to the bank a few yards from our sleeping bags. We hastily put more wood upon the campfire. Would they come in for the moosemeat—or for us? Although we had read that wolves were not given to attacking people in North America, we also recalled stories in which Russian peasants or lonely Arctic prospectors had come to grief after being surrounded by a pack of ravenous wolves. Usually, it would seem, it was very cold with snow upon the ground, and there would be less bullets than wolves. I thought about the Ghost Pack. Earlier in the summer, a trapper had told me about a large pack of wolves that frequently gave voice outside of a village near Anchorage—yet left no footprints.

The wolf pack, belonging to a canny race that has learned to give man a wide berth, did not visit our camp. Yet our edginess echoed the ambivalence with which mankind has regarded wolves for ages. Wild West thrillers to the contrary, there have been few, if any, unprovoked fatal attacks by wolves upon humans in North America. A Canadian newspaper once offered a standing reward of $100 for evidence of such an assault. It was never collected. James Curran of Sault Sainte Marie offered a similar reward, and eventually, after receiving no takers, he declared that "Any man who says he's been et by a wolf is a liar!" For twenty-five years the U.S. Fish and Wildlife Service made an active study of all reported wolf attacks, sifting clues and interviewing witnesses. Not a single report could be substantiated. Naturalists speak warmly of wolves, praising their intelligence, family structure, and ability to communicate with each other. Numerous people who have raised wolves have described their affectionate and playful natures.

Why then, do wolves play such sinister roles in our folklore? They are the villains of nursery stories such as Little Red Riding Hood. In isolated villages of New Mexico, people recount stories of witches who change into wolves even in this day and age. There are numerous accounts of werewolves, myths lingering from distant times as well as actual case studies of men who, under the delusion they had become wolves, have attacked and killed people.

In 1892, a brigadier general of the British Indian Army wrote that wolves "are generally cowardly beasts, but they not infrequently take to killing human beings." The zoologist C. H. D. Clarke, a specialist on wolves, has written that in 1875, 161 people were killed by wolves in Russia, a figure that was deduced from available records and assumed to be typical of the era. An Associated Press dispatch of 1962 described a Turkish village that was besieged by attacking wolves.

To understand the various ways in which wolves are viewed, it is necessary to look more closely at the wolf itself. Of its domestic cousins, the wolf closely resembles the German shepherd, although it has larger feet, longer legs, and more powerful jaws. A full-grown timber wolf ranges in size from 65 pounds to 125 pounds, sizeable variations occurring more on a geographical basis rather than individuals within the same range. Professional trappers have always found wolves to be elusive, intelligent opponents. As well as thoroughly knowing the country in which they range, their ingenuity in doubling back, crossing water or bare rock, and otherwise confounding trackers is legendary. Many North American Indian tribes regarded wolves with awe and admiration; through totem and clan ceremonies they honored the wolf spirit as being one of the most powerful in the natural world. Navajo Indians identified the cunning of the wolf with sorcery. In discussing the customs of his people, Johan Turi, an elderly Lapp, described a herder who had captured a wolf:

> . . . and when he has half-killed him, then he begins to curse and swear and say, "You have eaten my draft-reindeer and my reindeer cows, now eat some more, cursed breed. . . ." But the wolf hunter who often kills wolves, he does not shout at the wolf, nor swear at it either, he knows that the wolf kills only does what it must, and that he may not kill more than he is allowed to, just as there is a limit to the waves of the sea, how high they are allowed to raise themselves! (From Johan Turi, *Turi's Book of Lappland* [London, 1931].)

Wolves usually mate for life, and the pack is primarily an extended family. A typical pack might number from eight to fourteen wolves, although smaller groups may split off from time to time and then rejoin the full pack at a later date. A pack hunts in territories which may exceed 100 square miles, although 20 to 50 miles are more usual. Perimeters are defined by urinating upon trees or other fixed objects. Wolves are affectionate with each other, communicating in a variety of ways including yelps, whimpers, barks, howls, sounds inaudible to the human ear, nose touching, and tail wagging. Food is sometimes brought to elderly or disabled wolves by other members of the pack; orphaned cubs are frequently adopted.

While wolves eat a variety of small mammals, and even a certain amount of grass and berries, various members of the deer family, including elk, reindeer, and moose, are their principal prey. The pack is ideally suited for this sort of hunt. On Isle Royale in Lake Superior, members of a wolf pack have been observed to congregate immediately before pursuing a herd of moose. They touched noses and uttered short yips, as if planning strategies of the hunt. Wolves have fine eyesight, a superb sense of smell, and can lope steadily for hours without tiring. They attempt to wear down and eventually cut out weaker members of the herd—young, old, or disabled animals. When at bay, deer and their larger cousins slash out with sharp front hooves that can eviscerate wolves and other predators. The wolves attack with patient, deliberate teamwork. If the pack succeeds in bringing down its prey, they gorge themselves upon it and do not resume hunting until they are once again hungry. This is in contrast to packs of feral and domestic dogs, which may slaughter an entire flock of sheep while feeding upon little or none of it.

Wolves once ranged from the Arctic to southern Mexico, throughout Europe and much of Asia, as well as Africa north of the Sahara. They were exterminated in Britain during the seventeenth century and during the nineteenth century in Germany. Numerous wolves once roamed throughout the United States, but today only northern Minnesota harbors any appreciable population. Far more were killed by professional hunters or trappers paid privately or by the government to lay waste to any "varmints" that posed a threat to livestock. Since 1830, when Massachusetts first set a bounty on wolves, it has been estimated that more than a hundred million dollars has been paid out for wolf scalps or other evidence of their demise. By any accounting, a great many wolves and people have lived in proximity over much of the United States. In this light, it is remarkable that we have so few accounts of wolf attack.

Several early-day travelers in America have remarked upon wolves following them out of curiosity or trailing hunters in hopes of feasting upon flesh left to rot. Whereas Indians took virtually everything but the bones of the game they killed, wolves soon learned that white hunters might kill only for the hide, or the tenderloin and other choice pieces of meat. Buffalo shooters would sometimes down an animal to obtain a single delicacy, such as the tongue. Reflecting upon his trip across the Great Plains in 1859, Horace Greeley remarked:

> It is very common for these wolves to follow at night a man travelling the road on a mule, not making any belligerent demonstrations, but waiting for whatever might turn up. . . . Of some twenty of them that I have seen within the last two days, I think not six have really run from us.

In more recent times, naturalists venturing into regions of Northern Canada or Alaska where wolves have rarely, if ever, been shot at, report encountering wolves which display more curiosity than fear. Throughout the rest of the continent, however, wolves soon learned to avoid man. No doubt it is this elusiveness which caused a number of otherwise reasonable men to refer to the wolf as "cowardly," although it seems odd to define such behavior as anything more than common sense.

Stories of wolves attacking humans in the United States have been with us since Colonial times, although in most instances the victim managed to escape unharmed. In 1761 a party led by Daniel Boone was "violently attacked by a pack of fierce wolves which they had difficulty in beating off." We read of a Dr. Thompson who, when lost in the wilds of Pennsylvania in the early nineteenth century, drove away the wolves which beset him by flailing at them with a legging soaked in ammonia—in all probability a defense unique in wild animal encounters. In other journals we learn that wolves threatening the Indian widow of trapper Pierre Dorrien retreated at the sound of her voice, of several pioneers who were treed by wolves, and how trader Joshua Gregg repulsed the attack of a wolf by waving his large black hat at the animal's "gaping jaws."

Ross Cox became separated from his fellow trappers while traveling through Oregon Territory in 1812. He was wandering about, lost and starving, when in his own words:

> About dusk an immense-sized wolf rushed out of a thick copse a short distance from the pathway, planted himself directly before me, in a threatening position, and appeared determined to dispute my passage. He was not more than twenty feet from me. My situation was desperate, and as I knew that the least symptom of fear would be the signal for attack, I presented my stick, and shouted as loud as my weak voice would permit. He appeared somewhat startled, and retreated a few steps, still keeping his piercing eyes firmly fixed on me. I advanced a little, when he commenced howling in a most appalling manner; and supposing his intention was to collect a few of his comrades to assist in making an afternoon repast on my half-famished carcass, I redoubled my cries, until I had almost lost the power of utterance, at the same time calling out various names, thinking I might make it appear I was not alone. . . . The wolf remained about fifteen minutes in the same position; but whether my wild and fearful exclamations deterred any others from joining him, I cannot say. Finding at length my determination not to flinch, and that no assistance was likely to come, he retreated into the wood, and disappeared in the surrounding gloom.

The wolf's lack of inclination to press the attack would seem to belie the bloodthirsty image which Cox's prose propounds.

John Steele, in his book, *Across the Plains in 1850,* also describes an adventure with a wolf. He was south of Fort Laramie when:

Presently a large whitish wolf made its appearance; then two more; their howls were answered by others, until the gulches echoed in one continuous roar. As the day faded they became more bold, coming nearer, until I found it would be impossible to keep them at bay during the night without a fire. It was a moonless night but the stars shone out, and turning my back on the constellation of Ursa Major, I started for camp.

I cannot say that the wolves followed me; they were on all sides . . . the infernal chorus grew awfully discordant at a near approach. I would then fire my rifle and pistols among them, reloading as I ran. At the report they would scatter, and for a while keep a greater distance; but always there was a bitter fight among them after a shot, and I believe that the wounded were at once devoured.

In the open ground it was not difficult to keep them at bay; but in the deep gullies as I looked up into their glaring eyes and saw how easily they might spring upon me, I realized that, like David, there was but a step between me and death. However, I kept in the open ground as much as possible; but at best, it was a terrible night, and O, how I longed for the morning.

Towards morning, while following a long, high ridge, most of my pursuers left me.

Considering the scarcity of reported wolf attacks and the number of people who emerged from such adventures without injury, it would appear that the American frontiersman was in considerably more danger from a number of other creatures, such as ticks bearing the often-fatal Rocky Mountain spotted fever. During the last half of the nineteenth century, periodicals and books provided innumerable vignettes of the Old West and the Far North for avid readers. Although we read little about the perils of the tick in them, we are often reminded of the menace of the wolf through illustrations which depict homesteads besieged by a howling pack, or a snarling individual wolf advancing upon a man armed with a knife or pistol.

Yet there are a handful of accounts which assert that people have been injured or even killed by wolves in North America. Peter Freuchen, the polar explorer, once met an Eskimo woman at the village of Iglulik, Greenland, whose face and a shoulder were severely scarred. She had, he was told, been walking to the home of a friend which was a little over a mile away when a wolf sprang at her, biting at her fiercely. She fainted, the account continues, which scared the wolf away. Obviously, the wolf was not driven by hunger. Irritation rather than hunger was apparently the motive for an attack which reportedly took place near a cabin on the Little Snake River of Colorado in 1881. The eighteen-year-old daughter of a trapper had set out to drive in some milk cows. When she saw a gray wolf sitting upon a knoll beside the trail, she yelled, hoping to frighten it off. It remained motionless and growled. The girl then hurled a rock at the wolf, which charged her, biting her arms and legs. She screamed, and her brother, who was nearby, shot the wolf.

In their book *The Viviparous Quadrupeds of North America*, published in 1851, John James Audubon and John Bachman relate the following incident:

Although Wolves are bold and savage, few instances occur in our temperate regions of their making an attack on man; and we have only had one such case come under our own notice. Two young Negroes who resided near the Ohio, in the lower part of the State of Kentucky, about thirty years ago, had sweethearts living on another plantation four miles distant. After the labours of the day were over, they frequently visited the fair ladies of their choice, the nearest way to whose dwelling lay directly across a large cane brake. . . . One night, they set forth over a thin crust of snow. Prudent, to a certain degree, the lovers carried their axes on their shoulders, and walked as briskly as the narrow path would allow. Some transient glimpses of light now and then met their eyes in the more open spaces between the trees, or when the heavy drifting clouds parting at times allowing a star to peep forth on the desolate scene. Fearfully, a long and frightful howl burst upon them, and they were instantly aware that it proceeded from a troop of hungry and perhaps desperate wolves. They paused for a moment and a dismal silence succeeded. All was dark save for a few feet of the snow-covered ground immediately in front of them. They resumed their pace hastily, with their axes in their hands prepared for the attack. Suddenly the foremost man was assailed by several wolves which seized on him, and inflicted terrible wounds with their fangs on his legs and arms, and as they were followed by many others as ravenous as themselves, several sprung at the breast of his companion, and dragged him to the ground. Both struggled manfully against their foes, but in a short time one of the Negroes had ceased to move; and the other, reduced in strength and perhaps despairing of aiding his unfortunate comrade or even saving his own life, threw down his axe, sprang on to the branch of a tree, and speedily gained a place of safety among the boughs. There he passed a miserable night, and the next morning the bones of his friend lay scattered around on the snow, which was stained with his blood. Three dead wolves lay near, but the rest of the pack had disappeared and Scipio, sliding to the ground, recovered the axes and returned home to relate the terrible catastrophe. (From John James Audubon and Bachman, John, *The Quadrupeds of North America* [New York: V. G. Audubon, 1851–54].)

In April of 1933 a sixty-year-old prospector and trapper named John Millovich left Fairbanks, Alaska, for a cabin he maintained on Beaver Creek, a tributary of the Yukon River. When he failed to return after a period of time, two friends packed into Beaver Creek, thinking he might be ill or have had an accident. On the trail in, they noticed a number of wolf tracks, but gave them little thought, as wolves were common in the region. Close to the cabin they found Millovich's body. Much of the flesh had been stripped away and his torn clothing was strewn over a wide area. The snow was churned with the prints of numerous wolves. The dead man's friends surmised that he had been surrounded and killed by the pack while on his way to the creek for water. Yet there were no witnesses. Millovich might have been killed by the wolves; on the other hand, he might have been stricken by a heart attack or stroke and subsequently devoured. We will never know.

It is documented that wolves will feed upon human corpses. A description of a smallpox epidemic among Indians living on Delaware Bay in 1750 notes that wolves not only fed upon bodies but attacked sick and weakened Indians in their huts. Fur trader David Thompson described a similar situation during another Indian smallpox epidemic on the Great Plains thirty-one years later.

Another attack, which occurred in the 1870s at Fort Larned, a United States Army post on the Arkansas River, should be considered. Records state that:

On the 5th of August, at 10 P.M., a rabid wolf, of the large grey species, came into the post and charged round most furiously. He entered the hospital and attacked Corporal ——, who was lying sick in bed, biting him severely in the left hand and right arm. The left little finger was nearly taken off. The wolf next dashed into a party of ladies and gentlemen sitting on Colonel ——'s porch and bit Lieut. —— severely in both legs. Leaving there he soon afterward attacked and bit Private —— in two places. This all occurred in an incredibly short space of time; and, although the above-mentioned were the only parties bitten, the animal left the marks of his presence in every quarter of the garrison. He moved with great rapidity, snapping at everything within his reach, tearing tents, window-curtains, bed-clothing, etc. in every direction. The sentinel at the guardhouse fired over the animal's back, while he ran between the man's legs. Finally he charged upon a sentinel at the haystack, and was killed by a well directed and most fortunate shot. (The corporal bitten at the hospital later died of hydrophobia, though the other two men who were bitten recovered from their wounds and never showed signs of the dread disease.) No wonder the cry of "mad wolf" has struck terror into the hearts of people throughout its range.

This, then, is by and large the summation of wolf attack in North America—escapes from wolves assumed to be intent upon mayhem, a handful of occasions where the wolf had been shot, otherwise provoked, or was rabid, a few unwitnessed events or old second-hand tales.

There is a rich body of European wolf folklore. One of the most frequently heard tales is of the Russian nobleman whose troika was pursued by a pack of ravenous wolves. To appease them and make good his escape, he first discarded fur coats, then the family retainer, and finally his wife, although some versions have the wife pitching out the nobleman. Baron Münchausen's version of the story has the wolf leaping at the baron, who ducked! The wolf landed upon the horse and ate his way into the harness, whereupon the baron drove him on into St. Petersburg.

A modern-day epilogue was reported in the *London Sunday Express* for May 13, 1962:

WOLF PAWS AT VASILY'S CAR DOOR—FROM INSIDE

The Soviet weekly paper *Izvestia* has been telling readers the astonishing story of a man's singlehanded encounter with a savage wolf, a tale as old as Russia herself, but with a modern twist.

Says the paper's Crimea correspondent: "Vasily Plashkin was driving one night along a lonely road from Sevastopol, in the Crimea, to fetch a hunting party from a remote village in the steppe.

"Suddenly he saw in the distance dozens of flickering lights, sharp and glittering, caught in the rays of his headlamps.

" 'Wolves,' he thought to himself, pressing hard on the accelerator.

"As he approached, the wolves, instead of scattering, ran ahead of his car. He surged forward—right into the middle of the pack.

"The wolves dashed frantically right and left of the car. But one of the animals hit his bumper and was bowled over.

"Vasily got out of the car cautiously when he saw that the coast was clear, and looked at his 'catch.'

"It was a huge, brown-grey wolf, lying inert in the roadway.

"He pulled the huge beast into the back seat, and continued his journey.

"But he had barely gone 25 miles when he heard a strange noise from the back seat.

"He turned, and almost fainted with terror. The 'dead' wolf was standing upright on the back seat, breathing balefully, its enormous jaws extended and snapping.

"Hardly knowing what he was doing, Vasily braked to a halt and jumped out of the car.

"He slammed the car door hard behind him, and as he leaned against it he realized he carried no weapon of any kind with him.

"Inside the car, the enraged animal was battering against the car's windows.

"At any moment, thought Vasily, the glass would break.

"The night was cold and chilly, and Vasily began blowing on his frozen hands wondering what he should do.

"Then he noticed the exhaust fumes coming out of the exhaust pipe —he had forgotten to switch off the engine.

"Suddenly an idea struck him.

"He rushed round to the back of the car, pulled out the box of tools and a length of rubber hose.

"He hacked a hole in the body of the car and connected the hose to the exhaust pipe, then pushed it through the hole he had made.

"In a few minutes the interior of the car was filled with suffocating fumes.

"The wolf tossed about and finally quietened down, overcome by the poisonous exhaust fumes.

"Then Vasily continued his journey, with a dead wolf in the back of his car—and the best hunting story of his career."

Although there is a touch of whimsy to some European wolf stories, real or imagined, others are tales of pure terror. There is a stark reality that underlies the wolf mythology of Europe and Asia. Over the past few centuries, hundreds of people on those continents have been killed by wolves. Responsible studies indicate that a wolf or wolves killed a woman in Haute-Vienne, France, in 1918; a girl at Cara in 1914; 161 persons in Russia during the year 1875; 19 people in the vicinity of Poznan, Poland in 1814; as well as numerous other people in France, Spain, Germany, Russia, and Poland during the last century. A king of France, Louis d'Outremer, son of Charles the Simple, is said to have been slain by a wolf. Shelters were built in 1577 in the Scottish highlands during the reign of James VI so that travelers, caught by nightfall between towns, would have sanctuary from wolves.

In his monograph, *Dogs, Jackals, Wolves and Foxes,* published in 1890, St. George Mivart states that: "A large number of Indian children are carried off each year by them. Their depredations are facilitated by the superstition of the people, who are very averse to killing a wolf, thinking its blood injures the bearing of their fields."

Tradition has it that Milo of Croton, who on six occasions won the wrestling crown at Olympia, attempted to pry apart a cleft tree. The sides sprang back, trapping him in a vise, and wolves subsequently devoured the helpless athlete. It has been speculated that the boldness of the European wolf derives, at least in part, from feeding upon victims of the plague, or the Hundred Years War and other conflicts in which the dead or seriously wounded were simply left upon the field of battle. It has also been pointed out that the European wolf, in seeking livestock when game was scarce, was often opposed only by the children who herded them, armed with little more than sticks and stones. In North America, on the other hand, game was more plentiful, and domestic herders were usually armed with rifles.

Yet neither explanation is entirely satisfying when comparing the behavior of the wolves of the United States toward man, say, with the habits of those of France or Turkey. They are even less compelling when one considers that hard evidence of wolf attacks upon man in northern Europe is as lacking as it is in North America. This in spite of the fact that the wolf of northern Europe, like that of North America, tends to be larger and more formidable than the southern European wolf. In the opinion of C. H. D. Clarke, a noted wildlife expert, most people killed by wolves in Europe died of bites from animals which themselves were victims—of rabies.

After carefully analyzing the medieval epic poems which depict infamous wolf "beasts," Clarke concludes they were all rabid. There are a great many wolves in Rumania—over five thousand were taken during a single year in the 1950s. E. Slubczakowski, who has studied Rumanian wolves for years, has stated that only rabid wolves attack humans. People recognized the symptoms of rabies in wolves and domestic dogs long before Pasteur developed his treatment. Pasteur at one point administered it to nineteen Russians bitten by the same wolf: sixteen were cured, while the others were so badly mauled that they died anyway. Parenthetically, Pasteur's treatment in all probability saved the life of the author's mother after she was bitten by a rabid jackal in India.

On May 5, 1962, the following story went out upon the Associated Press wire service:

WOLVES ATTACK VILLAGE IN TURKEY, KILL BOY

IZMIR, TURKEY (AP)—A score or more of wolves, believed to have rabies, attacked a hamlet in Buca district last night, killing a nine-year-old boy and biting or mauling 14 other persons.

Press dispatches said the wolves attacked the 18-dwelling village of Kaynaklar four times during the night. The villagers fought the animals for seven hours with axes and scythes.

A medical team rushed to the village, placed it under quarantine and inoculated the residents against rabies.

Data on European and Asian wolf attacks tend to support Clarke's rabies theory. There are, of course, other unanswered questions. Although people have died as the result of bites from rabid foxes, skunks, and domestic dogs in North America, there are few records of people being killed by rabid wolves, although they exist. The previously cited attack by a rabid wolf on personnel of Fort Larned is conspicuous in its rarity.

Common rattlesnake. Few creatures have inspired as many myths and tall tales as the rattlesnake. (From Richard Lydehker, The New Natural History)

Snake charming is an ancient art that has been practiced in Asia and North Africa for centuries. Cobras are the most frequently used serpents as they are large, and—very importantly from the snakecharmer's point of view—not particularly fast when striking.

"The Snake Dance of the Hopi Indians." Drawing by H. F. Farny from a photograph by Cosmos Mindeloff. (From Harper's Weekly. Courtesy of Museum of New Mexico Press)

"Baskir Cossacks Attacked by Wolves." From a drawing by *Gustave Doré.*
(Illustrated Times, February 21, 1857)

"Bear Hunting in the Rocky Mountains," drawing by the nineteenth-century artist-journalist team of Frenzeny and Tavernier. (Culver Service)

"Roping a Wild Grizzly," 1877, painting by James Walker. This dangerous sport required exceptional skill and nerve from the vaqueros. (The Thomas Gilcrease Institute of American History and Art, *Tulsa, Oklahoma*)

Cattlemen tracking a grizzly bear to its den. Painting by William Cary. (Courtesy of American Museum of Natural History)

In his drawing, "The Dangers of Prospecting—a Scene in the Rocky Mountains," Paul Frenzeny depicts an untimely meeting with a grizzly. (From Luceris Beche and Charles Clegg. The American West)

Possibly the most interesting facet of the rabies notion is psychological. Our literature tends to reflect those things which we intensely love, hate, celebrate, or fear. Little has been written about the terrors of being attacked by a domestic dog with rabies, although it is a very real danger. Much has been written about the terrors of confronting man-eating wolves, which has less basis in reality. It is, apparently, less frightening to contemplate a domestic animal gone mad than a wild animal stalking man as a source of food.

Even if Clarke's rabies theory does account for most fatal wolf attacks, we are still left with that most frustrating and tantalizing of natural phenomena—the notable exception. In the case of wolves, this was the Beast of Gévaudan.

The Montagnes de la Margeride, a brushy highlands, lies in the south of France some sixty miles from the Mediterranean. Robert Louis Stevenson, leading a pack donkey, wandered through this region in 1878, remarking upon the villages, the people, and the countryside: "Moor, heathery marsh, tracts of rock and pines, woods of birch all jewelled with the autumn yellow. . . ." In the eighteenth century, as now, it was a pastoral region of villages and hamlets with stone, thatch-roof houses. In the early morning, children drove sheep or cattle out to unfenced pastures which merged with a scrub forest. Numerous wolves roamed the region, and herders and their dogs frequently had to frighten them away from the livestock. On June 30, 1764, Jeanne Boulet, a fourteen-year-old girl, was killed by a wolf near the hamlet of Ubas in the Margeride. In early August another fourteen-year-old girl was killed in the Gévaudan region—no great distance from the scene of the first tragedy. When a fifteen-year-old boy also fell victim to a wolf during the same month, personal village grief began to spread into an undercurrent of terror which swept through the region. Parish records indicate that children of the region had in the past died of bites from wolves or their own dogs, very likely rabid, but these killings were isolated incidents.

Before September was over, three other children and a woman of thirty-six had also been killed by a wolf or a wolflike creature. There began to be talk of the supernatural, of a Being sent by God to punish sinners, and old tales of werewolves were revived. The governor of the province of Languedoc sent Captain M. Duhamel and forty dragoons into the besieged region. Wolf hunts commenced almost immediately. The captain and his band began to work their way along the numerous ravines which gash the region, seeking wolf runways. Although their hunts produced a number of dead wolves, none was what was now being called the Beast of Gévaudan. Several other people were attacked: some of them died. It was noted that the Beast, given the opportunity, would feed upon its victims, something which rarely happens if the animal is infected with rabies. Dragoons kept watch over the bodies of victims to no avail; the Beast, instead of returning to his kills, made fresh ones.

On the sixth day of the new year, 1765, by order of the Bishop of Mende, prayers were offered for deliverance from the wolf in all the churches of the diocese. That same day, almost as if to mock the services, two more people were killed at sites a goodly distance from each other. Did this mean there were two Beasts? Or was it, as some people maintained, not of this earth and therefore able to travel with the wind?

By now, many families were sending their animals out to pasture in one large herd, so that there would be more children and dogs to defend each other. Six days after the day of prayers, a group of five boys and two girls were attacked near Vileret d'Apcher, where a twenty-year-old girl had lost her life in October. A twelve-year-old named Pontefaix and two companions of the same age, armed with homemade pikes, tried to fend off the wolf. Brushing past them, it bit one of the smaller boys on the cheek. Driven off by the older boys, it leaped upon another small child, only to be forced away by shouts and jabs of the pikes. The wolf now clamped its jaws upon the arm of its first victim and started to drag the screaming child away. Pontefaix and the other children pursued it to a mudhole, yelling, throwing stones, and striking it upon the head with the frail pikes. Snarling, the wolf released the boy and drove at the tormenting pikes. Although it left toothmarks in the wood, the boys held their ground and the wolf retreated.

Word spread quickly throughout France. A mere child had successfully defeated the Beast of Gévaudan! Honor was heaped upon him; poems were written about his bravery. As though setting the pattern for all too many novels of the following century, he was whisked away from his peasant home to be reared as a gentleman at the expense of the Crown.

Meanwhile, Captain Duhamel and his dragoons were having a frustrating time of it. Great hunts were organized. The month after Pontefaix's hour of glory, 20,000 men beat through the forest and scrub. Noblemen, including Lafayette, came to try their luck at slaying the Beast. Rewards totalling 9,400 livres—a fortune—were offered. To Duhamel, it must have seemed that the Beast possessed a sense of diabolical revenge: wolves would be killed and then the Beast would kill people, mostly children. It is interesting to note that only one adult male was killed during the whole reign of terror.

Duhamel, feeling the pressure, tried everything, including dressing sheep in little girls' clothing as decoys. He was getting backlash from the local people, who were tired of being called from their farming duties to unsuccessfully sweep the woods, and, like parents the world over in a similar situation, were probably suspicious that the exotic dragoons from the outside world might compromise the virtue of their daughters. The Sieur de la Barthe complained that "The dragoons treat Gévaudan like a conquered country," and was critical of their horses which trampled the harvests and were, in his opinion, about as useful in wolf hunting as a chariot with a third wheel.

Duhamel and his dragoons were recalled. In England, the media being somewhat fuzzy at the time, it was reported that a wolf had put the French army to flight. Captain Duhamel was replaced by a Norman squire, M. Denneval, who was recognized by the French court as an official wolf hunter. Accompanied by his son, local people, and a pack of trained dogs, Denneval diligently set about his task. Poison was set out. Hunting parties reported not only seeing the Beast, but actually wounding it on several occasions. Yet the Beast continued to press its attacks. Four boys managed to drive it away with clubs and a homemade pike, but a woman of fifty perished and the wolf later returned to its kill.

When three months passed without appreciable success, the king, growing impatient, withdrew Denneval, and asked M. Antoine de Beauterne, a member of his royal guard, to take charge of the hunts. Although Antoine's methods were basically the same as his predecessor's, he enjoyed the services of fourteen gamekeepers and two leashes of hounds. He had been hunting for fifty years and was well known and respected. A number of noblemen, some with their own dogs, came to assist him. The Beast, known from numerous reports to be a huge wolf, continued to elude its pursuers.

In early September Antoine rushed to the village of La Vachellerie with gamekeepers and trailing dogs upon hearing that a young shepherdess had failed to come in from the pastures after dark. A trail of ripped, bloodstained clothing led to the girl's nude, partially eaten body. Some students of slang believe that our modern reference to men who regard women in a predatory fashion stems from this incident. Three days later a muleteer was passing through the Margeride Mountains when attacked by a huge wolf, assumed to be the Beast. He shot, but missed, and was knocked to the ground. Friends managed to drive the wolf away. Two days after that a child from the mountain hamlet of Pepinet was killed, even though armed with a crude bayonet. She was the Beast's third victim from that hamlet.

Many people of the region were by now more than ever convinced that Antoine and his dogs were fruitlessly chasing after a supernatural being. On September 21, Antoine and some fellow hunters drove some wolves into a tangle of thickets. When Antoine sighted a large wolf some forty paces away, he fired at it. Even though the charge had been so heavy as to knock him upon his backside, the wolf did not go down until hit by a shot from one of the gamekeepers.

As would later be verified by one of the senior surgeons of France, the dead wolf was 5 feet 7½ inches long and weighed 130 pounds—which in terms of the European wolf is very large indeed. The carcass was covered with old wounds. A nineteen-year-old girl named Jeanne Valet had previously thwarted the Beast by driving a bayonet into its shoulder. Upon viewing the corpse, she immediately identified it by size, coloring, and the scar of the wound made by her bayonet. Other people who had survived attacks by the Beast viewed the wolf and made similar positive identifications. The senior surgeon made a hasty embalming of the wolf's body, and it was rushed to Paris where the queen and the entire court viewed it with interest, although probably at a distance, as it was getting a bit odoriferous.

Antoine received acclamation, expenses, a pension, and a Cross of St. Louis. He and his son made some side money by exhibiting the wolf until it finally disintegrated. In the region of the Margeride Mountains there were prayers of thanksgiving and rejoicing.

On December 2, two children were attacked by a wolf near the village of Bessyre-Sainte-Mary. There were more attacks, then a death, and in February a footprint larger than that of the Beast which had been killed was discovered. Had the wolf killed by Antoine been the wrong animal? Was it indeed all along a diabolical creature which had now returned from the dead to punish them for their sins? Four people were killed between December and April, six in April, and five in May. The old pattern of twilight terror and daytime hunts resumed. The hunts were of a more local, limited basis, initiated by the provincial government, since as far as Paris was concerned the Beast of Gévaudan was dead. When one examines the evidence, it is obvious that there were two Beasts: many of the attacks which took place before Antoine's kill were too widely spaced to have been made by the same animal.

In June 1767, the Marquis d'Apchier was running his hounds in the woods and assigned a peasant, Jean Chastel, to watch for whatever might break from the cover. When a large wolf bounded out, Chastel shot it, and the marquis's hounds finished it off. It was a large wolf whose stomach contained portions of its last human victim.

The Beast, or the two of them, were finally dead. It would appear that from sixty to one hundred people had been killed by them, and a number of others attacked.

As previously mentioned, C. H. D. Clarke, an authority on wolves and a man who admires them, believes most of the documented accounts we have of European and Asian wolf attacks involved rabid animals. Yet he freely admits that the Beasts of Gévaudan were not rabid. In the *Natural History* issue of April, 1971, he makes a plausible case that the Beasts were actually a hybrid dog/wolf cross, an almost unique situation in the wild, although it has been done in captivity, and dog/coyote crosses are commonplace. He points out that in size, coloration, shape, and behavior the Beasts were very uncharacteristic of wolves as we know them.

Although the Beasts of Gévaudan may indeed have not been true wolves at all, there can be little doubt that they contributed to the myth that wolves as a species are human predators. The same must be true of attacks by rabid wolves in southern Europe. Stories of wolves have passed from generation to generation, being modified and reshaped as they pass from person to person. Legend, realities, and half realities have been mingled to form the dramatic, and the wolf howl in the night has come to represent blood-curdling peril to man rather than an essentially friendly animal communicating with its own.

Webster's Dictionary defines lycanthropy in two ways: (1) *in folklore, the power to transform oneself or another into a wolf by use of magic,* and (2) *a form of mental disorder in which the patient imagines himself to be a wolf.* The notion that man can transform himself into animal form under certain conditions is probably as old as man himself. It is still very much alive in those societies that have not been engulfed or at least intimidated by modern civilization. The transformations may involve anything from swans to lions, serpents to birds.

The magic may be invoked to assume the strength or other desirable attributes of the animal. Thus the Cherokee Indian, preparatory to embarking upon a long winter journey, sang a wolf song and howled, so that the spirit of the wolf would enter him so that he too could pass over the snows without danger of frostbite. In other tribes, ceremonial identification with the wolf assured wisdom and fleetness in the hunt.

Lycanthropy goes back to the very roots of European mythology. In the Norse creation story, two teams of horses were created to pull the sun and moon across the sky, so that there might be day and night. But trolls, creatures of darkness, hated the light and assumed the form of wolves to chase the horses across the heavens, hoping to devour them and thus effect a return to perpetual night. The horses, terrified, ran steadily, as they do today and ever will, pulling sun and moon behind them. Greek legend has it that King Lycaon of Arcadia, cruel ruler of a wild and mountainous region, served Zeus chopped portions of his son to test the god's divinity. In punishment, Zeus changed Lycaon into a wolf. Subsequently, as Pliny tells us, a member of the family of Antaeus would be selected by lot to strip and plunge into an Arcadian lake during the festival of Jupiter Lycaeus. The water would transform him into a wolf. If after nine years he had refrained from eating human flesh, he could change back into his mortal form which would have aged throughout the period of his transformation.

Considered as a mental disorder, lycanthropy offers some strange histories. The modern word *berserk* comes from the Scandinavian *berserkir,* ancient, ferocious warriors who wore bear and wolfskins. Such garments gave them the strength of these animals and an unstoppable frenzy in battle. Some berserkirs were great heroes; others terrorized the countryside, killing farmers and taking their women and valuables.

During the Middle Ages a number of people confessed to having traffic with agents of the Devil, who gave them the power to become werewolves. Pierre Bourgot, a French sheep-man, related how a mysterious horseman had promised that his master would protect his flock and provide him with money. "I renounced Christianity, kissed his left hand, which was black and ice-cold as that of a corpse. Then

I fell on my knees and gave my allegiance to Satan," Bourgot testified in court. Bourgot also asserted that "In a wood near Chastel Charnon we met with many others whom I did not recognize; we danced, and each had in his or her hand a green taper with a blue flame." After being rubbed with a salve, Bourgot "believed myself then to be transformed into a wolf. I was at first somewhat horrified at my four wolf's feet, and the fur with which I was covered all at once, but I found that I could now travel with the speed of the wind." As a wolf, Bourgot had a craving for human flesh; he told the court of killing four children and an elderly woman.

The trial of Bourgot took place in the early sixteenth century, a time of lycanthropic frenzy. The church of the period took witchcraft and devil-possession quite seriously, and felt the rack to be a good tool for exacting honest confession. There were large numbers of wolves in southern Europe; many were rabid. Quite likely some perfectly harmless maniacs were burned to death as werewolves after confessing to attacks that were actually made by rabid wolves. Yet there were other men and women of that time for which the records leave little doubt: believing themselves to be wolves, they attacked, killed, and cannibalized other people. There were a number of incidents in France alone.

In 1598 some men came upon the body of a fifteen-year-old boy in a wild stretch of woods in Brittany. They immediately pursued the two wolves which had been tearing at the body, but lost their trail in the dusk. They were about to give up the chase when they discovered a strange, half-naked man crouched in the undergrowth. He had long wild hair and beard as well as long fingernails. His hands were blood-spattered; he was shaking with fear. He told his captors that his name was Roulet and that he was a beggar. While in wolf form, he told them, he had killed the youth, but had been frightened away from feasting upon the body by their arrival. The two wolves they had seen were his brothers.

At his subsequent trial in Angers, Roulet repeated this confession, and added that he frequently changed himself into a wolf.

"Do your hands and feet become paws of a wolf?" he was asked.
"Yes, they do."

"Does your head become like that of a wolf—your mouth become larger?"

"I do not know how my head was at the time; I used my teeth; my head was as it is today. I have wounded and eaten many other little children; I have also been to the sabbath." (The sabbath refers to a witch's sabbath, which was widely believed in at the time.)

In prison Roulet behaved like a madman; at one point he drank an entire pail of water, and then for some time refused to eat anything. Initially sentenced to death, he was finally committed to an insane asylum.

A girl named Pernette Gandillon in the Jura region in 1598 believed herself to be a werewolf. When she attacked a girl picking wild strawberries, the child's younger brother tried to defend her with a knife. Pernette wrenched it away and slit his throat. Enraged townspeople, we are told, apprehended her and tore her apart. Pernette's brother and nephew admitted to being able to change themselves to wolves by rubbing themselves with salve. While in prison they moved about on all fours and howled. Antoinette, Pernette's niece, confessed to giving herself to the devil, who appeared as a black goat. She could, she asserted, create hailstorms. Pernette's brother, nephew, and niece were hanged and burned as sorcerers.

There were others, such as the stoop-shouldered recluse known as the Hermit of St. Bonnot, who admitted in 1553 to killing and eating a number of people who wandered into the forest that surrounded his hut. He did so, he said, while in wolf form. He was found guilty of witchcraft and was burned.

In the same general period, a ragged, emaciated youth of thirteen named Jean Grenier killed several children under the delusion he was a wolf. The courts, realizing he was utterly demented, ordered him confined for life behind the secure walls of a monastery. There he died after seven years at the age of twenty, a furtive, pathetic creature with little grasp of day to day realities, but still believing he had once roamed as a werewolf.

It would be interesting to trace what effects such cases of lycanthropy have had upon our modern precepts of insanity with regard to law. It is also interesting, and more generic to the concerns of this book, to speculate upon what effect the werewolf manias of the Middle Ages have had upon wolf mythology. Being attacked by a wild animal is frightening enough, more so if the beast has the audacity to feed upon its human victim; and all of it is compounded if the wolf is actually another human being working in concert with the forces of Evil. Small wonder the wolf becomes a villain in our nursery tales or musical classics like Prokofiev's *Peter and the Wolf*.

When the Pilgrims arrived in Massachusetts and discovered that there were wolves, they reacted with alarm. Community leaders of Barnstable County, Massachusetts, seriously proposed in 1717 to erect a six-foot-high fence to shut out the wolves that prowled adjacent Plymouth County. The citizens of Plymouth County vetoed the plan, apparently having little desire to have all the wolves congregate on their side of the fence. Spanish colonists settling in what is now New Mexico in the sixteenth century knew werewolf stories. Around hearth fires on a winter night old tales would be spun. In the subtle ways of oral tradition, rabies, the Beast of Gévaudan, and human dementia had now, unbeknownst to the storytellers, mingled as a basis for wolf stories which evoked fascination among the listeners, as well as causing them to regard the wild wolf of the New World with fear.

Still and all, it was not the myth of wolf's menace to man which has caused the species to be eradicated from much of the United States, but a matter of simple displacement. As Americans moved westward, the buffalo was all but exterminated and domestic cattle were brought in to crop the grass; mountain meadows once grazed by large herds of elk became the domain of vast flocks of sheep. Wolves, clever and adaptable, deprived of their natural prey, naturally developed a taste for beef and mutton. For the stockman, rifles proved less effective than poison, especially strychnine salted in the carcass of another animal.

Today it is estimated that only about a thousand wolves remain within the conterminous United States, most of them in the vicinity of the Boundary Waters Canoe Area of northern Minnesota. Yet in the backcountry of Alaska and Canada there may be as many as fifty thousand. Is the wolf in danger of extinction? Probably not, at least in the foreseeable future. There appear to be small but stable wolf populations in the mountains of Spain and Italy, while numerous wolves range through eastern European nations such as Yugoslavia, Rumania, and Bulgaria, as well as the vast stretches of the Soviet Union and China. The future of the wolf is probably more critical in North America. For caribou and other prey of the wolf to survive in numbers, as well as the wolf itself, large tracts of land must be set aside for their preservation. Should the backcountry of Alaska and Canada be opened up for large scale development of mineral, timber, and other resources without adequate protection of the natural ecology, the wolf, one of the most interesting animals on the planet, is in real danger.

Recently, a number of good books have detailed the habits of wild wolves and accented their unaggressive nature. Biologist Adolph Murie, in his monograph *The Wolves of Mt. McKinley,* remarks that "The strongest impression remaining with me after watching the wolves on numerous occasions was their friendliness. The adults were friendly toward each other and were amiable toward the pups. This innate good feeling has been strongly marked in the three captive wolves I have known."

After centuries of myth and misunderstanding, we are finally beginning to see the healthy wild wolf in true perspective.

10

A Solitary Beast

For two summers, I worked as a stream guard on the coast of southern Alaska. My job was to prevent fishermen from setting their nets so close to the mouth of a nearby stream that salmon would have been unable to ascend it to spawn. The first summer my wilderness home was a wooden frame surmounted by canvas. One afternoon I was lying upon the floor on a sleeping bag, reading a paperback novel. A rainstorm had just let up. I heard a woofing sound just outside of the tent frame and looked up to see a large brown bear squeeze through the poles of the entrance. It loomed over me, apparently as startled as I was. I jumped up, backed into a corner and grabbed a 30-0-6 rifle. Even as I pulled back the bolt, I realized the cartridges for the unloaded weapon were on a shelf at the other side of the tent, behind the bear.

The bear, in trying to back out between the entrance poles of the tent frame, had become momentarily jammed. At the sharp crack of the rifle's stiff bolt being thrown open, the bear exploded out through a corner of the structure, bursting through a shelf of groceries and the wooden slats of the frame as if they were paper. As I loaded the rifle, I watched the bear hump its way down the beach with a fine burst of speed. It did not pay another visit that summer.

The following salmon season, a fellow stream guard used an old miner's cabin as headquarters. The cabin had been built flush against a steep sidehill, and he was accustomed to hearing small creatures on his roof. One evening, as he was eating supper from a makeshift table of wooden crates, he heard an unusually loud racket on the roof over his head. He was about to step outside to see what was making the commotion when the thin planking of the roof gave way and a brown bear dropped through, landing on a plate of chili. My friend fled out the door and spent an uncomfortable and mosquito-haunted night in his skiff offshore while the bear rampaged through the cabin, gobbling up or otherwise ruining the better part of a month's supply of groceries.

Most people who live or have camped in bear country to any extent have similar stories. Bear are curious creatures with a highly developed sense of smell and an obvious relish for many kinds of food favored by man.

For every actual attack upon man there are probably dozens of encounters in which the bear is merely curious rather than aggressive. In his book *Grizzly Country,* Andy Russell described the plight of a woman on a wilderness pack trip in British Columbia. One afternoon the outfitter noted signs of a female grizzly bear and cubs, but figured the scent of the party and bells of the pack horses would put her to flight. Camp was set up. For several days Mary Faegre and her family fished, hiked, and took day trips on horseback. On the day of departure, Mary went back to a small pond in the forest to bathe as the pack horses were being loaded. She washed and stretched out on a flat rock, dozing in the sunlight.

She was thirsty when she awoke, and strolled over to a nearby stream. She had just knelt to scoop up some water with her cupped hands when she heard a rustle in the bushes and looked up to face a large grizzly. Fighting for calmness, she stood up and faced the bear. The fur at the nape of its neck was raised, but it simply watched her impassively. She called out. A stiff breeze, blowing from the direction of camp, carried it away. Remembering that the outfitter had cautioned members of the party never to run from a bear, she began to gingerly edge her way toward camp. Almost leisurely, the grizzly sauntered around her, blocking her route. The nearby trees had dry, downward sloping branches at their bases, impossible to climb.

Terrified, she began to move slowly in a wide arc as the bear silently followed a few feet away, still between the woman and the safety of camp. Step by step, they covered over half a mile as if dancers in some ancient ritual. By concentrating upon her movements, the woman was able to hold down her impulse to run, as if it were something attempting to burst out of an unlocked box. Finally, almost in disbelief, she saw a bleached windfall tree trunk that led to the branches of a large spruce. She wondered if the bear would cut her off from it, as it had the escape routes to camp. Breathing quickly, shallowly, she inched closer to the log as the grizzly followed. When her hand touched the log, she whirled and scrambled up it, clawing her way quickly up through the spruce.

She called for help, and was soon rescued. Although badly frightened at the time, she would return to the backcountry many times, and later told Russell that she counted the experience as a wonderful story to tell her grandchildren.

The grizzly, a subspecies of the brown bear, once was the unchallenged master of a domain that stretched from northwestern Alaska into the mountains of Mexico. It is essentially a solitary creature when not mating or raising cubs, roaming large territories in search of food. An adult grizzly, which may weigh a quarter of a ton or more, is possessed of great strength, capable of dragging the carcass of a bull elk for some distance up the side of a mountain. The muscles above its massive shoulders form a distinctive hump. In addition to its strength, the grizzly has a keen sense of smell, surprising speed, and is highly intelligent. As its scientific name, *Ursus horribilis,* suggests, the grizzly is fearless, unpredictable, and a fearful adversary when angered.

In spite of its formidability, most of the grizzly's waking hours are spent in peaceful foraging—stripping berry bushes, digging up roots, rolling over rocks and logs for grubs and using its long claws to tear up the ground in search of ground squirrels. The great bears are skillful fishermen. They rarely kill larger mammals such as deer or elk, although are never adverse to feeding upon the carcass of an animal which may have fallen behind the herd because of age or injury. Grizzly cubs are wonderfully playful, romping in mock fights and curling into balls to roll down hillsides. The adult bears are not without their own sense of whimsy; a naturalist once watched one of them deliberately slide down a long and steep snowfield on its backside with what appeared to be carefree glee. Mother grizzlies are affectionate with their cubs and fiercely protective. Outside of wounding a grizzly, the quickest way to draw the wrath of one of the great bears is to disturb a mother with cubs.

In 1975, a California university professor, Gordon Edwards, worked his way through some thick brush near Feather Plume Falls in Glacier National Park. He had spent more than twenty summers prowling the backcountry of the park and had authored *A Climber's Guide to Glacier National Park*. He heard the yipping of bear cubs and then a deep growl. Edwards tensed, then relaxed as he heard the cubs moving away. Suddenly, the grizzly sow came plowing through the brush at him. The entomology professor felt that if he remained calm the bear would realize he meant no harm and would leave. When she was only an arm's length away, he pushed at her with his ice axe. The grizzly, off balance, tumbled down the steep hillside.

Quickly regaining her feet, she came back up the slope in a series of short leaps, pausing now and then to glare at him. The bear jolted Edwards off his feet and gripped his left hand in her jaws. He tried to work his hand free, softly slapping the grizzly on the nose while saying, "Come on, let go, I won't hurt you." The bear was not biting hard; in less than a minute Edwards worked his bloody hand out of the bear's mouth and fell upon his stomach in the recommended posture of playing dead.

Growling, the agitated grizzly rushed back and forth, sometimes standing over the motionless man, once dashing off to smash at some small trees. Then she was gone. Edwards picked up his ice axe and camera. He headed down the mountain, stopping once to photograph his torn hand. After doctors at Cardston Clinic stitched up his injuries, he returned to the Many Glacier Hotel. The next day, after the story had gone out to the press, the modest professor found he had become an instant nationwide celebrity.

A Canadian guide, Leonard Jeck, and his two clients, Steve Rose and Dave Slutker, confronted a testy grizzly with cubs in Jasper National Park in 1968. The men had tethered their horses and were walking through a stand of thick spruce when the sow broke out of cover and bowled over Jeck. As they struggled, Rose ascended a thickly-branched tree and yelled to divert the bear. In theory, adult grizzlies never climb trees, but this one hauled herself up into the spruce, branch by branch. She dragged Rose out of his perch and they tumbled to the ground. Rose rolled on to his stomach. The grizzly tore at his back and legs.

Slutker, who had been strolling along a ridge some 500 yards away, snatched up a length of wood and courageously sprinted down to draw the bear from his friend. The grizzly wheeled to meet him, swatting his club away and tearing a section from his face. She fell on him, biting and roaring. Somehow Slutker managed to thrust his fingers into the enraged animal's nostrils and she abruptly heaved to her feet and lumbered back into the forest.

The three badly mauled men stumbled a mile and a half to their horses and rode back to camp. Jeck continued on to a ranger station and all three outdoorsmen were flown by helicopter to a hospital.

In 1670 Charles II, King of England, granted a charter to a group of noblemen who were to found the Hudson's Bay Company, a fur trading enterprise whose wilderness empire would stretch across an area many times larger than the British Isles. The charter was granted with much pomp and fanfare; that same year marked the unauspicious birth of Henry Kelsey to a working class family. At fourteen, Kelsey joined the Hudson's Bay Company and was promptly shipped to North America as an apprentice. Company records note that he was "a very active lad, delighted much in Indian's company," and that "poor and semi-educated as he was, he was the discoverer of the Canadian prairie."

Kelsey was twenty years of age when, in 1690, he set off alone on a solitary journey which would take him all the way into what is now the province of Alberta. For better than a year he traveled afoot and in canoes through largely unexplored territory. He was the first white man to see the buffalo of western Canada and was probably the first to be treed by grizzlies, although Spanish explorers had spotted the giant carnivores on the shore of southern California almost a century before. The young fur trader killed the two behemoths which had put him up a tree. In his journal we find the first English language account of the great bears, presented in verse form:

> And then you have a beast of severall kind
> The one is a black a Buffillo great
> Another is an outgrown Bear wch. is good meat
> His skin to gett I have used all ye ways I can
> He is mans food & he makes food of man
> His hide they would not me it preserve
> But said it was a god & they should Starve
> This plain affords nothing but Beast & grass. . . .

Kelsey, who started with Hudson's Bay Company as an apprentice with little more status than that of a slave, later became British governor of Hudson Bay.

Over the next century a number of English, French, and American trappers undoubtedly encountered grizzlies, but their experiences, if set down at all, were mostly as brief and matter of fact as Kelsey's. During the years of 1804 through 1806, Captain Meriwether Lewis and William Clark made their monumental trek from St. Louis to the Pacific Ocean and back, gathering a wealth of scientific information on the wilderness through which they passed. Their journals contain several references to the grizzly, sometimes referred to as the "white bear" in the parlance of the time. On April 29, 1805, their journal noted that:

> Captain Lewis, who was on shore with one hunter, met, about eight o'clock, two white bears. Of the strength and ferocity of the animal the Indians had given us dreadful accounts. They never attack him except in parties of six or eight persons, and even then are often defeated with a loss of one or more of their party. Having no weapons but bows and arrows, and the bad guns with which traders supply them, they are obliged to approach very near the bear. As no wound, except through the head or heart, is mortal, they frequently fall sacrifice if they miss their aim. He rather attacks than avoids a man, and such is the terror which he has inspired, that the Indians who go in quest of him paint themselves and perform all the superstitious rites customary when they make war on a neighboring nation.

> Hitherto, those bears we had seen did not appear desirous of encountering us; but although to a skillful rifleman the danger is very much diminished, yet the white bear is a terrible animal. On approaching these two, both Captain Lewis and the hunter fired and each wounded a bear. One of these made his escape. The other turned on Captain Lewis and pursued him seventy or eighty yards, but being badly wounded the bear could not prevent him from reloading his piece, which he again aimed at him, and a third shot from the hunter brought him to the ground. He was a male, not quite full grown, and weighed about 300 pounds.

A few days later, Captain Lewis and one of the hunters killed a grizzly weighing between 500 and 600 pounds, and their journal entry for May 14 once again reflects the awesome staying power of a wounded and enraged grizzly:

Toward evening the men in the hindmost canoes discovered a large brown bear lying in the open grounds about three hundred yards from the river. Six of them, all good hunters, immediately went to attack him, and concealing themselves by a small eminence, came unperceived within forty paces of him. Four of the hunters now fired and each lodged a ball in his body, two directly through the lungs. The furious animal sprang up and ran open-mouthed upon them. As he came near, the two hunters who had reserved their fire gave him two wounds, one of which, breaking his shoulder retarded his motion for a moment; but before they could reload he was so near they were obliged to run for the river, and before they had reached it he had almost overtaken them. Two jumped into the canoe, the other four separated, and concealing themselves in the willows, fired as fast as they could reload. They struck him several times, but instead of weakening the monster, each shot seemed only to direct him towards the hunter; till at last he pursued two of them so closely that they threw aside their guns and pouches and jumped down a perpendicular bank twenty feet into the river. The bear sprang after them, and was within feet of the hindmost when one of the hunters on shore shot him in the head and finally killed him. They dragged him to the shore and found that eight balls had passed through him in different directions. The bear was old and the meat tough, so they took the skin only.

Among the mountain men, the fur trappers who wandered the Rocky Mountains in quest of beaver during the first half of the nineteenth century, there were few who could not reel off personal experiences attesting to the stamina and toughness of a wounded grizzly. On the other hand, some of the mountain men themselves were possessed of a toughness and stamina which at times seemed to match that of the great bears.

In 1822 William Ashley, the lieutenant governor of Missouri, and Andrew Henry formed a fur-trading partnership. They advertised for "Enterprising Young Men" to "ascend the river Missouri to its source, there to be employed for one, two or three years." Most of the mountain men who would later become legendary figures were hired by the new company in the first two years of operation, including William Sublette, James Clyman, Jim Bridger, Thomas Fitzpatrick, Jedediah Smith, and Hugh Glass. In contrast to most of the company recruits, the majority of whom were little more than adventurous youngsters when they started out, Glass was a seasoned frontiersman in his fifties.

The mountain men possessed a fierce sense of survival. Smith and Glass were in a party which was attacked by Arikara Indians. Fifteen of their companions were killed. On another occasion Glass wounded a grizzly and as Clyman was to note in his diary:

> Hugh Glass . . . met with a large grissly [*sic*] Bear which he shot and wounded the bear as is usual attacked Glass he attempted to climb a tree but the bear caught him and hauled to the ground tearing and lacerating his body in fearful rate by this time several men were in close gun shot but could not shoot for fear of hitting Glass at length the beare appeared to be satisfied and turned to leave when 2 or 3 men fired the bear turned immediately on Glass and give him a second mutilation. On turning again several more men shot him when for a third time he pounced on Glass and fell dead over his body. . . .

The old trapper was badly mangled. The worst of his wounds were stitched up with mending thread, and the party briefly lingered, expecting him to die at any moment. Yet Glass doggedly clung to life. The country was swarming with Arikaras and Ashley decided to press on. He offered a reward to anyone who would agree to stay with the stricken man until he died. With the Indians on the warpath, this was no casual request, but after some hesitation Fitzpatrick and Bridger volunteered. After a day or so, either thinking Glass dead or beyond any hope of recovery, Bridger and Fitzpatrick set out to catch up with the main party, taking Glass's rifle with them.

Hugh Glass refused to die. When he emerged from the semicoma in which he had been drifting, he was parched with thirst. He crawled to a nearby spring. Fruit-laden branches of a wild cherry tree hung within reach; for ten days he subsisted upon the cherries and tart buffalo berries which grew in a thicket close enough to crawl to. Finally, staggering, falling, getting up again to lurch forward, he started off in the direction of the Missouri River. The nearest outpost of civilization was Fort Kiowa, over a hundred miles away. The maimed man had not gone far when he chanced upon some wolves which had just killed a buffalo calf. Desperate for the meat, he shouted and waved his arms, but the wolves only bristled and snarled. The trapper, using his razor as a fire steel, managed to fire the grass, driving the wolves from their kill.

He remained by the carcass for five days, eating his fill of the meat as his wounds began to heal. He then started painfully on again, at first only making a mile or two a day, later covering several. There are those who claim that he was eventually found by a band of Sioux who were foraging in abandoned Arikara cornfields and that they took him back to Fort Kiowa where in time he joined up with a party of French trappers heading up the Missouri. Others say it was the French trappers who came upon the gaunt, ragged figure with the ruined face as he stumbled across the prairie.

In any case, he headed upriver with the Frenchmen, seeking revenge. A war party of Rees attacked the small expedition; only Glass and one other man survived. The old trapper, tough as a buffalo horn, continued his lonely quest for the men who had abandoned him. By the time he finally caught up with them, months after he first shot the grizzly, his rage had cooled. When he finally approached the astounded trappers, a couple of whom at first figured him to be a ghost, he is said to have declared that he was not "dead yet by a damn sight," and for them to give back his rifle.

The ubiquitous Jim Clyman had noted the particulars of the grizzly attack upon Hugh Glass in his journal, and later in the same year he reported an incident in which Jedediah Smith had a close call with a bear:

> Grissly did not hesitate a moment but sprang on the cap^t taking him by the head first pitc[h]ing sprawling on the earth . . . breaking several of his ribs and cutting his head badly. . . . the bear had taken nearly all his head in his cap[a]cious mouth close to his left eye on one side and close to his right ear on the other and laid the skull bare to near the crown of the head . . . one of his ears was torn from his head out to the outer rim. . . . this gave us a lisson on the character of the grissly Baare which we did not forget.

As Smith calmly gave instructions, Clyman sewed up his gaping wounds, and even managed to save the dangling ear. In the brief years still left to him, Smith made the first overland journey from the American frontier to California, the first crossing of the Sierra Nevada, pioneered the South Pass route to the Pacific and was the first white man to traverse the length of the Pacific Coast from the Columbia River to southern California. He had survived his grizzly attack to become one of our greatest explorers. In 1831, Smith was killed by a Comanche while on a trading venture to Santa Fe. He was thirty-two years of age. Hugh Glass survived his grizzly attack to rebound from one adventure to another until the year after Smith's death when a party of Rees Indians lifted his scalp as he was crossing the frozen Yellowstone River.

Once the word got out that there was gold in the Rocky Mountains, prospectors began panning their way up remote canyons and chipping rock samples from ledges which no white man had ever seen before. In the summer of 1866, two partners, Jim O'Malley and Jess Timberlake, were working their way along the eastern slope of the Continental Divide of Montana when Timberlake suffered a mild stroke. The stroke numbed the fifty-seven-year-old man's legs and it was decided to lay over in a cave until his condition improved. The cave made a fine shelter; there was just room enough for a man to wriggle through the boulders which barricaded the entrance while high gaps in the rock wall let in afternoon sunlight. There was a creek below the cave and another cave, facing, on the opposite bank.

O'Malley made his helpless partner comfortable, hung up a yearling deer he had shot and built a slow fire to cure it. He turned their mule loose to feed and cooked supper outside of the cave. He carried the food into the cave where, after a while, the men bedded down. During the night O'Malley heard a commotion out in the draw. He poked his head through the entrance; it was dark, he could see little, but he could hear the hooves of the mule striking rock as it headed off into the night. The sound receded until there was a silence broken only by the rush of the stream and the occasional hoot of an owl. Timberlake ventured the mule might have been spooked by a grizzly while O'Malley felt a wolf or coyote to be more likely, as they had seen no sign of bear in the draw. In any case, there was no point in trying to trail the pack animal until daylight.

Shortly after dawn O'Malley looked out to see a sow grizzly and her two cubs making a feast of the deer he had been curing across the creek. The prospectors depended upon deer meat to supplement their store-bought provisions. O'Malley snatched up his light Henry repeating rifle and fired merely three times at the mother bear before his weapon was empty. The shots antagonized the bear. As O'Malley clawed frantically through his gear for the remaining box of cartridges, the bear charged across the creek and thrust her head into the narrow slot leading into the cave. With deep-throated growls she wriggled and shoved against the rock as if to force her way through by sheer strength. Unable to locate the shells, O'Malley jabbed at the snapping muzzle with his rifle barrel. The bear backed up and attempted to push aside the boulders with her paws, but they were too massive, too deeply rooted in the ground. She finally gave up and returned to her cubs, driving them into the cave on the opposite side of the stream.

The bears lingered in the vicinity throughout the following day, the cubs rolling and playing in the grass, splashing through the stream after frogs. The sow, while affecting nonchalance, was obviously keeping an eye upon the cave in which the prospectors were holed up. At dusk, O'Malley ventured out to build a cooking fire and start supper. He was intent upon the task when Timberlake, watching from the cave entrance, shouted, "Here she comes!" O'Malley dashed for the cave, slipping through the entrance just ahead of the grizzly. Her claws scraped against the rock at his back.

Although the bears were gone early the following morning, they returned later in the day; it was obvious they regarded the cave opposite that of the besieged men as home, at least for the time being. Without ammunition, there was no means of obtaining deer meat, and the two men eyed their small stock of staples with concern, wondering if they would last until either the bears moved out or Timberlake recovered enough to travel.

The prospectors settled into a strange, almost tranquil routine. In the chalky predawn hours, while the grizzly was off foraging with her cubs, O'Malley fetched water from the stream and gathered firewood for the cooking fire at the mouth of their cave. During the daylight hours, the bears retired to their own cave to sleep; yet the sow, still smarting from the minor wounds inflicted by the Henry rifle, was ever watchful—O'Malley had only to emerge from his cave and walk a few paces before the bear would appear at the mouth of her cave, growling and tensed to charge. The small glade between the caves was rimmed with thick brush. Once the supply of dry wood close to the mouth of their cave had been exhausted, O'Malley began cautiously to wander farther up and down the creek in quest of fuel during the early morning hours when the bears were apparently elsewhere.

One morning, while scooping up some dry tinder, he heard a faint stirring in the tangled undergrowth on the slope just above, and raised up to see the mother bear barreling through the brush toward him. As in a nightmare, he churned toward the entrance of the cave, some fifty yards distant. The bear caught him, cuffed him to the ground only a few feet from safety. She raked his hip with her claws and bit into his face and shoulder. In the sudden fury of the attack, O'Malley tried to play dead; it did not take much effort at all. When he regained consciousness, it was dark. He began to crawl slowly toward the cave entrance, hitching in a sideways fashion after a burst of pain let him know that an arm was broken.

Inside the cave, Timberlake tore up a shirt and managed to stop the worst of the bleeding. There in the darkness, perhaps for the first time in their lives, the two happy-go-lucky prospectors talked about death, the pinching out of some things they had liked, and by dawn were unwrapping those things like gifts they had never opened.

After four days, clocked by the shafts of afternoon light coming in through the high, tight windows where the boulders met the cave roof, O'Malley's hip healed enough so that he could hobble down to the stream for more water, and even clutch up enough brittle brush with his one good arm to get a fire going for hot food. Their supplies were almost exhausted. They had been forted up for twenty-seven days. The partners agreed that their only possibility of salvation lay in O'Malley's hiking out to Canyon Creek stage station, fifteen miles away. Binding his useless arm to his body, O'Malley set out, carrying only a knife and a few matches.

After covering about three miles, he paused to rest. There seemed to be some movement back in the thick brush. Thinking it to be a deer, the prospector momentarily thought of fresh meat, and the missing cartridges which were at the root of their troubles. He pressed on. After a bit, he paused again and glanced back at the way he had come. Something was moving through the brush.

The bear and her two cubs ambled out of the undergrowth and crossed a small clearing. He was being stalked. Fighting panic, O'Malley strode to the base of a large black oak and clumsily attempted to climb it. It was useless. With his arm broken he could not even begin the ascent. In desperation, he pulled off his sweaty jacket, dropped it, and hurried up the side of a low ridge. From the crest, he looked back to see all three bears tearing at the jacket, as if by destroying it they could also destroy its offensive odor and the man that went with it. When the jacket was in shreds, the sow paused, her fury spent. She gathered her cubs and started back in the direction of the caves.

Six days after O'Malley had left the cave, a rescue party arrived at the glade between the caves. The mother grizzly was sprawled out dead on the grass. After O'Malley had left, Timberlake had noticed a

225

rain jacket wedged up in a corner of the cave. In one of the pockets was the missing box of cartridges. Timberlake loaded the Henry, crawled to the slot in the rock, and killed the bear when she returned.

Timberlake later recovered enough to get about on crutches, and was hired as timekeeper for a Butte mine. O'Malley went off looking for gold again, but history is silent as to whether he ever found any.

Grizzlies were once plentiful in California. Members of Sebastian Vizcaino's expedition saw them feeding upon a whale carcass at Monterey Bay in 1602. The tracks, they reported, were "a good third of a yard long and a hand wide." More than 160 years later an expedition headed by Don Gaspar de Portola set out from San Diego to establish missions in the Monterey region. The party was not well provisioned, and consequently the soldiers were always on the alert for game. North of Point Conception they killed a grizzly bear near a tidewater lagoon with muskets and lances. This was probably the first grizzly killed in California by white men. They reported the meat to be "savory and good." They soon killed a second, smaller bear.

Close to the present site of San Luis Obispo they crossed a wide, swampy valley. Miguel Constanso, expedition cartographer, wrote:

> In this canyon we saw troops of bears; they had the land plowed up and full of holes which they make in searching for roots they live on, which the land produces. The natives also use these roots for food, and there are some of good relish and taste. Some of the soldiers, attracted by the chase because they had been successful on two other occasions, mounted their horses, and this time succeeded in shooting one. They, however, experienced the fierceness and anger of these animals—when they feel themselves wounded, headlong they charge the hunter, who can escape only by the swiftness of his horse, for the first burst of speed is more rapid than one might expect from the bulk and awkwardness of such brutes.

They named the valley La Canada de los Osos (Bear Canyon).

Once the Monterey peninsula was reached, a presidio was erected, as well as the Carmel and San Antonio missions. When supply ships failed to arrive as scheduled and the settlers faced famine, Governor Pedro Fages returned to La Canada de los Osos with thirteen soldiers to hunt grizzlies. Over a three-month period they sent nine thousand pounds of jerked bear meat back to the missions, saving the colonists from starvation.

Gradually, the missions began to prosper. In 1784 vast empires of rangeland were parceled out into land grants. Cattle multiplied quickly and there were soon thousands of them grazing in semiwild herds. The cattle were raised for hides. Most ranches had a *cala-veras,* a place of skulls, in an outlying location where the cattle were killed and hides removed. Like the buffalo hunters of the plains, the vaqueros took only the choicest cuts of meat; the carcasses were left for scavengers. Grizzlies began to drift in from the hills. Having acquired a taste for beef, they soon learned that cattle were easier to catch than the more wary deer and elk. It was observed that occasionally grizzlies would lie upon their backs in tall stands of grass, waving their paws to attract curious cattle to within striking distance. Grizzlies took to the meat of Spanish cattle with as much gusto as the Spanish settlers of Monterey had taken to bear meat.

In spite of the efforts of many Spanish ranchers to eradicate them, the grizzly population began to increase. There were an estimated ten thousand of them in California prior to 1830.

Most California ranchers possessed only inaccurate muzzle-loaders, if they had rifles at all. Their bear hunts were usually conducted from horseback with *reatas,* rawhide ropes. Usually three or four riders would pursue a grizzly, attempting to lasso its head or one of its legs. It was a tricky business. Once caught by a single *reata,* the bears often charged the horse and rider, or even sank their claws into the rope and pulled the hunters to them, paw over paw. Some bear hunters greased their *reatas* to prevent this, and bobbed the tails of their mounts so that the enraged bears could not seize them and pull the horses over backward. An American, William Garner, observed grizzly-roping near Monterey in 1846 and wrote of it:

> It requires an extraordinary degree of courage for a man to ride up beside a savage monster like a grizzly bear in this country, which is nearly as active as a monkey, and whose strength is enormous. Should a lasso happen to break . . . the bear invariably attacks the horse, and it requires very often the most skillful horsemanship to prevent the horse or its rider from being injured. It requires also great skill to know when to tighten the lasso, and to what degree, to prevent it from being suddenly snapped by too sudden a strain. The rider must have his eye constantly on that of the bear, and watch his every motion. Sometimes, either through fear, carelessness or inad-

vertence, a man may let go his lasso. In this case, another, if the bear takes off (which he is likely to do), will go as hard as his horse can run, and without stopping his speed, will stoop from his saddle and pick up the end of the lasso off the ground, and taking two or three turns around the loggerhead of his saddle and checking his horse's rein, again detain the bear.

Once the grizzly was secured by more than one *reata,* it could be pulled off balance and dispatched by either lance or musket, or securely bound for transport to an arena for a bull and bear fight. Writers have remarked that these battles to the death fed the Latin passion for violence, as with bull and cock fights, yet it should be noted that such contests were also viewed with wild enthusiasm by American miners in the mother lode country when they were staged there.

On the open range, the great bears became skilled predators of cattle. Unaccustomed as they were to defiance from their prey, they rarely backed off when challenged by the tough, sharp-horned bulls, and fights were not uncommon. Wanderer J. Ross Browne observed one of these struggles from the safety of a tree branch:

The grizzly no sooner got within reach of the bull's horns than he seized them in his powerful grasp, keeping the head to the ground by main strength and the tremendous weight of his body, while he bit at the nose with his teeth, and raked strips of flesh from his shoulders with his hind paws.

Suddenly the bull wrenched his head from the grasp of his adversary and retreated a few steps. The bull charged with such impetuous force that the bear, despite the most terrific blows with his paws, rolled over in the dust. By a well-directed motion [the bull] got one of his horns under the bear's belly.

The bull made another charge, was knocked down, and both animals rolled in desperate struggle, the grizzly biting and clawing, the bull attempting to break away, to get to its feet for another charge. The bull, although badly injured and wobbly, charged the mortally gored bear, and killed it.

Then, as Browne noted, "The bull uttered a deep bellowing sound, shook his horns triumphantly, and slowly walked off. As the blood streamed from his wounds, a death-chill came over him. Finally his body became motionless, and the victor was dead."

Another visitor to California, artist and writer J. D. Borthwick, witnessed a bear and bull fight at Mokelumne Hill, a boom town of the California gold rush. Posters were plastered upon trees and rocks.

WAR! WAR!! WAR!!!
The celebrated Bull-Killing Bear,
GENERAL SCOTT
will fight a Bull on Sunday the 15th inst. at 2 P.M.
at Moquelumne Hill

The bear will be chained with a twenty-foot chain in the middle of the arena. The Bull will be perfectly wild, young, of the Spanish breed and the best that can be found in the country. The Bull's horns will be of their natural length, and *not sawed off to prevent accidents!* The Bull will be quite free in the arena, and not hampered in any way whatever.

Borthwick wryly observed that the posters contained a disclaimer in which the fight promoters claimed to have had no part in the "humbugging" which had characterized a previous event. Two fiddlers entertained the crowd as it filed into wooden bleachers. Borthwick remarked that "The most conspicuous objects were the shirts of the miners, red, white, and blue being the fashionable colors . . . revolvers and silver-handled bowie knives glanced in the bright sunshine; and among the crowd were numbers of gay Mexican blankets, and red and blue bonnets; where here and there the fair sex was represented by a few Mexican women in snowy-white dresses, puffing their cigaritos in delightful anticipation of the exciting scene which was to be enacted."

General Scott, a grizzly of some twelve hundred pounds, had killed several bulls in previous bouts, and during his introduction and that of the bull, the assembly amused itself by placing bets with each other as to the outcome. The bull was at first a reluctant participant, and had to be lured into the arena by the waving of a red flag. Eventually the bull charged, and each animal fought as it would in the wild: horns and power of charge against enormous strength and lacerating embraces. The bull, as was usually the case in such contests, was finally killed by the grizzly. The proprietors, as was also the custom, then announced that for an additional fee, another bull would be pitted against General Scott, and three or four men passed around hats which were quickly filled. The new bull was also dispatched, and

the crowd filed out in high spirits. One of them remarked to Borthwick that it had been "the finest fight ever fit in the country."

San Francisco was aswarm with odd characters and filled with
strange sights during the second half of the last century; nothing
seemed capable of surprising its citizenry much. Yet when in the fall
of 1856, a tall, gray-bearded man took to strolling down the streets
with a grizzly bear or two trailing at his heels like obedient dogs, the
free-wheeling city took immediate notice. They soon learned that the
man's name was James Adams, and they began to flock to a dingy
basement on Clay Street where he exhibited chained grizzlies and elk
in a stall, as well as wolves, foxes, cougars, and other wild creatures.
The most imposing resident of the menagerie was Samson, a
1,510-pound grizzly which Adams billed as the largest bear ever
caught.

Still and all, it was the two tame grizzlies with which he prome-
naded about town which elicited the greatest wonder among observ-
ers. It was learned that the bears, Lady Washington and Ben Franklin, often carried Adams's camp gear in the backcountry, shared his
food and lonely campfires, and even stood by his side as he once
faced a threatening adult grizzly.

This is not to say that Adams was a sort of frontier St. Francis of
Assisi, as more than one sentimental writer has implied. By his own
account, he was not sparing of the rod when training wild animals,
and rightfully considered himself a bear slayer of some prowess. Indeed, he was fond of relating the hair-raising struggles in which he
overcame the mothers of Lady Washington and Ben Franklin with
rifle and knife in order to obtain the cubs.

Adams was born in Massachusetts in 1807. His family expected
him to join them in the dependable if uneventful business of shoe-
making, but the restless youth soon apprenticed himself to a trade
that was more to his liking—wild-animal training. After being mauled
by a Bengal tiger, it seemed that his hands were the only thing which
would still work as he directed them, and he returned, resignedly, to
constructing footwear. He still harbored adventurous notions, however, and when word of California gold electrified the nation, he
headed west. Like many gold stampeders, his visions of instant
wealth tattered out into a grubby struggle for survival. In 1852, at
forty-five years of age, he, in his own words, became "disgusted
with the world and . . . took the road toward the wildest and most

unfrequented parts of the Sierra Nevada, resolved to make the wilderness my home, and wild beasts my companions."

His words are as haunting as a half-remembered tune rendered upon an old player piano; Biblical prophets as well as modern day mathematicians who have given up a university chair to construct simple shelters and live in the most solitary reaches of desert, beach, or mountains, have said much the same thing.

Assisted by two Indians and a young Texan, Adams began to catch animals. When he located the den of a grizzly with two cubs, he shot her in order to catch the yearlings and train them. The young bears promptly ran him up a tree. He and his companions later roped them from horseback after five days of tracking. Adams gave the male to his friends, and started to train the female. He named her Lady Washington.

At the end of that summer a curious caravan set off from Adams' headquarters on the Tuolumne River in the high Sierras. There was a string of thirty horses carrying improvised cages in which there was a variety of smaller animals, as well as provisions for them. Trailing the pack train were other animals that Adams and his crew had captured: six large bears, four wolves, four antelope, four deer, two elk, and an Indian dog. Such a mixed parade of creatures—predators and prey—would have pleased a small circus owner had they circled his tent even once without incident. Adams and six Indians urged them over three hundred miles of rough wilderness trails. At Portland, Oregon, Adams loaded the animals on the *Mary Ann,* a sailing bark headed around the horn for Boston where his brother was to handle their distribution to zoos and wild animal shows. Adams had become genuinely attached to Lady Washington, however, and after all her traveling companions were safely shuttled aboard, Adams and the grizzly ambled back to the Tuolumne River.

A year later, after acquiring Ben Franklin in Yosemite Valley, Adams trekked over the Sierra Nevada and across the deserts of the Great Basin, accompanied by two Indians and the two grizzlies. They all came close to perishing of thirst. Ben Franklin's tender feet were so punished by sharp rocks and scorching sand that Adams constructed moccasins for him. Adams and the Indians hunted and trapped small animals. They arrived in Salt Lake City on the Fourth of July and readily sold their hides to dealers and the animals as pets. Camp was set up near Fort Bridger, and Adams began to sell deer and bear meat to passing emigrant trains.

On three consecutive nights a large grizzly came right into the hunting camp during the late hours. Adams, whose first instinct was to shoot it, soon changed his mind as he realized the wild bear was courting Lady Washington. Adams's fears that she would return to the wilds with him were unfounded, although Lady Washington was obviously taken with the stranger. Six months later she gave birth to a cub, which Adams welcomed into his inner circle by christening him Fremont.

It was on this same eventful journey that Adams tangled with a wild mother grizzly he had provoked; she flattened him with the swing of a massive paw and seized his head in her jaws. The hunter went limp. After regarding him suspiciously for a moment, growling, the bear returned to her cubs. Adams seemed to recover from his massive scalp wound and went on to exhibit his animals in San Francisco as well as in New York City, where P. T. Barnum billed him as the "old hunter of '49." Yet the scalp wound, suffered in the Rockies, reopened, continued to bother him, and finally killed him eight years after he had set off into the wilderness where he dispassionately shot adult grizzlies for their hides, meat, and cubs, which he raised and came gradually to love.

Prior to the 1850s, numerous grizzlies roamed throughout the American West, shunning only the harsher deserts. They thrived in mountains and thicketed hill country from Canada to Mexico, prowled tidal estuaries of the Pacific Coast, and even wandered for great distances out on the Great Plains, digging up rodents and feasting upon dead or incapacitated buffalo. By rough estimate there were more than one hundred thousand of the huge, solitary beasts. During the second half of the nineteenth century the trickle of prospectors and land-seekers headed westward to the Rockies or beyond came into full flood. As the country filled up, man and grizzly increasingly came in contact with each other, usually to the disadvantage of the great bear. The unreliable, low-clout muzzle-loader of the mountain men had been replaced with powerful rifles like the Sharps, as well as repeating rifles. Although the great bears were hunted for sport, their hides, and to some degree for their meat, they were mostly killed off because they were judged to be a threat to livestock. Nat Straw, a grizzly-hunter of New Mexico Territory, once remarked that: "A bear will travel thirty miles to find a good harvest of acorns; he will graze on clover like a cow, and he will get as fat as a hog upon piñon nuts, wild cherries, manzanita berries, and other fruitage, but once let him get the taste of cow or sheep meat and after that he is a confirmed killer."

Certain grizzlies became infamous among stockmen, were given names like Reelfoot, Red Robber and Old Mose, and were hunted in anger at their predations as well as a grudging admiration for their strength and cunning. For thirty-five years Old Mose terrorized cattle herds and outwitted hunters in a rugged region straddling the Continental Divide of Colorado. The huge bear reputedly killed over eight hundred cattle, as well as a number of colts and sheep. On occasion, Old Mose would sneak up upon a camp of prospectors or herders, then suddenly charge growling into the midst of them. As the grizzly never harmed any of the men he thus scattered, panic-stricken, for the nearest trees, it would appear he was merely bluffing or perhaps playing. He did not bluff, however, with men who managed to get close enough to put a bullet into him; he killed five of them before finally losing out to a pack of hunting dogs and riflemen.

Magnificent rogues like Old Mose notwithstanding, there is considerable debate as to just how much threat an average grizzly has ever posed to livestock, since many of their presumed kills likely died or were dying of other causes first. Be that as it may, once bounties were offered on grizzlies, traps and poison as well as rifles were used to kill the great bears and their numbers declined rapidly. They were gone from the Great Plains by 1880, from California by 1922, and became extinct in Arizona and New Mexico by the beginning of the Great Depression. South of the Canadian border, the only remaining grizzlies prowled the rugged spurs of the northern Rockies in Montana, Idaho, and Wyoming. The great bears found safety from hunters in Yellowstone and Glacier National Parks. For the most part, their lonely sanctuaries of timber, meadow, and brush were rarely visited, and their solitary habits seldom disturbed.

Increasingly, however, they began to have more contact with man. Garbage was routinely set out as an enticement to draw the bears into places of easy access so that they could be observed by park visitors. And the visitors themselves were no longer content to oh and ah from scenic lookouts or the verandas of rustic lodges; in ever greater numbers backpackers were using the trails which led into even the most remote corners of the parks.

Glacier National Park is a beautiful wild sprawl of soaring peaks, forest, and meadows. Over fifty glaciers hang above the valleys they have carved and there are numerous lakes. John Muir referred to the region as "the greatest care-killing scenery" in North America. In 1939 a hiker named John Daubney was attacked by three grizzlies near Piegan Pass. He was the only person to be injured by a grizzly in the first thirty years of the park's existence. There were no other reported attacks until seventeen years later, when a man was bitten by a bear while sleeping in the open.

Four years after that, two young seasonal rangers, Alan Nelson and Edomo Mazzer, hiked in to Okotami Lake accompanied by Smitty Parrett, the ten-year-old son of another ranger. On the way back from the lake they met two Swedish schoolteachers, Gote Nyhlen and Brita Noring, and the five of them leisurely proceeded down the trail together. They were crossing an open meadow when Mazzer, in the lead, spotted a huge female grizzly ambling up the trail with two cubs in tow. He wheeled back to his companions, shouting, "Bear! Bear! Bear with cubs! Get up a tree! Get up a tree!" The hikers scattered.

Mazzer and Nyhlen managed to climb into trees as the bear pursued Nelson and the boy. Smitty glanced back over his shoulder and saw that the bear was almost upon him. He dropped onto his stomach, trying to play dead, cradling his face in his arms. Snarling, the bear slashed at his head with her claws. Nelson had slipped behind the trunk of an old, half dead tree. He yelled, hoping to distract the bear from the prostrate boy. She charged him. Nelson tried to pull himself up into the tree, but the branches, dry and brittle with age, snapped under his boots. He was only about four feet off the ground when the grizzly sank her teeth into his buttocks and dragged him back to the ground. Like the boy, the seasoned ranger felt his best chance for survival lay in remaining inert. The bear bit deeply into his thighs.

The bear's attacks upon Smitty and Nelson had been violent and swift. She turned from Nelson to rush at the tree selected by the two Swedes. Nyhlen had scrambled to a safe height, but his friend was still at the base of the tree, momentarily paralyzed. As the bear charged, Brita Noring tried frantically to pull herself up into the branches, yet even though Mazzer shouted and barked like a dog from his tree, momentarily distracting the bear, the schoolteacher could only haul herself a few feet off the ground before the grizzly hooked its claws into her thigh and pulled her back to the ground. The bear started to drag her off into the thick brush, then returned to the still forms of Nelson and Smitty, growling, sniffing, and watching for any sign of movement.

Finally, apparently satisfied that there was no longer any danger to her cubs, the bear abruptly left. For more than twenty minutes no one moved or spoke, fearing the grizzly might return. Then Mazzer and Nyhlen climbed down from their trees. All three people on the ground had been badly mauled, especially Smitty, who had been virtually scalped and had a broken arm. Other than making them as comfortable as possible, there was little to be done for the victims; they could not be moved.

The terrifying possibility that the bear had not gone for good was on everyone's mind.

Mazzer and Nyhlen hurried down the trail to Rising Sun Campground, figuring that even if they came upon the bear again, one of them would get through. At the campground, they got into Mazzer's car and drove to the ranger station at St. Mary. Fifteen minutes after they had arrived at the ranger station, a nine-man rescue party, armed and equipped with stretchers, blankets, a wheeled carrier, and a radio, moved up the trail in the dusk. Support teams were forming behind them. Rangers hung lights from trees at Rising Sun Campground where a doctor began to set up an emergency first-aid station, covering picnic tables with blankets.

It was dark by the time the rescuers reached the scene of the attack. The victims were still conscious. All three of them had severe injuries, but the ten-year-old boy was in the worst shape. Nevertheless, he had managed to stagger over to Nelson and, after collapsing at his side, to inquire as to the condition of Brita Noring. It took the rescuers two hours to carry the victims down the rough trail to the makeshift first-aid station at Rising Sun Campground. After being treated there, they were taken to the Cardston, Alberta, hospital, where Nelson and Noring were soon responding satisfactorily to treatment.

Smitty Parrett was in critical condition, with broken ribs and arm, deep puncture wounds in his chest, a collapsed lung, and other wounds. He would lose an eye. Yet the boy had endured the horror upon the mountain, and he now clung tenaciously to life. He was soon to face another kind of ordeal—five years of operations, skin grafts, and pain. The time would come when he would once again pick up a normal schoolboy's life, and would return to hike in Glacier National Park.

During the decade between 1956 and 1967 nine grizzly attacks in Glacier National Park were reported. This in no way would indicate that camping in the park had become a more dangerous pleasure than in John Muir's time; thousands of people were doing it every summer without incident. Still, the sheer number of people who were now hiking and sleeping out in the park naturally increased the odds that one of them or a party of them would inadvertently seem threatening to a bear with cubs, or in some other way antagonize the free-spirited, unpredictable creatures.

In a number of national parks there are islands of private land, places which were homesteaded before the parks were established and whose original owners and descendants have refused to sell. Kelly's Camp, a cluster of summer cabins on the shore of Lake McDonald in Glacier National Park, is one of these enclaves. It is a beautiful spot. The narrow blue-green glacial lake is ten miles long, wedged between craggy peaks. In mid-June of 1967, Joan Berry, a descendant of the original homesteader, who manages the camp with her husband, was readying the cabins for the season's visitors when she noticed a lean and mangy grizzly rooting through garbage pails in broad daylight. It had an oddly elongated head. She was struck not only by the bear's exceptionally poor condition, but by its boldness. When she shouted to drive it away, the emaciated creature merely raised up on its hind legs and then advanced toward her. She hastily retreated. The strange bear began to visit the camp regularly. One evening, when the Berrys' German shorthaired dog barked as the bear was prowling outside the cabin, the bear charged the door, as if trying to break it down.

By late June the camp was filled with vacationers. One afternoon a birthday party was in progress on the porch of one of the cabins when the grizzly with the misshapen head ambled toward the celebration. W. R. Hammond, whose fifty-seventh birthday was the cause of the gathering, shouted at the bear. It continued to pad to the cabin and started up the wooden stairs of the porch. Yelling for everyone to get inside, Hammond hefted a heavy bench and heaved it at the grizzly. The bench clipped the animal on a foot. The bear calmly retreated down the stairs, stood up, snorted, then dropped to all fours and wandered off. The party had barely resumed when there were screams from another part of the camp. Hammond fetched his .25-35 lever-action rifle and started off in the direction from which the screams had issued. He had not gone far when he encountered his nine-year-old grandson and an older girl.

"Don't run, but walk as fast as you can," the boy whispered as he passed. Hammond saw that the bear was trailing them about sixty feet away. He fired a warning shot into the air. The animal paused, reared upon its hind legs, then dropped back down and vanished around the side of a cabin.

Rangers were notified of the grizzly's bold behavior, but by the time they arrived the bear had left Kelly's Camp; one of the rangers had spotted it shambling up the steep trail which led over a steep ridge to Trout Lake. The bear made other visits to Kelly's Camp, often startling the residents with its curiously casual behavior. Mrs. Berry, who had spent all of her summers around grizzlies, told an executive ranger that "We've got a sick bear, a crazy acting bear around, and wish you'd do something about it." Little came of it; the Park Service was understaffed. On a few occasions, hearing that the grizzly was prowling the camp, rangers arrived with rifles only to find the bear had slipped away just before their arrival.

The gaunt grizzly was also frightening backpackers on the trails to and beside Trout Lake. It would sometimes follow them for hundreds of yards, staying only twenty to twenty-five feet behind them. More than one group of campers scattered to climb nearby trees when the bear sauntered into their camp and rummaged through it, as they yelled at it and even threw rocks to no avail.

On the afternoon of August 12, 1967, five seasonal park employees arrived at a campsite on Trout Lake, having hiked over Howe Ridge from Lake McDonald. Four of them, Michele Koons, Denise Huckle, and brothers Ron and Ray Noseck were college students; they had already made several backpacking trips that summer. It was the first such excursion for sixteen-year-old Paul Dunn, who had arrived at the park only three weeks before on a trip with his parents and had taken a job as a busboy on the spur of the moment. An abandoned puppy that Denise had befriended rounded out the party. At dusk, as a supper of trout and hot dogs was cooking, Michele saw a bear gazing at them from the edge of the woods not ten feet away. She shouted a warning to her companions, and all five of them dashed up the rocky lakeshore. Ray Noseck scooped up the dog as he went. From some fifty yards away, they watched as the scrawny grizzly entered their camp and leisurely devoured their supper. After it had left, they briefly debated returning to the ranger station at Lake McDonald, yet it was now dark, and they had only one weak flashlight. In the end, they decided to remain where they were. They built up a roaring fire and laid out their sleeping bags around it.

Granite Park Chalet is only eight or nine miles from Trout Lake as the crow flies, although separated from it by the high serrated wall of the Livingston Range. The chalet, a fieldstone structure with timbered roof, lies close to timberline, and accommodates the overnight guests who hike in to it only two months of the year. On the same afternoon that the Trout Lake campers were driven from their supper by a grizzly, the advisability of sleeping out in bear country was being discussed at Granite Park Chalet. Robert and Janet Klein had planned to bed down in a campground a quarter of a mile from the lodge until they learned that grizzlies routinely made a nightly feast of garbage which was set out for them by the chalet employees. When questioned, the manager of the chalet told them that the bears usually made their late evening appearances and departures on the trail which led to the campground. He added, however, that hundreds of people had spent the night at the campground that summer and that "the bears haven't eaten anybody yet." The two men laughed. Janet Klein was still dubious about the idea of sleeping out, but the lodge was already booked solidly for the night. When another backpacker, Don Gullett, told them he planned to sleep close to a trail cabin which was some distance off to the side of the campground, the Kleins followed suit.

The Kleins cooked supper and were about to serve it when Roy Ducat and Julie Helgeson came striding down the trail from the chalet and asked where the campground was. Like four of the five campers at Trout Lake, they were college students passing the summer at mundane jobs in a magnificent setting. When the Kleins indicated the direction of the campground, the two youths were curious as to why they had not camped there. Janet Klein admitted she was afraid of bears. Roy and Julie buoyantly assured them there was nothing to worry about, and hustled off to make their own camp at the designated site. They ate the sack lunches they had brought, enjoyed the quiet, peaceful gathering of the high mountain night, turned in, and were sound asleep long before midnight, as were the Kleins and Don Gullett. On the other side of the Livingston Range, the campers at Trout Lake were also sleeping; their fears of a lurking bear had dissolved with drowsiness. Their blazing fire was falling to a bed of glowing coals.

Roy Ducat swam up from the depths of sleep. A voice was calling to him. He barely had time to collect himself, realize that Julie was telling him to play dead, before a bear smashed at him with its paw and bit into his shoulder. In spite of the pain, he forced himself to remain motionless. The bear left him to bite into the sleeping bag of one girl, but soon returned to sink its teeth into his left arm and gnaw at the backs of his legs. The bear swung back once again to the girl's sleeping bag, and now young Roy Ducat heard bones crunching. Julie screamed. "It hurts," she cried. "Someone help us." Her anguished cries seemed to be receding into the distance. Ducat managed to stagger up to the trail cabin where he collapsed beside Don Gullett's sleeping bag.

The screams had aroused a restless guest at the chalet; she interpreted the sounds as that of a woman struggling for her life against a human assailant. Soon a number of people, half asleep, stood on the balcony, listening to the dark silence of the forest below them. Finally someone bellowed into the void: "Is everything OK?"

A voice came back out of the blackness. "No!"

"What's the trouble?"

"Bear!" The response seemed to come more from the direction of the trail cabin than the campground.

A rescue party quickly headed down the trail. First aid was administered to Roy Ducat and he was carried back to the lodge. Joan Devereaux, a young ranger naturalist, managed to contact the Park Fire Headquarters by two-way radio. In a remarkably short period of time a helicopter was on its way, carrying medical supplies and an armed ranger. A landing space was cleared. While this was going on some women on the balcony heard a faint moaning sound off in the darkness. One of them thought it might be an owl. It was not until later that they realized they had been listening to Julie Helgeson, the girl the bear had carried away.

Shortly after the helicopter touched down, the armed ranger and several men started off to look for Julie. Roy Ducat was placed aboard the helicopter and whisked off to a hospital where his serious wounds healed in a satisfactory fashion. The grizzly had taken Julie some distance from the campsite. The rescue party was able to follow a blood trail for a little way, then lost it, and had to fan out in the darkness, flashlights probing the dark forest and brush where the grizzly might still be lurking. When they found Julie she was still alive, although horribly mauled. They carried her back to the chalet where three doctors who happened to be overnight guests worked over her. But it was no use; she died upon the makeshift operating table.

At Trout Lake, Denise Huckle awakened to hear a splashing in the shallow water near camp. Her puppy growled, gazing intently in the direction of the sound. For a moment Denise thought she could make out the shape of a bear in the darkness. As the splashing receded she woke her companions. Ray and Ron Noseck stoked up the fire. After they had climbed back into their sleeping bags, a grizzly boldly walked into the wavering light cast by the fire, scooped up a sack of cookies which had been left upon a log, and returned to the dark woods. For more than an hour the frightened youths fed the fire and speculated on whether the bear would return. Finally most of them drifted back to sleep.

Around 4:30 A.M. Denise heard splashing again. She looked up to see the bear hustling from the water to the camp. The fire had fallen to coals again. The puppy began to yelp and she stuffed it deep into her sleeping bag, knowing that dogs and bears are ancient enemies. The bear sniffed at the sleepers. Paul Dunn awoke to see the bear standing over him. He froze. The grizzly bit into his sleeping bag, tearing the fabric of his sweatshirt. The boy barreled out of his bag, ricocheted off of the bear, and dashed to a tree, quickly climbing to safety.

Ron Noseck and Denise scrambled out of their bags. Ron boosted the young woman into a tree, handed the dog to her, then followed them up into its branches. The grizzly sniffed at Ray Noseck before turning to Michele Koons. Ray sprinted for a tree, shouting to Michele for her to run. Paul Dunn yelled for Michele to unzip her bag and run, but the zipper was in the bear's jaws. She screamed, "Oh my God, I'm dead!" As she struggled to get free of the bag, the grizzly dragged her off into the night.

At dawn the four terrified campers fled back over the trail to the Lake McDonald ranger station.

A search party found the girl's mutilated body about a hundred feet from the ill-fated campsite. Rangers later shot the lean bear with the misshapen head, although not before it had started to stalk them. Examination proved that it was, without a doubt, the killer bear. At the Granite Park Chalet, rangers shot and killed three bears as they approached the garbage dump. The Park Service announced that the other killer bear had been taken, although there was no conclusive evidence that this was so.

When the story broke in headlines across the country, many people wondered if the same grizzly was responsible for both deaths. It would have been physically impossible. The sites of the two attacks, while not distant by air, are separated by thirty miles of trail and the eight thousand-foot Livingston Range.

The unthinkable had happened. In the same night, two different bears had killed human beings in Glacier National Park.

How could the twin tragedies have happened? Speculations flew back and forth. Park superintendent Keith Neilson postulated that lightning storms might have crazed the bears. Wildlife biologists responded that no evidence of such a link had ever been reported. It was true, however, that had the Park Service personnel not been stretched so thin by the fire-fighting demands of an unusually large number of blazes, they might have been able to devote more attention to reports of the bold grizzly with the misshapen head. Another theory, soon discarded, was that the bears had eaten some hallucinogenic plant.

The fact that the Granite Park campground was situated close to a spot where garbage was regularly being put out for grizzlies stirred a controversy which continues to this day. The Park Service decided to close all dumps frequented by bear, of which there were some in Yellowstone Park, as soon as possible. The zoological team of Frank and John Craighead had been studying grizzly habits in Yellowstone for eight years, tracking their movements with the aid of radio collars. It was their opinion that an abrupt closure of the dumps would force the animals, accustomed as they were to handouts, into more confrontations with campers. The Park Service biologists disagreed, and instigated a plan to close the dumps within two years. The Craigheads protested, arguing that the dumps should be phased out over a ten-year span. The research team had previously disputed the Park Service assertion that the grizzly population was growing, citing their evidence that it was, in fact, declining. Miffed, the Park Service demanded that the Craigheads submit their reports for official approval before being released. When the two scientists declined to do so, their research project was terminated.

Since then, although the Park Service has been monitoring bear activity in both Yellowstone and Glacier National Parks, and closing off certain areas when it is felt the bears pose a threat, there have been scattered maulings. A young woman was dragged out of a tent and killed at a popular campground in Glacier National Park in 1976.

There are those who feel that all grizzlies should be eradicated from the National Parks, as well as those who fervently hope that careful management will allow man and grizzlies to share the same territory without incident. Others, like myself, reject the first option and see the second as unrealistic. Grizzlies are magnificent creatures, loners who, when their solitude is disturbed, may well react with ferocity, although in most cases they will merely withdraw. The National Parks were created so that people might enjoy a slice of the natural world, as little modified as possible. Grizzlies are as much a part of this natural world as a dandelion, a stream, or an eagle. To destroy any single species is to irrevocably tear the fabric of the total ecology, to destroy the rhythms of subtle interaction.

People by the score die in automobile wrecks every year en route to the National Parks, yet no one has seriously suggested that vehicles be banned as lethal. For every person who gets crossways with a grizzly there are numerous others who come to grief in icy lakes, tumble off cliffs, or eat poisonous plants. If we kill off the grizzlies as posing too much danger to humans, are we also to prohibit boating and swimming in lakes, and run guard rails along every abrupt drop? There are risks, although minimal, in the natural world, and they should be accepted by those who enter it.

Can the grizzlies survive, even if they do not behave like Smokey or Yogi or Elsa the Lovable Lion?

I hope so.

Selected Bibliography

AUTHOR'S NOTE. This selected bibliography represents only the materials that I found most generic to the intent of this book. In the course of my research I discovered an astonishing amount of periodical material about the animals man most fears, from such obvious sources as *National Geographic, Canadian Geographic Journal, Alaska Sportsman, Natural History, Smithsonian,* and the like, as well as some less likely sources such as *Westways, American Heritage, American West, The New Yorker, Time,* and *Newsweek.* The more important of these peripheral sources are listed below, but rather than make a tedious listing of all of them, may I refer the interested reader to the *Readers' Guide to Periodical Literature,* available in any public library, where particular interests such as "bear" or "crocodile" can be further explored.

Some of the material in this book was related to me firsthand by people involved in the incidents; in such cases I have thoroughly corroborated the truth of the tales by checking with other witnesses.

GENERAL

CARAS, ROGER. *Dangerous to Man.* Philadelphia: Chilton Books, 1964.
CLARKE, JAMES. *Man is the Prey.* New York: Stein and Day, 1969.

RENSBERGER, BOYCE. *The Cult of the Wild*. Garden City: Doubleday, 1977.

TOPSELL, E. *The Historie of Four-footed Beasts and Serpents*. London: 1658.

CHAPTER 1, SHARKS

BALDRIDGE, H. DAVID. *Shark Attack*. New York: Berkeley Publishing Company, 1976.

BROWN, THEO W. *Sharks—The Silent Savages*. Boston: Little, Brown and Co., 1973.

BURGESS, ROBERT F. *The Sharks*. Garden City: Doubleday, 1970.

COPPLESON, V. M. *Shark Attack*. London: Agnus and Robertson, 1959.

COUSTEAU, JACQUES-YVES and PHILIPPE. *The Shark—Splendid Savage of the Sea*. Garden City: Doubleday, 1970.

DENNIS, FELIX (ed.). *Man-Eating Sharks*. Secaucus: Castle Books, 1975.

MCCORMICK, HAROLD W., ALLEN, TOM, and YOUNG, CAPTAIN WILLIAM. *Shadows in the Sea*. Philadelphia: Chilton Book Company, 1963.

MATTHIESSEN, PETER. *Blue Meridian*. New York: Random House, 1973.

POLI, F. *Sharks are Caught at Night*. Chicago: Regnery Company, 1959.

CHAPTER 2, BEASTS OF THE WATER

COUSTEAU, JACQUES-YVES. *Octopus and Squid*. Garden City: Doubleday, 1973.

COUSTEAU, JACQUES-YVES, with JAMES DUGAN. *The Living Sea*. New York: Harper and Row, 1963.

HALSTED, B. W. *Dangerous Marine Animals*. Cambridge: Cornell Maritime Press, 1959.

HEUVELMANS, BERNARD. *In the Wake of the Sea Serpents*. New York: Hill and Wang, 1968.

ROOSEVELT, THEODORE. *Through the Brazilian Wilderness*. New York: Charles Scribner's Sons, 1925.

SCHLEE, SUSAN. "Prince Albert's way of catching squid." *Natural History*. February, 1970.

SWEENEY, JAMES B. *A Pictorial History of Sea Monsters*. New York: Crown Publishers, 1972.

WOOD, F. G. "An octopus trilogy." *Natural History*. March, 1971.

ZAHL, PAUL. "Seeking the truth about the piranha." *National Geographic*. November, 1970.

CHAPTER 3, SOME AFRICAN BEASTS

BAKER, SAMUEL. *The Albert N'Yanza.* London: Macmillan and Company, 1866.

CARAS, ROGER. *Dangerous to Man.* Philadelphia: Chilton Books, 1964.

CLARKE, JAMES. *Man is the Prey.* New York: Stein and Day, 1969.

DOUGLAS-HAMILTON, IAIN and ORIA. *Among the Elephants.* New York: Viking Press, 1975.

GORDON-CUMMING, RONALEYN. *The Lion Hunter.* New York: Macmillan Company, 1924.

HUNTER, J. A., with DANIEL P. MANNING. *Hunter.* New York: Harper and Brothers, 1952.

NEUMANN, ALFRED. *Elephant Hunting in Equatorial Africa.* London: Rowland Ward, 1898.

PATTERSON, COL. J. H. *The Maneaters of Tsavo.* New York: Macmillan Company, 1927.

CHAPTER 4, MAN-KILLING CATS

ANDERSON, KENNETH. *Nine Maneaters and One Rogue.* New York: E. P. Dutton, 1955.

CAPSTICK, PETER HATHAWAY. *Death in the Long Grass.* New York: St. Martin's Press, 1977.

CORBETT, JIM. *Man-Eaters of Kumoan.* New York: Oxford University Press, 1946.

GORDON-CUMMING, RONALEYN. *The Lion Hunter.* New York: Macmillan Company, 1924.

GUGGISBERG, C. A. W. *Simba, Life of the Lion.* Philadelphia: Chilton Books, 1963.

GUGGISBERG, C. A. W. *Wild Cats of the World.* New York: Taplinger Publishing Company, 1975.

JACKSON, PETER. "Scientists hunt the Bengal Tiger—But only in order to trace and save it." *Smithsonian.* August, 1978.

LIVINGSTON, DAVID and CHARLES. *Narrative of an Expedition to the Zambesi and Its Tributaries.* London: John Murray, 1865.

PATTERSON, COL. J. H. *The Maneaters of Tsavo.* New York: Macmillan Company, 1927.

PUTNAM, JOHN. "India struggles to save her wildlife." *National Geographic.* September, 1976.

CHAPTER 5, SCALY THINGS THAT SHUFFLE AND LURK

BAKER, SAMUEL. *The Albert N'Yanza.* London: Macmillan and Company, 1866.

BEARD, PETER, and ALISTAIR, GRAHAM. *Eyelids of Morning.* New York: New York Society Ltd., 1973.

EARL, LAWRENCE. *Crocodile Fever.* New York: Alfred A. Knopf, Inc., 1954.

GORE, RICK. "A bad time to be a crocodile." *National Geographic.* January, 1968.

GUGGISBERG, C. A. W. *Crocodiles: Their Natural History, Folklore and Conservation.* Harrisburg: Stackpole Books, 1972.

HERODOTUS. *The Histories.* New York: Penguin, 1954.

KINGSLEY, MARY H. *Travels in East Africa.* London: Macmillan and Company, 1898.

LOCKWOOD, DOUGLAS. *Crocodiles and Other People.* Melbourne: Cassell and Company Ltd., 1959.

NEILL, W. T. *The Last of the Ruling Reptiles.* New York: Columbia University Press, 1971.

NEUMANN, ALFRED. *Elephant Hunting in Equatorial Africa.* London: Rowland Ward, 1898.

CHAPTER 6, KILLER BEES

Committee on the African Honeybee. National Technology Service, Springfield, Virginia, 1972.

GORE, RICK. "Those fiery Brazilian bees." *National Geographic.* April, 1976.

POTTER, ANTHONY. *The Killer Bees.* New York: Grosset and Dunlap, 1977.

CHAPTER 7, BEHOLD THE SERPENT

DUNSON, WILLIAM. "The sea snakes are coming." *Natural History.* November, 1971.

MACLEISH, KENNETH, with BEN COPP. "Diving with sea snakes." *National Geographic.* April, 1972.

MILLER, HARRY. "The cobra, India's 'good snake.'" *National Geographic.* September, 1970.

MINTON, SHERMAN A., JR., and MADGE. *Venomous Reptiles.* London: George, Allen and Unwin Ltd., 1971.

MORRIS, DESMOND and RAMONA. *Men and Snakes*. New York: McGraw Hill, 1967.

OLIVER, JAMES A. *Snakes in Fact and Fiction*. New York: Macmillan Company, 1958.

PINKERTON, JOHN. *Voyages and Travels: Bosman's Guinea*. London: Longman, Hurst, Reese, Orma and Brown, 1811.

POPE, CLIFFORD. *The Giant Snakes*. New York: Alfred A. Knopf, 1961.

SAINT-MERY, MOREAU DE. *Moreau de Saint Mery's Journey*. Translated and edited by Kenneth and Anna Roberts. Garden City: Doubleday, 1947.

CHAPTER 8, THE BELLED VIPERS

CURTIS, EDWARD S. "Snake rite." *Westways*. August, 1974.

DOBIE, J. FRANK. *Rattlesnakes*. Boston: Little, Brown and Company, 1965.

FERGUSSON, ERNA. *Dancing Gods*. Albuquerque: University of New Mexico Press, 1931.

FORREST, EARLE. *The Snake Dance of the Hopi Indians*. Los Angeles: Westernlore Press, 1961.

KLAUBER, LAURENCE M. *Rattlesnakes: Their Habits, Life Histories, and Influence of Mankind*. Berkeley: University of California Press, 1956.

LA BARRE, WESTON. *They Shall Take Up Serpents*. Minneapolis: University of Minnesota Press, 1962.

CHAPTER 9, WOLVES

AUDUBON, JOHN JAMES, and BACHMAN, JOHN. *The Viviparous Quadrupeds of North America*. New York: Arno, 1854.

BARING-GOULD, SABINE. *The Book of Were-wolves*. New York: Causeway Books, 1973 (reprint).

CLARKE, C. H. D. "The beast of Gévaudon." *Natural History*. April, 1971.

COX, ROSS. *The Columbia River*. London: H. Colburn and R. Bentley, 1831.

GOLDMAN, EDWARD A., and YOUNG, STANLEY P. *The Wolves of North America*. Washington, D.C.: American Wildlife Institute, 1944.

MECH, L. D. *The Wolf*. Garden City: Doubleday Publishing Company, 1970.

MIVERT, ST. GEORGE. *Dogs, Jackals, Wolves and Foxes*. London: 1890.

MURIE, ADOLPH. *The Wolves of Mt. McKinley*. Washington, D.C.: U.S. Government Printing Office, 1944.

TURI, JOHAN. *Turi's Book of Lappland*. London: Norwood, 1931.

CHAPTER 10, A SOLITARY BEAST

EAST, BEN. *Bears*. New York: Outdoor Life/Crown Publishers, 1977.

GILBERT, BIL. "The great controversy." *Audubon*. January, 1976.

HANNA, WARREN L. *The Grizzlies of Glacier*. Missoula: Mountain Press Publishing Company, 1978.

HAYNES, BESSIE DOAK and EDGAR. *The Grizzly Bear*. Norman: University of Oklahoma Press, 1966.

MCCRACKEN, HAROLD. *The Beast that Walks Like Man*. Garden City: Hanover House, 1955.

OLSEN, JACK. *Night of the Grizzlies*. New York: G. P. Putnam's Sons, 1970.

RUSSELL, ANDY. *Grizzly Country*. New York: Alfred A. Knopf, 1967.

TAYLOR, TED M. "Vanished monarch of the Sierra." *American West*. May/June, 1976.

WRIGHT, WILLIAM H. *The Grizzly Bear*. New York: Charles Scribner's Sons, 1909.

ABOUT THE AUTHOR

Michael Jenkinson first became interested in how people relate to the animals they most fear while working as a game warden on the coast of Alaska—haunt of the giant brown bear—twenty years ago. Since then, he has worked as a teacher, ranch hand, professional actor, and in public relations. He currently serves the state of New Mexico as projects coordinator of its Arts Commission. His previous books include *Wild Rivers of North America* and *Land of Clear Light*. He has published poetry and magazine articles in numerous publications. Married and the father of three children, his home is in Santa Fe.

DATE DUE